Book Two
of the *Lucy's Crypt* series

Poison and Exile

Poison and Exile

Published by Wendy and Wetherall in Australia, 2024

ISBN 978-1-7638350-1-6

 A catalogue record for this book is available from the National Library of Australia

Map illustrated by Kerrie Turner

Typesetting and Cover Design by:
Charlotte Mouncey, www.bookstyle.co.uk

Map illustrated by Maria Priestley and Kerrie Turner

Printing and Distribution Channel: IngramSpark

Book Two
of the *Lucy's Crypt* series

Poison and Exile

Katie Webster

Rumustica

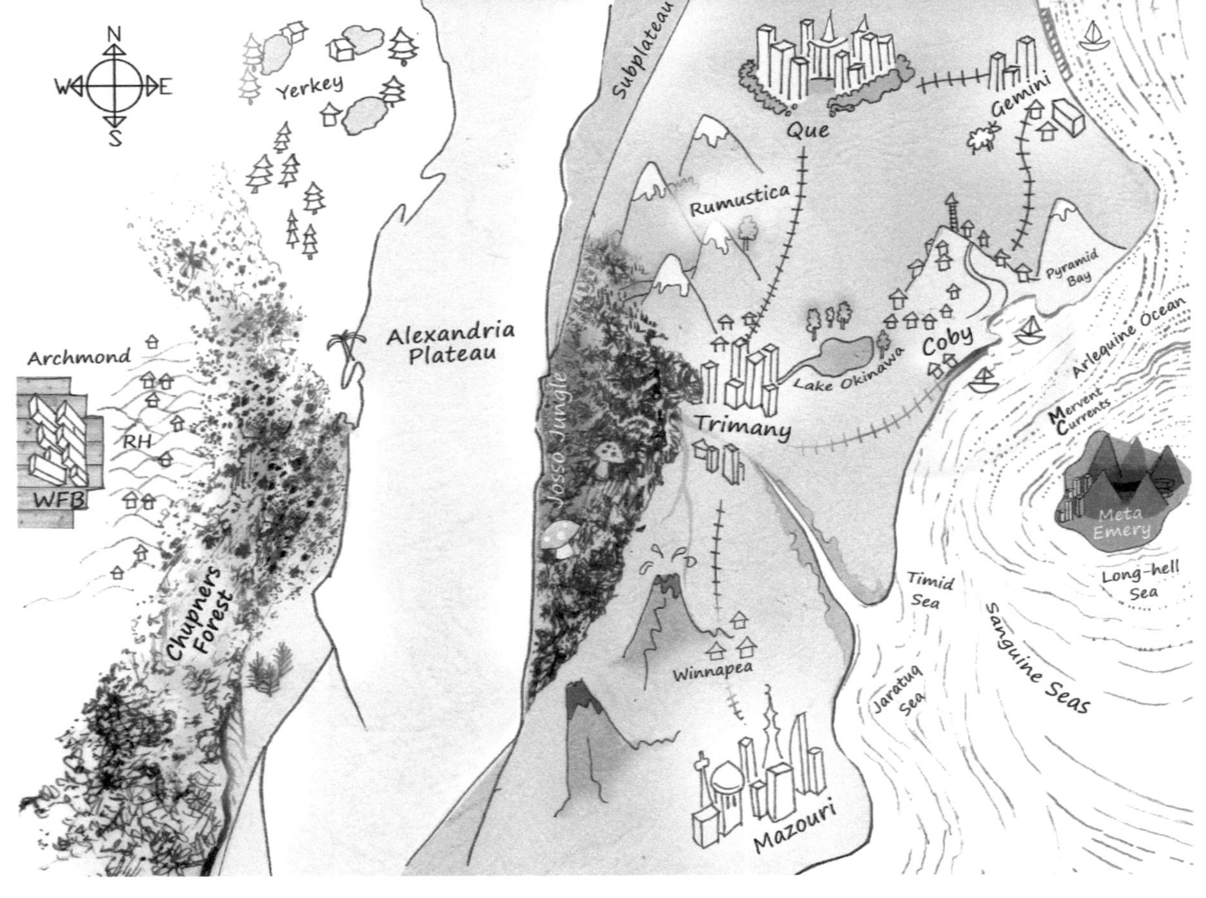

N
E
S
W
Yerkey
Subplateau
Que
Gemini
Rumustica
Pyramid Bay
Archmond
Alexandria Plateau
Coby
Lake Okinawa
Arlequine Ocean
RH
Josso Jungle
Trimany
Mervent Currents
WFB
Meta Emery
Chupners Forest
Timid Sea
Long-hell Sea
Winnapea
Jaratua Sea
Sanguine Seas
Mazouri

Eminence, I hope this finds you well.

I had very much intended to find an opportunity earlier to put a message together for you, but I'm afraid I have been in a limbo of sorts. The wind hasn't been blowing in the direction I'd like, and for many nights I've not seen a single albatross overhead.

Never mind. Enough prattle. I have found Lucy, we have reunited. Though perhaps not yet reconciled. She is in fair spirit, albeit a little moody, and I dare say it could be sometime before I am forgiven for having left her in the snow. But we have safely descended the scramble slopes at the edge of the frozen world beyond Yerkey and have now reached the plateau.

Lucy has undergone a tremendous adjustment since you last saw her. She is not the shy and weepy adolescent brought into this world some eighteen nights ago. She is slowly coming to terms with her new reality. However, no doubt it does not shock you to hear she has, still, a long way to go, and many skills to acquire before she can be self-sufficient.

As we expected, the past revealed to her in Yerkey has also had a profound impact. It is clear to me that remembering these truths about her childhood has affected her. As yet, whether it was for better or worse, I cannot say. She has a long way to go. She has been gifted a sword by the Reichi for protection, and I intend on teaching her how to use it. But rest assured, the prophecy and her destiny remain at the forefront of everything I do.

When I can find a path to return and debrief before you I will, but in the interests of maintaining rapport, I propose to stay beside her, at least until we reach the jungle.

Yours in the spirit now and forever,

X. Bear

Chapter 1

The Alexandria Plateau

*L*ucy steadied her breath and looked around but trying to get her bearings in this vast open darkness was unnerving. For one thing, the creature could come from anywhere. Its form seemed to blend so perfectly with the shadowy patches of the pitted desert floor, that when it set itself down it became invisible. More than that though, was the lack of landmarks to use in which to centre her direction. She was tired, obviously, a common theme, but she already harboured an innate wanting for a sense of direction.

'Where did you say to hit it again?' she called out to Bear. He was scanning the vicinity as well, but for all the powers and unnatural wisdom he had, his eyesight was no better than hers.

'The neck, I would think.'

Above them a clear sky let shine a myriad of stars so profoundly entangled with one another it was sometimes impossible to ascertain where one stopped and another began. The entangled clusters formed swirling patterns that looped into one another, but the similarity between these various clusters meant that they too were no use as a guidance post. Lucy wiped her hands across her shorts. The sweat that had gathered as she gripped the sword, ready and waiting, was from nerves not the weather. Although the Alexandria Plateau did impose a unique and intense heat, it was the dry heat of an oven, much of which rushed off every night after sunset. Very different to the persistent and damp warmth that would await her in Josso Jungle. As the creature finally emerged and she drew in fast quick breaths of this hot dry air, she momentarily longed to be back in Yerkey's frozen world.

'Okay. Hold steady. Do not hesitate. Do not hold back,' Bear said, as it moved into a sprint, almost launching into a gallop.

This was their third day of traveling across the plateau's inhospitable emptiness. This was not the first of these creatures they had encountered, unfortunately. Contrary to Bear's plans and ambitions for her training, Lucy had lucklessly crossed paths with one at a watering hole on their first day. As she raised her head from the tepid water, her face still dripping, she saw its confusing reflection on the rippled surface. A beast of a thing, somewhat ape-like, but with the golden and exuberant coat of a lion. It was perching on its hind legs, its gangly arms limp by its side, seemingly at ease. But its gaze was fixed squarely on Lucy, the deep-set eyes plainly exposing the animosity of its intentions.

'The sword, Lucy!' Bear had shouted. She had stumbled backwards, and then rushed to it, but she had never used a sword before. It was heavy. She had no arm strength and limited coordination. As it launched onto her, she had swung, but with the force one might put into a soft putt, not a life-saving swing. It barely even discomfited the creature, which drew back its gums to reveal a frightening set of fangs both wide and pointed. They drew down on her just as Bear shot a burst of faint blue-ish light at its neck.

Bear too was hoping for a more potent effect from his attack, but they were now a good way from Archmond Castle and the further they got, the less power he had. Luckily, the effect was enough to confuse the creature, who drew back in bewilderment as well as pain. Bear had shouted at Lucy again to get the sword, to kill it. But Lucy could only manage to stand in shock, and it was up to Bear once again to try and shock the creature with his energy. It was enough (thankfully that time) to confuse it to the point that it backed away and fled. But they were lucky. That one would have been old, he told Lucy. A younger more energetic omling (as Bear later revealed they were often called) would have devoured her and would have ignored his puny attempts to defend her.

This omling was just that. Its muscular hind legs propelled its torso with such velocity that its leap from the shadows sent it soaring, creating under the starlight, its own shadow over Lucy.

'Strike it!' Bear shouted, simultaneously willing his energy to his paw-tips ready to come to her aid. Defensively Lucy shot the sword upward in front of her, just in time for the creature to land across its blade. It let out a painful shriek as it fell backwards. Instantly, its blood, black in the night, began pooling beneath it. A spray of this same blood had cast across her and was starting to trickle down her chest and arms. She stared at both the omling and her defiled sword in shock.

Bear looked at her stoic figure with frustration. 'Finish it!'

Her breath was frantic. 'I can't! I can't!'

'You have to,' he said firmly.

But Lucy stood still. The creature writhed.

'I'm not a killer.'

'Then you're a sadist? You will watch it slowly bleed to death in agony?'

Lucy closed her eyes. Her right hand shook both under the weight of the sword and under the pressure she felt.

'Put it out of its misery,' Bear commanded, just as it began to screech in agony again, 'or you will be responsible for every moment of its suffering. And in any case, if you do not overcome your childlike squeamishness, it will be you bleeding to death on this parched dirt before long.'

Lucy drove the blade down toward its neck, missed, and hit its face. She wretched, but thankfully her stomach was empty. She drew her eyes nearly shut and drove the sword down four more times into its neck in rapid succession. She opened her eyes. It had stopped moving. It was dead. With a heavy gasp she dropped the sword and backed away, wiping the blood splatter from her face with her forearms. Bear let out a sigh, full of both anxiety and relief as he watched her little dog, Crumbs, emerge from behind a small rock.

'You'll have to get better at that. Quickly. That was half luck, again.'

That was the first time Lucy began to consider whether in fact she hated Bear. His lack of empathy. Was he really so oblivious about how horrible all of this was to her? No, she began to think, he can see how horrible this is, he just doesn't care. He was starting to float off in the direction they'd been heading.

'I'm not a killer, or a fighter, or a hunter,' she called to him.

'Then you need to become one, quickly. Tomorrow we'll go over some more of the techniques.'

That night they slept at what appeared to be the likes of some form of abandoned cattle station. Past a string of posts that had once connected barbed wire, but now stood as lonely markers, was a vacuous empty shed, half rusted away. Two enormous entrances, the likes of which once facilitated the passing of large machinery, exposed the shed to the elements from either side. Above the dirt floor, the remnants of animal pens were all up one side, although these too had mostly fallen apart. Pockets of starlight fell through the holes and speckled the darkness inside.

The Alexandria Plateau lay below the frozen tundra surrounding Yerkey. It was many miles lower in altitude, and they had faced a steep decline as the edge of the tundra (where Bear had mysteriously re-emerged to once again guide her way) gave way to cold grasslands, before they faced the barren and treacherous rocky decline to the plateau. But the altitude difference itself did not explain the sharp contrast in temperatures. In fact, nothing did. Both the plateau and the tundra seemed to be under the influence of their own respective micro-climates.

The Alexandria Plateau in particular had its peculiar cycles of drought and fertility. A century of regular rainfall and growth, where grasses and shrubs bloomed across the honey-bronze earth; then a century of drought and death. It had been more than fifty years since the last fertile season ended. In the decades before its end it had been prime cattle country. In the reign of King Xavier, a harmonious golden age of prosperity, farmers from Archmond, Trimany, Que and Mazouri, all had stakes in the fertile plateau. A variety of livestock were raised for sale in cities across the mainland and the island kingdom. Nowadays though, even abandoned cattle-stations had been reclaimed by the elements, and relics such as the one they slept in were few and far between.

There was a well outside the station though, which surprisingly still functioned, and Lucy was able to bring up brown groundwater to rinse off the blood. In the morning they distilled the brown water on a fire just outside the shed, a makeshift system which didn't catch all the condensation, but made Lucy glad she'd always paid attention in science class.

'There,' she said feeling pleased, examining drops of clear water from the canister, 'now you can't say I've been completely useless.'

Bear shrugged. 'Well if your dog could talk I'm sure he'd express some gratitude, but I've no need for your water.'

Lucy gave him a look, but she was feeling too pleased with herself to be bitter. 'His name is Crumbs. I'm sure you know that by now.'

'Rather stupid name, isn't it?' Bear remarked rhetorically.

'What kind of a name is Bear?'

'Well it's more a description really. Is that why you called him Crumbs, is he a morsel of food?'

'No, he was always eating my morsels of food.' Lucy watched Crumbs sniff around idly as she said this. 'Speaking of food, do you have any new ideas?'

'I do actually, but you're not going to like it.'

In fact, Lucy was less opposed to Bear's idea than he assumed. He thought they could smoke out (and then kill) some of the rodents from their shallow burrows. Given her squeamishness so far, and her (very) vocal opposition to violence, he thought he would need to tire himself talking her into sensibility. But she was hungrier than she was principled and needed more substance than desert plants or dried lizards.

Lucy's breath was rapid as they waited for the smoke to purge the creature (whatever it may be) out of its burrow.

'Calm down, you needn't be so intense about killing a mouse,' Bear said.

'You don't know it's a mouse, and it doesn't matter, you have no understanding of how horrible this is for me.'

Just as she said this a large snake shot out toward them from the sandy hole and Lucy withdrew in terror.

'Strike it you stupid girl!' Bear called. She hesitated in flux for a moment (they were expecting to trap and suffocate several mice, not decapitate a serpent) but then she grabbed the sword and sent it down on the serpent's head. Its body slithered around for several moments in the sand before it eventually fell still with death. She slid the sword back into its scabbard at her waist.

'Can we even eat this?' Lucy asked, between breaths of shock.

'Actually, I'm not sure.'

Later they did manage to find burrows filled with small desert rodents, and Lucy reluctantly participated in their demise. But the protein was well received by her poor malnourished body; there had been very little in both Yerkey and the plateau to sustain her. They were not able to work out whether the snake was edible, but they cooked it, and fed small portions to Crumbs, with Bear reasoning that even if it possible the flesh were poison, it could not be so concentrated as to kill her dog in such small morsels.

'Crumbs,' she had reminded him again, 'he has a name.'

Later that day, with the aid of the structure of this shed, Bear compelled her into hours of sword practice. Essentially he wanted to improve her aim, but equally he needed to get her wrists used to the weight of it. It was a slender sword, and meant for a female, but for a grown and practised swordswoman, not this flimsy, adolescent and currently malnourished girl.

'Okay, when you lift it, you have to be using the strength in your whole arm. So straighten your arm, and let your body take its weight,' Bear instructed.

'I am doing that,' Lucy whined.

'If you were, you'd be lifting it with much more ease.'

He had placed a stray piece of wood, perhaps something that had broken off one of the posts at the periphery, on a railing that ran across the sheet metal wall. It may have once been the frame for a bench or a pen. Now though, it was target practice.

She swung the sword down and missed the wood entirely. The blade left a serrated mark in the metal bar. She looked at Bear. He had his paws over his face, and without lowering them he sighed and said, 'okay, so it's about both weight and aim.'

He set her up again. Her posture, her position, her hand on the sword.

'Bring it down in slow motion first, perhaps? Maybe that will work. Judge the angle, and then practice it more swiftly.'

Lucy lined up the sword with the block, moved her shoulder back, slowly worked the angle, and then brought it down slowly to align it with the block. It seemed she had the angle right now. But when she tried to replicate that as some sort of attack, it missed the block by more than several inches.

'Try leaning with your hips, not your whole body. Focus girl - you can do this,' he said.

Lucy measured her shot again. She concentrated on using the strength in her whole arm, brought it down, and split the wood in two.

'There you go. Progress!' Bear belted proudly.

But with the second piece of wood, when she tried again, she missed and hit the metal again rather jaggedly.

Outside, in the mid-morning sun, the ears of a large male omling had pricked at the sound of the distant clanging, a rare indication of life. As it moved toward the vibrations, it had also picked up on a scent; her scent. It scrambled somewhat, on its knees in the terracotta dust, gathering what it could from the air. With another clang of metal, its eyes found and focused on the shed. This metallic rectangle on the horizon, glistening in the mirage of desert heat, became its focus.

Lucy was grateful that Bear had reappeared to guide her. But their reunion had not been exactly harmonious. Lucy had been upset that he'd so suddenly vanished in the snowstorm, when things were at the most frightening for her, as shadows and memories of her dark past surrounded and threatened her. It was also not as though he had come back after that part was over, when she was facing her past with Yinsoo in Yerkey's temple, or in the aftermath of that, when she was trying to process the trauma of realising that past. She'd had to deal with that all alone. And that in itself had further compounded her confusion about the conflicting stories from both Archmond's wizards, and Yerkey's spiritual Reichi, about how she had been brought into this world. She had relayed all this to Bear, but he had given little in the way of commentary or opinion, which only served to exacerbate her confusion. So she returned to the topic regularly, not willing to let the mystery linger.

'So… was this Yinsoo lady right? Was she or the Reichi the ones who were really behind bringing me here?' Lucy asked, as Bear lined up four more blocks for her to practice with.

Bear shrugged. 'You said she was quite certain about that.'

'Yes.' Lucy stared intently into the dirt ahead as she recalled the confidence of the woman in those moments by the fire, while the musky haze filled the temple.

'But Soleman and Ron were certain that they brought me here into this world, because apparently I am the one supposed to fulfil this prophecy that's so important to them. Yet, despite its supposed importance, they knew nothing about Yinsoo, whose grandfather had the prophecy. It's a bit strange, that she knew of them and their plans, but they knew nothing of her, or so it seemed,' Lucy said, swiping the sword horizontally through the air, managing to hit the first block off the metal railing. It shot off through the tractor-sized hole in the sheet metal and out into the glaring sunshine.

'Whose grandfather prophesied you,' Bear corrected, after nodding both in acknowledgment of her good shot but equally in instruction to continue. 'What you should understand is that to Archmond, this prophecy has become a bit of a symbol. Something to hold on to. People in Archmond have been restless for a long time. Nervous. Paranoid of another attack. There was a growing impatience of a sorts you could say. But they expect a lot, the Archmonders. The wizards knew about the prophecy, perhaps not where it came from, but they still knew of it, and they took it upon themselves to promise the kingdom they could ensure it was fulfilled. That it would restore the kingdom to the pre-Abigail world they enjoyed: unity between Archmond and the mainland, free trade, free movement of people between kingdoms, et cetera. They became committed to this promise to the people that they would bring the child here to fulfil that prophecy. I know they had tried before and failed. But this time, well I mean, they did a spell, and then you arrived.'

She grumbled with frustration as she missed the second block.

'Yet Yinsoo knew about my past. About dark things from a long time ago. And she admitted she sent me those notes. Soleman and Ron looked surprised when I asked about the notes.'

'Notes?' Bear queried, before pushing her on again. 'Come on. Focus. Keep going with your practice.'

Lucy sighed and swiped at the second block again, not only missing it, but almost losing her footing in the process.

'I found a series of notes, with these Celtic markings, back in Lockerby. The first two I couldn't read. The third one called me a liar. But the same markings were on the temple in Yerkey. It was following the notes into that windy parkland near the school that started all this. When I confronted Yinsoo about them, she claimed they were my invitation to come here.'

Bear huffed, and his eyes took on their cavernous galaxy voids for several moments, constellations sparkling away within them before he whispered faintly, 'interesting.'

Lucy laughed, finally managing to swipe off the second block.

'So Yinsoo's not making anything up. Maybe the wizards didn't do anything at all?' she suggested and turned to him for his input.

'I don't know what to tell you. They did a spell, then you arrived.'

'Did you see it?'

'The spell? Yes.'

'Tell me. Tell me what they did exactly,' she said, her left hand on her hip as she let the sword in her right rest against her side, its tip touching the soil.

Bear sighed, he had been instructed to keep the details from her, but more and more he couldn't see how it would hurt.

'They have rocks, boulders of emery, in the western garden behind the castle. The rocks connect with the sky, with the infinite they say. They had obtained a powder… I have no idea what it was… but they said they needed it to enhance the energy of the rocks. They threw the powder onto the rocks and chanted an incantation. The rocks lit up. There was a shot of light - into the sky. Then they went dark. A few days later you were lying on that carpet.'

Crumbs had been sniffing around the edge of the shed with increasing interest, and now began to growl softly at the bright world outside the enormous hole beside which Lucy's blocks were aligned. But both

Lucy and Bear were now too engrossed in this conversation of her origins to pay any attention to his concern.

Lucy grumbled for a minute, still trying to piece it all together.

'But when they did the spell, who did they think would arrive? Just someone? Yinsoo claims she sent the notes to me, personally, but I have no idea what led her to me. The wizards haven't told me anything about how or why they came to think I was the child from this prophecy, or why they wanted to bring me here.'

Internally Bear chuckled at the sudden distancing of herself from them by now referring to Soleman and Ronald as, 'the wizards'. The talk in the Rolling Hills and beyond had rubbed off on her, clearly.

'What does any of it matter as to how?' he said. 'You're here now, whether it was Yinsoo or Soleman.'

Lucy's gaze told him his answer was not sufficient.

'I can't speak for Yinsoo, but Soleman and Ron were doing the same spell on the night of the full moon, for many years in a bid to point them to the prophetic child. It was a similar spectacle to when they sought to bring you here. By the rocks they would chant over a small fire. Then they would read out lines from the prophecy and put a special parchment over the flames. The incantation made the flames curve intricately over the parchment. Rather than devour it, the flames burnt slender lines, making markings over it, different ones each time. They used the markings as a guide of where to look, through their lens into your world. The markings, they would resemble letters or symbols. Sometimes the markings made no sense or Ron would say they were too ambiguous so they would have to wait until the next moon. Sometimes they'd indicate a place, and they would look in that place and find nothing there. Every time this happened they put this down to the spell not being done correctly. They were in the wrong position, or they used the wrong fuel in the fire. But on the night they found you, the markings of the flames on the parchment had made a lock, and a bee.'

Lucy looked at him puzzled for several moments, before swallowing with an understanding, 'Lockerby?'

Bear nodded. 'They found old homes in Lockerby, and they liked what they saw in the oldest home. A girl, light in eyes, dark of hair, in a disturbing situation, and seemingly very alone.'

Lucy scoffed. They hadn't told her any of this. They had deliberately kept from her the methods they'd used to randomly select her as their saviour, and the methods they'd used to magic her into this world. What reason did they have to be so secretive? She couldn't help but become more cynical about everything they'd kept from her, both about her, this world, and about their own kingdom.

'And if the prophecy is fulfilled…' Lucy said, raising the sword up and trying to adjust to its weight as she pondered, 'they will be the heroes? They will be seen as rulers that can keep their promises? Is that all there is to it?'

Crumbs continued to growl, as the omling came alongside the shed, each breath making a faint gagging noise. Lucy and Bear were still too engrossed in their conversation and her practice to notice anything amiss, even as it began to scrape its claws into the red sand, cleaning them, preparing them for the kill.

Bear shook his head. 'Focus, Lucy, we can talk politics later. Right now, I have to get you up to at least novice level,' Bear said, sitting above her on a rafter, indicating the block again.

Lucy sighed.

'Remember, line it up, then use the strength of your whole arm,' he went on.

Lucy focused, steadied the sword backward, kept her arm straight, and swung toward the block, just as the omling launched through the tractor-sized hole in the shed. Lucy shrieked but immediately refocused and drove the sword further forward toward the omling. She struck it hard enough that it fell backward with a sizeable wound down its side, but it pounced forward again, sharp claws drawing into her ankle and pulling her leg to its mouth, causing her to fall backward. Bear shot the omling with a flash of light. It was enough for it to let go, and enough for Lucy to step back into position and send the sword straight down into the omling's neck with enough force that the head was nearly severed. The creature seized for several moments before it eventually fell still.

'Getting better,' Bear remarked with surprise.

Later that night, having left the cover of the shed miles behind in their journey southeast, they made camp beside a ring of large boulders. Several of the boulders, rusty red by day, imperceptibly charcoal in the night, had cracked, and then split in a sharp line down their centre. The extreme climate of the plateau having caused a weathering effect the likes of a godly sword. The carcasses of two desert rodents lay across the charred outskirts of the fire. There was enough left on them that they were more than skeletal; Lucy couldn't stomach the innards. The flesh alone made her stomach churn.

The evening was still. There was a welcome calmness to that emptiness. It was as if the evening were fostering its own clarity, in the still, starlit warmth. Lucy pulled her skin taut to examine the wound on her calf, and then the other on her ankle.

'You fared better than they did,' Bear commented, but she grimaced. The wounds, particularly the one on her calf, were painful, and fast infecting. In the morning, she would fail to notice how rapidly they had begun to heal.

'They were smaller than the first two,' she said dismissively. They were talking about the omling duo she'd successfully fought off several hours ago, in the moments before dusk fell.

'Yes. Probably younger, and fitter, so all the more reason to be proud.'

Lucy shrugged, she had other things on her mind. 'Why did you have to leave me in the frozen land? It was very frightful,' she added as she poked at the fire. Bright red embers burst up into the darkness, blurring into the net of stars above. They both recognised the comment as out of the blue.

'But I came back,' he said, defensively.

'Yes, you came back. After it was all over. When I was well outside of Yerkey, and all that torment was over.'

'It's the snow,' he said, scrunching up his face, 'it doesn't do good things to my coat.'

'What coat? You're ethereal. There is no coat.' She looked at him plainly as she spoke. She made a mental note to come back to this, but right now was wanting him to confess the true reason he suddenly left her. Crumbs lay between them, facing the fire. He sighed heavily, nuzzling his head further into his paws.

'This obsession with real again,' Bear huffed, 'besides, I got the impression they took care of you in Yerkey. That it was quite productive, and I was not needed. And, you've recovered from this, this, well you know…'

She knew what he meant of course, but she did not want to go along. 'Recovered from what?'

Bear looked away as he spoke, feigning nonchalance. 'You know, the memories, this thing that's come back to you.'

She arched back, raising her head, examining him. He shifted, anxiously.

'Well, we, that is, Soleman, Ronald and I… we knew there was something dark in your past, that it was going to come out at some point. I saw it coming, the shadows chasing us, you becoming lost in your head, and all the while I could sense we were getting nearer and nearer to the ancient settlement, the settlement known for its tenacity with the spirits, and I thought, well this has got to be it!' he said excitedly, as if she might share in the fascination and satisfaction he had from his accurate premonitions. She sat back a little, and her eyes fell to the cool dusty earth beside her. There was little life on the plateau, and what life there was lived below ground. They had nothing but the occasional crackle and roar of the fire between their silences.

'Don't worry, I have no idea what was in those memories, or what realisation came to you,' he tried to reassure her. 'That is between you and the Reichi. I will perhaps never know what it was that was revealed to you in their temple.'

'My father killed my sister, I saw it, and I've never told anyone.'

'Oh. Okay. Now I know.'

Another somewhat stilted silence resumed between them, but somehow the gravity of this did nothing to stir the calm stillness of the night air. No tension lingered in the space between them across the flames.

'How could I forget something like that? Seems impossible.'

Bear shook his head, and conjured a cigar for himself, which he lit in the fire. 'You were just doing as most children would, doing what you could to cope, to survive.'

She didn't take much comfort in this but went on, 'but then what I also don't understand is, how is that linked to me being here?'

Bear shrugged. 'Wouldn't knowing the truth make you stronger? Help you be strong in both worlds?'

Lucy rejected this notion entirely. She needn't have come to another world to deal with her past.

'How?' she said, challenging him and giving him a moment to respond.

'I don't feel any stronger. I feel awful,' she said when he didn't answer.

'Maybe now. Maybe now you feel awful. But… I think… I think you needed to accept the past before you could move on, and be any use to both yourself and this world.'

Lucy scoffed at this. 'Any use to this world? Don't you mean be any use to the wizards?'

Bear gave a look, which is to say he tilted his head and narrowed his eyes completely, he being a creature of limited facial expression.

'They only want me to be successful so they can impress their people. But it strikes me they're not being very good to all their people. The imprisoned people of the rural lands live in poverty, and from what I hear send all their produce up to the Wooden Floor Borders, because that's the only way they can get the medicine they seem to need. Meanwhile the WFB seems to exist in this kind of…surreal prosperity,' Lucy said, becoming lively. She was not vexed. Rather, she was enjoying her new-found observation. The veil of confusion was starting to lift, and the knowledge and understanding she was consuming, this, this was what made her feel strong. Bear agreed with her on this, but it would do no use to admit it.

'They're doing what they can. It's been hard for the kingdom to be self-sufficient. It was a big shock when the whole world, more or less, stopped trading with them.'

Lucy stared deep into the fire, then sighed and lay back onto the fur she now used as a sleep mat.

'But it doesn't change the point though, does it? Even if I could do this ridiculous thing, I'm just helping them. I'm not helping the world.'

'See it as you wish. For the meantime you still need to stay alive until you can find a way home. Yes?'

Home. She didn't reply for several moments and became lost in the idea of it. Home, how far away was home? How feasible was it that she could ever get back there? Bear's earlier description of the wizard's spell and the illuminated rocks then circled its way back into her mind.

'They told me they didn't have the power to reverse the spell, to send me home, but they never told me what the spell was. They also kept me from the western garden where you say those rocks are. Where you saw them conduct this secretive spell that brought, or well supposedly, brought me here. When they said they couldn't get me home, they were lying weren't they? They can reverse it, can't they?

They could send me home if they wanted to?' She was overcome, and overly excited.

Bear drew breath, and looked left, above, and right as if for answers. There was no correct way to respond.

'I don't know. If that's true they've never shared that with me.' He hesitated as to how to appease her. He wanted to be as honest as he could, given their rapport was starting to mean a lot to him. 'Maybe… maybe they're not sure how to do it, but they were scared you'd figure out a way.'

'Well, perhaps they should be scared. I might get better with this sword.'

'Lucy! You can't mean that!' he scolded her.

'I can. Look at what they've done. They have taken me from everything I know and thrown me into this horridly devoid land. It's not only immoral, it's heartless.'

Bear said nothing. He sympathised with her.

'Maybe I should change direction, go back to Archmond and test the power of these rocks for myself,' she paused as she thought on this plan. 'Would you help me - if I wanted to go back?'

'Lucy if they don't want you in that garden, I don't see how you can force your way in. No matter how good you get with that sword. And what would you do when you got there? Stand in front of the rocks and do what exactly?'

Lucy huffed. He was right, she knew.

'But if I did go, would you still help me?'

Crumbs whimpered beside them, his little paws pushing through the air in strides as though he was running wildly through the dreamworld.

Bear looked at Lucy, her face, a bronze sculpture in the fire-light, was stern in its petition of him. He sighed. 'In returning to Archmond, yes. Yes, if you decide to go back, I will still help you, my girl.'

For hours it seemed as though they might go to sleep. She wanted to. Sleep was the only relief and comfort she had anymore. The back of her throat was constantly scratchy and dry, and the outlook from Bear was that they'd be lucky to find even small wells of ground water over the next couple of days until they got to the watering hole, if it in fact still existed.

The well at the shed had been unused and filthy, but it ran deep. Given his dire forecasts they'd taken the necessary time to distil a good litre or so and fill her canister entirely before they left. She'd sipped it lightly, given she knew that she (and Crumbs) may be surviving on less than a few-hundred millilitres a day until they found the waterhole, if they found it. Her skin felt cooked already, and the limited intake of rodents she was consuming was making her both irritable and dizzy. Several more days lay ahead until they descended into jungle. It was a grim prospect.

Lucy tried to shift her focus by staring into the night sky. It was not her first time marvelling at it from out here. Why, she wondered, did the plateau itself have a different perspective on the celestial configurations that glittered above this new world. Never before the Alexandria, had she seen clusters of stars so plentiful and colourful: purple, red, green, pink, blue, and Amber. They sparkled at her rhythmically, as if they were performing a special dance only she could see. It was too beautiful to question. She simply let the performance play out and smiled back at them in appreciation. But as it seemed the night's weariness might overcome her, she remembered her mental note from earlier and asked softly, unsure if he was already asleep,

'You said in Chupner's Forest that you would tell me how you came to be. You said it was a story for another time. Is it another time yet?'

At this point, the night, late as it was, started to softly stir. A very faint breeze, tickling, blew in from the south.

'I can tell you all that I know. I don't know that it will give you much clarity.' Bear yawned.

Lucy was facing away from him, lying on the Indawara fur, under the coat that Yinsoo had gifted her.

'I'd still like to hear it,' she said.

Bear rolled over from where he lay on the stony earth. He questioned the point of this tale, but the relationship he was creating with Lucy was starting to become to him… something of importance. He glanced at her, or the back of her. Her hair was all dishevelled, her figure curled up into a ball. She's just a young girl, he reminded himself.

'I have little memory of it. Or that it is to say none. But I am told that I was once an inanimate object,' he began with a sigh. Pleasingly, Lucy did not react, so he went on with more comfort. 'I was gifted to the child you saw thrown from the Palace terrace in your dream. Gloria. I was hers.'

The fire had long since been put out, so there was nothing now to navigate their silences. But when Lucy did not speak for a while, he went on.

'I am told that after she died, I somehow, materialised…'

He saw her shift then, just a readjustment of posture, but she was awake, and she was listening.

'So, are you her spirit?' Eventually the expected question came. He knew she would ask this.

'It is not known. My opinion? No. I have no connection with this dead child - sad though the story is. The timing is questionable, but I feel nothing like a dead royal girl. I feel myself. So how the two are connected I do not know. But the story they tell about me is that a toy of hers, a plush cream bear, on the day of her burial, turned jet black and became animated with life. I remember seeing the screams as I opened my eyes. Everything that happened before that moment is a mystery to me. But I was vocal from day one, and I sensed my powers before I began to use them. I suppose starting out there, in that moment, made me feel I had some obligation towards that family, those grieving parents. So, while I'm not part of Archmond's government, I've been supporting their campaign for justice in the east for a long time.'

Bear was nervous. He seldom disclosed this kind of detail for fear of the reaction. Doubt, among many things he feared from the receiver.

But Lucy gave a satisfactory sigh and simply said, 'well, that is an interesting story. You are very unique. I'm tired now. Goodnight.'

Each day was a carbon copy of the last: waking with a crooked neck, sleeping with dehydration and pangs of hunger. Everything they saw was the same: the barren landscape with its burnt orange earth stretching into the horizon, the aqua sky and its sparse wispy white lines. It was disorientating at best, bewildering at worst. Just as maddening was the repetitiveness of their routine: waiting for the rodents, waiting hours; looking for wells where it seemed cattle stations might once have existed; then resting.

The amount of energy devoted to sourcing the bare necessities meant that the progress they made each day was pitiful. Bear had limited ability to speed things up. Other than guide their way, he could only promise to ward off the omlings if she truly was too lifeless to hold the sword. Luckily though, in the last two days, that threat at least had kept away. But even in her malnourished daze Lucy still suspected that he could probably help more if he chose to, but that in some way, for some reason, he chose not to.

They did find the creek. Or the watering hole. An almond shaped body of water about the size of a large garden pond. It drizzled south down the converged slabs of earth and dried up as it dripped into a miniature gorge below. The water spurred up from some underground bore. A bleeding crevice was marked by a black bubbled line in its deepest pocket, and it was deep. They'd seen it from some distance, but it was only as they drew within a hundred yards that she let herself succumb to an ecstatic acceptance, that this wasn't simply another mirage. Lucy tore off her boots, letting them fly through the air and tumble haphazardly to the ground, Crumbs racing ahead. The creek was cool at its depth, and warm at the surface. It had been more than a week since she'd felt the touch of water against her skin. The wells that allowed them to dredge up cloudy ground water never had enough spare that she could rinse the rusty dirt from her face and legs. This pond water was hard, mineral laden, and left a faint crystalline residue against her thighs where it lapped, but she embraced it all the same.

Bear watched plumes of grey mud balloon up from the bed all around her as she plunked down onto the shallow bank, completely disrobed.

'I don't know that we're entirely alone out here my girl.' Bear squinted as he looked around. He couldn't see any sign of danger, but the sun's glare glistening off sand and boulders meant he couldn't see much of anything in most directions.

'Watering holes being so rare… likely to make them fairly popular,' he continued.

'I don't care,' muttered Lucy almost inaudibly, dragging water toward her with cupped hands, running it down her shoulders and chest. She dragged herself deeper down the bank, until the water lapped up over her breasts and crept up toward her neck. The key come pendant, where it sat between her breasts, stirred with buoyancy, until it floated to the surface, the chain with it, and bobbed gently. She watched it for several moments, curious about how this heavy metallic pendant could float. Tiny aquatic life danced around it, attracted to it. A chorus of animated black specs moved excitedly amongst tadpole-sized fish, fascinated with this new entrancing addition to their pond. As she stared past them, she could just make out thin films of reeds, breaking through the surface of the black water on the bank across from her. But the serenity shattered as the pendant started to smoke, and small sparks frightened away the micro-fish.

'Get that out of the water,' Bear scolded as if she should have known better. Lucy yanked the chain back up, drawing it tight around her collarbone.

'Water isn't good for it,' he added, but adding little clarity. While his tone suggested this wasn't a terrible concern, Lucy still made sure to keep her chest elevated out of the water as she lay back and unwound her plait, letting her dark thick coils take in the muddy, mineral-laden water. She closed her eyes and let herself feel the water's kiss on nearly every part of her body.

'Oh I'm so glad I've found you! So, so glad!'

Lucy opened her eyes to see Soleman on the edge of bank. She shrieked and splashed wildly in the water, submerging herself deeper so the mud would conceal her.

'Good lord, what the devil are you doing here!' Bear scowled, moving Lucy's clothes to the edge of the bank where she could reach them easily. 'You'd better get dressed, dear. I don't think any appearance from His Eminence on the plateau signifies good news.'

'Quite right,' Soleman said in a sombre tone, turning around so she could dress. 'I'm afraid I appear to bring quite dire news indeed.'

As she dressed, she recognised from the blurred outline of his figure, that he in fact was not physically with them. Rather, like Bear who was present but without physical mass, he was just a vision, a hologram of sorts, however he was managing it. He was in formal attire, having just addressed his ministers on this same news hours earlier.

'The queen is aware of your existence, child, and more than that it appears she is aware of your journey. She has sent assassins out to hunt you, and we've word they've reached the plateau.'

He turned back around as he said this, and she felt then a sudden resurgence in awareness of her surroundings: the touch of the dry afternoon air on her wet skin, distant sounds, the patter of the paws of heavy beasts racing across broken earth miles away, perhaps?

'Assassins,' Lucy repeated, eyes widening anxiously.

'There's other things I wanted to tell you, though maybe now isn't the best time,' he added, nervously fidgeting, and letting out an exasperated sigh. Clearly, he could not contain himself, and so went on, 'there has been a crisis of missing children across Archmond since you arrived. Both on the WFB and in the Hills. I can't explain it but it… it also comes at a time when Ron's allegiance to our mission has come under some rather serious scrutiny.'

Having gathered her things, she began cleaning her sword with the water and wiping the blade with the edge of her shirt.

'Allegiance?' she questioned as she put it back in its holder.

'I don't know that I should go into the details now, I mean I don't have anything to suggest treason at this stage, and of course, of course I hope I'm wrong to even think that word,' said Soleman.

'Treason?' Lucy gawked, standing firm now, and alert.

Suddenly a look of terror rushed upon Soleman's face.

'Lucy!' Bear shouted.

She spun around to see an omling lurching toward her, the creature having crawled camouflaged across the rocky knolls around them. Whether she was becoming more agile, or whether the hostile news had pumped her up with fresh adrenaline, she didn't hesitate this time. She lunged toward the creature before it came any closer and drove her sword through its neck, hacking it across until its head dribbled forward, convulsing.

Soleman flinched. This was certainly a different girl to the sobbing juvenile he'd sent off from Archmond Castle. The aggression he now perceived in her was almost frightening. But as the creature began to slump backward into death, falling off her sword, they heard what he'd come to warn her about. A distant screeching, terrifyingly loud, echoed all around them. Lucy's breath became rapid. She turned to Bear. He looked up. High above, four large birds with a crimson hue circled. They screeched again and the plateau itself almost shuddered.

'Abigail's seekers,' Soleman said, swallowing hard, 'they've found you.'

'Hardly surprising, she stands out like glitter on this barren clifftop,' Bear replied.

Soleman disregarded the analogy as his expression now filled with dread. Shaking his head, he muttered, 'I have to go,' and at once his image was gone.

Lucy looked to Bear again for answers. She searched his face for 'what now'. But as she did, they both heard the re-emergence of what her fear thought it heard before.

Intrepidly, Lucy strode around the bank and up the knoll to where Soleman had stood before. Looking to the south, she saw what was making the rampant patter across the desert. Beasts, an entire pride of them. Their features were barely visible at this distance, but that also disguised the speed at which they charged toward her. In her initial confusion Lucy stared, transfixed.

'Sabre tigers. Time to go my dear,' Bear declared with a haunting certainty.

'Tigers? I thought you said there were only omlings on the plateau?' But even as she asked this, she was cognisant of the outline of a person, a male, behind the tigers, growing smaller as the beasts grew nearer and larger.

'The assassins,' Bear shouted. 'Come! Now!'

Lucy understood then and turned and ran, fastening the sword against her, shouting to Crumbs. She staggered as her clumsy feet caught in deep roots that still clambered up the bank. As she fell, her knees and shins grazed as she skid across gravelly soil. But she was quickly becoming accustomed to danger and pain. She jolted back up again, and raced toward Bear, until she and Crumbs were sprinting alongside his shadow.

'Where are we going?' she called to him.

'Not south anymore,' he answered with less certainty than she'd hoped. But he gave her something, shouting, 'there's an old salt mine on the edge of the plateau that drops into Josso Jungle. Or there used to be. It's been slowly collapsing into the jungle for decades, but in it may be a way down. I don't know. It's all I've got.'

When they reached the broken signposts at the mine's entrance, the sabres were well and truly at their heels. Lucy had been long out of breath and running on legs and lungs that seemed to move on their own.

'There!' Bear shouted. His voice turned them down a slender cement path still etched into the ground all these decades later. The path descended down a small hill and passed the decaying structures of storage sheds and processing units. Now, of course, there were only iron posts and pieces of sheet-metal to indicate anything ever existed. But they saw almost immediately the shaft, dark and shadowy.

'The mine!' Bear called, intending it to be informative, but shouting while remembering the urgency as he caught a glimpse of the sabres racing down the hill behind them. Lucy barely had time to question it as they stumbled over the pillows of sand dunes gathered up before the boxy dark entrance. The absurdity of it, the danger, the uncertainty of racing into a shaft decades in decay, was all but drowned out by the cries of the beasts behind them.

'Get back!' cried Bear as they cleared the entrance. His beam of blue light caused the roof of the shaft to crumble in on itself. There was no way in or out now. Lucy looked at him questioningly while Crumbs scampered out of the debris.

'Go!' he commanded gruffly.

They hurried further down the shaft, but the ground beneath them was descending sharply, and they could see very little. Bear's glow was only enough to show the perilous gradient at which the ground dropped away from them. After shakily scaling the decline they hit a flat hollow area and could feel the damp air open up around them. Bear floated around it rapidly, his faint hue folding across the dimensions. She watched him from the base of the decommissioned shaft, his tiny purple aura shifting back and forth frantically. He was panicking.

'We'll take the second tunnel,' he said, moving back in front of it. He like a beacon, guiding her to him. He the shepherd, and Lucy the sheep, following without question. She and Crumbs rushed across the hollow space, taking in the metallic whiffs of the cool damp air, and trusting that Bear knew the line between he and them was stable - as she could see nothing but his far violet light. They were still too filled with terror to communicate properly. Almost too panicked to talk.

'Where are we going?' Lucy asked, hurrying down the tunnel.

'I don't know,' Bear snapped, but then reconsidered. They stopped for a moment, 'I'm hoping to find the cable car, or what's left of it, to bring us down into the jungle below. To bring you down rather... I don't know where it would be, but this tunnel was the most eastward facing. And the plateau's cliff faces east.'

The wall behind him glistened in the halo of his lavender hue. Fragmented crystals glistened up and down the vertical grooves left by the machine that carved the tunnel.

'What kind of mine is this? Or was this?' Lucy asked.

'Salt,' Bear said, scanning the darkness as they came to a crossroads. Crumbs licked the sodium rich walls around them. Lucy watched him for a moment, as if allowing herself to take stock of where they were for the first time. The shaft had taken them a long way below ground, and they were still declining.

A thunderous echo, powerful but distant, reignited their sense of urgency. The sound of an explosion, followed by terrifyingly eager howls. The barrier Bear had created had been breached. Bear chanced on the tunnel to their right and she raced after him, but Bear's light faded every time he got far enough ahead of her. She was just as scared that she or Crumbs would fall through a cavity in the ground, she snatched him into her arms but holding him on her front and her heavy backpack only slowed her down further. She screamed for Bear to slow down, and he scolded her for giving them away.

They came into another cavernous space, where parts of abandoned machinery were poking out from under years of rubble and dust. The equipment and the rubble burying it filled the space entirely. Bear slowed to help navigate her over it, but some of the debris would shift and give way under her, and he grew more anxious as he heard the rhythmic thuds of the beasts making their way closer. His frustration overflowed as he watched her struggle to clutch a protruding beam from the buried mechanical digger to hoist herself up, while balancing the squirming dog in her other arm.

'Let the dog climb over himself for goodness' sake! He's probably better than you are,' snapped Bear as she stumbled again, and her distorted weight drew her down into a pit of sand between the excavator and the drill.

'I'm not letting go of him,' she insisted in a petulant tone, but she scampered over the final mound, and they scurried down the next tunnel.

The noises of the beasts grew louder, as the tunnel descended more sharply. They were running down intersecting tunnels which gave hope of losing her predators, but as her backpack bounced heavily on her back, in the pit of her stomach this sickening feeling permeated. A sickening, disgusting feeling. They were racing deeper and deeper into an inescapable death trap.

Suddenly she had the sense of the space around them opening up again, and she could see a clear reflection of Bear's illuminated image below them. She stumbled forward and the coldness of water lapped all around her legs. A reservoir. The ceiling above loomed low. She went forward and felt herself decline even more sharply and the water rise around her knees, until her boots felt the edge where the ground stopped. There was no time to think, she pushed off from the edge and felt the black water around her deepen and her feet could no longer feel the floor as her legs propelled her forward. She released Crumbs and he swam beside her.

They were halfway across this cavernous trench, Bear still lighting their way yards ahead, when they heard the bellowing confirmation that their hunters had finally caught up with them. She couldn't help but turn back, briefly. She pushed forward faster through the water with their image in her mind. Four beasts, five? Muscular figures of great cats. And she was sure that behind them was the figure of a slender man. She swam freestyle faster than she would have ever thought possible, tearing through the water, but that sickening feeling re-emerged with intensity. A sinking feeling that nearly sunk her. The futility of it. She could hear the pace of them through the rampant splashing of the water. Bear took in their image aghast, his shaky breath left her no confidence.

'Keep going, as fast as you can. Take any path that leads you east!' he shouted when she was nearly at the other side. He shot above them like a falling star back toward the beasts, holding them back with a criss-cross of blue light. He swivelled with great effort as they continued to try and circumvent it.

She knew she had reached the bank opposite only as her knees scraped across the rock. She gasped in pain but heaved herself up, hearing Crumbs shake himself dry. She swooped up Crumbs and ran on, but she couldn't see. There was nothing but hollow darkness. She had to keep close to the wall, her hand tracing it occasionally to feel where it turned away, but all the while her mind reminded her this was futile. Bear could not hold them forever. She was starting to feel too weak to continue.

Until she saw light. Its faint glow called from around the next bend. But its angelic beacon came in the same moment as she heard the return of the heavy patter of paws behind her. But now she had hope, and the hope fuelled her on. Bear had mentioned a cable car, and this opening, still so far below the ground as they were, must have been where it was. She pushed the last of her energy into her thighs, calves, and feet, and hurtled herself forward faster than she ever had before.

The tunnel turned again, and a sudden chorus of daylight over-whelmed and blinded her. She was going so fast it was almost difficult to stop. But as she tried to slow down and her eyes adjusted, frantically searching, she could see no cable car. There was no anything. There was a gaping hole where the mine stopped abruptly, and the cliff face had fallen away into the valley miles below.

The light had flooded in so suddenly, from a pale slither to a complete enveloping. She hadn't the time to stop and appreciate how sharply the ground beneath her feet disappeared, and she had sped right to its edge with all the energy of movement still charging through her. And as she turned to see the image of the beast lunging forward in the air mere metres away, the dread inside her couldn't hold still. She faltered, and then stumbled, and just like that her footing was lost. Still clutching Crumbs, she let out a blood-curdling scream as her body catapulted with dizzying speed down the side of the plateau. She was but a tiny speck as her body disappeared through the blanket of cloud that covered the jungle below.

❧

In the Mathilde Gardens of Verity Palace, the family pay homage to the dead...

'You are a remarkable creature, a survivor,' Abigail whispered, as she released the dove from her hands, and it took flight. Some of the staff had been mending its wing after it had become tangled in midnight blue ivy that clambered the walls of these same gardens: the Mathilde Gardens of Verity Palace. She had caught wind of this incident and insisted she take care of releasing it back into nature. They had brought the caged bird to her chambers, and she had kept it several more days to have its release coincide with today's memorial. Before they came down to the celebration, she'd had its feathers sprinkled with gold dust, (a surprise) and as it took flight over the garden walls, the gold trailed behind it in the air, glittering across the water and the reeds.

As far as Abigail was concerned the Mathilde gardens were lacking in sentiment. But they were that kind of perfectly preened and culti-vated beauty that most people seemed to enjoy, and it being a family affair, she had to take into account the preference of the majority. But she did not prefer them. She had spent her own time in remembrance this morning, in the untamed gardens that she alone adored. Between the palace and the rockface, near the Immar Wing, where the flushing green waters from the summit pooled and then trickled under a wall and off the edge of the mountain. The pond of mountain water was filled with mustard reeds and draped with willows. She had spent much time there as a child with her late sisters, so what better place to mourn the existence of family.

'Beautiful,' remarked Evaneigh, with a hand to her neck. 'Your mother would have loved it. Oh, and of course, of course I'm sure your father would have appreciated it too.'

'Not sure Joshua cared much for doves,' mused Norton, 'but he liked gold.'

This comment cost him a curious glance from his niece, but he saved himself promptly. 'He would be pleased with you my dear. At how strong you are. How well you've managed this enormous burden placed on you at such a tender age. The Kingdom thrives.'

Abigail smiled and moved back to where they'd gathered. Glass tables and light-stone chairs had been brought out into the garden and set up upon the grass area before the central path which divided it into quarters, each with a pond at the centre. An ink-wood tree stretched over the party with its slender black branches, the midnight blue ivy lapping over them, with star shaped leaves drooping down in the heat. Summer lingered on.

'It's a glorious day,' remarked Pykeros, taking in the clear sky and its wispy white clouds. 'I do love being up here on the mountain. The air is fresh and clear. It's always so dense down in the city this time of year.'

'You're always welcome to stay up here longer you know. You should. I'm sure your unit can manage without you. Or, actually even, you could be summonsed if they needed you,' said Evaneigh. It was spoken as an offer, an invitation, but her voice was softly pleading with him. Pykeros smiled at his wife but did not respond and poured himself another brandy.

'I can't remember the last time I went down into Lazareth,' said Locotier. 'We should go down soon, Norton, I feel as though we're missing out on all the action cooped away up here.'

'Plenty of action up here,' said Bevant, topping up her glass. She smiled back at him warmly. 'Though I'm sure there will be cause to go down soon to celebrate signing of the shipping channel arrangement with Coby,' he added.

'Oh?' Pykeros turned. 'So it's settled? I wasn't aware. Well done!' He directed his congratulations at Abigail who smiled humbly and glanced to Norton.

'Once the council approved the notion I wanted Coby notified at once. They are extremely pleased. I thank my uncle for his good counsel on this,' Abigail said, again tilting upwards to cast her eyes upon Norton who sat to her right at the head of the table. Her aunt and Pykeros sat to her left, and Bevant sat opposite beside Locotier. The attendants waited a good distance away, by the walls of the enclosed garden.

'I'm still not sure I understand what it is we've given Coby,' said Evaneigh. She had voted in favour of the proposition at the last sitting of the council, but only on instructions from her husband.

'It does a world of good to strengthen our alliance with them,' Norton responded to Abigail, 'they may not be the largest kingdom on the mainland but they have the largest harbour, and the most ships.'

'And are our closest neighbour,' added Bevant, 'anyone who wants to get to us, will have to go through them first.'

'Precisely,' said Norton, cutting into some game he'd put to one side on his plate, but now decided to finish. An attendant rang a bell to indicate their intrusion, before walking over with plates of cake. They put a piece down in front of each of them, with a candle waiting to be lit.

'Cake to honour the dead. It still seems uncouth to me,' said Pykeros.

Evaneigh looked down at the wreath poking out of its satchel by her feet. Pykeros had thought that was uncouth too. It had not helped to hear that. She had not made one on previous anniversaries, but for some reason this anniversary felt more poignant than others.

'Uncouth?' queried Abigail too softly for anyone to hear.

'Nonsense,' dismissed Bevant, 'we are celebrating their lives. And this is not cake for the dead, this is cake for the king and queen, for our predecessors. We need to hold on to the memories of great leaders. This fusion in the Dynasty Council, of the royal line and the merchant magnates, each of which have equally built this kingdom's glory, is held together by the monarchs, and it is a great responsibility.'

He paused to eye Abigail, who was staring transfixed into the pink sponge cake, the flimsy collar of her dress and her glossy black hair, lightly shifting in the breeze.

'A responsibility I'm sure our young Queen Abigail knows all too well,' he concluded.

Abigail looked up confused, she hadn't been paying attention, but she smiled, somewhat sheepishly, having caught the last line.

Pykeros scoffed. 'Spoken like a true royal,' he said. Evaneigh made a huff and elbowed him, but he shrugged, as if in jest.

'I have a match,' offered Locotier.

'No, no, I want to do it,' said Abigail.

There was a sort of collective drawing of breath. As though a nervous but controlled anxiety overcame them. Norton sighed, uncomfortably, but tried to hide it.

'Go on then,' Norton said, and pushed he and his wife's plate forward.

Evaneigh pushed her and her husband's plate closer to Abigail too. Bevant did the same. Excitedly Abigail took a deep breath. A chill ran over them all before she began to count as she went, lighting the candles with flames that emerged from her fingertips.

'One, two, three, four, five… six!' she exclaimed, delighted at herself. They relaxed a little that it was all over, but she couldn't help herself.

'And one for mother and one for father!' she exclaimed, pushing her hands together as if in prayer, and sending a burst of flames up into the air. Although the plume of flames shot straight through a gap in the ebony foliage, the residual heat eventually gave rise to small spot fires in the line where it parted the branches.

'Oh, Abbie! Now our oldest tree is on fire,' cursed Norton, waving over the servants. They came rushing with buckets and scooped water from the ponds, which they threw up into the branches.

'I thought it was a lovely gesture, Abigail. The tree will be fine. Don't worry about your uncle,' Evaneigh whispered to her encouragingly. Abigail smiled in thanks but felt wounded by her uncle's criticism. As the commotion about the flames died off, Evaneigh felt a spurt of courage burn within her and brought out her wreath.

'I…' she began but stopped, suddenly feeling so awkward under all the attention, 'I too, would like to offer something for my late brother and sister-in-law.'

She held out the wreath. It was made of leafy branches and red-flowering woody tendrils, but they had dried up and browned over the last few days.

Abigail recoiled. 'Ugh! Auntie! What is that?'

Evaneigh expected this reaction. She took the candle from her own cake and moved over to the first pond where she remembered playing with brother. They used to swim in it. Not that anyone believed her. These days it hardly seemed becoming to swim in for anyone, let alone a prince and princess. But when they were young it was bigger, there were no weeds or algae, and cascading slate rocks led down into welcoming jade water. He was so much older and he had better things to do, but still he had played with her. He'd get logs and old branches from around the corners, ones that floated, so she could clutch onto something as he dragged her around in the water. Evaneigh lit the candles on the wreath, and cast it adrift, pushing it toward the centre of the pond.

'This is for you Josh, and for you Laura. I miss you both.'

'What would my father have liked about tendril weeds?' Abigail asked confused, standing on a chair so she could see. Norton said nothing but shook his head blankly and looked on.

'Ahh, you two!' scolded Bevant, 'you're too young your Majesty, and Norton you weren't around. Our late king loved tendril weed. He used to build cubby forts and weave it around the entrances making traps for people. It was his insignia.'

Chapter 2

Josso Jungle: An introduction to madness

Twas brillig, and the slithy toves, did gire and gymble in the wabe.
All mimsy, were the borogroves, and the mome raths, outgrabe.
The Jabberwocky, Lewis Carrol, 1871

The silvery layer of fog that concealed the jagged canopy of Josso Jungle, did not have the consistency of mist. The fog was thickest where the scarcely penetrable jungle met the iron red plateau wall, which faded into terracotta the higher it rose, and became gold where it overshadowed the botanical wilderness beneath it. The fog's consistency was one of an unimaginable viscosity, a secret known only by the larger birds that had persisted in their attempts to pass through its thick milky grip.

When Lucy, clutching Crumbs, plummeted through its surface, she shattered the stillness like a shooting star through a placid midnight lake. But the mysterious mist reacted as though she were a pebble, sinking slowly through an opaque syrup. Its coordinating layers both parted and caught her, swiftly dampening the velocity of her plummet until she was merely slipping slowly through their gentle grasp. But this did not aid as she transitioned through to the fog's underside, where she began plummeting rapidly once more, still a pebble, but now falling unaided toward the jungle floor.

The terror and certainty of death that had all but paralysed her as she fell, both on the first plummet and the second, left her completely disoriented. So as she landed on her back, and her somewhat cushioned landing was immediately consumed by a cloud of purple haze, she had to wonder whether this was in fact part of death. As she blinked and noticed astonishingly that her petrified arms were still wrapped around Crumbs, and she could feel the surface of something soft and powdery beneath her calves, she considered that she was in fact, somehow, still alive.

She watched the haze lift and disperse, its naturally vibrant lilac hue becoming a deep mauve as fingers of it slithered into the shadowy underworld. As it thinned, she saw the spores within it, millions perhaps, suspended and drifting off in different directions. She had landed on what local botanists called an epi-alto-fungi, or more colloquially, a melody mushroom. They were named for the low-pitched, resonant bellows they made when releasing their spores, often followed by disturbingly conscious burbles of discomfort and relief. The consistency with which this occurred created a peculiar percussion through the jungle they proliferated. But their name did not take into account their enormity. The one whose fortunate position had been the miracle that saved Lucy from certain death on her second fall, was about the size of a small cottage, and it was smaller than many others.

Lucy coughed wretchedly. The spores had slithered down her throat and into her lungs. Crumbs wriggled forward and she swept the haze away with her arms, while her eyes adjusted to the eerie darkness beyond. The surface of the fungi was especially delicate and soft, this being the reason that she had not broken her back as she collided with it at great speed from the clutches of the fog above. But this same softness made the mushroom difficult to climb down from, as every movement seemed to sink her further down into its increasingly broken mass.

It took Lucy more than several moments for her to adjust to the light, or lack of it. The mess of botanical jungle, particularly in these parts, was in permanent shadow. The trees stretched high into the sky, crowding together until they were swallowed from above by the fog. But light had not been completely eradicated. As Lucy finally planted her feet on the mossy turf, she took in that light was being bestowed by the life that grew here. The most apparent change to the world around her was the transition from the plateau's overbearing daylight to the jungle's damp darkness, but the thriving wilderness by whatever powers, glowed like a dubious winter dawn.

The air was redolent of earth and moss and rain. Shelf mushrooms ascended like steps up tree trunks above her, outlining the enormous circumference of their hosts. Tiny fungi that circled around blossoms between tree roots, seemed to almost light the way in some parts like birthday candles. The most notable emitters of luminosity though, were the melody mushrooms like the one she landed on. In their array of pastel colours, they called as they croaked through the distant depths of the jungle like beacons to lost ships. The iridescent plants created an undergrowth not unlike the imagined drawings in children's storybooks. But it was muddied with all the cruel harshness of reality. Though the damp coolness was a welcome change to Lucy in her parched state, the persistence of the humidity would soon become a source of constant discomfort, and between the colossal trees, the terrain of tangled ferns, vines, and spiky epiphytes, would not be easily passed.

Lucy looked up to where the plateau would be beyond the fog. The creatures, whatever they had been, seemed determined to hunt her down at any cost. Best keep moving, Bear would find her when he could.

Lucy and Crumbs moved across the jungle floor, Lucy's legs being scratched and scraped by the dense undergrowth. Its darkness was periodically abated by speckled light from outbreaks of micro fungi and the faint glow of the enormous croaking mushrooms. There were areas that opened up and her feet moved freely on flat ground for a while, but there were no paths, and in time the tides of anonymous shrubbery returned. The only direction that seemed practical was straight ahead. Her eternal direction, east.

At the very least, the image of the plateau, which had very quickly been swallowed up behind fanning arms of shamrock and teal, was an anchor for west. If she could keep her direction perpendicular to it, she would continue east. She still suspected, bitterly, that these rocks hidden from her behind Archmond Castle could be her key to returning home. But she knew she would need help returning to Archmond for that purpose. More help than Bear could offer, which she would explain to him when he caught up with her. The nearest kingdom according to her map was Trimany, but she desperately hoped there would be at least something before that. A village like Yerkey maybe. Even another tribe, whose mercy she could throw herself on.

After a quarter of an hour, she noticed a small stream, or what may have been the runoff from a stream ahead. She fell to her knees beside it, rushing out her canister, and filling it. It was so shallow she had to press the canister down against the gritty bank to allow water to trickle in. Crumbs was under no such impediment, thirstily gulping up the water with his tongue. Lucy rushed it to her face, her legs. She'd been at the waterhole on the Alexandria only hours ago, but this water was not the stale hard water of a desert pond. It was shiny and clear, and cool to the touch.

Following the runoff took her in a direction that was slightly more north-east than east, but she kept or tried to keep an awareness of how far she was deviating and made note to correct it. She became aware of more intricate details as she went, and her eyes adjusted to the paled peppering of luminescence. The colossal trees at first appeared uniform, but they were in fact a variety of equally enormous tree species. Where the shelf mushrooms wound around their trunks like tinsel, she began to notice the bark on some being smooth and grey, while on others corrugated and chestnut. Other trees were nearly black, midnight in colour. Most were dotted with illuminated mush-room of some variety. Not all were plagued with woody or hanging climbers, but most had no substantial branches emerging until tens of metres above Lucy's height. The roots of many were large enough to build small bothies under, beside the light of the candle fungi.

The water trail continued through misty ferns, the land only ever so slightly moving upward. After what felt like weeks under the plateau's arid sky, the damp air on her skin was luscious, idyllic, and balmy. It was neither cool nor warm. Despite the bewilderment posed by the density of sprawling tendrils, bowing fans, and curtains of limply hanging vines, she felt her level of panic and distress start to fall away for the first time in over a week. She reasoned that the assassins may not follow. The beasts and their commander may fairly assume she had died in a fall that was, or should have been, impossible to survive. Now at least, there was fresh water, there was cover, there was shade. She had now learnt to use the sword, and she was learning to use courage. She let herself believe she would be okay.

After a further half hour of following the trickle of clear water, the dense jungle opened up to reveal a creek. She had to refocus her eyes to notice it in the dimness, with its glossy obsidian surface. The ferns and the shrubbery withdrew somewhat, revealing patches of gravelly soil, and layers of flat graphite rocks led down to where the shiny black water rippled and zigzagged away down crevices.

As she approached it, and Crumbs bounded ahead excitedly, she failed to notice how thickly a particular vine was coating the forest floor like carpet. It was not suspicious in its appearance: star shaped leaves striped with white and lime green. But the leaves bunched together near the rocky edge, and she trampled them unwittingly. A nefarious vapour sprayed up into her eyes, and instantly there was a sensation of burning pain. Shrieking, she threw off the sword and the bag. She rubbed her eyes but that made it worse. She couldn't see. Suddenly the stinging was not just blurring her vision but sending her into total darkness.

Horrified she stumbled forward toward the memory of the water, blindly throwing herself off the side of the rocks in desperation. She would later recall the anxious tension in Crumbs' rampant barking as she sunk into the cool water and began rubbing her eyes frantically. After a few moments, the water had rinsed away the poison and the burning stopped. Her vision would come back, but it was more than eight suspended minutes of pure dread before she realised this.

Sitting on the ashen rocks she'd blindly dragged herself up on to, scratching her forearms as she did, through watery eyes she took in the clearing and wondered what she should do now. She stared vacantly at the canvas of pointed green and white leaves running down the rocks on the opposite side of the creek. Like the rocks, they too submerged themselves beneath the creek's surface. Dragonflies darted in sporadic patterns above the stagnant water. In her vacant exhausted stare, her wondering soon turned to reflection. Crumbs had run around the creek to where she sat, and continued to lick at her, though of course this was of limited utility to the recovery of her blurry vision.

Things had been constantly perilous for Lucy, but the fear of, amid everything else that could go wrong, losing vision entirely, had in some ways made her take stock once again. It had been nearly a month now, she thought, counting the nights. Nearly a month since she had been ripped from her wretched, yet predictable, life in Scotland, and thrown into the chaos of this unbelievable world. A month was in all respects a very small amount of time, and yet… it wasn't. She felt different. She saw that there was something different about herself now. She was concerned by the potentially aimless wandering through the jungle, with no way of knowing where she should go, and yet… she wasn't. She was still at the whim of whatever people or creatures she came across, and yet she no longer felt helpless.

Having been separated from Bear in the fall, she was more alone now than she'd ever been, possibly in her entire life, yet she didn't feel it. Watching a distant melody mushroom croak, the arms of its cloud of pastel blue spores becoming more vibrant as they traversed above the creek and beyond, she chuckled, lightly, at how much energy she'd spent worrying about her problems in her *before life*. How important was it now, that Mary, who she'd likely never see again, made remarks about her shoes to other young people equally insignificant to her? Now that all her problems, all of them, were about survival, these things were so laughably inane.

Turning back to the present, she realised it had now been more than an hour since she landed on that mushroom in this beautifully eerie abyss, and Bear had still not emerged to once again guide her with his witty banter. *He must be making sure he isn't followed*, Lucy thought. She considered he was probably ensuring the beasts would not follow her, maybe even himself pretending to believe she was dead to convince them. He must know that she is still alive. He must be able to sense her in the way that he did before, in the way he found her again on the periphery of the frozen land. All would be well so long as he and his light and his wisdom joined her again by nightfall. She was scared to imagine this place any darker, once daylight no longer filtered through the mist above, however diluted.

The jungle buzzed and echoed with creaking wood and curious coos that could be mistaken by muddled ears for human voices. The sounds were not words, but they could be.

Agoo-na. Agoo-na. Agoo-na.

A series of tiny yellow leaves fell upon the creek. On bending teal stems emerging from the cracks in the rock beside her, an expansive white butterfly landed above bright, bronze centipedes, which crawled up and down as if on a collective mission. She watched them, and took in their work, but her eyes quickly drifted beyond them to a small slinky creature, squirrel like but larger, with ample arms and legs, scurrying up a tree. Perhaps now out of new habit, she immediately thought about killing it. For a brief moment she considered rushing to her sword. But she realised she would be too slow.

It was a good way up the young tree already, which being relatively small in this jungle context, was roughly four times her height. So instead, she watched it for several minutes. It paused to take her in and did nothing but watch her back for some time. It had beady black eyes on its black rabbit face, orange markings on its paws and collar. Once it took her stoic ease as assurance it began scampering the branches once again and feasting hungrily. She waited a while for the creature to finish its dinner and depart, before collecting her sword and cutting down a branch with a handful of the brown baubles it had feasted on. She smirked as she tore at the woody casing with her teeth, and the sweet juices ran down her chin. Despite the trepidation, she'd have no trouble finding sustenance here.

Lucy moved through the jungle into late afternoon. The land climbed and so did she. Beneath twisted branches festooned with mosses and delicate vines, she came through areas where ensembles of butter-flies, sapphire, ivory, and buttercup, fluttered in and out of shadows in the abyss. In slender stripes of pale light, where the mist parted high above, the brilliance of them shone against the endless emerald canvass. In parts where the luminosity of the fungi was strong, or the depth of the shadows eased, the butterflies were not the only colourful eye-candy. Caterpillars of robust reds, birds of brilliant shimmering blues, and amphibians of gold and bronze markings, peppered the dewy green lichen.

She was dazed enough by all the obscurity to distract herself from her tiredness, her worry, and her hunger. But these backdrops of unspoiled beauty were not the only face the jungle presented; it had another side. In pockets she found imploded melody mushrooms, grey and long dead, smothered by a wild and thorny carpet vine, and reeking with decay. While many beautiful birds, like the butterflies, shimmered in vivid contrast to the green wilderness, in pockets where the light touched their plumes of fuchsia, scarlet, and aquamarine, others horrified her with scars upon their bare, dimpled, torsos. With apparent hostility, they plucked out their remaining feathers as they stared her down.

As the day took a darker turn, the sun lost high above, preparing to disappear behind a horizon hidden from the jungle and its residents, Lucy understood that she and Crumbs should find refuge before it was too late. She had dried herself with Yinsoo's coat, but she was still very damp. She hurriedly pushed through the undergrowth in a bid to find a suitable spot to settle while she could still see, examining the landscape for clues and readjusting her direction several times - completely losing track of east. But her ability to read trickles of water, the density of trunks, and the incline of earth, proved fruitless. She had hoped to find a cosy corner, sheltered by rocks and giant leaves, but she gave up as the remnants of light began slipping away rather quickly, and slunk herself down onto a patch of dry ground between giant tree roots.

As she felt her energy start to leave her and heard the calls of wildlife transition from day to night, she wondered how long she could sustain herself without Bear's guidance. It of course occurred to her that he could appear at any moment, as unpredictably as he reappeared to guide her before she reached the plateau. Yet it also occurred to her that it was possible something had happened, it was possible there were things she did not know, and it *was* possible he would never again appear. But this thought scared her and so she dismissed it. She hung the damp coat over the knot in the bulbous root, so it would both dry and shield her. Then she lay down on and wrapped up in the Indawara fur and pulled Crumb's warm body close to her. He squirmed and grumbled a bit, but he too was hungry and weak. He let her shush him.

'Bear will be back again tomorrow, and we will find a better way to manage,' she promised him. But she said it one more time in her mind, as she promised herself.

Morning came and she found her exposed limbs covered in itchy mosquito like bumps. Bear had not returned, but at least the direction of light helped her again determine east. Land inclined so gradually she did not notice, but she was coming further out of the jungle's deepest valley, where the ceiling of mist was thinning, and the bioluminescence was no longer the dominant source of light.

She swiped at the green curtain before her, the blade slicing through the vines like water. At least Yinsoo, for whatever resentment she still deserved for her part in this mess, had armed her with something useful, Lucy thought. The most the wizards had given her was a flint, and no instructions on how to use it, as though her survival was a mere experiment. She had a bitterness in the back of her throat whenever her mind returned to them, and their duplicitous gestures of goodwill in the castle. Trapping her here with their lies about how she came into their world and how she might return.

She fantasized about what she would say to them when she returned to Archmond Castle and confronted them. Though of course she knew Bear was right and that getting back to Archmond itself was a daunting and unpleasant prospect, while forcing her way into their mysterious forbidden garden didn't even seem achievable. Even thinking of this forbidden garden, at how close she may have been back then, before all this perilous travel, to the only answer to get home, made her dizzyingly furious.

She contrasted this with how she felt about Yinsoo. She didn't trust Yinsoo because the woman was too mysterious to be trusted. But she did not have reason to suspect her of the same wrongdoings she levied on Soleman and Ronald. After all, Yinsoo was forthcoming as soon as she had the round-faced young translator. Lucy acknowledged too, with a heavy melancholic sigh, that Yinsoo had been right about her past. The relevance of that to this world and the prophecy she could not understand, but it was true that Lucy had guiltily buried away the details of her sister's death for all those years. It was true that this was wrong, and the truth needed to be heard. Lucy committed to herself, that she would return to Lockerby and put things right. Whatever the consequences were for her. That was the gamble of courage, the uncertain price of consequence. But she saw now too, that there had been deeper prices for her selfish silence.

A melody mushroom croaked somewhere nearby, its off-scarlet haze making thin lines in the distance some moments later. In slowing down to notice their progression, she barely escaped the entanglement of a large inconspicuous web. Its silver threads were stretched taut between fan-palms, and partially hidden by bundles of drooping curly leaves. Lucy cursed, and the jolt in her abrupt halt sent subtle vibrations across the web. Moments later its enormous inhabitant scurried down from the dark recesses of the foliage to examine its bounty. The hand-sized spider, black with orange stripes, searched around excitedly, before realising its grim disappointment, and planting itself squarely in the centre of web, rather than returning to the shadows, as if to make its displeasure known. Lucy backed away before it could surprise her any further.

It reminded her (once again bitterly) that until Bear returned with his guidance, her pace must be slow and careful. As she rounded the palms, a grey bird landed on a low epiphyte, and let out a powerful trill that caused its throat and the plumes of lilac feathers on it, to balloon out in front of him. It was as though he were laughing at her near calamity with the spider, and as he did so, he seemed to be echoed by a series of jungle calls. Ticking insects and buzzing dragonflies darted around her. Lucy froze for a moment, listening to Crumbs bark, and taking in the percussion of the mirrored sounds. It felt in that moment, that an entire assembly of jungle creatures were mocking her. Suddenly the jungle chorus of rustling, and cooing, and cawing, was intense and personal.

She spun in multiple directions, hand on the hilt of the sword, trying to glimpse just one of the laughing animals. But at best she could only see glimpses of fur disappear high above, or the swing of creaking branches where jumping creatures landed. She almost went to cry out at them, to shout at them to stop. But she restrained herself, and fell forward, putting her hands on her knees, nearly breaking out into laughter herself.

'Hold it together Lucy,' she commanded.

She spent the day foraging on fruits that animals had revealed edible. Her initial optimism was now rapidly waning. The fruit was plentiful, but it was not sustenance. As the day went on, hunger made her irritability rise, and the aimlessness of her journey became more glaringly apparent.

She parked herself by a tree again before dark, no longer motivated to go any further, and began to doubt whether Bear was coming back. When he had disappeared the first time, she was terrified, but she had (by all accounts) been rescued hours later. He then came back to her several hours after she began to navigate her way down the rocky wilderness, after Yinsoo more or less 'discharged' her from Reichi care. She hadn't accepted the story he'd given, but in both circumstances, he'd not left her alone for more than several hours. It was now close to two days, and she'd surely made some progress into the jungle, though whether she was going east or north anymore, she didn't really know. Lucy reminded herself that she hadn't known Bear for very long, and that anything with intelligence had the capacity to lie. Which then caused her to re-examine what he'd told her about Archmond, and its basis as her new direction.

After a time in despair, dwelling on these dark imaginings in her cocoon between the tree roots, she pulled herself up and noticed a creature emerging from a burrow on the other side of the tree. In fairness she had in fact heard it first, her ears having become mute to the white noise of jungle life, and able to narrow in on more immediate rustling and padding. Before it had even fully emerged, she was flooded with sound bites of commands she thought Bear might utter, if he were here, which themselves blurred with memories of his actual castigation of her on the plateau.

'*Kill it, stupid girl!*' she both imagined and heard him saying. The memory of his face, turning away in disgust, of how pathetic she was when time and time again she faltered when tasked with killing a rodent or clumsily struck an omling. Upon the sound of the scurrying creature, these imagined and remembered utterings now ricocheted through her mind like a challenge, and in the same instant she was furious that he had abandoned her once again. That he had left her in this new, baffling landscape, and that his promises of aid proved false, and that the only one in the world she knew she could truly rely on was herself.

Maybe I am stupid, but you are a liar, she thought fervently for a brief instant before seizing the sword and in a swift movement drove it down into the head of the poor emerging jungle burrower. The furry thing jolted wildly for several moments before it stopped completely, with death.

'Ha! Who's pathetic now? You can't even finish what you started. That's how pathetic you are!' she shouted into the darkness. Nothing but the eternal reverberation of insects responded.

'You think I'm just waiting for you to appear again? You're wrong. I'm fine! I'm going to be fine without you and your stupid sarcasm!' she shouted again.

Again, nothing answered her.

Panting in the silent darkness, Crumbs letting out a whimper of hunger, she shook away her silliness. She consoled herself with the fact she had managed to obtain a substantial portion of protein for herself and recognised that irritation was wasted energy right now. But her feelings of pride and glee were short lived, as she struggled in the dark with the flint against her sword. She could make sparks, but nothing would catch. She scrambled around the tree, not wanting to venture far, scrounging leaves and stems from the drier and flimsy growth nearby. But none of it was suitable tinder, and all of it was in any case too wet. She wouldn't be able to burn the flesh. She wouldn't be able to eat it.

She heard Crumbs begin to gnaw heartily on the dead creature's neck, which she could barely make out any more in the night. She pushed her back against the tree and slid down it, fighting off tears of self-loathing and frustration, as she cursed herself in her mind, listening to her little dog rip and tear at the burrower's flesh. At least Crumbs wouldn't go hungry. It was dawning on her damningly, that things were not as well as her brief dash with optimism had first supposed. She hushed herself though, as a glittering swarm of fireflies passed overhead, meandering the darkness like a band of traveling stars, and recognised she was being emotional. Bear would come, she knew. Two days were test enough. In the morning he would return to tell her she'd passed.

Late into the next day, wading across a wide river, Lucy froze as a sinking feeling rushed from the pit of her stomach. The rising irritation she had felt throughout the day, as she again failed to turn sparks into fire, and grew more depleted, sustaining merely on fruit, had in a single moment, given way to dread. Waking up to realise they were still alone, she and Crumbs had journeyed further north into the late afternoon and followed the sounds of rushing water to a wide but shallow river. Less than an hour earlier, in the eternal dawn glow that existed beneath the fog, she'd been able to make flames linger on the black curls of dead vine leaves for a moment or so, and she followed the sound of the water, hoping to capture river creatures small enough to singe in the fleeting heat. Eventually she had found this gushing tributary, but the tiny fish slipped through her hands, making her irritated. But her frustration, (worsened by feelings of rejection in Bear's continued absence) was swept away at the sight of two tusks, rising rather coolly from the river's turbulent current.

She was in up to her knees, which were being coated by the river's strange white silt. Jagged rocks scattered across the river's breadth, and between them white foam shot wildly from the gushes. Now, disturbingly steadfast, two brawny tusks, emerged from the foamy current to reveal a ferocious warthog. Lucy was frozen by the shock of her own naivety. She could not now fathom how the threat of wild and predatory beasts had been so far removed from her mind. The plateau had trained her, but the last few days of mushrooms and birdsong had made her complacent. She felt grossly unprepared. In the shock of it she couldn't think of the next move. But the warthog wasn't waiting for her.

Heavy hooves slammed into the flesh of her shoulders, cutting with their force as his weight submerged her below the surface. The back of her skull narrowly missed a large stone as her shoulders collided with the grainy riverbed, and water rushed up her nostrils. His mouth gaped open, letting out bellowing throaty grunts, while Lucy squirmed in her silent world below the surface. Awaiting her above, the foulness of his breath was worse than the foulness of the sores along his back. Crumbs watched helplessly from the shore, intermittently both barking, and howling with distress.

The warthog's initial instinct was to drown Lucy, as it did many of its victims, but it quickly wanted more from this interaction than just a corpse to feed on. As it drew back to impale her with its tusks, the release of pressure freed Lucy's arm, and she reached for her sword, trying to strike the creature's head. Her speed was stilted by the water. The alerted warthog swung its head into her forearm, and in the same instant the sword fell out of her hand and across to the other side of the river. She twisted as he moved to impale her, and his tusks caught on her shirt, before yanking her upward and throwing her into the air. It was her blood he was so desperate to see. Her blood and her pain. He had recently become enthralled with, and almost addicted to, cries of pain. When their bodies landed on the jagged rocks of the river, creatures like her could really scream, he had learnt.

It was an almost peaceful moment of airborne suspension, before gravity returned, in which Lucy outstretched her arm through a webbed screen of water droplets. Instinctively she grabbed at the thick vines, hanging like arteries from the mossy branches they festooned high above. Her fingers managed to grab at one, and to her relief it was strong, and it bore her weight. But her legs dangled with perilous proximity to the hog, who began rearing up and howling in frustration. Looking down, she watched the water part around his solid frame, stoic amid the turbulence. From above he was a stark contrast to tiny Crumbs, hidden beneath ferns on the edge of the bank, where masses of that noxious green and white creeping plant stretched across and then down into the water.

The terror of the warthog's continued guttural groans was followed by the terrifying sound of creaking wood above. She looked up. A grim sight. The network of vines ensnared two separate overlapping branches, rubbing them together. A precarious tension her added weight exacerbated. The top branch, which her vine wreathed and pulled, was hollow and dead. The vine would hold her weight, the branch would not. She had a further brief moment to appreciate this, before the branch snapped, and she fell back toward the river and the hog.

A stretch of vine went down with her, cut by the splintering wood, her fingers still wrapped around it. In that flash of intense fear as she fell, and the beast grunted with delight, something in her shifted, like never before. A surge of both rage and adrenaline rushed through her. She flailed her arms and managed to land on his back. He reared up to shake her off, but she saw the opportunity, digging her heels into his sides, and flinging the vine under his head and around his throat. By pulling back she was equally choking him and securing herself.

The hog squealed and came back down, allowing her to twist the vine, before he took off along the river, upstream. Crying out in panic she pulled the vines tighter, his disturbingly human skin blistering in the tension. He had a pinkish hue, blotched throughout with red, purple, and yellow, like a bruise. He flung his hind legs as he ran, still trying to throw her. She slipped, once, twice, three times, but using the vine as reins she kept herself from falling off him. She knew that if she fell under him again, she could have no hope. She desperately hoped that his silenced groans meant he was in fact choking to death.

As a pool of deep water approached, the warthog thrashed about more violently and using the power of its weight, slammed Lucy into the side of a boulder, before diving into the depths of the pool. The beast's plan worked, and the shock of the collision caused the reins to slip from Lucy's grip as they shattered the water's glassy surface. But the beast's pride and relief was fleeting, as he realised the tension on his throat did not ease. She had knotted the vines around his neck.

His enormous, caved eyes, from inside those hollow purple sockets, stared at her through a myriad of silver bubbles, as they sunk together in the waning velocity through the reeds. Lucy in turn, watched the warthog as he squirmed, twisted, and choked, desperately and violently, for those last few thrashing moments. There was a final jerked retraction of his head, and then gradually, almost peacefully, life left. His body bobbed and swayed gently. He was now a lifeless lump, with empty eyes, haunting the reeds.

Hamish had left his specimen of zea-flower as soon as he heard the ruckus in the Vivian's tributary. But he had followed the conniption with caution; Josso Jungle was a dangerous place. Precisely the reason for his expedition. Hamish was the oldest child and son of Mathew Mathers, and the family, hailing from Trimany, had both reasonable wealth and reasonable status. The Mathers name was not so much household known, but in certain esteemed fields, Hamish's father was known for his research and dissertations on previously unstudied cultures and habitats. The relative comfort and privilege of Hamish's upbringing afforded him the luxury of choice in how to spend his adult years. But choice is a rather illusive thing, and Hamish had somewhat deluded himself into thinking he chose to follow his father into field work of this kind, when in fact it was simply a path paved out for him from birth, and his choices had been influenced by the nature of the opportunities presented to him in crucial moments.

Hamish intended to record the details of the scuffle in his journal, which he had retrieved from his pocket as he slid behind the mossy trunks of the riverbank. The team had only limited and basic weaponry on hand, and although Hamish was trained in both hunting and combat, it was of course advisable to simply avoid altercations with the jungle's unknown beasts. In hoping to get a glimpse of the brawl, the opportunity he was seizing was an opportunity to record a wildlife battle as it unfolded, unadulterated. But Hamish, coming forward from behind the tree to observe the river, could not have appreciated, then, the significance this moment would have on him forever.

As the sleek figure emerged from the glossy black surface of the creek, it did so, to Hamish, in slow motion. His hair stood on end, his heart pounded anxiously, as if immediately and painfully recognising the betrayal it was about to commit. What emerged, victoriously, from the battle in the depths of the river-bend, was not a beast or even a warrior, but *a girl*. A young woman, whose features caught his breath in his throat and choked him. Perhaps it was the shock of it more than anything else. He expected to see a flailing, blood-covered beast, and instead he was met with blue eyes staring at him from under thick wet lashes, on a clear young face, beneath layer upon layer of silken black hair. With those rose lips and that glance of innocent (but he was dubious of the innocence) beseeching, he had to quickly assess and then reject the notion she was a siren. Hamish felt the blood rush somewhere it shouldn't have. A dark but equally sensual feeling came over him as he realised that he had unconsciously already betrayed his beloved, even though she would never know of these fleeting moments of feeling.

Lucy, looking back at Hamish, had the same pulsing sense of attraction. Though the attraction didn't necessarily resonate as sexual, simply magnetic. It was a shock to see a young but older man on the bank, and this shock gave his presence an angelic, dreamlike quality. When that passed, she quivered at the lingering sensation that remained. It was inexplicable, and she believed personally, impossible, to feel an attraction towards another person without them having said a word. And yet, this connection was somehow undeniable.

There was a synergy between them. A synergy they both felt, but would never speak of, and they would separately come to discount and deny the significance of these first moments and this first impression.

Hamish let out a laugh to shake off both his instantaneous infatuation and the awkwardness it might have created.

'You are not what I expected to see at all,' he said, and then, noticing the asphyxiated warthog bobbing on the surface among the reeds, added with a tone of incredulity. 'Did you do that?'

He was grinning, smirking even. Lucy looked at the pig and nodded slowly. Having now caught her breath, she realised that perhaps she could take some pride in this. It was no small beast that had just tried very keenly to kill her. But the beast was dead, and she was alive. This was no small thing.

She looked to Hamish and let out a small laugh herself. 'Yes, I did.'

But the lingering amusement and awe between them broke abruptly.

'Oh, you're hurt!' Hamish exclaimed. In shifting shadows, he hadn't first noticed the crimson colour against the sodden blue shirt and wet black hair. But now the blood was rushing heavily down from her shoulder. The warthog had managed to puncture her after all. As Lucy came toward the shore, although there was no sign of her needing assistance, Hamish rushed in up to his calves to help her up the bank. He lay his linen jacket on the ground and instructed her to sit on it. After he'd dabbed the wound with a tincture from his pocket, he tore a stretch of fabric from his shirt and instructed her to sit while he wrapped it tightly under her arm and around her shoulder.

'It's gotta be tight to stop the bleeding,' he said as she winced. Then he grinned. 'I think you'll live.'

Lucy replied with a polite, grateful smile.

'But more importantly, what in the world are you doing out here? Are you alone?' he asked.

Lucy realised in that moment, she needed to decide what to tell not only this man, but anyone she happened upon, as to who she was and where she was going. She recalled vividly in that moment, the warning from Soleman and Ron, to be cautious about who she gave her true name and identity to. They had implied that her name would spread across the world, and therefore she must be cautious about deciding whom she revealed her identity to. She was told that outside of Archmond, the cities and kingdoms were not united in their views on either Archmond or the eastern queen. But if she were to be dishonest, the more delicate task became explaining where she had come from, when she knew very little of this world. If she were to be honest, what would she say to people who possibly were not in favour of the prophecy, Archmond's ambitions, or people from other worlds. And only now, when the most predictable of questions had been put to her, did she recognise the need to have a simple explanation at hand.

'I'm… I was going to visit… some family… in Archmond.' As soon as the words left her mouth she heard the absurdity of them, and the long pause between his question and her response made them all the less convincing.

'Family… in Archmond?' he replied, puzzled, 'and you're what, walking there? Alone?'

The suspicion in his tone had almost become hostile, and his posture was also growing tense. He had been kneeling beside her, quite closely, in the crumbly earth, having finished fastening the bandage, but he was drawing back at this comment.

'Well… they're not family per se, not by blood, but they have become *like* family to us. Our little cousins, we call them. But I was traveling with my aunt and uncle when my horse was spooked, and ran off, for miles, and then it later threw me off, and… I have just been wandering in this jungle ever since.' She was more comfortable with this adapted version, and seemingly so was Hamish, letting his shoulders drop with ease, and rising to his feet.

'Well,' he patted the dirt from his trousers, 'there's no telling what may have spooked your horse, it could have been many things. But I'm afraid it doesn't surprise me. This jungle is not what it once was. It's not safe to travel through anymore. I'm surprised your aunt and uncle weren't aware of that. Seems a reckless route to take. How long have you been lost?' he said, offering a hand to help her up.

'A few days,' she replied meekly, taking it.

'Mmm, yes, you're not in a good way, are you?' he said examining her, though he could see nothing wrong with her physically aside from the wound, and the wet, muddy clothes. 'Don't worry though, I'm out here with a whole team, well, most of them are my family, but we've got plenty of supplies, we'll get you fixed up and properly fed.' He paused, unconsciously, to glance around cautiously before continuing. 'It's Hamish, by the way.'

'Mary,' she let out, as the caution about revealing her real name, swirled afresh through her mind. To her amusement he very lightly bowed in a casual manner that suggested this was merely custom.

'A pleasure,' he muttered, very quickly looking around again.

'I need to get back to my dog and my things,' Lucy said, indicating Crumbs, who had made his way upstream but was still on the other side of the river. Still partly obscured by the ferns, Crumbs let out a single bark as if recognising that he had finally been acknowledged. They travelled back downstream to where the incident began, Crumbs following across the way, and while Hamish (on insistence) waded across the river to fetch her things, and then searched the shallows for the lost sword, Crumbs hurried back to her, struggling in the current. Lucy was surprised when Hamish found her sword, thrusting it upward dramatically from the shallows.

'You found it! Thank you!' she cried, immensely grateful.

Hamish laughed, ascending back up the steep crumbling bank. 'A proper sword should be too heavy to drift away in river currents, it couldn't have gone far.' He handed it to her, and she slid it back into its scabbard on the sodden belt around her waist.

'Even if it is a woman's sword,' he added and winked.

Lucy sensed a certain level of flirtation, but it seemed more jovial than suggestive. 'Thank you for finding it, in any case,' she said.

Hamish looked around. 'We should get back to my camp,' he said with none of the jovial casualness she'd heard so far. Then he added, 'It really is lucky you found me.' Out of context this remark would have come across as arrogant, but in the circumstances, having nearly lost all resolve to go on in this lonely oblivion, Lucy felt the same. There had been a tremendous relief pulsating through her after his opening humour suggested she had in fact stumbled upon an affable stranger. Now his promises of comfort made him seem like a divine intervention.

As they made their way back to Hamish's camp, following the river, he told her about the purpose of the team's expedition. He explained that the jungle (even in his scepticism of her story, he assumed that she of course must have *some* knowledge of it) was not what it once was, but that it had over the recent years become tainted by the spread of unnatural substances. The team's particular expedition concerned a psychotropic plant, or weed rather, which was a nefarious adaptation of its original native form. As well as suffocating native species crucial to the ecosystem, it was also having some very disturbing effects on the wildlife consuming it. He went on to clarify that this weed was not the only problem being faced by the jungle, but it was a primary concern given the spread and impact of the plant, and it was the sole focus of their current project. But the project itself was simply an exercise of intelligence gathering, he explained. It was unwise to interfere at this stage, given what little they knew. This was their third trip in the jungle, into what was effectively the second stage of their project. Their concern was that although people understood the jungle was dangerous, the extent and threat of, what he called this 'new poison' was not widely known.

'It was probably behind whatever spooked your horse and no doubt what enraged that purple pig,' Hamish said, sweeping back vines with his hand, as though he were holding open a curtain for her. Lucy nodded thankfully, but his level of chivalry seemed unnecessary.

'The warthog?'

Hamish shrugged, 'I'm only guessing. I didn't see how it started.' He looked into the distance, shrouded by the warm mist. The scant pockets of the jungle's dim dawn glow were fast receding as the afternoon progressed. A thin film of blue-grey spores were cutting through the leaves high above them. 'But would you say he seemed keener to tear you apart than simply scare you off or eat you?'

Lucy nodded grimly, remembering those first few moments, when it seemed the slobbering thing could have swiftly ended her, but that it didn't want to.

He saw her look of dread, and nodded, placing a comforting hand on her shoulder. 'Don't worry, Mary, that's *precisely* why we're here,' he declared.

Hamish had a natural authority to his character that unwittingly put people under his spell. From as early on as adolescence his peers began to cling to his words, and social decisions were often put in his hands. It was never his intention to command or lead, but it was this very genuine reluctance, when coupled with his masculine charm, which made people so eager to follow him. In his late adolescence his powerful persona had most benefited him when it came to women (of which there had been a rather long string of lovers, before one peculiar girl stole his heart and left him in shambles) but in his mid-twenties he had begun to use this charm to get his way with most things in life.

'You know, I've never heard of anyone having such relations to Archmonders before. It's very unusual. Where did you say you were from again?'

'I didn't say,' she stalled.

He laughed. 'Right… so… where are you from?'

The stalling had served little purpose in finding an answer. She struggled to remember names on the map: *Coby, Gemini, Trimany, Que.* But her story would fall apart if she claimed to be from the same town as him, and yet it would be suspicious after this long pause, to put the question back to him.

'Gemini,' she answered.

'Gemini?' he repeated quizzically, and smiled politely, pursing his lips with suppressed disbelief.

'Aha,' Lucy nodded, smiling, but looking away again quickly. Her heart was racing from both an inexplicable desire to make the truth of her situation known to this stranger, and an equally potent fear that her lie might unravel and do just that.

'Our team is, ahh, we're all from Trimany. Hardly surprising being an academic city, and all the research laboratories there,' Hamish muttered a moment or so later. Hamish too was struggling with his own complex dichotomy of emotions: suspicion, compassion, and a sudden disturbing desire. As they continued, the blue film above thickened. The light took on its hue with the spores both more numerous and vibrant near their source; ahead on their right a slice of turquoise mushroom shone from between the bracken across the river.

Crumbs, a few paces ahead, stopped to chew on something by the base of a stunted palm.

Hamish pointed it out with alarm. 'Careful what he eats.'

'Hey, get off that,' she scolded lightly, lifting him up and pulling the object out of his mouth: a chunk of wood from a branch. There followed a low snigger, somewhere in the shrubbery.

'Hey, did you hear that?' Hamish whispered.

'What?'

'It sounded like laughter.'

'Oh,' Lucy glanced around, her eyes adjusting to the changing sources of light. As the eerie glow of jungle daylight faded, the encroaching darkness made the glow of the fungi more intense. Fireflies speckled the blackened undersides of the canopy, high above.

'I've heard that constantly, I, I assumed it was the birds…'

Following this was a series of caws, short and repetitive which did have a quality of laughter.

'Not that.' He rushed his own sizeable blade from its sheath. 'I heard a snigger.'

'Hey look,' Lucy said, holding up the chunk of wood she'd pulled from Crumbs' mouth, 'this has a chain around it.'

Hamish's eyes widened. His eyes scanned the darkness. He moved forward several paces, and then found the threat he suspected, lunging forward, and tackling a short squeaky man to the ground. The man squirmed and squealed under Hamish's weight and let out clamorous inhuman cries and babble, as though speaking a nonsense made-up language.

'Help!' cried Hamish, somewhat baffled by the fact that Lucy simply watched on passively as he struggled. She rushed over.

'In my pocket, there's some rope,' he said. He was kneeling on the man's back and had him pinioned but was still using both his own arms to restrain him. Lucy hesitated, but the pronounced urgency Hamish had declared overpowered her girlish nerves, and she slid her hand into his pocket and retrieved the rope.

'Help me hold him while I tie his hands,' Hamish ordered, and Lucy obediently gripped the small leathery forearms with the little strength she could muster, while Hamish bound the wrists tightly together. Between his nonsensical rambling, the man lifted his head and made to bite Lucy's leg. She gasped, flinching backward, but noted he was quite old.

'Down you deranged beast!' Hamish shouted, shoving the man's head into the dirt. He then bound his ankles and rolled him over.

'He's an Archmonder!' Lucy exclaimed.

'Not one of your *cousins*, I hope,' Hamish said dryly. Lucy shook her head.

Hamish examined the man, whose blabbering only paused momentarily before he riled up with greater ferocity and began spitting up at them. Lucy stepped back. Hamish grabbed the bound ankles and dragged the man under the nearest tree, examining him under the light of the shelf mushrooms. There was a dark gritty stain like a rash around his mouth, and his skin was blistered with oozing pus-filled sores.

'As I suspected,' Hamish said, hands on his hips, stepping back.

'What's wrong with him?' Lucy asked.

'That noxious weed I mentioned, these are the typical signs of its consumption, the rash, the sores... the delirium. A perfect example really.'

Lucy stared down at the old man. He had a pointedly long nose, and larger ears than most Archmonders. He was also scrawnier than most Archmonders, who tended toward looking soft and dewy. By contrast he looked frightfully dry and malnourished. Which if that was the case, he was not depleted of spirit, thrashing about wildly, snapping at the air with his teeth, as if he believed he could still roll over to them and take a chunk from her ankle.

Lucy was so entranced by his delirious yapping she didn't notice Hamish disappear and then reappear with the chunk of wood. He showed her that the chain on it was quite flimsy, but that it led back to a claw like trap, just beyond the next row of ferns.

'No doubt the work of our little friend,' Hamish said, sighing and shaking his head. 'They're deranged, but trust me they're cunning. Devilishly cunning. He probably didn't even want to eat Crumbs, just watch him bleed.'

Lucy recoiled in horror and turned back to Crumbs who was growling just out of reach of the madman. She lifted him up and embraced him while Hamish began to dismantle the trap. She took in the encroaching darkness pensively, wondering how many more madmen might be wondering the jungle.

'What is an Archmonder doing out here?' she asked.

'It is unusual,' he agreed, 'but he's not the first I've seen. It's possible they're crossing the jungle to attempt to migrate to one of the eastern cities, ate the wrong thing, and then never left.'

Lucy looked on as Hamish separated the trap's individual components, placing them into a satchel bag he withdrew from his other pocket, and then began adjusting the now gagged Archmonder, sitting him upright and crouching behind him. She was watching, but her mind was elsewhere, racing with new questions about Archmond. *Leave, why don't you just leave?* That's what she told Jock to do, and he'd scoffed at her ignorance. After barely surviving across the lifeless plateau, this is what leaving looked like. So heavy was the dawning of this realisation that she only realised what Hamish was doing when she saw the glimmer of a firefly in the mirrored blade.

'What are you doing?' she shrieked, alarmed.

'Mary, it's the only way,' he said, pushing the tip of the blade below the man's right ear. Now, the feeble old man seemed not to be deranged any longer, his eyes were wide with genuine sadness and fear.

'No! Stop. Put the blade down. There's no need for this. There must be something we can do. Take him back to Trimany. Study him, perhaps you'll find a cure. But to kill him like this is inhumane,' Lucy asserted sternly, trying to impute her words with as much authoritative conviction as possible.

Hamish's warm brown eyes pierced into hers for several moments, then he pushed the blade deep into the old man's skin and slit his throat with a swift motion. A vapour spray of blood splattered across Lucy's shirt and the bracken behind her.

Hamish let out a heavy sigh. 'Trust me, Mary, that was the *most* humane thing to do.'

Chapter 3

Poison And Remedy

Placebo, 1998

The two strangers were rather quiet for the rest of their walk to the camp along the river, the chorus of night birds keeping awkwardness at bay. Although Hamish did try to assure her more than once, that what he had done truly was the most humane option. He explained that the man would have been suffering, and that there was not only no known cure, there was also no known treatment. He also explained that there were no facilities to deal with infliction of that kind in Trimany, and that given his government's paranoia about contagion, the man would have been killed anyway, thrown into a pit and burnt alive, probably.

Each time he added a point of justification, she returned a passive smile. He took her silence to be disapproval, but in fact she was simply processing what all of this meant. Firstly, about Archmond, but also about the rest of her journey. It was true that she was horrified by what she'd seen him do, and it conflicted with her initial feelings of attraction toward him, sceptical as she was about those already. But it was more than that. Although she felt no particular affinity for the Archmonders, she had spent over a week among them, and as far as they saw it, she was *their hope* for a better life. To stand and watch as one of them was slaughtered in front of her felt like a gross betrayal to this hope - however ill-placed. But pitted against this was her instinctual urge to trust Hamish, which was matched only by a nervous reluctance to trust that very instinct.

'Ahh, here we are Mary,' he announced spiritedly. Towering over her at six foot something, he saw the welcome glow of the camp, nestled into the undergrowth, well before she could. But she did hear the delightful murmur of human life. As she saw the creamy glow of the tents, helpfully inconspicuous in a jungle littered with giant iridescent fungi, the death of the Archmonder was at once long forgotten.

'Those tents are enormous,' she gasped. Seeing their faint light like beacons of salvation she thought only of the comfort she now imagined to find inside. She had expected Hamish's camp might have food, the safety of numbers of men, perhaps somewhere for her to shelter from the midnight rainfall, but they were far more established than that.

'Well, we have a, ahh, a lot of equipment, and such,' he said, both surprised and pleased to have her talking again. 'It's quite a mission really, to set up. As you can imagine. There's no flat ground anywhere around here, so the first few hours are just clearing, and we can't clear anything without knowing if—'

'Hamish! For spirit's sake where the hell have you been? You know the rules are to be back *before* dinner,' a gruff male voice cut in. A man appeared from the shadows by the edge of the camp, wielding a large machete. He was acting as sentry, had heard their voices, and come around from the other side. His face was shadowed with the camp light behind him, but his irritation was morphing to amusement at the sight of Lucy.

'Oh… I see…' he said, chortling suggestively, but then turned back to Hamish. 'This better be a good story. Father decided to withhold dinner until a search went out for you, or you returned, one or

the other, and none of us wanted to go looking, so none of us have
eaten yet.'

The man paused to look at Lucy again, puzzled.

Hamish sighed. 'This is Mary. She was traveling with her family
when her horse was spooked and ran off. Now she's lost. I've said
we'd take her into our care.' He turned back to Lucy. 'Mary, this is
my older brother, Gin. He's just here because he wants to kill things.'

Hamish passed Gin and entered the camp. Lucy followed.

'That's not true. I like cutting things up and eating them too,' Gin
called, feigning offence, as he followed behind them.

'Hey! *Oh*, who is *that*? Did *you* hear that? Who's back in time to
change you? Yes! *Yes*, it's your pappa,' a female voice cooed from inside
the nearest and largest of the three tents as they entered the clearing.
An older woman then emerged from the tent, tanned and with grey-
ing black hair, carrying an infant in her arms. She hadn't seen Lucy
yet, who was a few paces behind Hamish and still somewhat lost in
darkness, but she beamed at Hamish as the camp light rushed over
him and through his golden hair.

She gasped dramatically at the infant. '*It is* your pappa! Pappa's
back, and he's okay, and he's going to change you.'

Everything after the first 'pappa' was spoken to Hamish directly,
with a more genuine almost amused warmth as she kissed him on
the cheek. Hamish smiled, taking the child, and only then did the
woman notice Lucy.

'Oh! Oh my god. What? Who is—' she began.

'That's Mary. She fell off her horse,' Gin cut in as he passed them
and continued toward the dying fire in the centre of the camp, poking
it back to life with his machete as he unburdened himself of it.

'She was separated from her family when the horse was spooked.
She's been in the jungle alone for days,' Hamish elucidated, bouncing
the child lightly in his arms. It had begun to cry.

'Oh, my goodness! That's horrible. Oh, you poor dear. Come sit by the fire and dry off the dampness, then we'll get you fed. What an ordeal you must have been through!'

Either from realising that she had now reached a point where she could finally give in, or if the words seemingly gave permission to do so, or simply made the gravity of the last few days dawn on her, she suddenly felt weak, and her knees began to buckle. Hamish, now nursing his son, stared perplexed at Lucy's sudden fragility as his step-mother led her over to the now spirited fire, helping her down onto a mat beside it. Meanwhile his son's cries continued and intensified.

'Hamish, he really needs to be changed. Would you? Please?' the woman directed.

Hamish groaned. The smell suggested she was right. 'Where's Star? I'll get her to do it.'

'Oh, you're hurt!' the woman noticed the bloodied bandage on Lucy's shoulder, 'Hamish. Mary's hurt!'

'Yeah, a pig - sorry - a warthog, attacked me,' Lucy muttered. The woman was kneeling beside her on the mat, gently prying back the bandage to examine the wound. She was clearly a good age. Her tanned skin was somewhat coarse, and her eyes creased significantly when her high cheeks formed into the wonderfully empathetic smile she gave Lucy just now. Age had dulled her blue eyes nearly into grey, but they had an enchanting tenderness to them. Lucy felt as though she could fall easily under her spell, that she would soon want to do anything to please her.

'I put some tonic on it when I bandaged her up,' Hamish said and indicated his torn shirt. He would not let his heroic aid go unnoticed. 'But I, ahh, I didn't very have much of it left,' he admitted sheepishly. The woman gave him a look of mock chastisement.

'Gin!' she called, 'will you fetch some tonic? And a washcloth, and some bandages. Poor Mary here's been gored.'

All the while the infant's cries had only become fiercer.

'Hamish! Please! Change him,' the woman snapped curtly. Then added in response to his last attempt to delegate, 'the little prodigy is asleep already. You'll have to do it yourself.'

Hamish sighed with dreariness and then disappeared into the other large tent. Between the two looming rectangular tents, both lit from within, a small triangular tent lay darkly, not four feet from the mats and logs encircling the fire.

'That's his sister, the little genius,' the woman explained, undoing Hamish's first attempt at a bandage. 'Her name's Star actually, which is quite fitting with how bright she has turned out to be. Sorry,' she paused to shake her head, 'I'm Lorelai, I should have started with that. I suppose you've met Hamish, and this is Gin,' she said as Gin returned with the medical supplies.

Hamish re-emerged from the larger tent and lay a towel on the ground to begin changing his son, whose cries had become almost ferocious.

'And the little *angel* we call Orran,' Gin added sarcastically. He sat on an unsteady but wide log the other side of the fire and watched his mother re-dress Lucy's wound. The fire made only a gentle orange flicker about them, and the lanterns in the tents were kept deliberately low. But even amid this insipid light at the camp's centre, it seemed that apart from fringes of emerald and violet tendrils, there was only blackness beyond. In her weary but equally charmed state, it felt as though the jungle had all but disappeared, and her new universe existed entirely within the confines of this quaint floating campsite.

'So, you been on your own now how long? A few days?' Lorelai asked.

'Yes, I, I think so, but I might have lost count,' Lucy said.

'You're terribly lucky Hamish found you, who knows what would have become of you otherwise,' said Lorelai, but then immediately felt she was being too grim. 'I mean to say, I'm sure you would have been fine. It is a dangerous place though. Hamish said you were traveling with your family, and your horse was spooked?'

Lucy did her best to feign an expression of recollection. 'With my aunt and uncle yes. I guess he must have been spooked, he'd never done that before,' she paused to play it out in her mind and then reiterate it to her new friends, she could sense Hamish in the background, half-listening, as he rewrapped his son.

'He riled up, for no reason, no reason at all. We were on a path of sorts - I think - it's a bit hazy - and then he just took off. It was a long time before he threw me off, we were quite deep into the jungle by then, and then he just kept going, galloped off without me.'

'Gosh. It is rather strange that your aunt and uncle would have wanted to be traveling through the jungle in the first place. Don't they know it's dangerous?'

'I don't think they planned to go into the jungle. At least they didn't tell me that. We were meant to pass by it, not go in it.'

'Oh dear, and I suppose all your things must have been on the carriage! Oh, to have nothing but the clothes on your back... in this place! It's a wonder your dog has stayed with you?' Lorelai exclaimed.

Lucy froze for a moment. She hadn't thought about Crumbs. He was no greyhound, and no match for a galloping horse. This really undermined her story. He had been sniffing around the edges of the tents and the clearing but had just returned to the fire and let out a hushed sigh as he lay down in the dirt.

'Yes, he ummm... he hates it when I'm on a horse without him. He just gets so yappy. Doesn't stop. It's impossible, to umm, get any peace,' Lucy said, and tried to seem natural as she inserted a light-hearted chuckle into the lie.

'You managed that whole ordeal, being galloped through the jungle, holding on to that dog?' Gin asked, more astounded than suspicious, but Lucy was nervous.

'Oh, no, no, no,' she said and chuckled again, stalling, 'he... Crumbs... has his own pouch... in the saddle.'

Lorelai and Gin were silent for a few moments in a mutually shared confusion, having not heard of such a thing, before Hamish returned with Orran and joined them.

'Well, you're *both* in good hands now,' he said, smiling warmly.

This seemed to steer Lorelai's questions back to her original, nurturing, agenda.

'And have you managed to eat anything?'

Lucy shook her head. 'Only some fruit I saw creatures eating. I managed to kill a small furry burrower thing last night, but I couldn't get fire to catch so I couldn't cook it. Not that raw flesh bothers him of course,' she said indicating Crumbs, 'so he was well fed.'

Lorelai now sat on a log, looming over Lucy who sat cross-legged in the dirt, nearer the hearth. Lucy's reference to hunting alerted Gin and Lorelai to her sword which they both eyed discreetly from their opposing positions across the fire. It was not unheard of for a woman to have a sword, but it was unusual, and such women were usually both much older and much broader than this little Mary.

'You won't get much to catch alight around here,' Gin remarked, 'the air is too damp, the mist and rain is perennial.'

'Certain plants will burn. I'll show you… tomorrow,' Hamish said.

'Let's get some real food into you straight away!' declared Lorelai, 'Gin, why don't you get one of the rabbits?'

'Okay, firstly, why are you always getting me to fetch things? I didn't come on this trip to be a kind of pantry-maid. Secondly, it's father's turn to make dinner. It was his damned idea to hold off until golden boy here returned safe and sound, which he did, so, now Lord Mathew can damn well cook? No?' He was finished his point then but went on to answer his own rhetorical question. 'Besides, it's late, and I've got a long night ahead of me.' Gin shifted back on the log to further indicate he would not be budging. Hamish grinned. Lorelai sighed and was turning toward Hamish when Mathew emerged from the tent behind them with two other men.

It was clear which one of the men was Mathew, because he looked very much like Hamish. They had the same alluringly warm eyes, square jaw, and slender, pointed nose. His father's hair though had broadly darkened, lightened of late only by wisps of grey. It was more a faded chestnut than a sunlit honey and fell in a ponytail down his back. Contrarily, and perhaps more evident in terms of Hamish's progeny, the other two men looked nothing like him, Gin, or each other.

Dr. Peter Sellis, an older, and in many ways more esteemed researcher than project leader Mr. Mathew Mathers (although being a botanist and chemist, and Mr. Mather's work being primarily in anthropology and ecology, their respective fields of research differed) had an ebony-coffee complexion and a tall, slender physique. His hair was starting to grey, which was about the only thing that gave away his age on his otherwise unblemished face. The third man, Geldie, was his (comparatively) young protege. He had slender eyes and a wide nose on a rather round face. He was stockier than the other two, with a deep olive complexion, but he had copied the hairstyle of Mr. Mathers.

'Ahh, Lord Mathew has graced us with his presence!' Gin mocked, but then eyed his stepfather seriously. 'Golden boy is back with a strange girl, so can we eat now?'

Mathew fixed his gaze toward Lucy for several intense moments before he nodded. While normally engaging and loquacious in his interactions, tonight he was tired and rather downhearted for his own reasons, so his words would be comparatively few. Geldie and Peter moved around to the opposite side of the fire, their work finally complete for the day. Peter sat himself down on a mat while Geldie sat on the log beside Gin, nearer the fire. Peter looked to Lucy with polite interest, while Geldie politely pretended to be disinterested, and instead fixated on the fire.

'I heard some of the commotion from inside the tent, but I had to finish my report,' Mathew said. 'I've gathered you're lost, or have become in need of help of some kind?'

He waited for Lucy to nod and let out a murmur of agreement before he continued, 'I'm Mathew, this is my co-researcher, Doctor Peter Sellis, and his understudy Geldie. I see you've met my sons Gin and Hamish, my partner Lorelai.'

'Yes, thank you so much for taking me into your camp, I'm so lucky Hamish found me,' she said, tactfully deciding to repeat the sentiments relayed to her.

'Yes,' Mathew muttered, looking into the fire wearily and mulling on Gin's demands for dinner, 'I will get the rabbit out. The rest? The rest, the ahh, the vegetables, bread and what have you, I guess that's all mostly cooked already. It might need to be warmed though,' he muttered, and then turned to go back into the tent, stopped, and said, 'Sorry, sorry, I'm a bit not myself. Your name was?'

'Sorry, it's L... it's Mary,' Lucy said, her eyes exposing a fear that the slip had given her away. She added out of caution, 'I'm sorry, I'm stumbling with words, I'm also a bit not myself.'

Hamish then went into the tent ahead of Mathew to fetch something, and while his father slowly brought out the equipment and food, Hamish knelt in front of Lucy and presented her with a piece of flatbread wrapped in paper. Lucy's eyes almost sparked with electricity she was so delighted. She almost couldn't take it from him, her hands were too weak.

'Eat,' he ordered. She obeyed. The sensation of the taste flooded her with endorphins, as if every cell in her sung with the knowledge that her otherwise doomed body would now be revived. And this was just bread.

Mathew hastily prepared the dinner with the usual fussing from his wife. Two rabbits, pre-skinned earlier, were spit-roasted along the top of the fire, while pots of miscellaneous vegetables hung from chains on a tripod in its centre. There was almost no discussion while everyone waited, this sudden shared lust for both sensory and appetite satisfaction consumed their collective thoughts, and they could do nothing but watch the flames turn the pink skin brown and then black. This hunger drew all energy that might otherwise be used for conversation.

But despite the silence, the campfire was alive with suspicion and unspoken questions. Geldie was by and large filtering through the day's findings in his mind, categorising them, connecting them, but even his focused mind could wander, and he considered Lucy several times. In sharp glances that were incidental enough, if caught, to naturally rise above her and into the jungle abyss, he quickly deduced her shabby and malnourished appearance. It was an objectionable sight, more so because he couldn't bear to comprehend the horribleness of several days alone in this jungle. But he further concluded that she was not his concern, but that of his seniors, and his thoughts returned to their research.

Peter, somewhat sprawled out on the mat and the dirt, polished his spectacles in a series of heavy sighs that were familiar to the team. He held the spectacles close to where they met Lucy's flickering image by the fire, just to the right of his line of sight. Hamish had assuaged his son's ferocious mood, and the bairn was now climbing from his lap down to the dirt floor and back up again. He used his son quite blatantly, as an excuse for making eye contact with Lucy, or an excuse for having his eyes on her figure, shimmering rose in the firelight. When Lucy's eyes caught his gaze, he would immediately divert to Orran, as if the contact were intentional, not accidental, and Orran was the reason.

'Who's that?' he would say to his entirely uninterested son, and point to Lucy. Gin was the only one who was fearlessly conspicuous in his examination. He watched Lucy intently and when she caught his gaze he threw in each question as it came to his mind.

'The dog, what's it called?' 'How long have you had that sword? Can you use it?'

'Time for rabbit,' Lorelai interjected, interrupting her son's last question, and the group's focus readily returned to hunger. Bread and pre-smoked vegetables were dished out into the clay bowls, the rabbit evenly divided.

'And you're sure Star doesn't want anything?' Hamish asked, appreciating his rather large helping.

'She's eaten far enough today, now she needs rest,' said Lorelai.

'She's exhausted because Orran's never quiet!' Gin snapped aggressively, who had himself not been able to sleep all day because of the child's inexorable wailing. But shortly after they had begun to gustily replenish themselves, the attention turned, rather expectantly, back to Lucy.

'Where exactly were you traveling from? When your horse was spooked?' Mathew asked, brusquely. There was a shifting of postures around the fire as his uncomfortable directness spurred an anxious anticipation in the team.

'I don't know where we were exactly, but I'm sure my aunt and uncle never meant to come into the jungle,' she said, trying to protect her story by shifting attention away from the details. Her left hand rested softly on Crumb's head after having given him a portion of her rabbit, feigning a relaxed disposition. But in truth as her body felt more physically revived, her mind began to fret with an anxious desperation. These people could be everything to her if they took her in: food, shelter, guidance. What's more, in the shadow of the last few days of pitiful loneliness, they represented comfort. She felt she had stumbled upon a golden goose. But the questions, in her mind, were proof that she had not been accepted just yet, rather, such acceptance was pending the results of this interrogation.

Mathew, on the other hand, hardly appreciated he was conducting such an exercise. He did not perceive Lucy as any kind of threat. Despite being armed with a sword, she was a small female, and he had his team of five men. All large and dutifully armed. His aspersions on the honesty of her character hadn't gone so far as to consider her dangerous. But it was obvious to all of them that her story made no sense, and he needed to at least attempt to get some clarity from her.

'Yes, I understand you might not have been aware of your precise location, but where were you coming from? Surely you know that much?'

Lucy swallowed hard. His tone intensified the pressure she felt to concoct a perfect answer, but her geographic ignorance made that impossible.

'We had been living just outside of Gemini,' she said, remembering this part of the lie she'd told Hamish earlier. But her evasion of Mathew's question was now apparent to everyone.

'Okay, you don't seem to want to tell us where you'd come from. Where was the intended destination then?' Mathew was not irate, not even annoyed, but anyone that did not know him would be forgiven for thinking this was so. His blunt words held no emotion, but Lucy trembled.

'Please, Mat! Stop interrogating her. After all, she doesn't know anything about us either,' said Lorelai coming to her defence. Mathew put his hands up in apologetic defence.

'I'm not trying to test her, but we all find it baffling that a young girl would be alone in this jungle. I think it's reasonable to try to get a clearer picture? How else can we help her get back to wherever she needs to be?' he said.

'We were going to Archmond,' she responded, somewhat stuttering now that she appreciated the ridiculousness of the lie she was forced to stick by, but added, 'to the Hills of Archmond.'

She felt the group air stir with incredulity. Even Mathew seemed stunned into silence for several moments as his mind struggled to comprehend what she'd said.

'Your family was traveling to Archmond? For what purpose? What business do Geminians have in Archmond?'

'I don't really know… why we were going there,' Lucy responded, sounding quiet and defeated, as though his question had been more a rhetorical reprimand than a genuine inquiry.

'Please, Mat, enough questions. It's all very curious, but we can take it up with her family when we find them,' Lorelai snapped hastily almost in the same moment Lucy answered.

Again, Mathew threw his hands up in bleak defence, determining then to ruminate on this overnight and come back to it in the morning.

Gin was not fazed by the subtle tension though, and keen to continue a less formal line of questioning on behalf of his stepfather asked, 'So, what's Gemini like? I've heard it's all green pastures, milk and honey… endless food. Pastures of sheep and oceans of fish. That's what they say.'

Lucy smiled sheepishly and shrugged as if to answer his question with a *maybe*. But she struggled to come up with anything generic to add. She worried Gin's question was a trap and was starting to feel the hope of being accepted slip away.

'To be honest,' she said, trying now to feign the impression of confession, 'we lived a good way out of Gemini, and were only there recently. We've moved around most of my life, usually staying in farming regions. My parents died young and then my aunt and uncle took me in. We move around a lot, but I don't often know where we are, or why we're there.'

'Oh! You're nomadic,' Hamish let out, almost unconsciously, with an unintentional sigh of relief. He laughed affably at himself for not piecing it together sooner. It was as though her words had now explained away all the abnormalities holding back his infatuation with her. In equal acceptance of her explanation, a relieved humour rushed across the rest of the team.

'That certainly explains a lot,' said Peter, speaking for the first time, looking to Geldie with a large, amused grin.

'Oh, I'm sorry,' Mathew sung, the shake of his head was also followed by a heavy humoured sigh as he slapped his hands down onto his knees, 'I understand now why you've been so mysterious with the details. But you mustn't worry. We have no problem with the nomadic here. I'm actually very interested in your people,' he said but then added cheerily, 'but, ahhh, rest assured! I'll leave any further questions for another day.'

Once it had been decided Mary's peculiarities were no longer enigmatic, but in fact perfectly predictable given what they knew about nomads (sword-wielding misfits who lived in small clans, moving from place to place, finding cheap temporary labour or surviving off the land) the conversation moved more keenly back to the present.

They discussed their various sightings over the day, made on their separate ventures from the camp. Mathew with Lorelai, Peter with Geldie, and Hamish alone (but only for half the day, having spent the first half at the camp, guarding his sister and son until Gin woke up). Hamish was the only one who hadn't recorded any sightings of the weed, with the rest of the team recording at least two to three thickets.

They discussed the similarities between the day's sightings and those of the previous days, in terms of where the weed had been growing. Peter was pleased that his hypothesis so far seemed substantiated. The alien invader's ideal soil density, sunlight, and spread, were consistent with that of its native relative. Though he cautioned Mathew that more tests on more samples of its noxious fruit would have to be undertaken before he could support any of the team's conclusions about the effects of its consumption.

Mathew paused to smile down at their wayfaring stranger, 'Miss Mary, you're probably quite lost in all this. Has anyone explained to you the purpose of our expedition out here?'

Now that he thought of her as nomadic, he had taken on a gentler more paternalistic temperament. This was coming from a desire to educate Mary, which was itself based on cultural stereotypes which painted nomadics as quite dim. But Mary, or Lucy rather, who knew nothing of this world, and nothing of nomadic stereotypes, could not perceive any condescension. She would take in all this information with, in her attempt to ingratiate herself to these people, unashamed eagerness.

'I have explained all,' said Hamish, who after having collected the bowls and handing out washcloths, was dismantling both the tripod and the skewer over the fire.

'In fact,' Hamish continued, 'our Mary has had quite a rude introduction into the adverse effects of the weed's fruit, cautious though you may be Dr. Sellis about ruling it so. That pig was hyped up on it without doubt.'

'Ahh, that's how you got this wound here?' Mathew said, his eyes trailing inquisitively down to Lucy's shoulder, before taking a swig of tonic. Lorelai had been arranging things in their tent, but she had come back out, and he handed the bottle to her.

'Admittedly I only saw the beast for a few short moments, but he was exceptionally enraged, and he had the same purple-red blotches on his skin,' Hamish continued, then whispered softly to Lorelai, 'Can I have some?'

'Where's your bottle?' Mathew asked, having overheard.

'I used the last of it to tend to Mary's wound,' declared Hamish defensively, but he was suppressing a soft smile.

'He drunk most of it last night with Gin and Peter,' muttered Lorelai. Mathew rolled his eyes and turned back to Lucy.

'This pig seemed particularly mad to you? And when I say that I don't mean angry. Did you notice a deranged absence in his eyes? Did he seem gleeful… whilst attacking you? Was there something… off?'

Lucy shuddered. 'I don't think he wanted to kill me quickly.' Her memories of it swam about a moment longer. 'There was something deranged in him,' she agreed.

Mathew threw a look at Peter.

Peter's eyes narrowed condescendingly. 'A sentient being! Should it not be allowed the same depravity of our species without the accusation of madness?'

Mathew refuted this with an abrupt laugh.

'A fit question for the anthropologist,' remarked Geldie, smirking.

'Indeed,' Mathew said, and eyed his colleagues, who were sniggering half-heartedly to themselves, and then returned to his new human specimen.

'We are mapping a weed called zea-weed. It is smothering the fragile flowers and mosses on the jungle floor and strangling the melody mushrooms. But it also bears fruit known to have psychotropic effects - at least on humans. It was actually created by *Her Majesty*,' he uttered the title disingenuously, 'in Meta Emery as a new fuel for the new army. It is supposed she was looking for a wondrous miracle cure for sickness, and an otherwise powerful stimulant. Because the fruit of the native zea-plant does have that effect, it has healing properties as Dr. Sellis here I'm sure will agree?'

Peter looked up and nodded, but he seemed confounded by the obvious nature of question. Everyone knew that zea-fruit paste was medicinal.

'But the native zea-fruit is inedible. Horrible acrid taste that in any case induces vomiting. That's why they administered it topically to wounds. But the palace, through its sorceress ruler, created a more potent *adaptation*.' Mathew said the last word sharply, darkening the inquisitive ambiance with a single breath. 'The zea-weed, which is both poisonous, and insidious. The intent was that it would rapidly cure sickness and wounds, strengthen soldiers. There's always good intentions. But as I said you can't eat the zea-fruit, the acidity was too high, most people simply vomited it back up again. So part of this development, of this new variety, was to produce edible fruit, but while edible, the fruit of the zea-weed seemed to make people go mad.'

Peter cut in, 'It wasn't about making it edible. I don't think the Dynasty cared how it was administered; they wanted a super potion. The palatable fruit was an accident. No matter though, they of course found with the new version, the weed, that administering it topically or through the blood, straight into a wound or a scratch or the like, as they had done with the native zea-fruit paste, caused the same incurable psychosis as eating it: hallucinations, rage, the whole basket.'

'Yes, so it was a failure really, no evidence that it had any additional medicinal properties than the zea-fruit, just these horrible new side effects, when eaten or absorbed topically. But they had been growing it here, before they realised, and when the experiment was abandoned, it had already spread—'

'Wait,' Lucy interjected, stricken, 'this weed, what does it look like? Does it spray you if you step on it? Sting your eyes?' She was remembering the vine carpeting the floor with the green and white leaves which had burned her eyes and nearly turned her blind.

'That would be Frost Leaf,' said Lorelai.

'Oh yes, yes, don't worry. The zea, the native version and the weed, is quite thick and thorny. At the very least it would be hard to accidentally walk through it. The fruit, if you want to spot it, they look like tiny peppers. They start out purple and go red towards the tip,' Peter added.

'Oh, good,' Lucy sighed with relief. Mathew and Lorelai laughed.

'But that Frost Leaf is a nasty thing,' Peter carried on, 'it can cause permanent blindness. Did it sting you?'

'Yes, the first day I was here. I couldn't see at all at first, it burned like fire, but I… I fell in water, into a creek, I just kept rubbing my eyes with the water and hoping.'

'You're a lucky lady. I'd say that creek saved your sight,' Peter said. The rest of them murmured in agreement. Lucy stared into the fire and swallowed hard in acknowledgment. The sabres, the fall, the stinging vine, the warthog and then to find Hamish and their team; she had been much luckier than they would ever know.

'But anyway, though Dr. Sellis is right that you wouldn't likely accidentally stumble into a thicket of zea-weed, it's been spreading across the jungle like an insidious mould.'

'Indeed,' Peter agreed, rubbing his chin. He had picked up a small twig and was making shapes in the dirt before the fire. The first was a crescent moon, but he rubbed that away and was now making a face. 'Because the zea-fruit was so acidic its propagation came from birds and burrowers using the fruit to build nests with, as far as we know it—' he paused, 'as far as we know it was never eaten.'

'Whereas the zea-weed,' Mathew continued soberly, 'supposedly has a sweet, citrus taste. This is why it's spreading - because creatures are learning to eat it. All kinds of creatures.'

'Yes, actually that reminds me-' Hamish remarked nervously, suddenly realising he should have mentioned this sooner, 'we found a ahh, possibly infected, Archmonder, on the way back as well.'

Mathew threw his arms wide, astounded. 'You wait until now to mention that part? Is all this in the report?'

Hamish looked away sheepishly before scooping up Orran, whose tiny, slobbery hands, were petulantly grabbing at Crumbs, despite Hamish's objections. 'No I haven't… I mean, I haven't had a chance. I'll do it at first light.'

Peter's scribbled face in the dirt was morphing into something more sinister looking: the nose a hollow heart, wide gaping eyes, the top of the head wide and round above the narrow square jaw.

'What happened with the Archmonder?' asked Geldie, taking a swig of tonic from Gin's bottle. Peter was staring back intently, also waiting for the answer.

'Well, we ahh, I… I had to, I had to kill him,' Hamish muttered quietly.

Geldie said nothing but his eyes widened, and Peter drew a deep breath.

'He was setting vile traps. He'd become sadistic. It was all I could do,' Hamish said defensively, but his elevated intonation exposed his internal confliction.

Peter and Geldie exchanged glances, but no one said anything else for several moments.

'I think it is high time I get some much-needed sleep. Excuse me all,' Peter said, groaning as he got up, his joints cracking. 'Very glad to meet you, Mary.'

Lucy nodded in return, noticing as she did, that the scribbled face had become a skull and crossbones.

'I should go too. Goodnight all,' Geldie said, following.

They sat quietly for several moments, eventually distracted from the lingering reproach of the researchers, by Orran's continued torment of poor Crumbs, who took it all with commendable tolerance.

'Mary, you might find you fit some of Star's clothes… she's obviously asleep… but we happen to have some drying in our tent. Do you want to come see? I'm sure you're ummm… I'm sure you're sick of being wet,' said Lorelai, determined to change the focus, standing above Lucy and offering her a hand.

'Oh, why don't you show Mary our equipment,' Mathew chimed as the two women walked into the tent. 'It might interest you to see just how advanced Trimany is on its field testing. Gemini may have its agricultural prominence, but we're leading the way in botanical research. See for yourself.'

From inside the tent, Lucy smiled graciously to Lorelai, pretending to both understand and be interested in the comparison.

Once alone, Lucy stripped down and wiped herself over with the washcloth Lorelai had left her, before squeezing into the long and modest dress of the team's only adolescent female. She laid her soggy soiled garments on a flimsy fold-out table, observing as she did the team's ensemble of scientific paraphernalia: specimens preserved in minute glass capsules and pressed between paper, magnifiers and prisms, vaporisers and dispensers, potions and powders, masks and goggles. She hadn't a half idea about most of it, but she found the image of it and the impression it created immensely inspiring. She had no reference point in their world against which to contrast this, but she had none from her own either. These people were like no one she had ever met, and she wanted to know everything about them.

When she returned to the fire, Hamish was just emerging from the opposite tent, having put his son to sleep, and Mathew and Lorelai said they too should get some sleep and bid them goodnight.

'Apparently he was screaming all through the day, but that should mean he sleeps through the night,' Hamish said, slipping his hands into his trouser pockets as he sat on the log with his brother.

'I'll move my shirts and trousers aside and you can have my bed until it's dawn. Hopefully the tyrant allows you more sleep than he did me,' said Gin, 'but first I just have to ahh… sort myself out.'

He wandered just out of sight into the darkness and after several moments of rustling shrubbery they could hear him urinating. She had understood by now, that Gin was their nightwatchman, and only needed the bed during the day.

Hamish offered Lucy some of the tonic. Tonic was a bitter-sweet citrus spirit they distilled back in Trimany, but it was consumed in many parts of the world, so he offered no explanation as to what it was. She took a gulp and was burned by its strength. Hamish let out a light huff of suppressed amusement.

'It's a strong brew. Listonderry,' he said, his tone softer now that it was just the two of them again. She grinned, nodding.

'He meant Orran by the way… *the tyrant*. He sleeps with me in the half of the tent I share with Gin. Peter and Geldie are in the other room. But I certainly won't keep you awake if he doesn't. I'm—' he paused because he wasn't being entirely honest with her or himself now, 'I think I will be asleep as soon as I shut my eyes.' He did not think that. He was too riled up by her existence, let alone her physical presence.

There was a silence then. Alone, the awkwardness rising between them was flickering sporadically with the sparks of this mutual unspoken attraction.

'Is your wife not here with you?' Lucy asked daringly.

Hamish shook his head, he tried to smile but it was a vain attempt to conceal his sensitivity on the topic. 'I'm not married,' he said eventually. But they both understood that wasn't really the meaning of her question.

Gin returned and the lingering chemistry seemed to evaporate. Lucy noticed now how different the two men were. It was clear they had no blood relation. Gin's features were sharp, wiry. His physique was broader and more muscularly defined than his young stepbrother. His hair was dark atop a long flat head. His eyes were deeply set and his nose prominent, imposing. Contrarily Hamish was baby-faced, despite his strong jaw. They shared several more swigs of tonic from Gin's bottle for several minutes before Hamish decided they should both get some sleep.

'If you feel yourself waking up because you're suddenly in need of some midnight conversation, I'll be here. All night,' Gin said, grinning, a thin film of turquoise spores stretching above the camp as they left him.

Settled in their beds, less than a metre apart but with Orran between them, Hamish shut his eyes, but he couldn't sleep. The notion of drifting calmly away now seemed impossible with the body of this alluring and mystifying girl in such close proximity to his own. And the notion of how sexually enchanting he found her disturbed everything he thought he knew about himself, and the woman he truly loved. Lucy struggled too, at first. Her head was spinning with the starry wonder that had been cast around her. She was enamoured by these people. All of them. By their intelligence and knowledge, by the nobility of their pursuit, and by the protection and safety being amongst them now offered. But not least of all, her head was spinning that this had all come about through the chivalrous charm of a captivating and handsome man.

For the second time since she arrived in this strange world, Lucy's night saw her transported into the intricately vivid world of her subconscious. Unlike her last dream there was no sense of telepathy. There wasn't even a narrative. Artificial and constructed scenes played out as though they were memories. She played a game of chess with Amber. Amber, still far too young to possibly comprehend the game, moved the pieces around on each turn with careful strategic precision. But Lucy still won, and tiny, three-year old Amber, with her hazel-chestnut eyes, stared her down in response. The stare of an aggrieved adult, not a petulant child. What's more, there was a distinct accusation of deceit and false victory in her countenance. But then in a muddled haze of movement she was now shopping with Amber, picking out dresses that Amber delighted in.

She was climbing a tree with Amber, a tree she'd never seen before, because it did not exist, and neither did the shiny plastic-red fruit it bore. But they continued climbing it anyway, and Amber aged somewhat as they did. Her legs lengthened, her cherub-shaped face narrowed into that of a girl's, she became five, then seven, then perhaps twelve? They dislodged a rainbow-coloured kite from the tree's top branch and were, in the same moment, walking through Lockerby toward a park to fly it.

The wind was strong. It whipped up Amber's unruly strawberry blonde locks as they walked down the main street, shifting strands into her eyes, and Amber, now three again, squealed gleefully, amused and bewildered that she couldn't see. But as Lucy parted Amber's hair back into place, she took in the sky; it was becoming very dark. The bleak afternoon wind was not for nothing. Amber beside her started to fade away, a picture going out of focus until there was nothing left. But the distant storm only strengthened and intensified its presence. On the horizon, above suburban rooftops at the end of the street, the menacing whirl of black clouds began to flicker with electricity. Debris and autumn leaves raced toward and past her in rolling gusts. Lucy realised she was completely alone on the street, alone in the town. Not a soul in sight. But then Hamish was beside her, where Amber had been, as though he'd always been there, and his presence did not seem out of place to her. He took in the storm with equal foreboding, but he took her hand, and without turning to her he said, 'I'll be with you the whole way, Lucy. The whole way.'

Lucy woke to the pleasant sounds of human murmur: quiet morning discussions amid careful shuffling designed not to wake her. The jungle's insects and amphibians were croaking away at pace, but those near the camp had been monotonous enough for her to block out. The tent was empty. Not just the section she'd shared with Hamish and Orran, but as she walked out, she saw that the other section was empty too. She'd searched her backpack and Hamish's belongings for something akin to a mirror, but she'd found nothing, then tried as best she could to untangle her hair with fingers and pink her lips and cheeks with pinches. She found Hamish sitting with Orran around the coals, the embers used to warm the tea fast fading. He seemed to be showing Orran a small sprig with a bronze caterpillar on it, and was speaking to him about it, not in silly baby talk, but in the way you might speak to a child old enough to comprehend such things. She caught the end of it.

'… and only when the caterpillar is just ready, when they have decided that it is time in their little life to transform, they will hang upside down from a leaf, with their liquid rope. Then they will cocoon in a special shell called a chrysalis they make from inside themselves, and in that shell, everything that the caterpillar was, dissolves.'

As he said the last few words, he looked at Lucy and smiled. Lucy sat down upon the log he leant against in the dirt. Orran, watching the caterpillar, was silent. His expression stern. As though it were possible that he were following his father's every word.

'And when the chrysalis breaks, what emerges is no longer a caterpillar! It has become something new. Something beautiful, that floats through the forest,' he lifted the edge of Orran's supple chin to point out the stream of sapphire butterflies passing the edge of the camp. It wasn't certain Orran could in fact see that far, but he seemed to delight at what his father tried to show him, bursting with drooling laughter, and waving his hands about ecstatically. Hamish laughed as well.

'They're so easily amused,' he said with most genuine adoration. Clearly, he was entranced with his son. Lucy smiled. She agreed, but she was too much in awe of how devoted Hamish was as a father, to think of anything else. Behind them, the remainder of Mathew's team shuffled about, getting ready for the day.

'There's no more tea,' Hamish said, somewhat apologetically, but he was not all that sorry.

Lucy was about to say she didn't drink tea anyway, when Lorelai strolling past said, 'Oh, you're awake! Let me get you some jek-fruit. Hamish, you want any more? We've got to eat it by today.'

'I'm okay,' Hamish responded, letting the caterpillar crawl onto his finger and then Orran's, much to the babe's delight.

'Just have a bit, it's a shame to waste it. Maybe Orran wants some more,' she pushed.

'No, he can't have that much sugar. I'm sorry, I can't eat anymore,' Hamish replied.

'Is it okay for dogs? Crumbs will eat anything,' Lucy said trying to be helpful.

'I think this is edible by just about anything,' replied Lorelai, gladly.

'She's awake! Finally… thank the skies!' cried Gin as he eyed Hamish. 'It's all you now, brother.' He disarmed himself of the machete and the crossbow, leaving them more or less in the dirt and without another word staggered into the tent to sleep. Lorelai brought out the fruit and more of the bread, which was much staler than Lucy appreciated the previous night.

'How old is he actually? I didn't even ask yesterday,' Lucy said when they were effectively alone again, the others preparing themselves and their equipment in the main tent.

Hamish grinned, finally flicked the caterpillar away, and rubbed Orran's rustic red hairs. 'He is close to two years old. But he has his father's mind, so I estimate he is only six years away from contributing to these expeditions and writing a dissertation of his own.'

Crumbs rushed into Lucy's lap, and Orran outstretched his milky hands, desperate to grab at the wriggly animal. They locked eyes as he did, Hamish and Lucy, and it became apparent to them both that the awkwardness of the previous evening had already merged into something more powerful. She would be forgiven in the intensity of his gaze, for thinking that perhaps he had been there beside her after all, as that storm rolled into Lockerby.

'And your sister, Star, is it?'

Hamish nodded, but considered the question, 'she's about thirteen, I think,' he laughed at his ignorance, 'I sound like a horrible brother, maybe she's fourteen, my father should know.'

Mathew emerged from the tent, tucking the ends of the flowing green shirt into his khaki linen trousers. 'Hamish we're about ready to leave, but Star still isn't awake yet which is a bit odd. I'm concerned she may be coming down with something. Will you be okay here on your own to look after her?' he asked, placing his knapsack on the log and fastening the ties on his belt, nodding briefly at Lucy.

'He won't be alone. I'll be here,' Lucy added. Mathew thought she was more vocal today, but before he could express his gratitude, Hamish shrugged off his father's concerns.

'She's going through a lazy phase. She's been sluggish the whole trip. But I think we have what we need,' he said blandly, but then added, 'although at this moment I need to… ahhh… Mary would you?' he held Orran out.

'Oh, yes. Of course,' Lucy said and gladly took the infant in her arms. He was small for two years she thought. But Hamish was right about him being bright. In the milky round face his hazel eyes pierced hers with a chilling sincerity and analysis. Hamish went to pee.

'I hope you slept okay,' said Mathew, turning away before she could answer as Peter and Geldie came up alongside him, and the trio appeared to exchange some final propositions about their respective routes. Lucy turned her attention back to Orran, and she remembered her dream then more vividly, and Hamish's hand in hers, and she wondered about why he wasn't married, and what that meant about Orran's mother. But then they heard a horrifying cry.

Hamish had walked into the bracken between his father's tent and his sister's, beyond which the land began to incline steeply. Not so much that he had to consider the stream of his urine, but it was fairly basic courtesy to get as far away from camp as was reasonable. Slightly uphill and aiming himself politely in a downstream angle away from the campsite, he took a deep sigh as he relieved himself.

Morning mist moved through the jungle rapidly, in clouds as thick as the colourful fungal spores. The mushrooms, at least, ceased to obfuscate things in the morning, which in relative terms gave the white mist an almost angelic clarity. But as he tilted his head back toward the camp, and focussed on his sister's triangular tent, some-thing was askew. Shadows on the canvas where there were not meant to be shadows.

His flow stopped. He froze. His breath became shallow, and he crossed the shrubbery and the ferns down toward the dark triangular tent. He was tremulous. He was only hoping to be wrong. But the shadows were what his sleepy morning mind had perceived them: great ferocious tears in the fabric. The tent had been ripped, clawed open from the back. He raced forward.

'Star!' he yelled, though his terror confounded his articulation, and the word came out as nothing but a rancorous roar. To his horror he was not wrong. He burst through her tent, and she was not there. Her sleeping bag held the same horrendous slashes from horrendous claws. He burst out the other side.

'Star!' he screamed. Lucy could have almost dropped Orran in the terror his voice created.

'What? What?' Mathew shouted but he too was already pink with panic.

'She's not there. She's not there! She's not *in there*!' Hamish said, his frantic body language failing to conceal his shock. A darkness that Lucy could not have imagined came over the camp. Gin emerged.

'What's going on?' he suppressed his urge to make light of everything when he saw their faces and saw the tent. 'Where's Star?'

Hamish suddenly couldn't breathe. Gin went to look in the tent.

'Oh… no… no… no,' he said shakily as he came out and seemed to transform into a different person himself, one more solemn and serious than could be expected from his initial impression, as he confessed the following, 'They look like baboon marks. I thought I saw a baboon yesterday, on the edge of the camp, watching us…'

'You what?' Mathew's anger was palpable.

'I put it in the report!' he cried defensively.

'You say nothing! And now where is my sister?' Hamish roared ferociously and took Gin by the neck.

'He doesn't know!' screamed Lorelai, whacking a thick but smooth branch into Hamish's own neck. He released his stepbrother.

'We are no use to her if we are seduced by rage!' Peter bellowed authoritatively. 'Now think, Gin, where did you see this baboon?'

Gin had fallen onto his knees in the dirt. He could barely speak. Despite being slightly shorter and more slender than Gin, the grip Hamish had put around his neck had caused temporary damage.

He whispered hoarsely, 'That way, upwards,' and pointed in the same direction Hamish had been standing, beyond the tent, 'but I'm not sure.'

At that moment, he felt nothing more than an intense desire to take Hamish's face and shove it into the hot logs of the fire. He was after all, bigger, and older, and stronger, and his stupid, thoughtless, arrogant stepbrother should be made to appreciate this fact. But he was kind enough to forgive him his ignorant burst of rage, at least until after they recovered poor little Star.

'We'll head in that direction now,' said Mathew, followed with, 'Men, arm yourselves.'

Peter tried to object. 'Baboons can live in packs of up to fifty or more, each of them about our size, and your own hypothesis is that many packs may be acting in ways that are sadistic or deranged because of this weed. While I am yet to agree, I have not ruled it out. Supposing she is alive, how do you suppose the five of us, will get her back from a pack of twenty or more males, that may be acting under psychotropic influence?'

'It doesn't matter. They have my daughter. I have to try,' Mathew retorted angrily.

'I am simply saying we take a moment to plan this out, and come up with a strategy,' Peter retorted defensively, hoping to calm Mathew into being reasonable.

'No, we need to hurry, my sister, she can't defend herself,' Hamish said, gripping Peter's arm.

Amid all that had been said, and she was very eagerly listening, it was the word strategy that gave Lucy a thought. She thought of the frost-leaf. She remembered how it burned and how she had thought this must be what pepper-spray felt like. And that pepper-spray itself was used to defend yourself by blinding your attacker.

'The frost-leaf, doesn't it burn your eyes? Blind you even?'

They all stared at her with the same bewilderment but gave no response, and then made to carry on talking. But she continued before they could.

'If there really are fifty or more baboons and they really are acting mad like that river pig... what if she dies in the struggle. What if we all die trying to save her? The frost leaf. All that equipment you have... could we squeeze out the liquid from the leaves, make a kind of... a kind of spray? We could spray them. You have masks? We can wear masks and spray the baboons. If they've been blinded, we could more easily kill them and rescue her.'

There was a stark silence. Mathew and Peter exchanged several glances before Peter eventually responded, 'That is a brilliant idea, or it would be, but the frost-leaf only grows in tiny hand-size patches. It is not so common to find quantities enough for this idea. You would need a whole thicket of it to produce enough liquid to blind a troop of baboons. And unfortunately, it just doesn't grow in those quantities.'

He turned back to Mathew and was going to suggest they each take a bow-and-arrow and carefully stake out the baboon camp, but Lucy cut him off yet again, determined.

'Yes, it does. It does grow in those quantities, in thickets. I saw a whole creek bed full of it. A huge wall of it, trailing off into the water, where the pig attacked me, not far from here. There was yards and yards of it growing along the river.'

Mathew, Peter, Hamish, Geldie, Lorelai, and Gin all examined her and then each other with the same dumbstruck hesitance. They'd all held the same steadfast inclination to reject ideas from a simple nomad girl, but now, if what she said was true, the genius of her proposal could not be denied.

Within an hour they were marching up the hillside through the mist to the dense pocket of sissara trees where Gin had identified the baboon camp. Lucy's guess about the functionality of some of the equipment she'd briefly glanced at had been correct. They would later whisper to themselves quizzically, wondering how a young girl, let alone a nomadic girl, could have possibly, out of thin air, created a plan that involved using an atomiser as a weapon. The devices were fairly novel in Trimany and were only just making their way into mainstream medicine. Of course, Lucy had never heard the term atomiser. Nor had she (as they later considered) simply deduced from glimpsing the component parts, the way they would operate to turn water and oil into a fine particle mist. She'd just recognised that the brass nozzles and tubes they connected to looked like the tops of the perfume bottles and dispensers she'd seen at home. And they were. When the mixture was ready, which took very little in the way of preparation, it was dispersed into about six bottles. In each bottle, the vertical tube was partially submerged in their makeshift pepper-spray and connected to the bottle's lid which housed another tube connected to a soft bulb, which connected to the nozzle. As the soft bulb was squeezed, Peter had briefly demonstrated to Mathew and Hamish who were not particularly familiar with these devices, the vacuum created by the passage of air pulls the liquid up into the vertical tube and pushes it out through the nozzle.

'Then,' he'd further explained as they watched the fine mist disperse, 'as the air and our potion pass through this mesh nozzle, it causes the potion to break up into small drops and mixes it with the air. This restriction built into the nozzle, also increases the speed in which the air and the potion mix, causing it to break up and the air to disperse more widely.' Peter handed the finished weapons over. He was too old to accompany them.

All donned in goggles and masks, Mathew, Geldie, and Hamish each held a bottle of the liquified frost-leaf toxins in their hands, fingers on the trigger, with at least two more strapped to their belts. Lucy and Gin, also suitably protected with goggles and masks, had both hands on their weapons: Gin his machete, and Lucy her sword. They'd objected to her joining them, Gin most adamantly, and Hamish nearly equally as opposed, but Mathew had the final say and he was too fixated on his daughter to care about the safety of this strange nomad.

'Very well, you're not my daughter,' he said dryly in the end, refusing to waste time on it any longer.

'You said she fought off the pig well,' Geldie had said with a shrug to Hamish, fastening his belt while Lucy marched past them, following Mathew and Gin out of the camp.

Whether it was the confidence of having several victories against beasts under her own belt now, or whether it was because Star was Hamish's sister, and his *little* sister, Lucy felt a courage and determination to help that she'd never known before.

They hoped that when the first few angry baboons to meet them were stung and blinded, cowering away, the rest would retreat in terror. But Hamish and Mathew feared it would not go down like this at all if their fears about consumption of the zea-weed were founded.

In the approach of mid-morning the opaque fingers of the mushroom-spore clouds were starting to slither their way around the trunks that preceded the dense pocket of sissara trees. The faintest hue of a teal cloud was lingering on the edge of their peripheral vision, as they stood waiting, watching an enormous and low cloud of tainted yellow unfurl from their right. The dawn mist was lifting, but a pervasive humidity remained, as high above the canopy the sun was emanating a powerful summer heat over the treetops.

Lucy trembled a little but tried not to show it, pride an equally strong opponent against fear. She tried to recall the final words of instruction or encouragement that Bear had uttered before each omling attack, but she'd never faced more than two of them. Without looking around she consoled herself that to one side of her was Hamish, hand on the trigger of the noxious spray, and to her right his burly stepbrother already had his machete raised, ready to bear down. Gin leaned forward and looked past her to the others, he was signalling to go right. He had staked out the baboon camp some twenty minutes earlier. But he hadn't exactly been able to obtain a great deal of information in the several moments he'd peered through a gap between the trees and confirmed that an innumerable pack of baboons were indeed situated in the clearing within.

It had all happened so fast, no one had stopped to truly question how sure they could be that the baboons had Star. To Mathew, the hour had felt like ten, as Lorelai and Hamish returned with Lucy from the creek, satchels filled with frost-leaf, and Peter began making it into a concoction with vinegar and warmed salt water. But in truth, as soon as they'd taken up Lucy's idea, it was a chaotic race to prepare themselves and the liquid. They more or less followed Gin up the hill mere minutes after he returned, gasping from the sprint, and confirming he'd found the troop. The haste and the panic made it seem like there was no time to plan their approach, no time to talk at all, but in hindsight there probably should have been.

As Gin turned again to indicate a parting of the shrubbery, that not thirty minutes earlier had allowed him to silently scope out the baboon camp's boundary, a weighty fist hit the side of his face and he felt a burst of pain as a ligament tore and bones fractured in his eye socket. Lucy drew her sword back and swung forward, as Gin swayed for a moment, and it came for her. The baboon was larger than she'd imagined, having never encountered a monkey in person, and foolishly falling into the trap of drawing on her own limited, not less, other worldly experience in priming her expectations.

Like the younger omlings it was nearly as tall as her, muscular, and stood easily on its two legs before it launched. Her blade struck its armpit so fiercely the arm was almost severed, and as blood spurted out spraying her and the others, Hamish was momentarily shell-shocked.

Both at this mysterious and shy beauty, now wielding her sword with all the vigour of an aggrieved soldier, and at the knowledge of what it meant for a single baboon to behave with such wild inhibition toward a group of adult humans, four of which were near double its size. But his shock was shaken off in the same moment, as its screeching and wailing summoned the rest of the cohort. The men steadied their hands on the triggers of the leaf-water-come-tear gas, all hope leaning on it, as the slender and flimsy sissara trees shifted and bent under the weight of the emerging baboons.

The lingering yellow cloud cast an obscure haze before them as the baboons charged forward. Hamish was first to fire the spray down toward one as it approached him, it shrieked with instant agony, staggering back away, hands over its face.

Brief elation. It worked.

But it did not deter them. In the same moment Mathew and Geldie were spraying down and around them as the pack launched forward. Gin, without the spray and on the edge, hacked wildly at baboons that made toward the team from other directions. He knocked one down, and then another, but they began to gang up on him as they saw their relatives wail futility against the mist being propelled by the other men. He let out a bellowing cry before he tore off the one from his back, and then ripped the other from his torso, hurling them both against four-foot roots of a nearby ink-wood. But he was not deluded as to the limits of his strength, and hurried to share Lucy's sheltered position, between Hamish, Mathew, and Geldie.

As the baboons hissed and shrieked at the sting from the spray, staggering back blindly or retreating in pain, the team edged closer to the natural enclosure from which they'd emerged. With their masks and goggles, they were sufficiently protected from the toxicity, but the mist combined with the now dampened yellow spores, worsened their vision, and slowed their pace.

In the haze, Lucy lost her position amongst them. A foot or so behind them, she stepped inadvertently to the right, and was forced further in that direction as two large baboons came at her from the left, having circumvented her comrades. She swung forward at the first but the other landed on her upper body, sinking its fangs into her neck. The first she'd hit was also neither immobilized or deterred by her strike, and she screamed in pain as it pierced her thigh. She froze for a moment not knowing how to defend herself. How to get them off her when she could almost buckle under their weight?

But in the next instant the baboon head on her neck twitched, and then rolled off its torso. Gin's machete stopped short of her skin. He tore the other from her thigh and she tried to ignore the stream of blood she glimpsed gushing down her leg. It seemed brute force was still no match for any skills she could ever learn.

Lucy and Gin scrambled back amongst the others, but there was a sudden quietness. The onslaught, for now at least, had stopped, and the team began to push through the flimsy olive trunks of the sissaras and into the clearing. Hamish, Mathew, and Geldie were all well onto their second bottle of the spray.

When they entered the clearing however, their premature sense of triumph was fast torn away. By moving through the sissara wall into the baboon territory they immediately lost their advantage. They were ambushed by hordes of females waiting for the figures to finish emerging through the bending trunks, and their ability to operate their noxious spray guns was almost impossible with no distance between them and the baboons. They knew then they should have remained outside the camp, patiently staking them out. They should have developed a strategy. Instead, in foolish eagerness they had thrown themselves into the clawing fire.

Lucy and Gin saw two baboons land on Hamish. He fumbled for his spray, but he couldn't manoeuvre it to aim at them while they pressed against his arms and legs, attacking him. No sooner though had they turned to go to his aid, than they were set upon with equal force. Lucy buckled under their weight, and they delivered blow after blow upon her, while she writhed beneath them on the floor.

In the same moment, Hamish's fingers released the spray trigger and reached for his pocket knife, puncturing the lung of the first ape as he pierced through her side, and then pierced right through the eye of the second.

Lucy squirmed beneath the baboons, suppressing her first instinct to call for help, as the sounds of men hollering in agony around her suggested they could not come if she did. She tried and failed to reach for her sword, pinioned under their grip. She struggled feebly to hold back their arms, as the hand that had just dug into the flesh of her collar-bone, just missing her jugular as she twisted, came down again to claw her face. Her grip on the female's wrist only managed to dampen the blow, the sharp leaden-nails cutting across her face. But as she cried out and saw the yellow mist shift in the centre of the clearing, the hordes of manila-coated primates camouflaged against it, a momentary glimpse of strawberry-blonde locks caught her eye and sent a charge running through her.

The image lasted only a second before blurring back into the haze, but just like when she'd fallen from the vines toward the wrath of the warthog in the frothy creek, time slowed and lingered. In that fleeting moment she recognised that the glossy locks belonged to a young girl, and that the position of her head, meant she was suspended off the ground, hanging, somehow, off something. But her rationality had gone in the impulsive charge, and she did not recognise this hanging body to be that of the girl they'd come for. With those wild, wavy locks, looking almost chestnut in the shadow, but glistening where the light touched them, to Lucy, this was Amber.

Suddenly Lucy felt herself spring up against the baboon's weight with seemingly impossible strength. She tore off one of the baboons by its neck, simultaneously breaking it, and drove her sword down into the face of the other as its widened jaw threatened to bear down. In retaliation, the rest of the baboons left the men and came for her. In another instant she was spinning around in this and that direction with more speed and agility she ever knew possible and striking the baboons with a strength that had come from nowhere. All fear had left her, and the searing pain of the fangs puncturing the nape of her neck only seemed to irritate her now; they caused no alarm.

The sword too, it seemed to her, had suddenly taken on an inexplicable sharpness as it combined with her frenzied spirit. It easily lopped off the head of one baboon and sliced through the innards of the next; sprays of crimson blood filled the yellow air. Still, they kept coming, but she found herself in a new and strange sensation of morbid bloodlust.

She was *enjoying* this.

Her anger had become vengeful, and she was enjoying exacting this punishment upon them. She wanted them to come, beckoned them even as males, their burning eyes regaining focus, bounded back into the clearing to fiercely defend their territory. She grinned, opening her arms encouragingly. She wanted them to attack with all the vigour and strength they were capable of, because it made it all the sweeter to watch them tear apart at the touch of her sword. The next contender to launch, and another attempting to sneak up on her from behind, were both bisected in sequential moments. She had probably never moved with such uninhibited confidence in her whole existence. By the time she eventually stopped to catch her breath, rasping for air, baboon corpses were strewn across the ground.

Hamish, Mathew, and Geldie were still only several feet in from the sissara boundary, looking on in shock. They had watched her, stifled with amazement and terror. While Gin himself had struck down a large number of the baboons, he towered over Lucy and was nearly twice her girth. Still her furore was unlike anything he'd seen in action… at least from a woman. They also hadn't failed to notice the unique edge of her sword and the way it cut the baboons like butter, and Mathew would later recognise it as coming from the snow village he'd once studied.

Lucy turned away from their bewildered faces and rushed to where the fleeting image of the girl had been. It was almost a profound sadness to realise that of course this girl was not, and never was, her sister. She was evidently well into puberty, slightly chubby, with a pale, peachy complexion. Limp and unconscious, she'd been stripped of all clothing apart from her knickers. She was covered with superficial scratches, but there were no serious wounds visible. A thick mossy vine that looped around a low branch perforating through the sissara boundary, was wound around her neck and upper body. Her upper half was partially slumped over the branch on an angle, and partially suspended in the air by the vines. Worryingly, her neck appeared to be taking a good part of her weight. By the time Lucy had climbed up the branch to cut her loose, the yellow haze had almost completely dissipated, and the others had seen what she had found.

'Star, Star!' Mathew cried as Lucy cut the final snag, and the girl fell into her father's arms below. She was out cold, but he could feel her breath. She was alive.

'I won't ever let you down again my sweetheart, I promise,' he said, stroking her hair.

'Come on,' said Hamish putting a hand on his father's shoulder and looking around, 'let's get her out of here.'

Arriving back at the camp, the haunting expression of equal parts concern and revulsion across Lorelai's face was enough to jolt Lucy to what a bloody mess they all were. It would surely take Gin weeks to regain full use of his right eye, and some careful attention to ensure it healed without ghastly disfigurement. Hamish's arms and neck were gouged and looking down at herself, she realised that her left leg was drenched with blood from the wound in her thigh.

Mathew took Star into his tent, along with Hamish and Lorelai, and laid her down, while Peter began to mix up a remedy for her revival. Lucy, dazed with delayed shock, watched on from the centre of the camp, her sword still in hand, while Crumbs licked at the dried blood on her ankle. Lorelai broke the trance, reappearing with a container of water and some cloth over her shoulder.

'Sit,' she instructed Lucy, 'we'll get your leg cleaned and bandaged, looks like it's stopped bleeding. Hopefully then they didn't sever the vein… you're not going to bleed to death in any case.'

The shaky words rushed out with an anxious quiver as the woman knelt on the dirt beside Lucy. 'Oh spirits, I'm so glad she's alive. We are so fortunate.'

'What did they want with her?' Lucy asked. She couldn't process the way she'd found her, half undressed, half knotted in vines, and half hanging by her neck.

'Oh, don't try to guess. Minefield of possibilities. Most likely a male took her, for whatever deranged reason: hallucinations, hunger, hatred…' she was about to say more but stopped and changed direction, 'but it's fair to guess it and its troop were, *are*, under the influence of *it*.'

She meant the poison weed. She finished wrapping the cloth tightly around Lucy's thigh, having cleaned it, and lowered the hem of the tattered dress back over the bandage, letting out a little sigh of relief. She looked up. Lucy had deep scratches on her face and neck too, so she rinsed the washcloth in the now bloodied water and put more of the tonic on it.

'Ugh,' Lucy winced.

'I know. But these scratches should heal just fine, as long as we keep them clean. We'll have to put alcohol on them. Often. It stings but they'll swell up with bacteria if we don't.'

Lucy bit her lip in pain but nodded.

'Actually, we should take a look at that pig puncture from yesterday too, put some more tonic on that,' said Lorelai, and Lucy braced herself, gripping down on the log with her fingers so hard that the rotted wood crumbled at the pressure. But a perplexing sensation came as Lorelai gently tugged at the bandage to reveal the wound. Nothing. There was no tenderness at all. No sensitivity. Lorelai's eyes widened, her face twitched in confusion, and then contorted. She shook her head and then pulled back more of the bandage, until she'd removed it completely.

'What?' asked Lucy, 'what is it?'

'Th-th-the wound,' Lorelai stuttered quietly in disbelief, 'it's… it's… it's almost completely healed.'

℘

In Archmond Castle, news of rural arrests vindicate the Imperial Lord.

Ron stared into the colourless remains of pea soup which had long since gone cold in its porcelain bowl. Behind him, the cerulean evening was flooding in from the wall of leaded windows that stretched up to the ceiling. But it was still darker in the room than out, and the blue evening spilled across the glossy ink-wood table in a grid of shadow and light.

The aide began to light the lanterns.

Ron pushed the soup away, conceding he wouldn't have any more of it. It wasn't usual to dine in the Council Room, but both he and Soleman had asked to take their supper here this evening amid news that a group of suspected deserters had been apprehended.

The group included eleven small children which was most troubling to Soleman. They had been detained in the castle cells, rather than the WFB prison, and were being interrogated that same evening. It seemed self-evident though, having been caught with all their possessions at the forest's entrance, that they were attempting to cross Chupner's Forest and make a life elsewhere. In the aftermath of the attack, this sort of thing was at first discouraged as wanton recklessness but was soon after made illegal. The increased segregation of Archmond into its two regions, made the once absurd notion of relocation seem, to some, the better of two hopeless options. The decision to criminalise that option was intended to steer people toward the other; remain and be loyal. Of course, those running Archmond reminded themselves regularly, that the law was of course in the best interests of the people; whether they knew it or not.

'For the attempt to be made so brazenly, so flagrantly! In the middle of the day, and with children, to put the children at risk too is—' Ron began.

'This,' said Soleman cutting him off, 'this is what troubles me the most. But it *was* brazen. In the middle of the day, dragging their carts through the town, did they think they would not be seen?'

He was standing in darkness at the far end of the table, looking back to Ron, who was seated in the centre between the windows. Ron couldn't make out Soleman's expression until the final lantern was lit. When it was, he saw Soleman's face was dark. Staring blankly across the table to Ron, he wore a beige tunic that although finely made, was presently crumpled and because of the hour looked like a nightgown. Soleman leant over the table, spreading his palms across it.

'I fear perhaps they wanted to be seen. That they're making a statement more than a getaway. It somewhat goes toward validating that theory of mine,' Ron said, a lingering bitterness on his tongue.

They locked eyes. 'I'm sorry I don't follow,' said Soleman.

Soleman of course knew what Ron was referencing, to what theory he was alluding, but he was not about to agree the point of validation.

'People. Leaving. Of their own free will in this public manner. It supports an argument that others might have done so before them, recently, and that the prompt for all this links—' Ron began but for the second time tonight Soleman made to cut him short.

'Oh, haven't you had enough trouble with that? In fact, haven't we both?'

'I still can't fathom that so much doubt could have been cast over me, after all my years of faithful service, based on such a frivolous accusation,' Ron continued.

'There was not this doubt you claim. There was only an accusation, but any accusation like that from a minister has to be investigated.'

'And it was found to be fruitless,' Ron said bitterly, looking away to the maroon tapestries he himself had commissioned on the far wall at the opposite end of the table.

'Yes, and now you are vindicated,' Soleman said blandly. His tone was unapologetic. Although the whole ordeal had left him conflicted about his own decisions, he knew this feeling to be baseless. It was in Ron's interest, not just his own, that the claim be looked into, even if only to prove it false.

'And yet the accusation still stings.'

'They always do,' Soleman sung, and then his eyelids dropped heavily, 'but you were not entirely blameless in bringing the attention to yourself. Making those comments about Lucy, I've said it before, but comments like those, well, I mean, they are somewhat out of order.'

'They were out of context!' Ron snapped angrily, 'I simply thought she may be the *reason* the children left, a catalyst if you will, not that she was involved in taking them. But that perhaps these children, rather than having been abducted, had perhaps run away, had gone after her even. I didn't suggest it was at her *instigation*… whatever this aide to Fogmyre thought he heard. He was mistaken and zealously so might I add. Beggars belief that this should be whipped into a paranoid frenzy about sabotage, and betrayal, and slander, and all that nonsense.'

'Ministers will always look for an opportunity to attack us. It's in their nature. You know better than to be so *frivolous* about how and where you have these discussions,' Soleman retorted.

Ron huffed and signalled for some water. Ministers were vexatious. Part of him accepted that was true, and that he had become too careless with sensitive talks of late. The lesson learned was a hard one though, and in the pang of resentment he remained reluctant to accept fault.

The incident in question was the accusation of Minister Fogmyre nearly several weeks earlier, in this very Council Room. The memory of it all unravelling was still too vivid in Ron's mind: Fogmyre's arm waving fervently beneath his navy robes, as he swore with all his might that Ronald Tobias was conspiring against the Government. The scandalous account being relayed by Minister Fogmyre was one of Ron being overheard in a castle-side tavern, slandering the very project promoted to save the kingdom from both its economic doom and its crumbling reputation: Lucy Crypt. It was the Minister's personal aide that overheard the boothed conversation between Ron and his, thus far unidentified compatriot, where he apparently explicitly suggested a connection between the missing children and the prophetic heroine. But the initial allegation was exaggerated beyond that. The Minister's accusations, gaining traction, led to a formal inquiry where the same Minister later happily revealed that his own office had uncovered movements of his Imperial Lord beyond the clink gates the day before the girl's arrival. Travel beyond the clink gates was untraceable and therefore who knew how *far* beyond Ron had gone. Given Ron didn't deny the comments he was heard to have said in the tavern, in the flurry of finger pointing this was entangled into the original accusation and had even Soleman questioning, for the first time, his partner's loyalty.

'Surely you can see how these things, as they stack up, start to paint a picture?' Soleman had seethed to Ron in his chambers, at the height of the controversy, when he himself had not the full picture.

'When viewed through the lens of suspicion, many ordinary things seem suddenly unusual,' Ron had responded dryly. That comment alone had not been enough to quell his concerns, but it was enough for Soleman to back down, and wait for the inquiry to finish. Soleman had said, although he didn't know if he believed it at the time, that he still fledged unfailing loyalty to his co-ruler whatever the outcome of the inquiry. The findings of the inquiry of course though, were nil.

But it seemed the doubt itself had left an irreparable crack in the foundation of their relationship, to be ever avoided, so Soleman tried to gently steer the conversational air away from the memories of these tenuous times.

'Which is the missing child that was associated with her? Peter?'

'Pepper. He has no remaining family. His friend Daniel also disappeared, but there have been none other from the WFB, the rest of the children have all gone missing from the Rolling Hills.'

There was a knock at the door. The aide opened one of the elongated timber doors only slightly ajar, and turned back, 'tis Master Ingress.'

They nodded and Aramor came through.

'Aramor!' called Ron warmly, 'have a seat. You missed my latest grumble about Minister Fogmyre.'

Aramor was cheery, having just had supper with a woman he planned to soon ask to marry him, and the evening had gone exceptionally well. As he'd seen her off from the castle gates she'd planted an impassioned kiss on his prickly cheek, and though he'd removed most of the lipstick, his cheeks were still as rosy as his shirt, glowing equally with embarrassment and delight.

Soleman and Ron knew nothing about the evening's date, but they knew he was courting a woman from a noble family who lived near the castle. Aramor was young, and his interest in women and marriage engendered trust, because it made it unlikely he would covet either of their roles, which required celibacy.

'Oh yes, horrible business, certainly could have been handled better,' said Aramor, planting himself on the nearest chair. Ron cast a conceited gaze in Soleman's direction.

'But I've actually interrupted with more troubling news,' Aramor went on, doing his best to quash his gleefulness and give the report with the sincerity it deserved. He tilted his head toward the aide, who was leaning over a counter beneath the tapestries and slotting the stems of goblets between the fingers of his left hand, clutching a terracotta jug with the other.

'Jacque!' Soleman called, a generic name given to male servants whose actual name was unknown. The man turned. 'That is all for this evening please, but have the guards remain stationed.' The aide was puzzled momentarily, but replaced the jug and the goblets, bowed, and left.

A few moments after the door boomed closed behind him, Aramor went on. 'Intelligence suggests there's another group, this time of about six or more young men, preparing to leave through the forest tomorrow.'

'Tomorrow! Six! Men!' Soleman exclaimed, flustered, 'in one day *two* groups, this could fast become an exodus.'

Ron caught his breath in his throat.

'Yes, and apparently the group we apprehended earlier do know these men. They're connected. It seems the talk in the Hills after the girl lef… when Miss Crypt left, was that if she can go through the forest, why can't they?'

'That's preposterous. She's had a spirit guide, and even then, what she's survived thus far is a miracle,' Ron blurted. He was half amused given this is exactly what he'd suggested, but still frustrated that no one had listened.

'*Or* prophetic destiny,' Soleman corrected sharply, with a gaze of derision, but then turned back to Aramor. 'They don't see that there is a difference between her travel and theirs? The prophecy of course means that she alone is one of the only people who could safely make that journey.'

'Yes, but you know as well as we all do, Eminence, that many in the Hills don't believe the prophecy,' said Aramor.

'Well, the fact that she's an Easterner, or looks like an Easterner, at the very least means she won't be targeted like our people would be. Such fools. They need to appreciate how dangerous it is at this time... And to put the children at risk!'

'There are no children reported to be in this second group, Eminence,' Aramor corrected.

'No, no, I know... I meant... I meant the first... oh, this whole business is such anarchy!'

'Well surely if we impose the harshest penalty, it will—' Aramor began before Ron cut him off with the raise of a hand.

'We were just discussing that earlier, and even when we suspected this to be some new ideological rallying, we decided a vigorous penalty would only cause more furore and outcry. We need to show restraint. Reason. Compassion.'

Aramor stood up, 'I had already sent agents to wait for this second group and apprehend them, do you want them to be recalled?'

'Yes... well, no...' Soleman began and then pressed his fingers against the bridge of his nose, torn, but then suddenly looked up. His eyes were blinking, tinkering.

He turned back to Aramor. 'Don't recall the agents, but send a message. Have them pursue the group, covertly, until they're well into Chupner's Forest.'

'And then?' asked Aramor pensively, examining his master with unease. Soleman looked at Ron, and as Soleman's eyes pierced Ron's with intensity, Ron understood what his partner was seeking to propose. Ron drew a sharp breath, but then nodded, warily.

'The group aren't aware we have this intelligence on them yet, are they?' Soleman asked.

Aramor shook his head.

'It is unfortunate but... perhaps the only way we can make the people understand what danger might befall them if they try to leave, is if they experience that danger first hand. Get the agents to work with the Indawarra if they can - they have my authority to make considerable offers to the tribe, but these young men should be made to realise just how dangerous leaving Archmond can be in these trying times.'

Chapter 4

Halcyon Days

Lucy caught Star's eyes again, gleaming at her. Steam from the water's surface wafted between them, in curls and clouds that were haphazard but constant. A narrow trail of crushed bracken and orchid petals led out from the spring. In its thermal waters, the two girls were alone. For the most part, the steam was as erratic as their chatter, but at times became so thick that they were obscured from each other for more than several seconds, amusing Star greatly.

'It's pretty warm, isn't it?' she asked, as she caught Lucy's eyes and lost them again. Both the water and the steam it made were making their features flushed. Star's face was particularly red, and beads of sweat rolled down from her forehead. The phenomena of the thermal spring was both fascinating and luxurious to Star, but Lucy was vexed by the heat. It was warm enough already, in this region they had travelled to, near the Vivian River. After Star's rescue, there had been a decision made to pack up camp and return to the riverboat. This was the only compromise Mathew could see between abandoning the project altogether or continuing to put the team (by which of course he only meant Star and Orran) at risk. Reflections would be had about the decisions to bring Star and Orran in the first place, but they were here now, and no one wanted to see the weeks of preparation and data wasted.

The riverboat, the River Princess, was commissioned from and captained by a man called Maleek from Trimany, who occasionally took hunters and fisherman up the Vivian. The River Princess was a secure enough vessel to be safe from jungle inhabitants, no matter how deranged. Of course now, while the data collected so far wasn't entirely a waste and they could extrapolate to a degree, they had to shift their scope. Their field work continued but was limited to regions within half a day's hike from wherever the River Princess moored, which itself would continue north east down the Vivian every other day.

The thermal spring, an hour walk from where they currently moored, had been discovered by Mathew and Hamish on an earlier expedition. Peter's laboratory confirmed the water sample they returned with was rich in healing minerals, the reason Lucy and Star were here.

'Maybe a bit too warm,' Lucy said. Star was pushing herself up, trying to float, but the water would trail across her face and into her eyes and she'd burst up, laughing a little. Lucy couldn't help but be affronted by the maroon ligature marks around her neck. It had been two days since Star woke up, and she seemed to have brushed off her near-death encounter as though it were a minor sporting injury.

'You seem very relaxed,' Lucy remarked.

'Why wouldn't I be?'

Lucy paused before responding, looking up into the curled lime leaves and the wispy ashen beards of the palms, skirting the edges of the rock wall high above. She opened her mouth to speak but stopped cautiously, at a loss.

Star could guess though. She looked away shyly. She didn't like to be pitied.

'Aren't you relaxed?'

Lucy laughed nervously. 'Not really, I'm hot. But I'm also nervous being undressed and letting go of the sword after what happened.'

Star shrugged. 'Being naked is unavoidable. We've got to bathe. Hamish and Gin are keeping watch. There's only one path in or out of here,' she said with a shrug, pretending not to recognise Lucy's concern. She was right though, the pool was enclosed by sheer rock face on nearly all sides, save for a small mud-bank and its path of crumpled bracken leading back into the jungle, at the end of which, Hamish and Gin waited.

'Also, the sodium and magnesium in the water will help us heal…
or rather, it will help me heal at least.'

She looked at Lucy quite inquisitively then, taking on a somewhat
precocious countenance. The suspicious curiosity of a woman many
years Lucy's senior was being reflected back at her from this girl several
years her junior. There was the echoes of the team's new wariness
about Lucy in Star's tone, but the relationship between them was
anything but distrustful. Far from it. Star was developing an idolisa-
tion for this beautiful nomadic girl that her brother seemed secretly
infatuated with.

Lucy pursed her lips and rolled her eyes cheekily, giving a very slight
shrug. It was inexplicable. Lucy's wounds from the incident had almost
healed, and she was at a loss to explain it. But the shock and bafflement
of this realisation had already settled in her. When the warthog's gouge
had transformed into a scab the next day, she had (fearfully) persisted
to Lorelai and the team that the wound had probably just appeared
deeper than it actually was. She knew this wasn't true. But now they
had all seen that the baboon's bite gash on her thigh was unmistakably
deeper than the pig gouge, and in two days it had completely sealed
over. The bloody claw marks across her face that threatened to leave
undesirable scars, were now faint lines, barely visible.

Earlier that morning, when Mathew interrogated her about it, and
in the same breath revisited his suspicions about her sudden uncanny
ability to use a sword, her eyes had become wet. It was not a crumbling
to the tone of his voice, instead she felt a rise of panic at the thought
that she might lose the safety of this team, be cast out on her own
again. Star had watched the conversation unfold sympathetically.

'Anyway, if beasts do come, I bet you could still jump out and
defend us with your sword,' Star said, pausing to giggle, 'even if you
are naked.'.

Lucy knew it was only a joke, but she glanced neurotically at her
sword and clothes on the rocky edge. They were still there. Along with

Crumbs, fidgeting, watching them intently, teetering on the edge of jumping in or staying out.

Star was fascinated with the accounts of her brothers, about how wildly this girl suddenly began to attack the baboons. Her father had said nothing to her about it, seemed to only discuss it in surreptitious under-breath conversations while Mary was out of earshot, which further ignited her fascination. She had heard of swordswomen, and women soldiers, but she'd never seen or met a woman that could fence or fight, and she had imagined them looking more like men.

'When are you going to teach me how to use it?' Star pleaded.

Lucy laughed. 'I only said I would show you how I use it, but I can't teach you anything, I don't know anything to teach.'

Star shook her head in disbelief, and leaned back, letting all her wild chestnut-blonde hair float out in the tepid water around her, 'so many half-truths Mary, so many secrets…'

'Oh, stop creating tales in your head,' Lucy said, and splashed her. 'The other thing that makes me nervous though,' she said, wanting to tactfully change the topic. Lucy looked down, bubbles gathered around a dark seam on the rock-wall some ways below the surface.

'Don't fret. The ground would quiver for days before anything ruptured, it's only a small spring. The jungle isn't volcanic, the magma stream is thousands of lines below the surface, it only gets dangerous where it starts to surface, closer to Rumustica. There's the other hot springs, on the other side of the river, but they're heated by magma chambers that connect back to Mount William in Winnapea, so they're too hot to swim in. But these are pretty safe, see, feel the bottom with your foot.'

'No thank you,' Lucy replied.

Star chuckled at this, 'it won't burn! It's just a bit hot.'

'All the same,' Lucy sung.

Above them a gust rustled the canopy, streams of mid-morning light shot down to the spring, blinding Lucy. She shifted back. 'A chamber beneath us connects all the way to Rumustica?'

Star nodded. 'Mm, you would have gone through Rumustica, or past it, coming from Gemini? And seen all the mountains? Do the summits all look dormant still?'

Lucy tried to recall the relative relationship of those two places on the map.

'Yes, we would have passed through there,' she agreed, but hesitantly, swallowing hard.

'Well did you, or didn't you?'

'No, we did, but I wasn't paying that much attention to the summits.'

'Oh. Well, what is it like?'

'Rumustica? Oh, it's what you'd expect, you know, mountains…' she tried to recall descriptions of the place from Yinsoo's book, but all she could remember was rather unhelpful descriptions of the nesting habits of various birds, and even then, not their actual names, '… and lots of those pretty orange trees,' Lucy said, remembering that much.

'Nomadics supposedly travel everywhere. I thought you'd have been to Rumustica hundreds of times,' said Star.

'Oh, no I have. When I was younger. I guess that's why I wasn't paying attention, you know, I've seen it all before.'

'You don't have much to say about it though, or anywhere really,' Star said, she was disappointed by how little this worldly lady was able to tell her about her travels. It seemed secretive, which was frustrating, because she thought the relationship between them was different, that Mary trusted her.

Lucy tried to feign a look of offence. 'What else is there to say? I don't know. I'm just not, I'm not very good at descriptions. It's always better if you see a place with your own eyes anyway, without letting someone else's idea of it influence you.'

Star nodded, as if accepting that the point was valid.

'But come on, you weren't really going to Archmond were you? You can tell me! I won't tell anyone,' Star said, she was upright now after again floating on her back. She had come uncomfortably close as she asked this, and Lucy could smell the metallic whiffs of minerals mixing with her skin and see the perspiration forming on her flushed youthful cheeks.

'We were going to Archmond!' Lucy insisted, regaining some personal space as she edged backward.

'But nobody has friends in Archmond, not anymore, not since way before… before you know, the attack.'

'Well,' Lucy said casually, as she tried to bring back the air of warm familiarity she'd cultivated between them, 'I'm pretty sure that's how long my aunt has known these people, since way before. They live right on the outskirts of the farm lands, I think we just… wanted to see how they were.'

Star narrowed her eyes with suspicion theatrically, but then spun around in the water, playing with Crumbs who had finally joined them.

'But I still don't know why you'd go there, even for an old friend. It's just too awful. It would be too depressing. And frustrating, that there's nothing you can do. Not when it's their own government making them suffer.' Star stared wistfully at Crumbs, paddling around them as she spoke, but as she raised her eyes she was surprised to be met with an expression of intense worry.

'You do know about Archmond, don't you?' Star asked, curious now.

Lucy tried to shake off her worried look. 'Yes, yeah, I mean, I know that they're all sick, in the Hills,' she muttered, failing to feign disinterest as her tone accidentally inflected at the end.

'But they could be better! If those corrupted wizards let them. But they don't want anyone to get better, or to think that they're better. They don't want to open up the border between the Hills and the city, or give the farmers a reason to stop underselling themselves.'

Lucy didn't catch the meaning of all of that, but she rejected the first notion.

'Why would they not want people to get better? I don't think Soleman and Ron *want* people to be sick,' she said dismissively, forgetting herself as she used their given names so casually, but Star failed to notice.

'Oh Mary! *Come on*. They've made indentured workers out of nearly eighty percent of their people. They say seventy something percent of Archmond live in the rural area, below the WFB, and that's where all the produce comes from. But around the same percentage of all the produce goes up to the upper class… mind the pun.' Star grinned at her wordplay rather proudly. It was evident she'd used this before.

'And they pay the rural people virtually nothing for it, largely in that medicine that makes them feel better. It supposedly inoculates you against the lingering poison from the attack, which was ten whole summers ago anyway, but it doesn't. It's a band-aid, that's all it is. It doesn't actually make anyone better. Actually, my papa says a lot of young people aren't even sick anymore, especially children born since then. Well, that's what a lot of people suspect but it's hard to get any real information. But, regardless, the farmers have no choice, they're forced to comply with the arrangement, by peer pressure, as well as military force. You see, because there's no newscasts there, the majority of people in the Hills still believe they need the medicine made on the WFB, so there's enormous pressure on farmers to go along with the arrangement, for everyone's sake. If everyone was better, the whole system would collapse.'

Mottled light fell again across the steamy spring as the canopy shifted above. The jungle's deepest darkest valley with its silver cover was miles behind them, and while the enormous dense canopy still loomed over them from every direction, raw daylight danced through the forest in fleeting angelic wisps.

'Sounds awful, I don't know why they don't just leave. My aunt wants her friend to leave,' Lucy said, and pushed her torso backward out of the water to sit on the rocks. She embraced the coolness of the air on her skin for a brief moment but was quickly self-conscious again and slid back down in the water.

Star sighed. 'Yeah that's the way Archies are. But they can't anyway, they'd be imprisoned. They made it against Kingdom law.'

'To leave?'

'Yes! Spirits, where have you been Mary?' Star said and laughed.

Lucy shrugged, squinting, and shielding her face from a barrage of droplets; Crumbs splashed wildly as he paddled up to her.

'But it's a shame because if they had ov left, years ago that is, they could have been helped. Some did. Leave that is. They made a medicine in Trimany that could eradicate the poison from the body in one dose, *if* you weren't exposed to it anymore. But Archmond weren't interested. Typical arrogant west. They said they had it *under control.*' Star rolled her eyes. 'Of course it would be harder to leave now, it being against their law, but also, it's so unheard of now to see an Archie in the east. They'd stand out. It would be like…' she made a face of comic alarm.

Lucy didn't really know what to say in response. All of this sounded completely at odds with the impression that Soleman and Ron had given her. She had suspected them of hiding things from her, but what this loquacious young girl was saying sounded undeniably cruel, and it was hard to fathom the men she met being capable of that. Yet she couldn't question Star's honesty, and she was speaking as though this was all common knowledge. All she knew was the further away she got from Archmond, the sicker she felt about it, and them.

'But some people have left. Who knows, maybe your aunt's friends will get out,' Star said.

Lucy smiled.

From beyond the chartreuse curtains, they heard the deep rumble of men laughing, followed by an exchange of loud, animated anecdotes. The girls smiled, equally amused.

'You know,' said Star, 'it's a shame about you being nomadic, because I think my brother really likes you.'

Lucy was affronted, but she blushed intensely, her cheeks all the redder.

'What? No, no, I think your brother is just trying to be kind to me, after, what I went through.'

Star's coquettish grin brightened. 'Oh, he does want to be kind… very, very kind! I know my brother. Trust me, he is *besotted* with you.'

'I'm sure that's not true,' Lucy replied, smiling, her eyes focusing on the dense vegetation, beyond which the louder parts of Hamish's conversation could still be heard.

'It is! And we think you'd be good for him. We all think it's time he get over this woman, whoever she was, that left him with Orran. He needs a wife, and at least we know you could defend yourself, and Orran, and I suppose any other children you both might have.'

Lucy was lost for words. Was the girl actually proposing this? Questions as plentiful as the thermal bubbles rose and popped in her mind. Orran's mother had *left* Hamish and *left* her son? And had Hamish's family discussed the possibility of some kind of relationship between herself and Hamish? Had they discussed this *with Hamish?* Had they talked of marriage?

Lucy's eyelids fluttered, and she shook her head.

'I think you're getting a bit carried away there,' she said, and wanted to blame the girl's youthful naivety, but she was too struck by how mature and intelligent Star was to do that. For some reason, the only question she asked was the most obscure one.

'What do you mean, *it's a shame I'm nomadic?*'

'Well, you know, your family will already have a husband arranged for you.'

Lucy scoffed, forgetting in that moment that she in fact was not nomadic.

'Ahh they certainly *do not*.'

Star rolled her eyes condescendingly. 'Oh, they certainly do.'

'I think I would know if I was arranged to be married.'

Lucy was annoyed now, and Star was starting to sense it. Star remembered then, other things she'd learnt from her father and his colleagues about nomadic tradition, and that in some clans, the girls were not told of the marriages in order to prevent them running away.

'No, you're right, of course you would, I'm sorry,' she said, with a half-smile, the patronising pity in it all too apparent. Star couldn't help but feel sad that this seemingly strong woman, this beautiful woman, was so ignorant of her own doomed destiny.

'Well, I hope you're not forced to marry someone you don't want to. You're very pretty. You could have any man. Unlike me. I'd have been better off in a culture that had arranged marriages,' Star remarked meekly. 'No boy will ever *want* to marry me.'

'That's not true, of course they would,' Lucy said tenderly. 'You're a lovely girl. Clever, kind—'

'Boys don't want girls that are clever and kind. They want girls that are beautiful, like you,' Star moped.

Lucy examined her then, considering her response more carefully. Star was not striking to look at, and in the spring with her flushed face and wet hair plastered across her round head it was not the best version of her, but Lucy did not think of her as ugly. Far from it, the girl had the same baby-faced features of her brother, perhaps with rounder, chubbier cheeks, a more padded figure, and an otherwise sweet simpleness to her. She was in no way displeasing to look at.

'Boys don't know what they want,' Lucy said eventually, 'but men, a good man, will want all those things. And you are all those things. Beautiful too.'

Star blushed, delighted to hear the words but too awkward to acknowledge them.

'Come on,' she said decisively. She had the same innate aptitude for authority as her brother. 'We'll head back so we can eat.'

They dried and got dressed and meandered back down the crushed bracken path to rejoin Hamish and Gin.

'So, it was pretty warm huh?' Hamish said, grinning, rustling the matted caramel hair on Star's flushed red face.

'Oh, spirits, it was so very hot,' she replied, widening her eyes for emphasis. He nodded at Lucy and turned to Gin. 'Shall we head back? Or do you want to jump in?'

Gin snickered. 'No, thank you, the river water will do me just fine.'

Making their way back to the river, a bird with mere scraps of red feathers on its exposed torso, landed on a flimsy branch just ahead of them. Its dimpled body was covered in the trademark purple blotches of zea-fruit ingestion, and its yellowed droopy eyes, which watched them approach with terrifying intensity, indicated the onset of psychosis.

Star shuddered. 'It's so horrible when they peck themselves bare.'

'Worse when they start going through the skin, come on, make haste before it swoops us,' Hamish said, just as they neared the branch where it perched. A piercingly aggressive caw came from its mustard beak as they passed.

As the lofty vanilla frame of the River Princess came into view between the trees, and the dark undergrowth became sparser as they neared the bank, Star rushed ahead excitedly.

'Come on, let's sneak up on my papa and scare him!' she'd whispered before making a brisk jaunt over ferns and mushrooms. Lucy thought that the girl seemed to flutter between appearing twenty-five, and then twelve. She stopped a few metres ahead, looking back, disappointed that Lucy hadn't followed.

'Oh, ahhh—' Lucy began, making to go toward Star, but Hamish cut her off.

'Gin can sneak up on father with you,' he said. 'I should try and teach Mary how to make the fire again.'

Lucy was thankful he didn't see the knowing look that Star returned, and then bashful because it was her he was looking at instead.

'Do you remember the bark we need to find?' he asked when they could hear the clamour of Gin and Star ascending the gangway in the distance.

'The messy bark,' she guessed tentatively, but she couldn't recall whether this was actually the bark used to make the anti-nausea tea or the fire.

'That's correct. Now go find some, and some dead leaves and twigs and things, and I'll show you again how we arrange it,' he instructed. She nodded, half wanting to be irritated by the commandment, but liking him enough to allow it. When she returned, he showed her the best way to arrange the bark, the twigs, and the decaying leaves. The sexual intensity between them was reinforced when the accidental brush of their hands created a sparkling awkwardness that lingered some, only to be dismissed by shallow murmurs of suppressed laughter.

'You have to promise not to use this skill to set fire and wage war on small villages. You're dangerous enough with the sword,' he joked, but immediately regretted it, looking up to see her perplexed face. *Promise not to wage war? What a bizarre and outlandish thing to say, where did that come from?* He derided himself. He scattered the arrangement he'd made, and then gestured for her to attempt to replicate what she'd seen.

She began, but stopped, staring past him. A hushed little gasp escaped her lips.

'Look,' she pointed to the copper-wood tree behind him. He craned to see a rabbit-sized rodent, brown, black, and yellow, with a large buck-toothed grin and a flat bushy tail, descending the trunk.

He watched it for a moment, the way he watched all the wildlife, cautiously, making sure it was not afflicted by the madness. It froze for a moment as it registered their presence, its chest rising and falling rapidly: a typical natural reaction.

'A marikot. They're very rare,' he said, turning back to her, watching her replicate the arrangement.

'I know.'

'How do you *know?*' he rebuffed.

'How do you think?'

His eyes glazed over. 'Star.'

'There's a drawing in one of her books,' Lucy went on, 'and she was horrified when I confirmed that was the creature I'd killed, before you found me. She said they don't, what was the word she used, oh yes,' Lucy paused to chuckle, '*copulate*, very effectively.'

Hamish nodded, grinning at the word, and in being satisfied with her arrangement, handed her the flint and his knife.

'She's very proper when she talks about these things, which is a relief really at her tender age. But, yes, the ahh, the females, are only ready for some *copulation* if we use Star's nomenclature, for a brief window between the seasons. Mere days really, and the men have a tough time finding them in this confusing place before that window shuts.'

'Yes, she told me that too,' said Lucy. Hamish crouched around the pile closer to her. He took her hands in his to reposition them so that the flames would catch the tinder as she struck the flint. Aboard the River Princess, Lucy had seen him put an oil to his neck and face after he shaved, and as he leant over her collarbone to reposition her hands, she could smell it. It was musky, warm, and spicy.

'And yet,' his eyes met hers and he couldn't help but feel the synergy between this conversation and their unspoken union, 'they find a way.' He was pleased when she didn't look away, but he removed his hands from atop hers, and sat back a little. They watched the fire take hold for a moment.

'Well done,' he acknowledged, adding, 'you know, you're not like other nomads I've met.'

'How many have you met?' she queried cheekily, pushing her tongue against her front teeth, as if almost conceding to his implicit accusation.

'Not many,' he admitted, very quietly, as he was suddenly overcome with a searing urge to kiss her and an unnerving inkling that she knew this and wanted him to. But the presence of the River Princess and his family was looming in the periphery of his mind and the forestscape. He let the urge slip away as quickly as it had come over him.

Lucy's heart fluttered, flummoxed, terrified. She wasn't sure if she was reading his eyes correctly or if she was deluding herself. She wasn't entirely sure if she wanted him to kiss her. She couldn't deny that she felt a powerful attraction to him, but the absurdity of her situation was too potent on its own to be paired with love and lust.

'You know, it would be useful to have a short survey of the wildlife, the marikots in particular, now that we've seen one. It's not why we're here, but the repository in Trimany can always use the data. Perhaps you'd like to, ahh, join me? A long walk tomorrow, and we can try and spot them?' he said.

Lucy was staring into the fire she'd created, a soft curl in her lips. Despite Star's insistence about Hamish's affections for her, and the growing alchemy she felt between them, there was also something from him that pulled against this theory and gave a very reluctant impression.

'What are you two *doing*?' Star's shrill call from the deck severed their privacy, 'Mary, aren't you going to come and look at the horses?'

She was referring to a reference book of horse breeds from Gemini. Something Lucy was trying to avoid looking at ever since she was cornered into fabricating that her own disobedient horse had come from Gemini.

'If the governess lets you of course,' Hamish added.

Lucy grinned. 'I'm sure she'll make an exception.'

But the promising walk would never eventuate. Although the next day as planned, Hamish returned early from his field work eager to be alone with Lucy, under the guise of conservationism, there was a crisis with the pump in the vessel that Maleek needed his assistance with. Thenceforth, fate seemed to intervene to stop their scheduled walk day after day. As if the powers that be were keeping them apart.

But as time drew on, Lucy's place among the expedition team started to settle. Mathew and his team, while still not wholly convinced in the completeness of what she'd told them about her past and her strange healing abilities, once again became too immersed in their project to care.

The days passed Lucy by with beautifully predictable repetition. They roused early to attend to morning preparations, of which Lucy was tasked with collecting buckets of the river's azure water, which impossibly still held some of its rich colour even when filtered and put into pots on the fire. While those heading off on field work packed their bags for the day, Lucy would wait for each pot of water to boil, before swapping it out for the next, and pouring the first into containers to cool and drink for the evening and the next morning. Adjacent the fire, Star would cut fruit and bread, and wrap them into five packages.

Mathew, Lorelai, Peter, Hamish, and Geldie would set off each day, often in pairs or threes (but usually Hamish preferred to go on his own) and return, in staggered groups in the late afternoon or evening, to consolidate their findings. As Hamish usually set off on his own, this meant he would return on his own, most days earlier than the others. Although Lucy continued to dismiss Star's remarks about his affections for her, her heart would flutter and her nerves alight each time his figure emerged through from the emerald abyss and navigated the palms toward the shore where the River Princess waited. Then the two of them, like magnets, would be more or less inseparable as the evening closed in. Much to the private amusement of Gin and Star.

During the days, Lucy was equally inseparable from Hamish's little sister, who clung to her as keenly as Crumbs had done when he was a pup. But they had many shared tasks. They would clean the camp cookery from the breakfast and ready it for dinner. They would carefully wipe down equipment used for examining specimens and package it properly. They would wash the team's clothes and hang them around the deck, and of course the deck and the cabins themselves needed cleaning every other day. They would collect edible plants, dark mushrooms, root vegetables, and fruits which grew around their mooring.

They would collect grasses on the Vivian's banks where the River Princess was moored and take in the intense birdsong that filled the trees all around the shore as they did so, taking turns to try and spot the maker of each song. Gin would glance down on them occasionally from the bow, checking all was well. Now that they had exchanged the vulnerable canvas enclosures of camp for the Princess's sturdy wooden cabins, they could sleep peacefully without the need for an armed nightwatchman. This left Gin free to sleep when he pleased, which was at night. Gin was not a researcher and had no interest in surveying botany with the others, preferring to fish or lounge on the deck, which meant there was no anxiety about Star during the day, as long as she didn't wander far, and there was certainly no concerns about Lucy.

There were many unmemorable days. And there were days of an ordinary nature whose essence nonetheless seemed determinedly poignant. One such afternoon, about two weeks after they had begun living on the River Princess, Lucy and Star swam in the sunshine, in a relativity calm pool of water outside the grasp of the river's many exuberant currents. They were playing a game that Star had invented, to see who could gather the most stones from the riverbed in one breath. Star named it amphibians, on account of the fact it was a test of your ability to stay underwater.

'I got three,' Star said between gasps. She had not long burst from the shimmery surface. A sheer brown river weed, crumpled all over, was caught in her hair. It wasn't clear if she'd done that on purpose, as a childish way to look the part, or if she'd been so determined to find stones that she foraged in the reeds.

Lucy didn't ask. She nodded, took a deep breath, and forced her body beneath the glassy surface. The water became turquoise, strikingly green, and then clouded as she descended. Sand, leaves, and plankton, swirled around chaotically in violent thrashes that were the offshoots of the rushing white currents to her right. She kind of enjoyed seeing how ruthlessly things were twisted beneath the calm surface, and how easily she could navigate it. She was used to turbulence after all. Wildness and violence had always been just to her right.

There were a great many large rocks on the riverbed, but the purpose of Star's game was to find stones, the more the better. But the rules were as fluid as the conditions, and Lucy sought out more of the salmon-coloured pebbles she had picked up at the beginning, filtering for them below the mud. She only found one before her lungs were giving in. She shot up.

'One!' Star rejected mockingly.

'But it's pink,' Lucy retorted.

It was late in the afternoon. Mathew and Lorelai had returned before the others which was unusual, and the girls could hear the clamour of activity and conversation coming from the riverboat. They were a good thirty feet from the shore, but the river stretched another hundred yards across. The setting sun, now just above the horizon, was starting to cast everything ablaze in its bronze glow. It cut across the choppy river, making shadows. As a frothy burst of dark water splashed her face amid the gold glow, Lucy somehow understood this simple moment was precious, as if it were already a memory she was looking back on.

'Mary!' they heard a voice called from the deck. It was Mathew. 'So we know you're quite confident with that sword?'

Bobbing in the ripples, she looked at him curiously, but he didn't need an answer.

'How would you like to go hunting tomorrow with Gin, around this time? Need to keep your wits about you?'

Lucy wiped her wet hair from her face and nodded. From the deck Mathew could only just make out her obvious delight. For Lucy this had nothing to do with the prospect of hunting. The invitation signified respect, trust. As she caught Star's goofy smile in the corner of her eye, all satisfaction and victory, she knew Star thought so too. Star treated Lucy like a stray dog she was trying to adopt, and the more her father piled Lucy with enduring duties, the more it seemed like her plan was working. Lucy saw Mathew turn to Gin, who spread his hands out in front of him in defeat, having said all he had to say on the matter. Mathew disregarded the objection and turned back to the girls. 'Well come on in then. Better come in and get a briefing.'

As the girls swam back to shore, Lucy saw Gin rise and gesture to Mathew, before looking down at her nearing figure. In a quasi-serious stance, he was warning her that she better not screw anything up.

To Gin's dismay, when the hunt came, Lucy was not a hindrance. She was alert and stealthily still when he instructed, and she followed his instructions with precision. When he drew his index finger up, tilted to indicate the direction of the boar they were stalking, she was able to freeze at once and even her breath became silent. He'd given her a hunting knife to use in lieu of the sword, and when the boar was ensnared in a very feeble trap he'd set, and he called on her to help him restrain it, she was on its back and slitting its throat a moment later.

Henceforth, hunting became another task, one she shared with Gin alone, which like the tasks she shared with Star or undertook on her own, proved that she had a role to play in this expedition.

In the now pervasive warmth of the jungle's higher plains, where they were no longer shielded in coolness by the silver fog, the hunts left her sweating with exertion. But the warmth and perspiration was not arduous for Lucy, not after the ordeal she had faced on the Alexandria. Nor was the work and the routine of the work, the repetition of each day, tiresome for Lucy. Aside from still being dazzled by the wild brilliance of the world around them, which rearranged itself every other day when the vessel moved north or east with the bend of the river, the work she did and the routine that went with it further grounded her role in the team. Having a role in a team of people she admired was exhilarating. Belonging to people she admired, was exhilarating.

Lucy and Star would also spend each noon lounging on the deck, where the sunshine, glorious in its full emergence, fell across them and the Vivian, whose rich blue waters glistened like shattered gemstones at its touch.

Although the adults agreed the friendship was having a positive effect on Star, the truth was her teenage insecurities were exacerbated around Lucy. This was both because Lucy was beautiful and also because of the mystery of her, which was exotic and interesting when she compared it to her ordinary upbringing in the bland city of Trimany. This kind of thought drove a subconscious desire to impress upon Lucy, what she deemed to be her own uniqueness, a desperation to prove that she was special too. Star was too young or perhaps too immature to appreciate that she was simply trying to prove this to herself. As they sat upon rocks along the marshy embankment and waited for the bread to cook over the fire, or dried grasses in the sun on the deck, Star would fetch books or equipment from the cargo hold and try to casually introduce them into conversation, to demonstrate her knowledge.

'Have you seen one of these before Mary? Do you know what it does? Look in the top! See,' she said, as she presented Lucy with something not unlike a microscope. She tried to bury her embarrassment when Lucy said she had seen something like it before.

'Have you ever seen anything written in native Mazourian?' she said on another occasion as she showed Lucy an old, papery book, with red writing. 'My father got this on one of his expeditions. He can even speak a little native Mazourian. Maybe I'll get him to show you at supper.'

To Star's great pleasure, Lucy was impressed with this book, as well as some of the history books about Que, and with the botanical manuals that her father had co-written with Peter. This was on a particularly moody day, in a shadowy tributary off the Vivian, where black and copper branches formed a tunnel above the narrow channel of water. They were sitting on mangrove roots, their feet lost below the surface of the dark water. Both an orange and a pink mushroom nearby were painting the upper air with rich colourful clouds. The melody mushrooms were less frequent beyond the Josso's misty valleys. They didn't grow as easily in areas where daylight was often able to find its way to the jungle floor as wind and animals shuffled treetops above. But there were evidently a great many regions still gloomy enough to sustain plenty of the luminescent fungi and yet in these regions, only scraps of mushroom appeared.

This was because the melody 'shroom was also a victim of the zea-weed. Wherever it grew alongside them, its roots both suffocated and starved the mushrooms, and their colours would fade to grey, and they would gradually cave inward. This was another significant problem for the jungle ecosystem, given the imploded mushrooms were no longer able to release their spores and propagate. The twofold effect of the diminished number of mushrooms, was the loss of vital nutrients the mushrooms provided for nearby trees and other plants as they decayed, but equally while they were alive, the bright glowing fungus enriched the soil by helping to break down other dead plants. As each strangled mushroom might prevent a hundred more from sprouting, it appeared the loss of luminescent fungi could be rapid. Once she had understood all this, Lucy took in the swirling clouds of spores with a greater appreciation, and the pink and orange ceiling above their chatter in the mangroves was an enchantment, not a bother.

'Papa isn't a botanist, that's Peter's area really, but Peter hasn't explored like my father has. The nature of the plant, its biochemistry, its family, that's Peter. But where the plant grows and how it grows differently or how it's used differently across the world, my father has collected the most accurate data on that in his lifetime,' Star explained. 'Sure, there's anecdotal musings from botanists in different kingdoms but, that's not the same as someone who has set out to study environments, and the wilderness surrounding these kingdoms.'

'You seem very proud of him, your father,' Lucy said.

Star didn't answer, but her face puckered, trying to hide that very pride.

'I'm going to study botany *and* environments, I'm going to combine what Peter and papa do,' she said decisively.

On another occasion, when they were back in the brighter world by the Vivian, Lucy was equally impressed when Star showed her how to tell which grasses were edible using some of Peter's equipment. Star remarked casually, that she had no use for that method anymore, because now, now she could tell just by looking at them.

But the more things Star showed and explained to Lucy, the more struck Star was by the simplicity of the topics that impressed or interested her. It dawned upon Star that this girl was more ignorant about the world than anyone she'd ever met from east of the plateau. It added a new dimension to the mystery that surrounded this Mary girl and the way she'd been found by her brother. Star began to test her by showing her very basic things, such as the last newscasts from Trimany from before they left (which they'd only brought to wrap the glass trinkets in any event) with reports on Meta Emery. It seemed that just as this girl knew very little about what was going on in the west, she knew even less about what was going on in the east.

'Meta Emery isn't a place you can just visit,' Star said, mockery in her tone, when Lucy (feigning nonchalance) asked if Star had ever been to the floating markets the newscasts referenced in their trade report. Shockingly though, when Star went on dismissing the notion of 'visits' to the island and made casual reference to that infamous move by the queen to militarize all aspects of it, Lucy had tilted her head and given a blank but curious expression. If she'd been told any of this in Archmond, she couldn't remember it now, but she didn't think she had.

Star was astounded. 'The schools, the hospitals, the farms, even the stores and the markets and the taverns, they are all run by the military. It's the first time in history this has ever happened. You must have heard this before? That's why everyone is concerned about the island, about *her*. Come on, Mary, you would have heard this before. That's all anyone ever talks about these days when they mention Meta Emery.'

But Star had seen that Lucy was visibly embarrassed and distressed at realising she did not know this key fact, so she tried to retreat from her momentary incredulity.

'Oh, well, I guess it doesn't really affect us. Politics is politics, right?' she'd said, trying awkwardly to lighten things up. 'Ahh these grasses are nearly dried.'

But Star had found a moment to quietly raise these growing concerns with her father.

'Papa really, something is very strange with Mary. She knows nothing of the world. She didn't even know that she probably has a husband arranged for her already, and thought her family really was taking her to Archmond. Isn't that strange?'

Mathew was deeply suspicious of Lucy, but his suspicions were taking a different direction to his daughter's, and he didn't want to frighten her. 'Perhaps she does not have a husband arranged yet?' he suggested.

'No, papa, I think this goes further than that. She said she never met her parents. You said her sword is from Yerkey. What if the nomads kidnapped her as a baby? Maybe they killed her parents in Yerkey! What if they've been keeping her prisoner her whole life, and she doesn't even know it! Maybe they were going to sell her to Archmond!'

'Now Star, your imagination is making quite a few leaps there isn't it? Is that really the most logical conclusion? Perhaps it's more logical that they neglected her education and that perhaps because of this, she doesn't talk much, and doesn't know as much about the world? Hmmm? Not everyone is as bright as you.'

'But, papa, what I'm saying is we can't let her go back with them! She can marry Hamish and live with us,' Star persisted.

Mathew's eyes widened with amusement, 'I think that's a matter for Hamish and Mary to discuss. Sweetheart, she isn't a pet, you can't keep her. She doesn't belong to us.'

'She doesn't belong to anyone at seventeen, she can make up her own mind,' Star retorted.

Mathew was on the cusp of agreeing with his daughter and suggesting Star ask Mary what she wanted to do, but this could cause issues. He caught himself and said instead, 'When we get back to Trimany, we'll send the word out through relevant nomad contacts that a young lady by the name of Mary has been found, lost, and her aunt Asha Mosley should send for her at our address.'

Star walked away from the conversation determined to bring the matter up again.

But from Lucy's vantage, she had never belonged anywhere as much as she belonged here, with them. The hours she spent scrubbing the deck, the tense hunting ventures with Gin, the added skills he taught her with the knife and her sword, the sweat and strain on her fore-head and shoulders as they navigated back through the jungle with the haul, it was hard work, but it was wonderfully satisfying. Then there was her almost ritualistic purification of water each sunrise, and the muddy business of knotting the mooring ropes around roots of the mangroves, it was messy work, but it was important. Her ability to complete each vital task, as the days went on, told her she was no longer in their care, she was contributing, she was *one of them*. And crucially, Hamish seemed to think so too.

Although their walk seemed perpetually delayed, he regularly pursued her company, and this drove an almost star-crossed delusion in Lucy's mind. On one afternoon of many where their private walk was thwarted, he brought her back an aftonamanarris. A rare and exquisite flower, Lucy was taken by its beauty, and thanked him for it before she even knew what it was. Soft black petals, closed to the tip, were marbled with shimmery magnolia veins.

'Well hold on, I didn't give it to you just because it was pretty,' he said as she held it by the stem and turned away to look for a vase below deck.

'Sorry?' she responded, shyly, her cheeks already red.

'Come back and I'll show you.'

Lucy brought back the flower. It was all closed up tightly, the way tulips and violets did at night. Hamish waved his hand over it, lightly and then looked at her willingly as a magician would before the trick, to show that the boundaries were real. He then took Lucy's hand by the wrist and moved it over the closed velvet petals.

'What is…' Lucy exclaimed.

Hamish chuckled. 'It's technically known as an aftonamanarris, but we call it a maidenflower,' he said. And then, to her astonishment, at the movement of her wrist over its clenched petals, the flower began to open.

'I don't understand…' Lucy exclaimed, and turned to him, wide-eyed. He beamed tenderly; this was exactly the astonishment he hoped to achieve. The image of his warmed smile in that moment, would stay with her for all her years. A maidenflower, he went on to explain, would only open in certain phases of the moon, or, at the close scent of a female.

One evening, after an unusually hot day, Lucy and Hamish sat alone on the deck, the only two people aboard the River Princess still awake. As the receding vibrance of sunset softened the atmosphere, a marmalade glow was left piercing through the increasingly blackish silhouette of treetops across the river. The hum of insects fell into an unwitting harmony.

A rare chain of private moments befell them. A moment that at first seemed as though would be singular, and then seemed perhaps extended, became another and another. But because it was never clear when the chain would end, the uncertainty was too much to let their talk delve deep.

The heat had been taxing on those that had ventured out on surveying expeditions; Peter, Mathew, Lorelai, Geldie, and Hamish. But Hamish, somehow, was not as overborne as the others. This was likely because his efforts had not been as astute as that of his colleagues, and he'd covered only half the area allocated to him that day. He was passionate about the cause, but he saw no reason to overexert himself.

Star had escaped the day's unusually high temperatures by spending most of it swimming beside the boat. But while the water had kept her cool, the amount of sun absorbed by her pale skin had made her sleepy. So she too, like the others, had retired before the sun had even set.

With Maleek unlikely to ever leave his quarters, the only potential interruption that threatened to shatter their privacy, was Gin, who had ventured off for a sunset hunt. He could be back at any moment, either because he was victorious, had given up, or changed his mind, all of which were equally likely options.

Hamish had finished somewhat of a diatribe on his aunt and two cousins whom Star enjoyed the company of but he found nauseating. Lucy had listened along eagerly and intently, but when she didn't reply with a similar anecdote of her own about a nuisance relative or family friend, he began to be suspicious.

'You don't speak much of your family,' he postured.

Lucy shrugged.

'Do you miss them? It's been some time since you were thrown from that horse. It's a long time for them to be worried for you. That must make you anxious?'

Lucy nodded. 'It does, but there isn't much I can do about it.'

Hamish sighed, discomfited by her answer. 'But you seem so comfortable with that reality. Is it normal, in your clan, to lose each other, and to just make peace with it? To then just make your own way.'

Lucy thought about this for a long time. It was clear that Hamish thought such an attitude unusual, and she had thus far been inclined to follow his lead when it came to attitudes and beliefs so as to not give herself away. But here she considered that nomads were expected to be unusual as a start, and if she were to acknowledge something unusual about her own personal relations with her family, that would only pave the way for another lie to conjure and weave carefully with the ones she'd already told.

'Normal for nomad clans is hard to define. But it's not so unusual, this,' she said eventually. 'I mean to say, the connection I have with my family is still there, and we know we will find each other again, eventually. But I believe that they know I will be okay, and make my way back to them in good time. They also know it's possible I may just… find my own path. I'm that age. I would never just completely forsake them entirely though, that's not part of our culture. I have to let them know I'm okay. But when I reach them again, I may have a new path.'

'So then, you may choose a different path? To the nomadic path?' Hamish tried to sound casual.

'Well, I hadn't thought of it before, but some do, so I guess, sure,' she answered.

Hamish nodded, trying not expose the whirlwind of imagined possibilities now circling inside him.

'What kind of path do you think you would choose, if you weren't going to follow the nomadic tradition?' he posed.

Lucy laughed. 'I don't know, I… well, I've never had any other options before, so I guess that's why I've never thought about it.'

'Before?' he queried.

Lucy blushed, she hadn't meant it in the way he'd interpreted it. Before him. Before this. Before the expedition. She went to say so, but he beat her to it.

'What about now? What about, Trimany?'

Lucy gave him an inquisitive look. It was unclear exactly what he was proposing, or suggesting, exactly.

'Would you consider living in Trimany? With us?' he asked, and this time, the puppy-dog look in his eyes and the sentimental tone in his humble question was clear. The marmalade glow behind the branches across the river was swiftly fading to lavender, and the only light between them now came from the torches either side of the deck and the lanterns that hung just inside the gully.

He reached out to her then, slowly, and touched her hand. The tips of his fingers stroked across her wrist and wove down to her own fingertips. She wanted to say that she would, that she did, that she had. She would not want to say how much she had wanted to hear him ask her that. In fact, she had no idea how to respond. Where to start? How to explain? That in this moment she wanted nothing more than to stay with him and his family forever, but that she had a mother somewhere in another world. She was about to answer, but the clanking of the gunwale and the grunting of a dying animal broke their silence.

'Spirits!' Gin cried, heaving the blood drenched sack, which in the dismal light was only blackness on blackness. Grunting and squealing came from the thing which writhed inside the canvas. 'I thought the bloody thing was dead! I got him with an arrow, straight to the neck, and it choked a while, and splattered up blood and all that, then it went quiet. So I sacked him, and the whole way here not a grunt, and just as I get back he kicks off. Get me the hammer will you my brother?'

In both the blistering and the temperate days that followed, sleep overcame her each night, more soundly than she had ever known possible. She had never slept more peacefully than she did in the musty cabin she shared with Star, taking comfort in the sounds of the weather following its own predictable routine. The jostling of late afternoon thunderstorms would almost always be followed by a darkness that would soothe and settle the sky. In the bunk below Star, Crumbs would nestle into Lucy's arms, and the wood would creak rhythmically as the Vivian's current rocked the boat gently amid the soft night rain. Everything was perfect with her new family, until Bear returned and spoiled everything.

Lucy had continued to throw herself energetically into expedition life and was savouring the scarcity of each moment all the more after it was announced they would return to Trimany in several nights. She was savouring one such moment with Gin, who having taught her more swordsmanship, was now teaching her about fishing on this particularly humid afternoon. The laundry had been minimal, and Star had fallen into a nap as she settled Orran for his, while Lucy had wrung out and hung the clothes. Gin loved fishing. More for the sport of it than for the catch. So it was convenient that he was good at it, and could therefore use it as a reason not to assist with the chores undertaken by his stepsister and Mary. Fishing resulted in food, or could result in food, therefore it was more important.

He showed Lucy how to bait the line, and how to cast it. Lucy knew these things. She had gone fishing before, in lakes and streams around Lockerby. But she didn't say so; she was enjoying the lesson too much.

'In the Vivian all you're likely to get is troy. That's all I've been catching. But I have had bites from a few mink-tails. They're a bit slippery, but no better tasting so it doesn't matter,' he explained.

The wild river before them glistened intensely, but the afternoon sun was pulling away and the glare was receding with it. Gin was of course not her preferred brother, but she still liked his company. It was unclear whether he had ever been married in the past, it certainly wasn't spoken of, but if he had ever had an appetite for romance, he gave the impression that it was long behind him. Without anything precise you could pinpoint, he somehow gave the impression of being perfectly at ease in his bachelorhood and perfectly satisfied with the pursuits he built his life around: hunting, fishing, and carpentry. But he did have a softer side that appreciated nature and immersing himself in it, even if it wasn't through the same scientific lens as the others.

Time dragged on through the afternoon and they barely had as much as a nibble from either the troy or the mink-tails. Conversation had lulled to a complete halt. Lucy was bored and had lost concentration. She was leaning her head into her hand with her elbow on the railing, staring at the shifting branches of a nearby fern, when Gin excitedly drew her attention further across the river.

'Mary! Look! In the current, mid-stream, can you see that? In the middle, just there, they're just starting to appear!'

Lucy shook her head. She squinted, but nothing in the mirrored glare of the rushing water changed.

'Keep looking,' he instructed, leaning the rod against the gunwale. His gaze was exuberant. The sun slipped away a little more, and the light on the river became softer still.

'THERE!' he yelled, and she saw it then. A school of fish, hundreds and then thousands. They were the colour of deep champagne, shooting across the blue water like arrows upon its surface. In another moment, the water was foaming and churning with the onslaught. They had come from nowhere.

'Midas,' he said, and scoffed in disbelief. 'An army of them.'

'Catch one!' she pleaded, enchanted.

He shook his head. 'They're too fast, and they're not interested. They're on a mission.'

She heard his words, but they glossed over the tip of her consciousness. Her awareness was on the turbulence that had so rapidly overcome the entirety of the Vivian's surface. He nudged her, so she would look at him, and he could recognise the same wonderment he felt reflected back in her eyes, and they'd have then shared this moment between them. She marvelled at how his eyes were suddenly full of a childlike joy that in many ways betrayed his stiff character. But it was right to be bewildered. For as far as they could see in both directions, the melodic sapphire surface had been transformed into a churn of white and gold, as the fish tore down through its current.

A thought burst into her mind as she took them in; the change in the water, the sudden emergence of the beautiful fish, encapsulated so succinctly what was happening to her. Change could be sudden, it could be turbulent and chaotic, but with the right perspective, it could be astonishingly beautiful. She laughed as this thought came to her, intoxicated by how happy she was, and knew that Gin, as he too let out a laugh, would never understand it. As the school slowed, they watched the army of gold dart beneath the rich blue surface for a time that fell into a daze, that felt as much like an instant as it did an hour, taking in what was self-evidently a spectacular phenomenon. Their shimmering scales were already disappearing when Hamish made himself known.

He had returned earlier than usual from the daily expedition, having only finished off his packed lunch a couple of hours ago.

'Hello hello, what's got you two so transfixed?'

Lucy's ear pricked at the sound of his voice, her posture stiffened, but she daren't turn around.

Gin waved him over. 'Phenomenal, an army of midas,' he said, but the school had largely passed and it was only shifting lines of yellow stragglers that rushed beneath them now.

'Well, there was,' Gin corrected.

'Oh right,' Hamish said, glancing down, but he had no appreciation for what he'd just missed. 'I've had to come back because I ran out of water and these large cats wouldn't leave the stream, pond, whatever it was, the only nearby water source. I waited a while, but they weren't going anywhere, and they looked rather large.'

'I thought we shouldn't drink the water unless we boil it first,' said Gin.

Lucy's hairs stood on end, remembering the sabres from the plateau chasing her into the salt mine and cornering her in the black reservoir, Bear's demonic glow as he held them back in the darkness. She realised that was the last time she'd seen him.

'What kind of cats? How large were they?' she asked.

'Oh, I'm not sure, I actually didn't get too close, I was a bit concerned about them. They were quite big, but don't worry they tend to stay in their own camps. It was a good two hours walk from here. Anyway,' he said, turning to Gin, putting a firm hand on his shoulder, 'seeing as I'm back so early I thought we could go for a brotherly stalk?'

'We could, but—'

'Just a quick one, we're heading back in what… a couple of days? Supposedly? And we've hardly done *any* hunting. You've had more jaunts with Mary,' Hamish pushed.

'The little gifted one is asleep with the noise maker, so Mary would have to get the fire and everything ready for dinner on her own,' Gin replied.

'Oh, but Maleek is here… somewhere? Right?' he said to Gin, then turned to Lucy, 'Mary, that's okay, isn't it? Just tonight. Just so Gin and I can have some brotherly time together.' Hamish didn't really give her a choice. 'You'll just have to gather the messy bark like I showed you to make the fire. Have some hot water going, and make sure the grill and the boning knife are clean. I'm sure my father and Lorelai will be back in the next hour or so anyway.'

Lucy nodded. Hamish's petitions were always made with a brightness in his eyes and the makings of a soft smile across his face. It was what made them so easy to oblige, you were always lulled into compliance, sweetly. Besides, the items he referred to were already clean. She and Star saw to it that everything was always cleaned.

'I dunno young man,' said Gin, craning his head around the portside, 'there are some fast moving clouds comin' this way from the north, storms could be early.'

Gin came back around to see Hamish's expression start to become strained and then petulant, but before Hamish could do his best to persuade Gin to go anyway, the sound of a foreign voice threw the significance of a brotherly hunt into disarray.

'Yes. Very likely. From high above, the lightning already crackling across the tops of those copper-wood giants in the distance, I'd say we'll be inundated in minutes. Saturated,' Bear said, materialising in the centre of the deck, just a few feet above them all.

Lucy fell still with dread as Crumbs let out a woof of disturbance before wagging eagerly, and the men stumbled back in alarm. Her face grew red. How desperate she had been for him to come back to her those days when she faced this dark misty chaos all alone, could not begin to compare with how desperately horrified she was that he had returned now, at this juncture.

Hamish and Gin were speechless and afraid, which told her at once that these transparent floating creatures were as inconceivable here as they were in her world; well, perhaps not quite.

'Lucy,' Bear said, letting out a dramatic sigh of relief, 'what a pleasure it is to see you alive and well, and Crumbs too.'

Lucy only stared back somewhat in shock, somewhat uncertain of how to proceed under the watchful eyes of the brothers. She heard Hamish mutter, 'Lucy?' almost inaudibly, under his breath.

'I remembered his name this time, see,' he added, meaning Crumbs, as she said nothing still.

'What are you doing here?' she whispered with shock.

'Looking for you, of course, why else would I be here?' He was taken aback by the question, but he very quickly began to understand his presence was unwelcome.

'Now? Now you're looking for me. I was a wreck for days. This place is madness! I didn't know where to go, what to expect. I called out for you. You didn't come.'

'I was looking for you, truly, believe it or not but you're actually difficult to track in this madness as you call it. And while I could sense you at first, I wasn't sure if I was what led them to you in the first the place, I wanted to know if that may be the case, so I waited.'

'And?'

'Well, I still don't know, but they did leave the jungle.'

'Hamish just said he saw some big ca—'

'I heard. No, not the same ones, don't fret. They did come down into the jungle looking for you, after they found a safe way down, but they gave up very quickly. They left but… I doubt that's the end of it.'

'And what about all the other things that could have killed me here? I was thrown into this deadly place, quite literally thrown, completely blind.'

'You had come such a long way on the plateau. I had to have faith you could use that sword and survive.'

'How did you know I didn't die in the fall? And survival is difficult when you don't know who or what will come after you,' she snapped.

The noise by now had woken Orran. The sound of his cries paused their argument as they all looked toward the doorway where Star stood sleepy-eyed, holding the watery-eyed cherub. Orran was distracted from his tears by the attention and stopped crying.

Bear looked at Star and Orran for a moment, then shifted back to Lucy. 'Yes, I appreciate that Lucy, but as I said there were the *other* concerns. It was a choice between two risks. But then I became aware you two had found each other, and I hoped it would prove to be as serendipitous as it seemed.'

Then more voices came. Muffled conversation in the distance. Mathew and Lorelai were returning from their expedition. This was also much earlier than usual, but so was the storm today, and they could both read changes in atmosphere.

Lucy didn't know precisely who he meant by 'you two' but the exact words he used didn't register until later the next evening. All she heard was that he was passing the baton so to speak, or felt his obligations discharged, which is what she then accused him of. Her tone was unwarranted though, if that was what he'd intended it had worked out perfectly in the end, hurt feelings aside. She was only frustrated now because his flamboyant return jeopardised exactly that handover.

'Hardly,' he rebuffed to the comment of abandonment, 'but it is true that you will be much better served by human guidance. Magic tricks can you only get you so far. What you need more is perspective, and connections. Which I cannot give you. But I didn't come to say goodbye.'

'Well why did you come?'

They heard the clamour of footsteps on the gangway. Mathew could see at once that a tense conversation was unfolding on the deck, but it took him several more moments to notice the floating form at the centre of it.

'Spirits,' Mathew whispered. Lorelai said nothing. Bear ignored them both, and though the brothers registered their arrival they were too fixated on the ghost bear to look away.

'To see you, see how you are,' he regarded his answers as obvious, 'and to tell you that my assistance is still on offer. And more pressingly to warn you that while the immediate threat has abated,' he considered his words, appreciating he had accumulated a small audience, 'not to let your guard down entirely. They have not completely given up.'

He looked around, the eyes of the group were darting between him and Lucy. He had been immediately aware that his presence had damaged something, but that damage was all but done from his first breath. Might as well finish it then.

'My assistance and guidance remains on the table, if and when I can find you, which will be easier once you are out of this jungle. But for now, I see I have rather rudely interrupted.' He then turned to the rest of the team. Peter and Geldie were making their way down the bank in the background. 'I apologise to you all for this rather sudden intrusion.'

He then turned back to Lucy, 'I hope you'll later see this is exactly the interference I was avoiding by… well… avoiding you.'

'Bear, wait!' she began as he started to flicker, but he was gone. In the resounding silence, and the darkness of the early storm, there remained six sets of eyes on her, but the only ones she cared about were Hamish's; they were equal parts confusion and contempt.

Chapter 5

Disillusionment

*'If knowing where you're going is preferable to being lost, ask. Rabbit knows a thing
or two and I myself don't need a weather vane to tell which way the wind blows.'*
Cheshire Cat, *American McGee's Alice*, 2000.

'You've seen this before, I know you have. Show me. On the map,
show me where,' Mathew commanded Lucy, pointing to the map
sprawled over the dainty wooden table between them.

They were in the galley. It was late. The River Princess rocked
rhythmically with the tide the same way it did every night, yet somehow tonight, every creak of wood was a thump to the heart. Lucy
looked up, fretting. In the opposing diagonal corner, stiff against the
ivory-wood panelling, Hamish averted his eyes. Across from him Star
yawned. The light from the oil lanterns swayed, starboard to portside,
portside to starboard, back again.

She'd never noticed how much leather plastered this seldom-used
communal space. It covered the long stretch of lounge, which wound
its way along the back and side walls of the adjoining compartment
where Hamish and Star sat, and after a short stretch of ivory-wood
panelling above the lounge, it continued again between the panelling
and the ceiling. Nor had she ever noticed how much the swaying
light from the lanterns above the windows made her nauseous. It
was strange because it was this same swaying rhythm that sent her
into a sound sleep every night. Then of course she remembered, that's
where they all should be. It wasn't usual to remain awake long after
sun down, that's not how expeditions worked, she'd learned.

But Mathew was waiting for an answer, and he pointed to the map again, leaning in, his greyish ponytail slipping forward over his right shoulder. A gold band with what appeared to be a clock-face on it slid down his wrist as he tapped the map. A watch? She hadn't noticed it before. And now in the pendulum rolls of dim light it was too difficult to see if it was indeed a clock-face, and if it was, whether it counted time the same way her world did. But she realised then in that moment that of course they must, count the time that is, in some way. Maybe her world had more in common with this place than she initially thought.

Swallowing hard, she cast her eyes back to the map and its title: *Escallia Wimbers*. This was their world. The only world they knew, understood, and believed to exist, and they wanted her to identify where within it she originated.

Though it clearly depicted the same place, the world on this map was slightly different to that illustrated on the map from Toby's shop. The Alexandria looked much narrower, and Meta Emery was much larger, as were the Kingdoms of Gemini and Que. This one also had Yerkey on it, very faintly. But these discrepancies seemed an irrelevant thing to marvel at considering the temperature of the room.

'I'm not…' she began.

Mathew's finger directed her back, authoritatively, to the centre of the map. He'd already heard what she was about to say and had already dismissed it.

She answered anyway, 'I'm not from this world.'

There was a collective exasperation from the room.

'Lucy, I'm not going to accept that answer. That's complete and utter nonsense. You've lied to us, and you've been found out, and now it's time for the truth,' he asserted, coolly. Mathew's eyes as he said this, as the lanterns cast their glow across them, pierced her in a way she had not encountered before. He was interrogating her, but not like an enemy, like a father. An authority that cared but was nonetheless disappointed and demanded answers.

That look in itself was all too much for Lucy. She threw her head into her hands, she didn't know what else to say.

'I fail to see the point of this. Given the elaborate nature of the lies so far, I don't see how we can believe whatever she comes up with next,' Lorelai quipped. From thenceforth Lorelai would only speak about Lucy, and not to her. Despite her sweet nature, she had a particular aversion for dishonesty, and had no capacity to forgive the deceit of strangers.

'I'm giving her an opportunity to come clean,' Mathew retorted, twisting around on the foldout wooden chair to face his wife, who was standing pensively behind him. Lorelai kept his gaze for several moments, pressing her hand over her mouth and squeezing her chin, until she shrugged and joined Hamish on the lounge, in the adjoining compartment.

Mathew turned back to Lucy. 'Well?'

Lucy took her head out of her hands. She couldn't help but let her eyes travel once again to the back corner and glimpse Hamish's chestnut blonde head. He was looking into his lap, where his khaki pants were overlaid with his white linen shirt. His face was obscured by shadow.

'I've told you *the truth* and you don't believe it.'

'The problem is, now that you've lied to us, and you were quite, as Lorelai says, quite elaborate with all your lies, about your aunt and the horse and all of that, now it's hard for us to know whether to believe you about anything you say, and in the face of that reasonable scepticism you're telling us some story about other worlds,' Peter chimed in. He was sitting across from Lorelai, on the opposing side of the lounge-wall. A lacquered foldaway table separated the two sides. Behind Peter in the left corner, Star hugged her knees close to her chest, watching the events unfold with vested interest as well as intrigue.

Geldie had retired for the evening, as had Maleek, not that he was interested. Gin sat on a stool between Mathew and the lounge. Like Hamish, he'd said nothing, but in contrast to his brother, his mute stare on Lucy had been constant.

'I know, I know,' Lucy said. She was crying but silently, and Mathew was the only one close to enough to see it.

'They told me to do that. They told me not to tell anyone where I was from, or that *I was* Lucy,' she said the last bit with uncertainty trying to recall, 'they said I had to be careful because people and cities were still choosing sides.'

'Who did? The wizards?' Star piped.

'But before they brought you in, to do this mission, where were you right before then?' Peter asked.

'I told you! I was in Lockerby, in Scotland, where I grew up,' she huffed, 'and it's not a mission, I haven't been—'

'And you can't even say in which direction that is, on the map?' Gin asked.

'Oh my god! No. It's not on your map. Or off your map. I come from a world where all the places are known. Every city, every kingdom, every country, every continent,' she was getting flustered now, 'it's all one giant sphere. There is nothing left unexplored. No one comes from anywhere in the world that is unknown. This, this place, it doesn't exist where I come from. Where I come from none of this is possible, none of you are real,' she ranted at them.

There was another wave of murmuring.

Peter stirred, shifting himself upright. His face often looked gaunt, but in the swinging shadows this was even more pronounced. He clutched the lacquered table, which made Lucy think perhaps her own nausea wasn't entirely psychological.

'Mat, I don't know how many times we can ask her the same question and get the same response, I mean she obviously...' Peter began but faltered, realising he was about to contradict his last rebuke of her.

'I believe her,' Star said. Attention shifted and you could feel the room almost sigh with an eagerness to quash her youthful naivety, but she went on to clarify before they could deliver a patronising retort.

'I believe that this is what she thinks is the truth. Listen to her. You can hear it in her voice. All the time before when we were asking her about Gemini and her aunt, and the trip to Archmond, it was all so uneasy and vague. She was so… cautious. Now she is repeating herself clearly and fervidly. This is clearly what she believes. It doesn't mean it's true. But think about it. Archmond has shut itself off for years, the conduct of the wizards and their preparations to retaliate against Murder's Echo have been kept well-hidden. Who knows what they've been plotting—'

'Star,' Hamish cut in, mockery in his tone wanting to halt her line of reasoning.

'No listen,' she pushed back, 'I'm not saying she's from another world. I'm saying maybe she thinks she is. Remember, Papa, I thought maybe she was kidnapped? Maybe she was, years ago. Maybe she's been brainwashed, and she can't remember her past, and they've got her to believe this story about other worlds and a place called Scotland and… what not.'

The room fell still as they took in the young girl's wild thoughts and kneaded them out.

Peter tilted his head. 'It is not unprecedented for the wizards to brainwash someone. They've been accused of it before.'

Mathew sat back in his chair, 'You mean the incident with the minister from Coby or…'

'With their own citizens,' Star said.

'That's not really the same thing,' Gin scoffed.

'No, no, but it's still relevant. But, yes, the minister from Coby is what I meant,' Peter said.

Star's remark was in defence of Lucy, but it had the effect of side-lining her participation in the discussion. Now they were all talking about her, not to her. The incident they referred to was a minister from Coby who went to visit Archmond shortly after the attack, and returned so fundamentally aligned with Archmond's views, rumours soon spread he'd been hypnotised or brainwashed by the wizards.

'What's the first thing you remember of being in Archmond then?' Mathew asked, changing tack.

Lucy's heart pounded to think of it. To remember waking up so utterly terrified and disoriented. 'I woke up. On red carpet in the middle of the street, in the middle of the day, it was hotter than I'd ever known.'

'And then how did the wizards find you?'

'They were just there. People were screaming at me, they were angry, and then I looked up and they were just there. Looking down at me, smiling,' Lucy was feeling more disturbed the more she recounted it.

'And when did they tell you about this mission you were to go on?' Mathew went on. Evidently this gentler technique was much more effective.

'The next day. After I'd stopped crying. But it's not a mission, they haven't really said exactly what they want me to do. I mean they want to overthrow the queen, and first they talked about this Princess Cherry—'

'She died during the attack on Archmond, ten summers ago,' Mathew cut in, chuckling. His brow furrowed and he shook his head as he arched back, frustrated as well as perplexed.

'Exactly, they said they thought she might have, eventually they said that, but then they didn't really explain who else might be supposedly able to take the queen's place. This is what I'm saying. There's no mission. They say it's a prophecy, and the girl in the prophecy will suppress the sorceress, and that they brought me here because they believe I am that girl. They seem to think something will just *happen*.'

'And what did they tell you about your life before… before you came to Archmond?' Peter asked.

'Nothing!' Lucy insisted, 'they don't know anything about Lockerby. They said very generic things about me being sad, or having a difficult life. I can't remember exactly. But they don't know anything about my life. They didn't plant memories in me.'

But it was too late, Star's theory had very swiftly captivated them, and provided a comfortable middle ground between Lucy being a liar or a lunatic. She was a victim of an established reprobate. Peter, Mathew, and Lorelai exchanged knowing looks.

'I think it's time we call it a day,' said Mathew wearily, rising. Others followed. Shuffling footsteps. Lucy looked up to see Hamish and Star still in the left and right corners of the adjoining room.

Hamish didn't know why he had lingered. He realised he had nothing to say. It was all too bizarre, and the only thing clear was that the girl couldn't be trusted. But it was more than that, the deceit felt personal. He went to leave.

'Hamish I'm sorry, I didn't want to lie to you, to any of you, I was just scared,' she gasped.

'Can I even believe that?' he asked softly, examining her, but he turned away before she could answer, and Star followed after him.

Lucy woke later than she usually did the morning after her inquisition. It was warm, and the world outside was still. She couldn't hear the familiar splashing of the river against the hull, or the chattering of the team. A silent warmth. Crumbs whined anxiously, it was hours after he should have been fed, and his attempts at licking her awake had been unsuccessful. She sat up with a slight alarm. She looked at him.

'I'm sorry,' she muttered, 'I don't know… how late is it? How long did I…' but she slipped on the dressing gown Star had lent her and left the compartment before finishing the thought.

She found the boat empty.

Out on the deck, the sun told her that it was in fact well past dawn, and the lack of human noise meant that they'd all departed. The insects, however, seemed rowdier than usual, and the air buzzed and clicked almost mechanically.

Squinting in the abrupt rudeness of daylight that sparkled off the Vivian, she found Maleek on the bow deck fastening some contraptions. He regarded her by nodding, 'Morning,' she greeted.

'Morning,' he responded, almost under his breath, and made to leave, taking the contraptions back to the bridge. In recent days, before yesterday evening, being emerged in this new pattern of life with these people and the security she'd let herself feel in being one of them, had allowed her attention to tune entirely with the world around her. Aside from capricious daydreams about Hamish, her awareness was completely consumed by the chaotic diversity of the jungle; its colours, its rhythm, its darkness and light. But now that she felt her acceptance crumbling beneath her, she could consider nothing beyond the immediacy of their social sphere. Maleek's apparent avoidance troubled her.

She saw Star on the riverbank. The lid of a pot on the fire beside her was rattling. The water had nearly boiled. Orran was secured into a bassinet beside her via a white mesh cover that rose up the sides and was presently opened at the top. It was high enough that he would struggle to climb out. She was shushing him as his cries pierced over the crackle of fire and the chorus of insects and birds. He was reaching up, desperate to roam around in the dirt and the grass.

'Not now little man,' she sung softly, and turned back to tend to the pot.

'Where is everyone?' Lucy asked, coming down the gangway.

Star looked up, heaving the weighty pot onto the ground, and releasing the two claw grabbers she used to move it.

'They set off. A while ago. You overslept.'

'I know. I must have been in a deep sleep, I didn't hear a thing. Why didn't you wake me?'

Star shrugged, 'I supposed you might need the rest.' But they both knew that wasn't true. It was awkward now, and of Star's many aptitudes, social pretence wasn't one of them.

'But where's Gin?'

'He went with Hamish. He's going to try and hunt while Hamish spots zea pockets.' Star threw a handful of dirt into the small fire, turning the red coals to smoky ashes.

'Why wouldn't he ask me?' said Lucy, hurt, remembering the successes over the last few trips; a hog, and then a plump flightless bird known as a yakko.

Star looked at Lucy with bemusement.

'Right of course, they all hate me now.'

'They don't hate you. They're just nervous. They don't trust you,' Star sat down again beside Orran and folded down the white mesh cover, lifting him out. He drooled and babbled with delight as he began to pull at the grass and lift it to his mouth. He looked every bit the cherub, his supple baby skin and auburn hair taking on a heavenly hue in the morning light. Star sighed, snatching the grass from his hands. He began to wail.

'I can take him,' Lucy offered, pensively. Star handed Orran to Lucy, with somewhat watchful eyes, but then began to dismantle the other parts of the fire.

Orran tried to curl around the side of Lucy's torso, peering at something beyond. She touched the back of his pale hand. His attention shifted. His supple but strong fingers gripped around her thumb, and then his eyes peered up at hers, very curiously.

Lucy felt the air rush out of her. She realised then she had never paid a great deal of attention to the distictive features of this child. And in that, had never really appreciated how strange the boy's eyes were. A wondrous hazel, but deeper than hazel, a mahogany without being brown, brimming with light and life. Lucy knew she had few memories of toddlers and babies to draw upon for comparison; the memories of Amber as an infant were misty and shape-shifting. So she dismissed her own marvel as maternal ignorance. And as she did so, the more troubling thoughts returned.

'What about you? Do you trust me?' Lucy asked.

Star hesitated pensively. She was seated cross-legged on the damp mossy ground between the smoky ashes and the bassinet, her brown dress flowed past her folded knees to the dirt, enveloping her legs.

'I don't think you're… lying,' she gave her careful response eventually.

Lucy remembered more of the conversation from the previous evening.

'Oh, that's right, you think I've been hypnotised, brainwashed?'

Star turned her palms skyward, the two options, to her, were self-evident, 'there's no *other worlds*, Mary,' she caught her mistake with mild amusement, 'Lucy.'

Lucy sighed and looked away, she didn't want to revisit this pointless conversation. She realised apart from the fire, there was nothing set up. Normally there were fold out chairs, materials drying, equipment and benches.

'Where is… everything?'

'It'll be a very basic dinner tonight, we're leaving in the morning, and continuing back to Trimany.'

This information left Lucy looking a little shaken.

'It isn't because of you,' Star said, somewhat soothingly, 'it was time we head back anyway. You heard my papa say that a few days ago, didn't you?'

Lucy nodded.

'We've observed about all we can, there's only so much data we can compile in one trip. We have limited supplies. Lives must go on, and so on and so forth.'

Again, Lucy nodded meekly. It was true that the researchers had discussed their respective conclusions several nights ago. Most concluded the spread was worse than they'd hypothesised, and the diversity of species feasting on the fruit was larger than anticipated. The marikots, thankfully, seemed not interested. The effect on the other plant life was more significant than they'd anticipated (the mushrooms particularly, as more and more they found that the weed both dominated and suffocated the melody mushrooms it encountered) and the creatures that did enjoy the fruit seemed to be those that travelled the greatest distances, like the baboons and the birds, spreading seeds as they did. For Hamish and Mathew, the concern remained greatest for the animals eating the fruit, as the madness seemingly spurred them to not only terrifying behaviours the likes of nightmares, it drove them one way or another to death, and stopped their reproduction in the meantime.

'What will you do with the data?' Lucy asked, all of this circling in her mind.

'I think Peter is hopeful it will mean he can get more funding. He needs to spend time working on a poison that can kill the zea-weed without harming the native zea, or anything else. If that's even possible, he'll need to spend all his time on it, and recruit others,' Star said. She took Orran back from Lucy's arms, sat him in the grass, and gave him a stick to play with. He battered it into the ashes excitedly. A reddish blonde wisp of hair curled down his past his eye, Star tucked it behind his ear.

'I should get him inside and try and settle him for a nap. Besides, I still have some washing that I have to…' she stopped as she noticed Lucy's anxious stance. The girl was pressing her fingertips nervously into each other, her eyes fixed despondently on a line of red caterpillars ascending a nearby root, 'that *we* have to do.'

They went back aboard the Princess. Star disappeared for several minutes while she tried to settle Orran in the cabin. He'd been riled up into making continuous 'ook' noises as they ascended the clanky gangway. Then, pitying her for missing breakfast, she fished out some food for Lucy from the dry stores that had been packed away. Lucy ate fairly quietly before taking the laundry to scrub out on the deck, but as they were leaving tomorrow, there wasn't much to be done.

'So, what happens with going back to Trimany? With me, I mean, am I coming with you?'

'Well, we're not going to leave you here. Papa might want to consult with people he knows that work with authorities, about, I guess, what we should do,' her sweet voice broke as it navigated the awkward territory of this idolised friend becoming a subject, 'but we would never leave you here, in the jungle. We're not Mazourians. Maybe he thinks there's a way we can help you. Maybe.'

Lucy was relieved at that answer and pulled a sheet from the basket of dirty clothes between them on the table, and dipped it into the bucket of sudsy water by her feet. The sheet had been used by Gin to carry home the yakko they caught and was covered in blood. Star soon ducked back down into the compartments for several minutes before returning.

'He's out now, for an hour or so at least,' she uttered in her precociously maternal voice, as she emerged back onto the deck. She was holding a mortar and pestle with some fruit in the centre. A flimsy paper-bound book was pressed between her middle finger and the mortar.

'I need to make his lunch,' she explained, resting everything down on the table. Beside her, Lucy continued to rub the sheet over the washboard, the colour of the soapy water was becoming pink; she would have to change it soon.

Star fiddled with the mortar for several moments with frequent glimpses at Lucy before she slid the booklet across the table. Lucy didn't fail to notice that Star avoided eye contact as she did this. In contrast to her usual eagerness to relish in Lucy's expression when she shared things with her, like history or geography, this time she was uncomfortable.

'What's this?' Lucy asked.

'The very middle. It goes across two pages. Read it,' Star said, and having peeled the yellow fruit, began to pummel it gently with the pestle. But her hazel eyes darted nervously over to see if Lucy was doing as she'd instructed.

Lucy could read this. The calligraphy was unfamiliar, but she could make out the words.

'This is translated, of course. The only original text is in Yerkaen,' Star explained, softly, seeing that Lucy was already reading it.

The time will come when the new power rises in the east. From tragedy comes horror. Peace cannot be sustained where vanity and greed are prominent. Long before, a time of impossibilities stirred in the sky and beyond. A fusion of realities, and a fusion of truth. A fusion of time and times. When power grows it darkens, its shadow will cast across the world like tendrils, driving out the light of peace. But shadows can be expelled with light. Light will drive out shadow. A light that came of improbable fusion, for only the same thread can be used to sew the silk together. But noble men must seek out this force of light, youthful, dark of hair and clear in eyes, suffering in the oldest place. Whom can bring light? An ember of light grows from tragedy. From a conquered kingdom, into ours, the destiny of the alien light is to recolour our world. The blood they carry will subdue the power of the east, and their light will drive out the darkness.'

Lucy's eyes darted over the words several more times trying to comprehend them. She understood instantly, but this couldn't be, this couldn't be what she thought it was. It was too…

'Is this…' she blurted.

Star nodded. 'Is this the same as the one the wizards showed you?'

Lucy stared at the text in shock, then shook her head. 'They didn't show me anything. Or maybe they did. Some kind of scroll. They said it was important, but whatever it was I couldn't read it, the letters were all —'

Star cut in, nodding. 'It was originally in Yerkaen, so this is one of several translated versions. Although it isn't very broadly translated. No one really cared about it until Archmond started harping on about it. But there are other versions. Some speak in terms of *he* the whole way. This one is gender neutral. Another version I read said *suffering in an ancient abode* instead of *the oldest place*. Oh, and instead of *force of light* it said *bringer of light*, and I think it said something like, *a land of many battles*, instead of a *conquered kingdom*. Anyway, not that any of that really makes a difference I suppose. But given it reads differently every time it's translated who knows what it really says. The Yerkaens maybe. But all of it's pretty ambiguous, regardless.'

Lucy shifted her posture, squinting, and held the pages out in front of her with the deepest disturbance. She never believed in the idea of this prophecy, or that she was its subject, but she had let herself believe the men that set her on her way genuinely did. That belief was now difficult to reconcile with the text before her. There was nothing at all in those words that could found a belief that she was actually connected to this obscure and shady prediction.

'This says, ugh, it says…' she thought before putting it down, her hands shaking, 'nothing. It says nothing. It's all nonsense. There is nothing in that, that has anything remotely to do with me, apart from having dark hair and light eyes.'

Lucy had left the sheet, still somewhat bloodstained, on the washboard. Star pummelled away at the hard fruit, but she checked it, and its consistency was nearly edible for a little bairn.

'I know. I've always thought that. So have most people in Trimany and the other cities. That's the reason why we don't believe in it,' Star laughed, 'because it doesn't actually say anything. Not really. I mean light and dark, that could be applied to so many things.'

Lucy took several deep breaths and looked up into the curls of intertwined ebony and jade vines dangling over them high above. There was a creature moving among the branches they concealed, but the brown leaves were too thick to make out what. She tried to compose her thoughts.

'And so, there's no reason to think the Queen of Meta Emery is this dark power the world needs to be saved from?'

'Well, to say that we need saving from her is a bit dramatic, but Queen Abigail isn't making many friends lately, and let's just say I'm glad I don't live in Meta Emery.'

'Why's that?' Lucy had reluctantly gone back to the sheet, if only to try and steady her mind by thinking about something else.

'I'd be married off to a brute in a few years for a start,' Star said, 'she's put this system in place, called offerings, where the young women attend these balls from sixteen to twenty four, which is where the elite soldiers from the Red Army select their brides like prized cattle. The girls basically have no choice. So, girls aren't allowed to marry anyone other than a soldier who picks them at one of these balls, until after they've turned twenty-four. If they get to that age, and they haven't been selected by anyone, then they can marry someone else.'

'Ugh, I see,' Lucy murmured, disturbed.

'Actually though, everything she's doing with marriage is horrible. She also brought in laws that force people together if they don't marry by a certain age, and forcibly dissolves marriages that haven't produced any children. It's about population you see. The Dynasty Council believes the numbers are in decline, but people say she's just trying to grow her army.'

'The Red Army?'

'Well, the PeaceKeep too. So, everyone at a certain age is automatically enrolled in the PeaceKeep, remember I was telling you? Because the PeaceKeep now run everything in the Kingdom. But the Red Army too. Peter says he heard that one of the armies, I can't remember whether it was the PeaceKeep or the Red Army, is being fed this nutrient she's developed from a successful version of the zea-weed.'

'Successful?'

'It supposedly gives you all this extra strength, without any of the maddening side effects, if you can believe that. Peter says there is no evidence the zea-weed actually gives anyone any extra strength, just madness. Nasty, insidious weed.'

'Well, hopefully Peter develops a way to poison it,' Lucy said.

Star grinned. 'Hopefully. Anyway, as I was saying, I wouldn't want to live in Meta Emery, and they shouldn't have attacked Archmond, but like my papa says we really should just mind our own business, respect the sovereignty of the island and its people. Certainly not for Trimany to be making any kind of proclamations about what other kingdoms should or shouldn't do, or who should be running them, like Archmond going on about reinstating some dead princess.'

'Cherry?'

'That's her name. But no, the world doesn't need to be *saved* from Meta Emery, and the only ones that can save the people of Meta Emery, if they even want saving, is the people themselves. They need a revolution, not a ghost.'

'Well, I think your father has a point about people minding their own bus—'

'An albatross!' Star launched up from her seat, her neck craning upward to the sky. Lucy saw the fragments of a white shape disappear behind tree tops.

'What?'

'An albatross!' Star repeated, and in an instant, she was racing down the gangway.

'Star, wait, where are you going?' Lucy called, but Star didn't stop. Lucy hesitated. Crumbs twitched by her feet. She didn't want to leave

Orran unattended, but Maleek was around, somewhere. She only had a second to consider the choice, but instinctively she grabbed her sword and raced off after the young girl before she lost sight of her altogether.

Persistent fist-sized swarms of tiny black flies kept buzzing before Lucy's eyes, obstructing her as she chased Star through the undergrowth. A manila carpet of fallen fronds crunched beneath her feet. As she pursued her, Star's small figure kept disappearing behind enormous billowing leaves, some of which were turning yellow in this sparser, sunlit, pocket of jungle. When Lucy eventually pushed through the last curtain of decaying vines and sweetpalm spurs, in the middle of a small glade was the largest bird she had ever seen.

Dappled white and cream, the bird's head was hidden under a wing large enough to conceal a pelican. It hadn't yet appreciated the presence of the two girls. Brown and gold palms encircled them, but behind the bird, a mossy rock-face led up to another level of the jungle.

'An albatross,' Star whispered very quietly, leaning into Lucy's ear. 'He may have some news.'

'News?'

'Yes, news. As in what's being reported in the newscasts?' Star looked at her astounded. 'The albatrosses are the only journalists that cover—' But she was sharply interrupted.

'Oh my!' his beak opened to reveal a deep and unfamiliar accent. 'Well, hello there little women. Who do we have here? I have to tell you sneaking up on an old fellow while he's preening can be considered exceptionally bad manners in some cultures. And by some, I mean nearly all. But I guess we *are* in the jungle.'

Lucy felt the world around her almost pulsate at the shock of this suave voice, emerging from the beak of this towering white bird. As he sat upright, he was taller than Lucy, and his torso was wider than the two girls combined. His large beady eyes flicked between them, awaiting any semblance of a polite response or a greeting.

Lucy steadied herself. Just when she thought the reality of this world had settled in her mind, something impossible rocked her again. She remembered suddenly and fleetingly, the white winged creatures landing on the terrace at Archmond Castle. She was right to connect the two.

There were effectively two kinds of albatross in Escallia Wimbers, those that could understand the common tongue, and those that could both understand it and speak it. All albatrosses could of course speak their own language and communicate with each other, but only a select few could speak the common tongue, which Lucy thought of as English, and they knew only as common and often gave it no name. It was the language of all the world's kingdoms apart from Mazouri, or small and irrelevant settlements such as Yerkey. Nearly all albatrosses that could speak the common tongue, whether it be a learned ability or genetic gift, became cross-country journalists. They would communicate both with fellow non-speaking albatrosses, other birds and humans, and fly between regions selling the information on.

On the mainland, it was practice for all albatrosses to be self-employed. This was a necessity for trust. Of course, depending on how the kingdom was run, it was sometimes the governments who paid for this information from the albatross, and passed it on to the people how they saw fit. But any albatross seen or even rumoured to be in the employ of any government, would find difficulty in selling his stories. Certainly, most cities on the mainland had an independent printing press who bought the scoop, and Archmond for all its dubious practices of late, also still maintained one. There was one kingdom though, that in recent years acquired a good many albatross into the royal government, and that was Meta Emery. This was another 'random' fact known by Star, who also was steadying herself from shock, but not from the fact the bird was speaking, but from the band on his ankle.

'That's the band!' Star turned and pushed Lucy. 'Don't talk to him, quick, let's go.'

'What?' Lucy pushed back against her, confused, but about the talking bird more than the instruction.

'Pfft, this?' the albatross extended his foot, just above which sat a red band, with a simple golden crest imprinted into it, 'please. I just haven't got the pesky thing off yet. But I assure you, I am no longer in her Majesty's service. I am, as of very recently, a freelance journalist.' He bowed in slight self-mockery.

'Don't believe him, let's go, come on,' Star said, pulling on Lucy's arm.

'Believe? What is this band?'

'It means I used to be enslaved, oops, I mean employed, by Her Majesty the Queen of Meta Emery. But as I said, I'm no longer in her service. Though it does stir up some professional curiosity as to why the idea of that distresses your little friend so much.'

Star became more frantic then. 'Lucy let's go!' But she realised her slip-up immediately, rushing her hand to her mouth, which of course further exposed what she was trying to conceal.

The bird's glassy yellow eyes tweaked, and he tilted his head, seeming to grin, which was most disturbing to Lucy who had never known birds to take on human expression. But the dividing line in his yolk beak certainly did curl upwards.

'*Lucy?*' he repeated, and then waddled round to properly surmise her. 'Hmmm a young woman, with dark hair and blue eyes, in the enchanted jungle, with a sword…' His tone was laced with sarcasm, as he had pieced it together before he finished.

'Say, you wouldn't happen to be, *the Lucy*, would you? The one the queen thinks has been brought here from another world, on a mission to *kill her*?'

'Maybe.'

'Oh, my feathers!' He pressed the tips of his wings together, expressing some sort of divine gratitude. 'My first scoop as a freelancer and I come across the most infamous girl in a generation. Well, I've clearly prayed to the right gods, haven't I? No need to answer, that was rhetorical,' he added when Lucy went to speak.

'As it happens,' the glee on his freshly smug face was now indisputable, 'I'm on my way back to Archmond now. First to the Hills, but I will then make my way to the WFB and see if they'll entertain me at the castle, which I'm sure they will. Though now perhaps I might just go straight to the Arched Standard, cut out the middle man, give myself more legitimacy. I could go to the Hills Herald, but it's hardly more than a rumour mill from what I hear of late... Oh but either way, a quote from you would absolutely make my career. Launch me from the depths of shady jungles into the headlines! You see, it's quite difficult starting out as an independent, especially being later in years and needing to shake the stigma of being pre-owned by the east, which rattles people, as you can see,' he indicated Star with the tip of his wing, who was still tugging on Lucy and hissing at her not to talk to the bird.

'Please, humour me, just give me a little soundbite, one quote. In fact, think of this as a messaging service. Do you have any messages for the Archmonders about the progress of your mission?'

'Actually, yes, I do.' Lucy was suddenly inspired.

'No, Lucy don't'! Star shrieked, pulling at her wrist tightly, but Lucy pulled away just as violently.

'You can tell the Archmonders I'm not on their mission. Tell the people of the Rolling Hills the prophecy is a farce. There is no saviour. The wizards lied. The only people that can save the Archmonders, are the Archmonders themselves.'

'Lucy enough!' Star shouted, rather loudly this time, and then turned to run off. Lucy was desperate to get more from the bird, but she recognised that right now Star was her only remaining ally in the team. But before Star disappeared completely the albatross made one more announcement.

'Very well, run along suspicious creatures,' he sung cavalierly, skilfully hiding the rippling excitement rushing through him at this groundbreaking exposé Lucy had so generously allowed him. 'Might I say though, if your plan is to continue down river I wouldn't go through Trimany if I were you. It's about to be invaded.'

Already part way through the palms at the edge of the glade, Star halted at this and turned back to gauge the bird's expression. Lucy, stoic and sword in hand, felt the force of his allegation through her bones. Nonchalant to their distress, he dipped his head in a respectful gesture, and having now successfully removed the red band from his ankle, took flight.

❧

In Verity Palace - the Queen seeks her cousin's favour.

'Mr. Obsidian,' Abigail called from across the gravel forecourt. Bevant turned, bemused and curious. He had been examining a crimson creeper that wound its way up the ceramic pot and the tightly pruned conifer within it, just as it was designed to do. This was replicated across each of the pointed conifers that lined the walls around the palace entrance, but the creeper in this pot was mysteriously slighter and less virile than the others.

Bevant's role in the Dynasty Council included maintenance of the palace and its grounds. Every member of the Council governed a region within Meta Emery. His, by birthright, was Obsidian. Obsidian, the region, comprised the small territory before the palace gates, as well as the territory beyond the gates at the base of the mountain, and continued up the goods railway that accessed the palace, to the palace itself and all its gardens, waterways, and fixtures. It was somewhat of a dubious governance though, given that the true ruler of the palace was of course the queen. Although others had argued that the same could be said of any region of Meta Emery. And while he sometimes lamented not having his own region to rule, he was consoled by the knowledge that a division of the PeaceKeep reported to every other seat of the Dynasty Council, but it was the Red Army that reported to him. The entirety of it.

174

While Bevant had a good many landscapers reporting to him, of whom had gardeners reporting to them, he had a personal affinity for all that grew, and took pleasure in inspecting the gardens himself from time to time. Although outside the palace, these somewhat public gardens, (insofar as they were accessible by those permitted beyond the gates but not necessarily into the palace itself) were rather demure in contrast to the exquisitely cultivated displays that lay within, and thus not his favourite.

The queen this morning donned an uncharacteristically plain dress of soft copper shadings. It was straight; no petticoat, and free of frills and trimmings. This was a deliberate change of tone, and transparently so, to the man whose favour she sought. Bevant was known to be objectionable to excessive displays of wealth and royalty. He like her, was royal by blood, but he took it on as some sort of self-evident badge, a distinction that needn't be proved and was lurid and petty to display. Nevertheless, her plain copper gown caught the morning light across the mountain very prettily. It was early, but activity was starting to stir at the palace entrance. Supplies were being received into delivery docks and servants shuffled around independently to each other. It was on this basis she had worn her bonnet, despite the early hour, as it was protocol if appearing in public without her crown, and beyond the palace foyer was, arguably, public grounds.

'Mister? Why the formality?' he asked, offended.

She cast her eyes about. 'Well, for the sake of common ears,' she suggested.

He shrugged. 'No one is paying attention at this hour, they're all still half asleep.'

'The aloigayria, how is it progressing?' she indicated the crimson vine. She looked about twelve-years-old today, not alarmingly younger than her usual appearance of about fourteen.

'Did you dream up an interest in horticulture?' he asked, dryly.

'It would not hurt if I had.'

'And that's what has brought you out at this hour?' He looked across to the edge of the forecourt, to where the mountain dropped away; yolk yellow dawn was cracking over the black rock. The air was crisp, but the sky above was blue and clear, a delightful change from mountain mornings that were usually shrouded in mist.

'No, actually, I thought we might talk, and I supposed I would find you here.'

'You supposed? Or you looked at the schedules?'

'Perhaps I did both,' she replied. He turned up from the aloigayria, letting it slip out of his hands, and faced her directly.

'Candid of you to admit,' he teased, playfully.

'Well, if I am interfering, I shall leave you in peace.'

He beamed at her then. 'Not in the slightest your Majesty. Your presence is a delight. I was about to peruse the lilies,' he said and then outstretched his arm toward the stony archway to their right.

They crossed under the dark archway into a more secluded courtyard which curved around to where the palace met the boundaries of mountain rock. They admired the dew on the blood lilies that bloomed up from baby's breath in chequered squares across the courtyard, interposed with squares of shiny black pebbles of the rock that was his namesake.

Slowly, she began to move the discussion toward the source of her attendance, by raising the subject of Trimany and the events that had led to the dispatch of the two companies of soldiers to the midland city. It was the Red Army that attended to foreign missions, and so of course Bevant had organised the dispatch once the Council had voted on the matter. But the whole business instigated from intelligence no more credible than rumour.

'I do not want to think that they would conspire against us. We may not have an alliance with them as we do with Mazouri, or an accord as we do with Coby and Gemini, but Trimany is not one to get involved in the governance of other kingdoms,' Abigail proclaimed, thinking out loud.

'Alliances can shift,' said Bevant, 'remember that. But in any case, Abigail, what do you expect will come of this, ultimately?' he was careful to check that they were alone before he addressed her so informally. 'Do you think there's anything to this tip off? Do we really think your sister is somehow alive, and all of a sudden living in a Trimanian suburb? And that the city is actively hiding her? I mean we had a similar tip off several winters ago that amounted to nothing, more or less. Everything we know tells us that the treacherous whore burned to death in the fires of Archmond... quite fittingly.'

'Bevant, please,' Abigail chided him, 'this is still my sister we're talking about,' she sighed, melancholy, 'but no, I agree. I think we all recognise that is probably the case. The tip off does not concern me so much as Trimany's changed attitude of late. Trimany's refusal to honour the simple request, which would merely involve sending officials out to do some door-knocking in that particular province, is fast appearing symbolic of something far more sinister.'

'Sinister or stubborn? Let's just hope this was merely about resources as they say, and they'll let our army search the reported suburb themselves, and there will be no trouble.'

'They had better,' Abigail snapped bitterly. 'After everything that's happened lately, if they refuse to let our army in to search for a suspected enemy of the crown, I could easily consider that in itself an act of war.'

By everything, she meant discussions that Trimany's government had been having with Archmond in relation to reinstating a rail network between the two kingdoms. The line had been damaged by bad weather several decades ago, and the deterioration continued for several years while a dispute about who would foot the cost of repair remained unresolved. The attack on Archmond a decade ago had then demolished the entirety of the line from the Rolling Hills to the edge of the forest. But over the last few years Archmond's position in the world had changed and it was in desperate need of imports. It had agreed to co-ordinate and fund the entirety of the repair, if Trimany assisted and was amenable to opening up trade between them.

Abigail had written to Trimany and voiced her dissent about the project, asking Trimany to remain united in imposing sanctions against Archmond until it retracted its heretical claims against her rule.

In truth though, the biggest obstacle to the line being reinstated was the tunnel that had partially collapsed on the southern tip of the Alexandria Plateau. So, while the two governments entertained very promising talks on the topic, if the joint venture was even agreed, the planning alone of works needed to restore the tunnel would take a year in itself.

'War can be destructive, but it can also be productive,' Bevant commented, touching the soft dark petals of a blood lily. 'Certainly if they are minded to be provocative against us, then inaction itself may weaken Meta Emery.'

'I only ask that Trimany investigate the rumour, in line with what is customary practice between civilised nations. I would do the same if petitioned,' she said, and then sighed, vexed. But she cast her hazel eyes up to him and he could see beneath her heavy eyelids, that it was not the insolence of this inferior kingdom that troubled her.

He knelt by one of the squares and tussled the tiny obsidian stones with his hand. There was a deep rust moss below several handfuls that had not been turned in some time. He made a mental note of this, meaning to raise it with the senior landscaper. The dark stone wall that enclosed the courtyard was blocking the glare of the rising sun. He noted that in the absence of daylight the courtyard seemed a dreary place, the dark stone walls, its chequered ground mostly black. But in this charcoal canvas, the red of the blood lilies and the white of the baby's breath sung with intensity. Beyond the archway to where they had stood before, he could see blinding stripes of morning light were cutting through the air in a daze before the palace entrance, prompting workers to raise their hands and forearms to shield themselves from the glare as they communicated with one another.

'And leaving the Council aside for a moment, what is it that you would want done with your sister? If the intelligence proves correct, and she is in fact alive, living in Trimany?'

Abigail took a deep breath and turned onto a path perpendicular to the one they were on.

He looked at her simple slumped figure, in the plain dress and the white bonnet, with some sympathy then.

'Well she is a threat to our kingdom,' Abigail said, matter-of-factly, twisting back to face him, 'I have to put my personal hopes and feelings aside. Any threat to the kingdom must be dealt with in the same way. I understand that.'

'Indeed, and indeed why we've sent assassins after this other threat, another young lady,' Bevant noted.

'*Yes*,' Abigail agreed tentatively, this was the reason she had wanted to speak to him. 'Are you also due to inspect the repairs to the cistern this morning?'

He understood her meaning. She wanted to be perfectly alone.

'It was the very next thing on my list, Majesty,' he said with a sly grin. 'Shall we go inspect it now?'

They walked silently to the end of the courtyard and through a door which led into a truncated marble corridor. At the end of this corridor, steps led down to the reservoir which stored water for the palace's some nineteen-hundred occupants. High altitude catchments funnelled rain and melting snow from the summit and redirected it here. In the chamber below the Winter's wing, bestowed to her uncle, the sound of rushing green mountain water pouring into the reservoir was incessant. They seemed to use water at the very rate it was replenished, and had only ever once in her lifetime, needed to use the levers that redirected the channels and stopped it from overflowing. The cavernous chamber was lit with skylights. One had recently cracked, and this was the repair work she had alluded to.

'So,' he said, his deep voice echoing, but now he could be certain they were alone, for he controlled access to the cistern, and no one would be down here at this time, 'it is not the apprehension of your sister that alarms you, but that of this girl?'

Abigail clasped her hands together. 'If my sister isn't already dead as we've believed, then she soon will be, and as unfortunate as it is to have such a relationship with one's sister, it is what it is,' she began, then noted she hadn't seen her sister since before she was *actually* eleven years old. They trailed the walkway beside the reservoir, toward the broken skylight, some twenty yards ahead. You could see the beam of light in the distance, breaking through unfiltered, dust floating within it. Beside them, the sound of the water lapping against the marble was a sweet contrast to the distant roar of it funnelling in.

'But this girl…' Bevant encouraged.

'By accounts of the albatrosses she is not an Archmonder. By that, I mean, she looks like us. But still, how could Archmond have materialised a common girl? Or taken her from some other city? They just don't have the means to, which is so curious because—'

'Because maybe she is from another world?' Bevant finished, but his question answered itself with its condescending tone. 'Abigail, come now, you cannot believe that. What proof is there that such a thing is possible?'

Abigail shrugged. 'Many things seem impossible, until it is proved they are not.'

Bevant rolled his eyes, and let out a heavy sigh, he could sense an uncomfortable request was coming. They had reached the broken skylight and he looked up toward it, thinking of when the glass could be cut to reseal it. 'And so… ?'

'Is it possible to get a message to the assassins, to instruct that she is not to be killed or harmed on apprehension?'

Bevant was aghast. 'The orders for the mission are set by the Council. It has been voted on. I'm unclear as to what your Majesty is asking?'

'Yes, I am aware, the orders were for the threat she poses to be eliminated. I just want to ensure she is brought here alive, first.'

'This is something that should be put to the Council. You're asking to amend the order.'

'No, it is the same order. I'm simply saying the threat can be eliminated *here,* as opposed to out in the field.'

Bevant rubbed his fingers across his eyebrows, troubled. 'To what end?'

'I mean, really, apprehending her is still eliminating the threat anyway, is it not? Once she is apprehended, she is no longer a threat. I'm not seeking to change the order, I just wanted it… *executed…* differently, specifically.'

He dropped his hands and leant back against the pale marble wall. It was cold against his back, particularly given the light nature of his corduroy coat and muslin shirt. He took a deep breath and consumed the scents of the cistern: metallic and mineral.

'Again, I say, to what end? What purpose does that achieve?'

'Well there are questions that need answering,' Abigail said, arms spread outward, as she became somewhat defiant in her posture and her voice firmed. 'She would have information on Archmond that is crucial to us here and now.'

'Information that I'm sure Thomas is suitably able to extract,' Bevant suggested, wearily.

Abigail sighed irritably. 'Please do not mention his involvement in this I am upset enough about that as it is. I am sure he can get some information, but it is not the same thing. There are things she can tell us that only I may be able to extract from her.'

'Is that so? Your Majesty, you do have a persuasive way about you, but I wouldn't think you are the only one in the world able to talk to this girl and get her to open up, if she does in fact have anything useful to say. What is this really about? Is this more of, please do not be insulted, but, a personal fascination?'

Abigail pursed her lips. 'Perhaps it is. Is that so bad? Perhaps I can have more than one reason for pursuing something. It does not mean that my position is invalid. Bringing her here alive does fulfil the orders. But it can give us more as well. I do not want to go through the trouble of raising this with everyone. Please, cousin,' she stopped, noting in her anxiousness that the nearby dripping of water, was pulsating as awkwardly as a ticking clock, 'can you not just get a message to them that I want her brought here, alive?'

Chapter 6

Fast Moving Clouds

'I dunno young man,' said Gin, craning his head around the portside, 'there are some fast moving clouds comin' this way from the north. Storms could be early.'
Gin Mathers, Chapter 4, *Halcyon Days.*

The night Lucy left them, the emerging moon had the most glorious full light. Hamish would always remember that part of it. The River Princess sped down the Vivian in a chilling race to return to Trimany as soon as possible. Leaning over the gunwale and clutching the maidenflower he'd given her, that in the emotional haste of her departure had been left behind, he took in the light on the frothing black water below and remembered Lucy's love of the moon.

It was undoubtedly cruel of course. To expel her like that when she wanted so much to return with them. But while the decision wasn't his alone, as he stared into the moonlit river racing them by, Hamish rehashed the many justifications keeping guilt at bay. First and foremost, the ultimatum was a dire one. While it was cruel to send her back into the jungle alone, if she truly was this this girl that Archmond proclaimed as prophesied to kill the Queen of Meta Emery, then no doubt she was an enemy of that same queen, the forces of whom were rumoured to be invading his city.

Those forces, being the Red Army, were known, of late, to be both unpredictable and brutal. If the River Princess sailed into port, and that port was already controlled by Red Army soldiers, the risk of them identifying Lucy had to be considered. Were there not already assassins after her? If discovered with her, no doubt those same assassins would consider the entire team collateral kill. Therefore the chances of their immediate execution, his little Orran included, were all too real. Given the jungle was not littered with these soldiers, in many ways Lucy too, was safer there. Secondly, he also reassured himself that they had provided her with more tools than they'd found her with: a better, *proper* flint; a hunting knife; rope; a bedding roll; and stores of food, including both bread (albeit very stale bread) and dried meats. Thirdly, while the act of casting a young lady out into the wilderness might otherwise be seen as unforgivable to most Trimanian gentle-men, this was no ordinary young lady. This particular young lady had demonstrated, quite deftly, that she was not at all helpless. And lastly, what his father opined, and Hamish hoped to be true, was that the most dangerous wildlife was well behind them, inhabiting the darker jungle valleys further west.

Still, he did worry for her, amid the lingering sexual frustration that was the dominant and conflicting reaction he had to making her leave. But he still worried. The chivalrous part of him did, and he would be haunted if anything happened to her out there on her own. But if anything had happened to his son because of her, and her presence among them, implicating them all in this political scandal, he would have never forgiven either her or himself. So, the decision was ultimately a fairly straightforward one. They hoped the bird was wrong about war, but they could not risk the bird's warning being correct, and sail into Trimany with the queen's enemy on their boat while Trimany was filled with the queen's soldiers.

But her true identity had rocked him more than he had been able to say, and as he clutched the black embossed petals in his hand, he only hoped she had taken heed of the pertinence and precision of his directions. North. Admittedly she was a mess as she left, her eyes wet as she tried not to cry, her responses scrambled. Seeing her that way at least had diluted his sexual desires or abated them. But he was persistent with her, *go north.*

'So, where does the sun set?' he asked her more than once, assuring himself that she could follow such directions.

'And so which way is north? You need to know because you must go through Rumustica,' he'd told her, repeatedly. Through the mountains, away from Trimany. But her eyes told him she was too frazzled to appreciate the importance of these details, and once she was gone, she would find her own way. He could only hope that way would be north.

❧

'Come on, Crumbs,' Lucy muttered irritably, 'leave it. We'll hunt something proper in a little bit.' He ignored her and persisted. 'Leave it!'

He had been chasing some sort of tiny rodent that scurried beneath the leaf litter as they passed. She wasn't normally so terse with him, and his beseeching eyes told her so. She turned away, but she would feel guilty about it later. They had walked for hours in the deep darkness the previous night and slept fairly roughly, and this morning they were both hungry. As they walked amid the consistent mechanical chorus of insects, and Lucy mulled on her loss and bitterness at being forced away from the only people she'd ever admired, she found herself thinking about her friend Asha. Funny that, because she had never felt as close to Asha as she had to Hamish and young Star these last few weeks.

Yet the comforting memory of Asha was in her consistency and reliability. Asha had always been around. Their relationship had brought limited intimacy, but Asha had taken up the posting of mild friendship, and kept it, for over a decade. That might explain why in the whirlwind of welcome and then rejection from the fascinating clan of the Mathers family, that Lucy found herself in a melancholic nostalgia for the steadiness that Asha once brought, and was in her predicament, now gone. But the colours and lines of her friend's face kept shifting and contorting with each attempt to picture her or mixing with the more recent and vivid memories of Star and Hamish and distorting in that way. Asha became Star became Hamish became Mathew in her mind's eye. And it was Hamish and Star, Lorelai and Peter, and all of them, that she didn't want to think about.

She had more immediate problems, of course, and tried to keep her eyes peeled for the edible dark mushrooms she'd learnt to forage for. She had a better flint now, (and tried to repel the image of Hamish's sombre eyes as he pressed it into her palm) a day or so's worth of dried food, and now knew the plants that made suitable tinder and kindling, so she at least didn't fret about how to take care of herself. They had taught her a good deal at the very least.

She did find some edible mushrooms and while she sat to roast them by one of the Vivian's many tributaries, and ate them with the bread they'd given her, Crumbs was able to pin down some golden amphibians. Reluctantly, she took some that he'd caught and roasted them herself. They weren't any more horrid than the rats of the Alexandria. Their flavour was if anything, rather fishy, but this was well and truly drowned out by the smoke from the messy bark.

As she ate, she thought of Bear, and wondered if he would now, once again re-emerge to guide her. Now that there was no contentment to fracture. Somehow, she sensed he would not. Call it intuition, but, somehow, she sensed she would not see him for some time. She was still too bitter about his having left her alone those days in the jungle to allow herself to admit that this, too, upset her.

She found her thoughts drifting back to Pepper and Hult, the only other *almost* friends she had made in the strange time she had been stuck here, and how they disappeared so suddenly too. Of course, then, naturally, she had to consider that immediately before this, the wizards had asked her to leave their castle and go off on her own as well. Should she consider whether some of this was not circumstantial, but was more about *her?* And then if so, what was it that she was doing wrong? None of these events seemed linked in her mind. But she considered that it was possible they were, and whatever the linkage, she was just too dim to see it.

The shifting edges of a pink film of spores were drifting languidly above her. The melody mushroom itself was a white-spotted vermilion. She had passed it some yards before the stream, and it was the only echoing croak she had heard since they crushed the bracken to rest. Its familiar resonant bellow still just as disturbingly conscious, with its burbles of discomfort and then relief. The jungle had thickened and darkened around them the further they moved from those botanical banks of the Vivian, all dappled with light. Certainly the splendour the jungle had taken on these last few weeks was completely vanquished the moment she had been exiled. No longer was the assorted bird call a wonder, or the kaleidoscopic colours of the crawling insects and butterflies magnetic. It was once again a dazzling obstacle, but an obstacle nonetheless. She had been promised that if she heeded to north, the jungle would soon pass. But then what?

As her thoughts scattered, she chewed her bottom lip bitterly and tried desperately to remember home. To remember her mother. But the more she tried, the more her mother's face, like Asha's, swirled and blurred in her mind. Even the memories, which had so dauntingly attacked her on the frozen tundra before Yerkey, were now almost impossible to recall. Everything except Amber, and that fateful moment, and her actions afterwards. Now it was Amber she remembered, and the rest of her life she had buried away. Oh, how everything in this world was upside down. But to not be able to see her mother's face, this was a new kind of confronting.

'Emotion will serve no purpose now,' she remembered Hamish's words urging her as he was saying goodbye, 'you must be practical.'

This had irritated her because she wasn't being emotional. In fact, she had not shed one tear, not even since she turned suddenly and left them all behind. Star was the one who sobbed uncontrollably on the deck, but somehow it seemed okay if she cried.

Lucy realised now, with the clear-minded benefit of rest, time, and food, that when he'd walked some distance away from the River Princess to privately bid her farewell, what he had not said. He had not asked her to come find him later. He had not asked her to inquire about whether the invasion rumour was true when she got to the nearest town. He also had made no promise to come look for her when things were better, when they were safe. He had simply repeated directional commands (no doubt getting her as far away from his family and their happy lives as he could) thanked her again for her help with Star, apologised that it had to be this way, and said goodbye. She wondered then if she'd been wrong about him, and everything she thought she felt between them. And why not? She had been wrong about so much else.

She and Crumbs set off again, crossing the wide stream which took them some time to navigate. Without the light from the sky, its shallow waters were almost invisible, and the depths of the slippery stones beneath them imperceptible. When the land sloped upward at points, or she deliberately traversed rocky slopes to higher grounds, they would come to parts where the sunlight between the shifting canopy showed the extent of the lime lichen covering the rocks and the trees. It may have, in other circumstances, been a wonder, but it only reminded her of how wet everything was here. She tired of every part of her being incessantly damp, and almost felt she could miss the inexorable dryness of the Alexandria. *Almost.*

But it was certain that she had become immune to the jungle's frightening chaotic beauty. The billowing leaves were a nuisance. Even the roaming fingers of colourful clouds that signalled nearby melody-shrooms, which would have sparked whimsical wonder with Star, (*'Hey what colour would you say that was? Maybe it's a peppermint mushroom! How big do you think it is? Did you hear that? Where do you think it is?*) were now just garish stripes of loneliness. All the glitter had been washed away. The halcyon days were at an end. But she wasn't scared anymore. They had left her, or discarded her, richer than they had found her, whether she appreciated it or not. It was during this pessimistic insistence of being unafraid, that she found, or rather ran into, Leo.

Meeting Leo

It was fortunate she didn't entirely collide with him. Given the enormity of his paws, and his frayed but stern claws, this would have instantly been the end of her. She hadn't heard him because he'd been quiet for some time; out of breath, defeated. His deafening roars and moans the previous night had vibrated the swooning monstera and silenced the other creatures. But Lucy in her bitter determination had travelled a great distance today. She'd been too far to hear his deafening bellow the previous night.

She had climbed upward, with great difficulty, out of the enclosed valley that in the murky light she was not aware she had been led into. But upward, risking the precarious instability of rocky ground and steep slopes, provided hope that higher ground would lead to a thinning of the jungle. Above the valley, the jungle was just as dense. But closer to where the tops of towering trees swayed, there was some light, albeit sparse and grey, and the sun's position could be gauged. She was optimistic about her idea of north.

Her optimism shrunk away when she tripped over the giant black foot, its outline barely discernible, and with a chilling howl, jagged claws came down toward her from within a black mess of fur.

The next few moments seemed to all happen at once. Crumbs barked ferociously but ducked out of sight. The roar erupted again but Lucy had pushed herself up and darted backward, and an enormous black paw tore down into the earth and having missed her, ripped up a thicket of thorny carpet vines, exposing new blooms of zea-weed beneath it. And then nothing. Stillness. Lucy's heart pounded. She looked at the nearest trunks as an escape, but their branches begun several metres above her, and in the panic of the moment there was no way she'd summon the agility to scale them. She could run, she would run, but how fast was this beast, still hidden, whose paws were the size of her head?

Instinctively she pulled out the sword. There was no way she could defeat something so large but maybe, if she pierced it, it might retreat. The sword's appearance seemed to have an effect on the weather. A strong gale high above sent the trees swishing, and the daylight that shot down glimmered off the blade and cast away the shadows before her. The creature could be seen now; an enormous bear, towering in width and height, black and white in colour, with miserable patches like running mascara over his eyes… a panda?

'Get back, get back!' he wailed. She was momentarily jolted by the sound of his voice, but after the albatross, the shock this time didn't last. She steadied her breath, looking him over, she wasn't sure how to proceed.

'Stay away from me or I'll cut you,' she cried, hoarsely.

'Get back, go away, stay away from me!' he cried. She was confused by this and then heard as his stance shifted, the faint sound of rusted metal jangling. She lowered her eyes, and then realised in this bright-ness that reflected from the vorpal blade, that blood was splattered across the bracken and thorny carpet vines between her and the beast. Then the information clicked together.

'You're hurt? Are you trapped?' She had suddenly remembered that insidious little Archmonder, but could he have possibly travelled this far? They were more than fifty miles from where Hamish had slit his throat. Or were there simply more of them?

'Well, if you think that's enough to kill me, well, well it isn't! I can still fight you, I can still rip you apart… and *I will*,' he roared.

Lucy lowered her sword. She stepped two paces back and to her right and could see the chain now, and the horrid teeth of the trap that skewered into the beast's foot. She was out of his reach, and he was trapped.

'I don't want to fight,' she said plainly, directly, looking into the dark shadowy eyes. 'How long have you been here?'

The panda suddenly realised she was not here to hurt him, but he seemed confused by this, so it took him some time to respond.

'More than one night, but I'm not sure it's three, or just two, or five. I don't count real well, and I've started to go mad. Like everything else in here,' he said, sullenly.

'Did you eat any of the fruit of that weed?' Lucy used her sword to point to the zea-weed and its pepper-shaped fruit.

The panda shook his head profusely. 'Never, never, never! Devil's weed,' he hissed.

'Listen, I don't want to hurt you. I'm alone out here myself,' she began, but the panda looked toward Crumbs who'd now come out from hiding.

Lucy rolled her eyes. '*We're* alone out here then. But we've been trying to find a way out. I didn't set that trap, I promise you. But I think I know who did. And I might be able to get it off you, if you let me. But it could hurt and I… I don't really know how to do it. But I'll try, if you want me to? If you can brace yourself?'

The panda looked at the small girl as she set her sword down and stretched her arms out, and her even smaller companion. He nodded, gritting his teeth, and turning away. When she knelt down to look at the trap, in the darkness she could find no lever for release. Its surface was rough with rust. Only the base of its teeth were visible, the rest were keenly embedded into the poor panda's ankle.

She drew breath. The only way was to try and pry it open with her hands. But if her strength was not enough, or the contraption did not work the way she imagined, it would snap back and hurt him even more, after she'd just asked him to trust her. She looked up at him, terrified of her task. He was not watching. His neck was twisted away, and she felt that all of him was tensed.

Shakily, she slid her fingers between the oozy, blood-soaked teeth on either side of his ankle, took a deep breath, and began to pry the trap apart. At first it would not budge, and she cried out with exertion as each failing attempt jolted her wrists. But eventually she began to pull against its inertia and the teeth started to slide out of the wounds. Her weak arms were trembling against the force of its spring that wanted to slam tightly shut again. She grunted again, her face going red with all the strength she could muster until it opened further, and the teeth were out.

'Pull up your foot!' she shrieked with urgency. 'Hurry!'

The panda did and in the same moment Lucy screamed in pain and let the trap fall shut. Her hands, before her, soaked in panda blood, were trembling from the exertion and they ached immensely. She wondered now if she could even hold a sword, let alone use one. She exhaled.

The panda beside her, was now curled over on himself licking the wound. Lying back between the ferns, she spun around, facing him, watching him for a few moments while she caught her breath. No one said anything for several minutes. She was aware of the vibrations of the insects again, thousands of them, high-pitched and perforating the background. Their constant cacophony had been mollified in the intensity of the task.

'Where will you go now? Do you live here or were you passing through,' she asked him eventually, once it was clear he was okay.

He drew back dismissively, 'I live everywhere, I live here, I live there, I live down in those gullies.'

Lucy nodded singularly to accept the comment, even though she wasn't really sure what he meant. She didn't want to offend him with thoughtless questions.

Softly, it started to rain.

'Sorry,' she said, craning up to feel the trickle of droplets on her cheeks, as they ricocheted off the leaves, 'I don't know anything about pandas. I've never met a panda before.'

'A what?'

'A *panda*,' she said the word very hesitantly, worried she'd offended him after all.

'What's a panda?' he asked, suspicious.

'Well, that's what you are, aren't you?' She considered there was probably a different word for it here and wondered where in his life this creature of common tongue might have heard the correct word in this world for his kind.

He twitched his nose at the idea and stood up. His coat shook off the settling rain as he moved, and she appreciated its density, wondering how hot he got in this tepid place. She could also see that the trap had not damaged the ability for his leg to bear his weight. The teeth had been about an inch long, but his ankle was easily eight or more inches in diameter.

'I don't think so,' he said, reaching up into a nearby tree, pulling branches toward him and scanning them for low hanging fruit. 'How can I be, if I don't know it? Can't be something without knowing it.'

Lucy went to reject his broken logic but decided to change the topic. 'Do you have anyone waiting for you somewhere? A family, a pack, a herd?' She didn't know what the correct term was.

The panda shook his head, plucking bulbous brown and red fruit off the second tree, and letting the flimsy branches snap back creating a rustle across all the surrounding foliage.

'Got no bear kin. No bear would want anything to do with me, not in my condition,' he uttered, and then ate gustily.

'What condition?' she asked, when it was clear he wasn't going to elaborate, and watched the magenta juices of the fruit run down the white fur of his neck.

'Well just look at me,' he mumbled through his mouthful, and gestured across his fur, 'not white, not black... just a mess of both. It's why my mum abandoned me. Couldn't live with the shame.'

Lucy shrugged. 'Oh, well, in my world, we would call you a panda. All pandas look exactly like you, black and white, even the markings on your eyes are the same. We don't think it's messy. Pandas are special. Rare. They're considered precious.'

'What's preshos mean?' He struggled to pronounce it. 'Is that another word for freak?' he asked cynically.

'No!' Lucy tried not to laugh but now the childishness of his self-pity was becoming somewhat amusing. 'It means... wanted. It means people want to have you or be near you or take care of you.'

He thought on this for a long moment. 'Your world, aye? Where's your world?'

Lucy's eyes fell into thorny ground cover, 'I don't know.'

'You tryna get back there?'

Lucy nodded.

'But you're lost?' he figured.

'I guess I am,' she agreed, soberly, 'but right now I'm trying to get to Rumustica, or just get out of this jungle really. I'm sick of being in this dark wet circus.'

'Oh, yeah? Me too!' exclaimed the panda, but it seemed as though the notion had only just come to him, 'I was already getting sick of this place before I got caught in that thing. It's not the same as it once was. It just keeps getting weirder and *weirder*. All the animals eating that devil weed these days, it makes 'em wild and crazy. Some Archies came through all weird. Some soldiers came through looking for stuff a while ago. Some of them went weird. It never used to be like this.'

Lucy had her own idea then. 'So, you want to leave too? Maybe we can leave together then? I'm no warrior but I have a sword and have hands that can use it, well, not right at this moment,' she rubbed over her aching fingers, 'and I can make fire too. I'm sure that might help you, somehow, sometimes? Do you know the way out of here? I'm told it's north? But I've lost which way north is.'

'North is to Rumustica,' the panda agreed, before looking around, appraising his position, 'the sun sets in the east, north is behind me.'

'Well, how about it? Do you want to go together, to Rumustica? Do you know the way?'

He considered the notion nonchalantly. 'Yeah, it would be good to get outta here, get some proper sunshine. Yeah, I know the way.'

She felt a huge relief wash over her. 'Great,' she said, exhaling with relief.

'What's your name by the way?' she asked, after coughing and patting her throat. 'I forgot to ask before. I'm Lucy.'

The panda smiled, almost flattered, as if some secret compliment had been bestowed by the unveiling of her name.

'Hello, Lucy,' he half burbled through a giggle.

'What should I call you?' she repeated the question, wondering if he had a name. Wondering then also, if he was alone out here, from what reference did his words come?

He mulled over her question though, and as he did it was apparent that he did not have a name that he knew or could recall and had begun to muster one from the depths of his imagination. His face tinkered with recognition more than once, before contorting with dissatisfaction and softening again. Eventually he said, 'Leo. My name is Leo.'

Lucy only smiled back warmly. 'Nice to meet you, Leo,' she said with a respectful nod. And that was it. That was how Lucy met Leo.

The three compatriots hadn't gone very far before Leo suggested that she and Crumbs ride on his back. Lucy took it as an indication of his kind nature, but in part this was motivated by his frustration at how long it seemed to take the feeble girl to move through the jungle. His enormous figure bent and crushed everything other than the towering jungle trees, whose girths were far wider than even he was. Moreover, as they ascended, either up slippery lichen slopes, or steep crumbling ground, he manoeuvred with ease in places where she struggled and slipped.

But when they stopped to rest, he was impressed by how quickly she could get large amounts of water from the stream and bring them for drinking. He was delighted by her fire, and the way it dried things like his fur, and he remembered that he had seen and enjoyed fire once before. He was fascinated by the way her nimble hands made things out of things. He could bend and impress upon the jungle as he went, and it rarely scared him, but the contraptions she created, for drinking, for scratching the teeth, for eating, and for shelter, he had not seen much of this kind of thing before.

He thought to himself as he settled off to sleep, full of warm contentment, beside that same shelter she'd constructed from sticks and fan palms, that he would try and keep this friend forever. But he remembered, with a stir, the last time he had a friend, the friend from whom he'd seen fire, all the many moons ago when he was only a youngster. That had also been a creature who was feeble and clever like Lucy, and it had died, as feeble things do, and so he did not want to get his hopes up.

They set off early the next dawn, and so covered a great distance over the morning. So much so, in fact, that by midday, Lucy started to feel finally, that this seemingly infinite jungle universe was starting to wane. The forest remained all around them, but they had ascended to a level that was brighter and sparser.

Surprisingly, to herself at least, Leo's company did not seem to ameliorate in any great way, the severity of her spiraling surliness and cynicism. But when she dwelled on this more, it seemed only fitting that she would continue to grieve what she thought were the only true friends she'd ever made, and what promised to be the first (or maybe only) love of her life. The company of this equally surly bear was unlikely to even serve as a replacement at the very least, let alone heal deep wounds at best.

As the morning became noon, she found herself looking around at the trees; they were slighter. Riding along on Leo's back had an easiness to it that seemed to send her inward. She was so self-absorbed she had almost failed to appreciate how easy this journey now was for her, thanks to the generosity of this strange bear she had happened upon. But now, coming out of her thoughts into the world, she noticed also that there were no longer any mushrooms or event faint iridescence of any kind. Even the lichen was no more.

It was simply too bright for iridescence now. The darkness and the mist was behind them. She breathed in the air and could taste that it was not wet. Looking up through the trees with a great infectious smile, she realised not only could she see the sky, but for the first time since she swam with Star in the Vivian's azure waters, she could take in vast patches of it and let the daylight kiss her eyelids.

'The sky and the sun!' she exclaimed to Leo, the only thing she'd said in hours. Crumbs was fidgeting in her grip. She had become used to Leo's galumphing sway, as he had become used to the pressure of her and her dog as they held tight grip on the fur of his neck.

'Yup, should be plenty more a that soon,' he replied, and she felt his body vibrate as he spoke.

'What is actually in Rumustica, besides trees and birds and rocks?' Lucy asked, considering it for the first time.

'Think that about covers it. Why do you want to go there?' he responded.

He couldn't see it, but Lucy's stare then became introspectively poignant and bitter. Hamish's cold commands were only days ago, but they felt like weeks, and still there was no reason he gave as to why she should follow them.

'I don't know. I was told I must,' she said, and Leo accepted this without further question.

In the early afternoon, they navigated what unbelievably appeared to be a track: a wide stretch of dirt, empty of vines and bushes and bracken, at least two feet in width that bent this way and that and led them on. This unlikely path, in an absurd end to her whirlwind, month-long venture in Josso Jungle, seemed to very gradually, lead them out.

The land at the jungle's sharp end, appeared to be another world existing beyond an ethereal, sunlit, curtain. At the path's end, where the straggly remnants of jungle stopped abruptly, a carpet of teal grass blanketed an undulating landscape that was more Scotland than Escallia Winters. This *was* Scotland in summer, or the end of a warmer spring, when the wisteria bloomed, when the robins were plentiful, and the meadows glistened greenly amid a clear crisp sky.

'Let me down,' she said to Leo, and he craned toward the ground and let her slide from his neck.

She looked up, and she squinted. Could it be possible for the sky to really be so blue, and so *vast*? The rolling grasslands spilled out before her like the promised land. She looked at Leo, and Crumbs, and the foreboding walls of jungle darkness just behind her, in a bid to assure herself this was certainly not Scotland. The sun in the sky was booming. The cerulean canvas above her was scattered with voluptuous cumulus clouds like mounds of volcanic plumes turned white. The teal grass was peppered with rocky outcrops, and ashen trees; mist-woods, with pale foliage. Just as plentiful on the landscape where the black trees with auburn foliage; the ink-woods. They looked the same as she'd imagined in her mind, when she'd deceptively described them to Star, pretending to recount a memory from life, instead of information from Yinsoo's book. But, now, here they were, just as she'd described.

'Is it insane to say that the sunshine feels delicious?' she asked Leo, having done a sort of ungainly pirouette, and Crumbs raced toward her, feeling her joy for the first time in days.

'Not as insane as cutting off your own foot and eating it,' replied Leo, and she decided not to continue the conversation.

They stopped at a lake to wash and drink. There were a great many in Rumustica, which Star had once told her, and they had already passed several before this one, but they weren't (in Leo's view) the right kind for stopping at. He gave no justification, but given he was carrying her, she had no cause to complain.

The lake's still waters sunk between three hills and were surrounded by stretches of long yellowing grass, where rabbits and other small mammals frolicked and hid. They ate a rabbit that Lucy caught, and roots that she pulled from the aqueous mud by the bank. Leo didn't much like rabbit, but he tolerated the roots. They did not rest for long.

'Leo, where did you learn to speak, well to speak the common tongue?' she asked him later that afternoon.

It was windy. The sun was setting to their right as they continued their progression north. Unwittingly, they were venturing up into a gradually rising range of mountains. They were traipsing along a path that formed between a series of disconnected boulders, interconnected by soft floral bushland, and slight, flimsy trees that managed to root themselves in crevices part way up rock walls. They were following the distant but distinct droning of rushing water that called them nearer. A waterfall might mean a cave or other enclosure, suitable to camp the night.

'I had a teacher. He was my friend. He taught me young,' Leo replied with a sorrowful sigh.

'A human teacher?'

'Well, he wasn't a bear, he was one of those roundish folk, from, I forget what it's called.'

'Archmond?'

'Yeah, that's it. He found me all alone because my mother had gone and left me, and he took to feed'n' me, and then he started telling me words, and getting me to make sounds not like my sounds, but like his sounds. He said his sounds were *words*. He was clever. He was ganna make up a farm somewhere near the coast he said. Fishing and farming. That's what he said.'

'What happened to him?' Lucy asked tentatively, but Leo was prevented from answering by the scene and events that then unfolded. They suddenly found themselves in a place of serene and splendid beauty.

They rounded a bend and came into an opening among the rocks where they could just make out the pool of water being replenished by the waterfall from above. To their right the land fell sharply down, and the view took in valley after valley. But the sun now hung low in the eastern sky, casting Rumustica's valleys ablaze, and the scene before them was momentarily cut with stripes of its warm red light. Lucy squinted, and stretched her hand outward to block the sun, as the petals and leaves of early autumn blew around her in perfumed gusts of air. Around the rocky pool, a flowering plant like wisteria, but apricot in colour, also bore chains of overripe fruit. The air was redolent with it.

Leo stepped forward and with their backs to the sun Lucy's eyes adjusted, and she realised with a shock that in the centre of this pretty pool, a girl was floating, naked. Her hair, long, and the colour difficult to discern with all the reddish light, floated around her. She was pale, slender, and probably older than Lucy by a few years at the very least. Her ears being submerged must have been why she hadn't heard them approach, as she was clearly alive; sweeping her arms back and forth in the water and smiling to herself, her eyes closed.

'Hey!' Lucy called out, her hand on Leo's shoulder urging him to keep a good distance, so as not to intrude on the young lady's privacy.

'Hey!' Lucy called again. The young lady didn't stir.

'Hello! Excuse me! Miss!' Lucy called even louder this time, and then plucked a seed pod from an overhanging branch and tossed it into the pool, just ahead of the woman. The water rippled around her. Her eyes opened then, and she came up some but was facing toward the waterfall and not the imminent sunset behind her where Lucy sat atop Leo.

'Hello there!' Lucy called out. The woman heard her then, because she turned her head, almost as quickly as a flinch, and with the same reactionary speed, she shot out of the pool, snatching a cloth from a branch and disappearing into the rocky bushland on the opposite side.

'Wait,' Lucy began, but she was already gone. Lucy need not say one word to Leo. He knew exactly what she was thinking and exactly what she wanted. Without so much as a whispered breath between them, in the same moment that the woman disappeared among the flowering trees, he shot off around the pool and after her.

Lucy was taken aback by how rampantly Leo was able to move, she hadn't thought of pandas as great sprinters, but he thundered across that crumbling bushy terrain with ever greater strides and bounds. She clutched tightly into his fur as he rushed down the steeply sloping hillside, Crumbs trailing after them, but the woman at the bottom had already mounted a horse and was galloping away across the valley. Lucy's heart fluttered with something unspeakable, incomprehensible: she had to get to that young woman. It was no moment for logic. There was no examination of why, or of the practicalities that might justify this sudden immense desire, there was just desire.

'Keep after her,' Lucy implored.

And so, he did. In sunset's strawberry haze they pursued the young woman in and out of pockets of woodland and bushland. Across Rumustica's undulating hills they would lose her and find her again in turn. It was a chaotic pursuit, and all the while Lucy's heart beat faster with a sensation she could not appreciate: *find her.* The glare of the sunset blinded them in a rhythmic procession of glare and shadow. They would lose her to the shadow of the hills, but they would pause to listen for the gallop of her horse, triumphant in this silent serene mountainscape.

They would scan the valley below them with each new hill they came to the crest of, and in some marvel of fate Lucy would glimpse her again. But it felt like more than chance. It was that Lucy could almost sense her, could sense where this woman was going, that saw them finding her time and time again. After every few breaths of motion she felt as though she could feel the frightened panic of the young woman's heart, and she would steer Leo in that direction where it pulled. And each time, momentarily without fail, they would see a flash of her long hair or her cream dress. And then the chase would continue. The woodlands darkened as the afternoon drew on, but colour lingered around every corner, and in flashes of it, was the cream dress on a mottled horse.

When the sun had finally set, in twilight's fading whimsy, it seemed over the next hill they might soon lose her to the impending darkness. But Lucy, still full of adrenal instinct and desire, edged Leo up and around the side of a steep rocky hillside, high above the valley.

When they got their bearings and scanned the scenery, there, in a pokey corner valley below, a woodland looked empty and still. But Lucy could sense something; whatever was driving her on was driving her toward that sharp depression. This drive was more than a desperation for food and shelter, she assured herself briskly; she hoped it was given how severely she felt the need to pursue this female stranger. She studied the landscape. They had somehow climbed quite high onto this rocky mountainside, either that or the valley had very suddenly fallen away beneath them. To the north and to the east, the valley jutted out with mountainous peaks and pocket woodlands well into the horizon, between the shadows of slender lakes. Remnants of pink and orange swirls still lingered on the horizon's mountainous border.

She looked down again into the small corner of the valley beneath them. On this windy evening, the trees bent and swayed more than they usually did, and Lucy saw a momentary slither of grey, a shade too blue to be rock. It was lost again behind the trees the same second she saw it.

'Down there,' she whispered to Leo. It seemed improbable, because the hillside was steep, and having ridden horses herself in her youth, she couldn't see how a galloping horse could navigate this passage. But in their haste, they had come a cumbersome route, and grassy pastures also gradually sloped up into the micro-valley. The rocky cliff that they'd found themselves on was not the only way in.

When they emerged into the valley some fifteen minutes later, it was still light enough to see. The twilight was not yet drowning in dark, cobalt shadows, though an indigo film was just starting to wash over everything.

They walked through a pine grove to where Lucy had seen the fleck of blue-ish grey swept up by branches, but there seemed nothing but trees down here, and it was silent.

Nothing stirred.

The trees were sparse enough that she could clearly see the sky starting to twinkle with starlight. The wide space between their trunks was empty. But as she again followed her instincts back to the centre, she saw the dense thicket of mist-woods and conifers that she had for no good reason, disregarded just before. This time she pushed through them.

Her instincts were correct. Enclosed and hidden within the hedges of slender trees, was a glade that housed a weatherboard cottage.

'Whose house is this?' asked Leo, rather loudly, as Crumbs rushed excitedly to the entrance.

'Shh,' Lucy responded, carefully approaching the open doorway, hand on her hilt. She took a step inside but cautiously. Inside was dark. It seemed empty.

'Hello,' she called out, quietly, the empty cottage and impending nightfall was starting to frighten her, 'there's no horse here either,' she said to Leo stepping back outside.

'Where else could she have gone though? A house in the valley, and she's not in it. Must be hers. Someone else's, they'd be in it you'd think,' Leo reasoned.

Lucy tilted her head, surprised that she agreed with him. 'Maybe if we wait here, she'll come back.'

'Girl!' Lucy called out toward the trees and their shadows, 'please come back, I promise I won't bother you, I'm no trouble, I just want somewhere to sleep.'

The wind tore through the willowy branches.

'Maybe if she don't come back, we can sleep in there anyway,' suggested Leo.

'I will sleep in there,' Lucy corrected, turning back to him, the detail of his face was fast being lost to dusk, but for now she could still see him quite clearly, 'you wouldn't fit through the door.'

'That's mean,' whined Leo.

'It's not mean, it's just the truth,' Lucy replied, peering this way and that into the trees around the cottage. Leo gasped, but when she turned back to muster up an apology for her factual statement, she saw he was pointing behind her, back at the cottage.

Emerging from behind the cottage, two delicate hands gripped the weatherboard corner of the house. The girl, the young woman rather, leaned outward to peer at them, very tentatively. She stepped forward a little more, but she still clung somewhat to the side corner of the cottage. A demure face, a slender, delicate frame.

At the sight of her Lucy quivered. All her hairs stood on end at once. Inexplicably, she knew instantly who this was. Her mind tried to doubt it with rationality, but the knowledge was instinctual, and caught in her throat the same way as those intense instincts that had led her here. There was enough light that she could, at this closeness, truly appreciate the colour of the girl's long wild hair. It was the softest, pinkest shade of red she had ever seen.

This was the missing princess. The princess everyone thought was dead.

Standing there with her fragile gait leaning against the cottage, her almond shaped eyes scanned Lucy with an inquisition full of a fear that was somehow enchanting. Her eyes were mesmerizing, her complexion was creamy and bright, and her tall slender figure with those endless legs was so feminine, that the beauty of her not only left Lucy momentarily speechless, she felt her own sense of self-worth diminish in her presence.

'You're the missing princess,' Lucy whispered, astonished.

'I am not,' she replied quickly, her eyes darting around, checking if others had come too. But her initial denial didn't register with Lucy.

'What are you… what are you doing out here?' Lucy asked looking around at the cottage, the chipped wood of the weatherboard, the moss growing on parts of the roof. She took in the girl's tattered dress. She certainly didn't look like royalty. The once white dress had a yellowish tint of age. It was stained with beige marks at the collar and the hem.

At nearly twenty-seven years of age, she was a good deal older than Lucy, but her precise age was imperceptible on sight alone, because she glowed with a particular vitality.

Those almond eyes of hers narrowed in on Lucy. 'Who are you?' she asked. Her countenance was frightened, defensive.

Still grappling with pangs of regret from starting out dishonestly with Hamish and the others, Lucy told the truth.

'My name is Lucy, I was brought into this world by the wizards of Archmond: Soleman and Ron,' Lucy said.

'Archmond?' the girl repeated, stepping forward a little. The word seemed to pique her interest and disarm her at the same time.

'Yes. The wizards wanted me to find you, to have you take the throne from your sister in—' Lucy began but the girl snatched up a wooden stake from the ground and pointed it toward Lucy.

'No! Never! I am not going back there. I am no longer playing that game.' This inadvertent admission of identity was voiced with as much conviction as she could muster, but her voice, like her body, was trembling.

Lucy put her hands out in front of her. 'Okay, wait, listen. I was brought into this world by the wizards to find you, but I don't care what they want anymore. All I want now is get home, back to my world. I'm not going to do anything. Everyone I've met so far thinks you're dead. That doesn't have to change. I just want somewhere to sleep.'

The girl relaxed her stance. Still gripping the stake, she let if fall limply by her side.

'Your world?' she asked, a moment later. Lucy nodded.

Cherry looked around then. She took in Leo for the first time, looking him up and down.

'Hello, my name is Leo,' he said proudly. It had been many long years since he had a name to introduce himself with, or anyone to introduce himself to.

Cherry darted back in shock. 'It can speak?'

'Yup,' Leo said, nodding.

Lucy laughed. 'I guess talking pandas aren't so common in this world either.'

'What is a panda?' Cherry asked.

Lucy shrugged. 'In the world I come from that's what we call these white and black bears; pandas. But Leo had never heard of that word before either so...'

Cherry looked him over quietly for several moments. She blinked. Those enchanting almond eyes of hers, with their golden brown colour, took Lucy in with curiosity once more, but then she turned back to the fascinating new creature.

'Where are you from?' she asked Leo, but it was put so delicately it suggested he may quite reasonably be disinclined to answer.

'I think am from this world. 'Til I met her, I was in the jungle, but it's getting a bit weird in there, and I needed some air.'

Calmer now and no longer feeling threatened, Cherry asked about the city that had once been her refuge.

'What is it like in Archmond now?'

'On the Wooden Floor Borders, the people seemed well, most of them, but in the Hills they're sick,' Lucy said.

'From the attack?' she guessed glumly, looking at the ground.

'That's right.'

'Oh,' Cherry said, quietly, still tremulous, and then clasped her hands in front of her, as if waiting to see what else Lucy wanted.

Lucy exhaled awkwardly. 'Listen, I am trying to get home but right now I'm… I guess I'm somewhat lost. I haven't slept under a roof for two nights and I am so tired. I know I've no right to ask you this but please, could I come in and rest? I won't be any trouble. I can help in any way you ask, I…' Lucy trailed off, begging did not come naturally to her.

Cherry in no way wanted to take Lucy in, but she knew she couldn't refuse her. The girl looked ravaged, and if she had been in the jungle as the strange talking beast claimed, then she may well have been. Cherry had been through the jungle once down the river by boat, it was no place for a young girl. Cherry nodded with a forced a smile, and then Lucy followed her into the cottage.

Inside, with the lanterns lit, the cottage appeared both well-built and well-kept. There was an outdoor water tank connected to a pump that provided running water, though Cherry was frugal with the amount she put in Lucy's cup. The kitchen was well stocked: pots, pans, knives, ladles, bowls, whisks, plates, cutlery, mugs, and saucers. There was a spice rack on the wall lined with jars of varying sizes, their contents obscured by the brown colour of the glass. A wood-stove at the kitch-en's centre was used for cooking as well as warming, evidenced by the pan sitting atop it.

On the other side of the cottage was a bed, and a floor layered with overlapping rugs and scattered with large cushions. Tiny potted plants lined the windowsills on that side. A round iron table seemed to act as a divide for the two spaces.

'How long have you lived here?' Lucy asked.

'I am not sure exactly,' Cherry muttered.

'But you live here alone?'

Cherry looked up and nodded. She was looking for something in a chest beside the bed. Lucy was still so utterly perplexed by all of this. 'But I don't understand. Why are you living out here?'

'Because I *hoped* no one would find me,' she responded, tersely, pulling a blanket from the chest, pushing the garments and other things back down and slamming the chest closed again.

It was indeed a clandestine setting. In the context of the Morgessen Range, that Lucy and Leo had unknowingly traversed as they pursued the princess here, the V-shaped valley where the cottage lay was but a microcosm. It was merely a slender but widening depression part way down a sheer slope, which deceptively from afar presented as a ledge atop a perversely steep crevice with an impenetrable thicket of trees. It was only on close inspection, that the gentle pastures leading up to the level grove revealed themselves.

In the resounding echo the thumping wood of the chest made, Lucy got the clear impression that questioning the princess's reasons for being here was not welcome, and it was already apparent that her presence itself was not particularly welcome either.

Lucy nodded and looked around. 'And so you built this?' she asked, changing tack.

Cherry shook her head, lightly. She was still sitting stiffly on the edge of the bed, the blanket in her lap. She barely looked in the direction of the young girl, sitting by the table, or her dog, now sniffing around the cottage. She glanced occasionally out the window at the shadowy outline of the panda beast, glumly curled up at the base of the mist-wood tree that leaned over the babbling brook.

'I just found it. The door was unlocked and there was everything in here, but there was no one here. I waited,' she said, looking across the flickering candlelight toward Lucy then, but looking away the instant their eyes met, 'but no one ever came.' After an eerie pause, she added, 'In a way I am still waiting.'

Cherry set about fixing something for the two of them to eat. She did so in silence. She filled the pot with water and placed it over the wood-stove, increasing the heat. She fetched vegetables from a wooden box on the far side of the kitchen's bench, which was overlain with a wet cloth. Then she took a wooden board and a knife and began cutting them. All the while neither of them spoke. Lucy was brimming with questions but she kept objecting to them as she phrased them in her mind. Cherry made her extremely uncomfortable, and what's more, it was clear that her presence was an intrusion. So she drew breath as though she were about to speak several times, but ultimately said nothing. Crumbs, on the floor beside the wooden chair where she sat, in the middle of the cottage between the kitchen and sleeping area, whimpered petulantly, excited by the smell of food.

But while the awkwardness for Lucy was unpleasant, it was outweighed by the pleasant sensation of being inside. The warmth of the fire amid the fresh night wind, the smell of salted food and the feeling of ease that came with once again being indoors, filled Lucy with a sleepy contentment.

As they ate the boiled vegetables and the stale unleavened bread, Cherry observed her new guest with reserved intrigue. While Cherry did not relish having to provide hospitality to this strange unannounced guest, she was interesting to look at. Cherry had been living in her mountain cottage for over two years, and yet it was Lucy that seemed like the wild one. Covered in small cuts and bruises, with her dark hair smelling of mildew, it was believable that she had spent a good while in the jungle beyond the valley.

Lucy sensed the judgment in Cherry's brief glimpses. 'Perhaps there's somewhere I can wash before I sleep?'

Cherry merely nodded, but she didn't elaborate on where or how Lucy might do this.

'You say you come from another world. How is that? How did you get here?' Cherry asked after they had both finished their food. Unlike everyone in Mathew's team, there was not the slightest implication of disbelief in Cherry's tone, and her eyes were wide and waiting on an answer, as if Lucy might be about to give her directions to the nearest town.

'I don't know,' said Lucy, disturbed, both because the question plagued her as well, but also because Cherry's acceptance of her origins was in such stark contrast to her aggressive interrogation aboard the River Princess. She was unsure how to absorb it.

The candlelight flickered. Cherry looked away. Her silence suggested that Lucy's answer was unsatisfactory at best, or disappointing even. So Lucy added more detail.

'A man in a parkland near where I live, well where I used to live, a man I'd never seen before, grabbed my hand and opened a metal latch in the ground that I'd also never seen before. After that I woke up in Archmond. Soleman and Ron told me that they brought me here, to help them to find you really.' She paused there, feeling out the reaction to that part, but Cherry did not seem rattled and was still looking away. 'But then again, an old woman in Yerkey also told me she brought me here, or invited me,' said Lucy, shutting her eyes, and shaking her head, still amused by the absurdity of all the conflicting information.

Cherry stood up, collected the plates, and began to wipe them over with a wash cloth by the sink.

'Where is Yerkey?' was all she asked.

Lucy was frazzled at this, of all things, being the princess's only question, and took a moment to respond.

'Ahh, it's a settlement. A large one but an ancient one in the frozen tundra.'

Cherry, having now cleaned over the plates and the knife and the cutting board, only sighed with a weary disinterest, and said she would sleep soon, implying that Lucy should too.

Later, as Lucy lay awake in the bed, glad for the girl's warm body beside her after having washed herself briskly in the cold brook, the significance of the evening finally dawned on her. She had accidentally done the impossible. She had achieved exactly what Archmond asked her to do. She had *found* Princess Cherry, a person nearly everyone believed to be dead, and whom Archmond wanted so desperately to be queen. And yet, the exiled princess would not go to Meta Emery, and she had no intention of being its queen. What was she to make of this?

Outside, the distant wail of the wind continued, jostling the tops of the trees as it skipped over the valley and up the rocky hillside behind them. The frogs in the brook croaked in turn.

Chapter 7

Sweetness and light

Cherry :// *Cherise ://* *Cherie : sweet fruit, darling, sweetheart.*
Lucy :// *Lucinda : //* *Lucia : of light, bringer of light, light.*

*L*ucy roused early the next morning. Despite the blessed warmth and softness of the bed for which she was so grateful, she was too aware of the imposition her presence created. Too aware of herself in the bed. She was conscious of every breath, every movement, every sigh. When the morning light started to fill the cottage, the sleeping figure beside her did not stir. Lucy rose, determined to dampen the imposition of her stay, and changed from the nightshirt the princess had lent her, into the spare clothes in her backpack, gifted from Star.

Outside, in the milky light of dawn, Lucy took in the blue-grey cottage properly. Yellow roses bloomed on wild unruly bushes, either side of the front door. To the left of the cottage, an extensive kitchen garden, with vine-covered lattices, fruit trees, and rows and rows of alternate vegetables, was bustling with tiny visiting birds. Behind the garden, in the far left corner of the cottage, the curvature of the red water tank could be seen. Its slender pipe, or pipes, as they joined together, jutted awkwardly toward the kitchen window. On the sill of this window, the two frogs from the brook, (on the opposite side of the cottage) now sat and overlooked the garden, silently.

She realised too that the princess's horse *was* here. In fact, there were two horses, grazing freely in the pasture beyond the water tank, behind the cottage. They grazed about in the stretch of long grass that lay between the back of the cottage, and the steep valley walls that closed them all in. But the cottage was more functional than Lucy could even then appreciate. Against the back wall of the cottage a chicken coop provided much needed protein. The brook, dotted with mist-woods, supplemented the water tower in providing a constant source of fresh water for drinking and bathing, trailing down from the mountain lake above. There was also a soft stretch of grass in front of the cottage, where on clear days the glade allowed pools sunlight and blue sky, before the surrounding conifers and ink-woods of the grove sealed them in from the north. Within that very grove, was an endless supply of wood and forest fruit.

Before she set off, Lucy first went to see Leo. 'Leo,' she said, gently rousing him.

He grumbled as he woke up. 'What? What? Are we leaving?'

'Shush, the princess is still sleeping. And no. I am going to hunt down a small mammal or a large bird or something. It's better you stay here though, you're not very… well… quiet,' she said, quietly.

'Well, I don't want any rabbit again, I don't like eating things with eyes,' Leo whined, disgusted.

'Fine. I'm sure I can bring back some of those roots again.'

'They were okay,' he sulked and then stood up, stretching, and scratching his head. 'Maybe I'll find some fruit in these woods.'

Lucy shrugged and went to leave, Crumbs at her heel, when Leo called out, before remembering himself and asking quietly. 'Should I come back though? After?'

He was so painfully insecure in his question she almost changed her plans and went with him to find fruit, but she was determined to be a valuable guest and not a burden to her royal host. As to his question, she knew if she left the decision up to him, he would read that as a lack of wanting on her part.

'Of course,' she said instead firmly. 'We can compare what we've seen in these woods.'

Leo liked that answer, and with a dopey smile, he turned and went galumphing off through the conifers.

As Lucy made her own way off through the conifers in the opposite direction, she discovered the gradual pastures that sloped down from this eclipsed pocket of narrow woodland, into the sweeping hills and greater valleys of Rumustica. Cherry's minute valley was a V-shaped fracture in the Morgessen Range, one of the more extensive mountain ranges across Rumustica, though not nearly the tallest. The valley faced north east, looking across a wide network of valleys consisting of undulating meadows and lakes, toward the Dolomire Ranges. The unique vantage meant from the eastern edge of the pasture sweeping down from the hidden valley, you could look north west and glimpse the boggy pass between the Dolomire and the end of the Morgessen Range. From the western edge you could look east and see past the eastern peak of the Dolomires, to the hills beyond them. There were somewhere between seven to eleven distinct mountain ranges in Rumustica, (depending on who you asked, given there was debate as to whether the peaks just east of the Alabaster Range should be classified separately, and similar debates surrounded the Karrichore Range) thirty-three lakes, and around fifty peaks. Naturally in the fresh dawn Lucy knew none of this, nor the names of the defining landmarks she anchored herself with.

She made her way down into the expansive valley and staked out the furry creatures of the grasslands and the birds that dotted the black branches of the ink-woods, but they were too small and too fast. She also loathed seizing upon anything particularly small or vulnerable, as it made the hunting feel all the more monstrous.

She crossed the grasses and moved through an area of young bushland, where, by a natural pond, she saw a flightless bird with a plumpness and a gobble that was not unlike a turkey; a yakko. She set upon it deftly, but it broke from her clutches, and she was thereafter too put off by its scurried panic and terror and ultimately made her way back to the grasslands.

Just as the morning brightened into full colour, she managed to pin down a perot (a long slinky ferret type creature) before it could scurry back into its burrow. It was hardly the game to offer royalty. Returning with it felt like failure, but time had run out, the yellow sun was high over the green hills, and the princess would be awake now. She told herself that tomorrow she would not be so squeamish with the fat gobbling bird and they could have drumsticks with spices. She could almost salivate at that thought: spiced poultry, company, fire.

As she traversed back up the slopes and came back into the woodland again, she muttered things to Crumbs, in the way she often did when they weren't stalking prey or hiding from danger. She was justifying the use to be made of the meagre perot, and the meat that could be carved from it, and the flavour it would take on over smoke. But as she muttered something about how they would cook the perot, she heard her own voice echo back to her.

'I can make a spit over the fire,' she heard her own voice say, more than several moments after she'd said it. She looked at Crumbs, just to check that this world had not somehow bewitched him as well, but by her feet he panted, his slobbering tongue outstretched. Then she heard it again, her voice, and saw a warm pinkish light floating between the conifer branches just above her eye level.

'*I can make a spit over the fire.*'

She shuddered. This was not like when she heard the sassy bird speak, or the doleful panda, this was but a light, and it was *her voice*.

The light, about the size of a marshmallow, hopped across the spindly spines of the branches, considerately and deliberately, with consciousness. Then it paused, and she almost felt as though it was both breathing and looking at her, as the light dimmed and brightened to the pace of her own breath. Then in the next second it shot off through the trees, and was gone, like a shooting star.

When Lucy arrived back at the cottage, still dazed and exhilarated from the phenomena, Cherry was in the garden. She seemed surprised but not startled by Lucy's return.

Listlessly she rose from her knees in the dirt, putting the cultivator down beside her, and waited for Lucy to come closer before she spoke, as if unaccustomed to raising her voice.

'I thought you had left,' she said, still vague and indirect in her manner, but then added, 'At first I did. But I saw your satchel was still here. I suspect you would not leave without that.' By this she meant Lucy's backpack.

Lucy looked around, 'Leo isn't back yet?'

Cherry shook her head lightly, then her eyes fell, saw the limp perot in Lucy's hand and gasped.

'What happened to it?' she asked, both wincing and drawing her hands to her mouth, but before Lucy could reply she then saw the knife. 'Did you? Did you do this?' The question smacked of disbelief. It was clear she was aghast.

'I…' Lucy was taken aback by the reaction, 'I wanted to bring us something substantial for supper as a… as a contribution. I can prepare it all. I know how to build a large fire, and I know how to skin an animal. Well, not this animal specifically, but once you've done one—'

'Skin it?' Cherry's eyes stayed on the creature. 'That is horrid.'

'Well… we can't really eat it… otherwise,' Lucy replied sheepishly, sounding confused.

'I will not eat this,' Cherry said, flabbergasted, before coming closer and taking the dead creature from Lucy ever so gently.

'All that is. All that was. All that will be,' she whispered into its dead ears, before walking off with it through the garden. She picked up her spade from the cluttered wooden table beneath the window where the frogs had earlier sat and crossed the garden to the space between it and the unfenced paddock where the horses still grazed. She began to dig.

'What are you doing?' Lucy asked gingerly, walking between the rows of potato flowers.

'I am giving him.' Cherry checked it was a him. 'I am giving him a proper burial,' she muttered, still digging. Her tone was cold, but no more so than it had been thus far.

Lucy didn't know what to say. She considered that perhaps this particular animal or this type of animal had some sort of significance to the princess, one she should have known about? Lucy wondered if she should ask. Cherry certainly acted as though her outrage needed no explanation. But at this moment Leo returned and he came around from the front side of the house, the thumping of his gait perforating the awkwardness.

'Hallo,' Leo called, sonorously. The white fur of his neck was painted red with fruit juices, so it was clear he had found what he sought. Lucy shot him a half smile, but then turned back to Cherry, who was now patching up the dirt with the back of the spade. She whispered something softly over the grave. It was inaudible, and intentionally so.

'What did you say?' asked Leo boorishly, but Lucy gave him a look and he was quiet.

Finally, Cherry stood. 'There is enough to be feared by everyone in this world, without the creatures having to fear us as well.'

'I… ahhh… I'm not sure I understand your meaning,' Lucy replied.

'I will not eat anything that ever had a head and legs and breathed and feared.'

'Me neither!' agreed Leo, spiritedly.

'I… I didn't know that,' Lucy began, intending to apologise, but she stopped because it was clear her ignorance would not assuage the upset. She felt cheated then too, because she too had so hated the act of killing, but she had been forcibly taught to desensitise herself from it, to prove herself worthy by doing so, and now having done so, was being punished by someone more like her original self.

'It is too hateful,' Cherry went on in little louder than a whisper, 'I grow enough food to keep from hunger. No creatures need to die.'

'I'm sorry. I just wanted to help. I felt I couldn't very well eat your food without providing some as well. I didn't think to grow anything… If I'd known you didn't eat animals, I wouldn't have…' again she found herself unable to finish her thoughts.

Cherry said nothing but threw a soft, almost insincere, smile in Lucy's direction. She walked back over to the table, returning the spade, and then went back to the dirt where she'd left the cultivator and began finishing the harvesting she had started before Lucy's return.

Lucy would later learn just how diverse Cherry's garden-come-hobby-farm was. Aside from the variety of hearty vegetables, legumes, and sweet fruits, in days to come she would be introduced to Cherry's goats, when they returned as they did periodically, from their traipsing over the adjacent mountain. Cherry maintained they were in fact not hers at all, but were free, and allowed her to milk them in exchange for her care of the lush grass they ate, and the tranquility they enjoyed in her stream. The chickens, Cherry claimed, were also 'free' but they wandered less than the goats, and she sheltered them in their coop behind the cottage only for their own protection from the likes of hawks and sharp-toothed predators.

Much to Leo's disappointment, Lucy decided to sit inside the cottage to escape the tension lingering in the garden air, rather than cross to the brook on the other side of the cottage. For a while he sought her attention by splashing his paws in the brook and making water droplets land on the window pane. She was cheered by his playfulness, but she remained inside, wounded by her interaction, and confused by the situation she found herself in. Crumbs though, decided to prefer

Leo's company to that of his now moody master, so Leo's loneliness was abated.

Contrary to the initial impression of stoicism she created, Cherry was quite a joyful young lady. She had developed an uncanny ability to see the best in both others, and in situations. Rather than lamenting about her exiled existence, she had taken to seeing it as a precious gift of peace, not bestowed on many. She had made similar resolutions as a young girl about her life as a foreigner in Archmond. She took great pleasure in many simple things: water, sunshine, nourishment, and sleep. She was slow to anger, but kept her misgivings to herself, and seeing all emotion as weakness, showed it only to those she truly trusted. In some ways, in their reticence and distrust of others, the two women were more similar than they would ever come to realise.

Lucy sat at the iron table for a while, listening to the barking and the splashing, and the periodic thud of the cultivator into the ground. The contrast of both the outside's gaiety and its airy brightness, against the shadow of the cottage, was at first dreary. For a while, all Lucy could do was stare through the open door into the blue and green of the outside world and wonder how it was possible that she found herself here. But eventually Lucy's attention was drawn to the book at the centre of the table.

Strange that she hadn't noticed it before. But it could not have been there when they ate the previous night, because its imposing size meant it took up nearly the whole table. It was clearly ancient, its leather binding heavily worn. She went to open it but hesitated. Perhaps this would be another social folly? Everything she had done so far seemed to have unsettled her host. Lucy looked outside the kitchen window to her right. The beautiful girl was now adjusting a vine on the trellis. Even this finicky task was being done with such poise that Lucy felt uncouth just being seated. She sighed, realising they were worlds apart. She should read the book anyway.

Lucy thumbed the pages. They contained passages of seemingly unconnected script, sometimes with diagrams on the opposing page. The text was centred, and somewhat rhythmical if you could make sense of the grammar. While most of the words she could gauge, the markings like apostrophes seemed to break known words into new obscurities.

'What is this?' Lucy asked.

Cherry came inside just as Lucy had turned to a page that was revealing the nature of the book. Caught red-handed, Lucy could only make her curiosity known.

Cherry's gaze fell upon the book. If she was irritated by Lucy handling it, she didn't show it. She came to the table and with her index finger on the page Lucy was reading, flipped the book shut so Lucy could read the title. It seemed patronising, but her temperament didn't suggest she meant to be.

'Lores of Terra,' Lucy read out the title.

'It was here when I got here, like everything else,' Cherry muttered, and went to wash her hands, 'but I have been reading it,' she added moments after.

'These read like spells, or curses,' Lucy exclaimed.

'They are. Charms. I have been trying to learn them, use them.'

'You're a witch?'

Cherry turned back, her expression seemed to regard the question mockingly.

'But you're working magic?' Lucy rephrased.

Again, Cherry derided this notion. 'I just follow the instructions, but not very well it seems. I did a concealment spell over the cottage, or rather I tried to.'

'You don't think it worked?'

'Well, you found me, did you not?'

Lucy nodded rather hesitantly. 'I did but, it was by such chance, and the...' she stopped to listen outside. She could hear the horses neighing, she could hear the chickens, the brook. She remembered the incessant croaking of the frogs the previous evening.

'I almost didn't find you, this valley seemed so hidden—'

'The spell did not make the valley,' Cherry cut in, but quietly, as if to herself.

'But when I came down here there was no sound. It was so eerily quiet I could have thought there was no life here at all. But today, I can hear everything.'

Cherry sat opposite Lucy and put her head in her hand. 'Maybe it only half worked,' she considered.

'Which would mean you can make some magic,' Lucy suggested.

Cherry looked at her then, and it seemed they were making progress because her almond-shaped hazel eyes did not dart away.

'We all have our own magic,' she said eventually with a wry smile, 'like you with your cuts and bruises yesterday, and today you are new again. I cannot do that.'

Lucy was stricken for a moment but then looked at her arms. She had stopped taking stock of her cuts and their healing. She had become used to it. But it was true that she had been very scratched by their ascent out of the jungle the previous morning, and today her skin bore no markings. But the talk of magic then suddenly reminded Lucy of what she had been brimming about an hour earlier.

'What other magic is in this forest?' Lucy asked.

The princess shrugged. She seemed to know but found the answer tiresome.

'I saw a light,' Lucy elaborated, 'when I was coming back this morning. A small bouncing light that echoed my voice.'

Contrarily, this got the princess's attention. She sat up straight. 'A light? Where was this bouncing light?'

'Just at the edge of the woodland where it slopes down again.'

Cherry went to the doorway of the cottage and peered out. 'Just one?' she asked. She was excited rather than alarmed.

'Just one.'

'Hmm,' Cherry murmured with an amused grin, and went to fetch a glass of water. 'Sounds like a lotus sprite, but I have not seen one in a long time. I have been looking for them. I had thought there were no more.'

Cherry smiled and stared out the window. It was nearly noon now and the frogs had left the windowsill. She brought a glass of water to Lucy and disconcertingly watched her drink it. Then she fetched a basket from the corner of the cottage and emptied the rags from it onto the bed. She came over and handed the basket to Lucy, then walked toward the door.

When Lucy didn't follow, she turned from the doorway, hand on her hip. 'You said you wanted to help?'

As days turned into nights, neither Cherry nor Lucy ever mentioned the prospect of her departure, or any potential onward travel plans. In fact, the talk between them contained nothing substantial at all. The comfortableness around each other grew, but Cherry remained taciturn, and the conversation was as minimal as it was trivial. After teaching Lucy about the garden on the first day, Cherry taught her about pickling, and showed her where to fetch wood nearby. As several days went by, they unconsciously fell into a routine. But they set about their tasks with limited intimacy. It was in no way acrimonious, but the rapport between them remained fleeting and stilted.

But despite this stunted growth in friendship, from as early as their third day together, Cherry started to see the benefits of Lucy's presence. As it turned out, Lucy's sword, the sharpness of which cut through branches like butter, made the collection of firewood much easier than the use of the rusted axe that had, like most things, come with the cottage. And despite her apparent wildness, Lucy had some wisdom, and had taught Cherry about sharpening blades and preventing rust. The former of which was something Lucy herself had only recently learnt from Gin.

Leo too, remained in the vicinity of the cottage day after day, lingering, with no sign he would ever leave. He had no reason to. This was home now as much as anywhere else had ever been. He had no propensity for making long-term plans. He had no more expectation of this being permanent, than he had any expectation of it being transient. Expectations in this sense did not occur to him. Such long-term ideations were not part of the repertoire of his internal processes. The days came and the days went. But for now, he was glad to have the company of both the humans and the other unspeaking creatures that surrounded them.

One night, when Cherry stirred in her sleep to the sound of a sharp noise (that she later reasoned was likely just the yawning of a nearby branch) she found herself returning to sleep easily, readily. This was a welcome change. In the past she might have rushed to the window to wait or slipped covertly from the back door of the cottage to hide with terror in the trees and watch to see if the men in red uniforms had come. But now she sunk calmly back into slumber with the knowledge the girl sleeping beside her had a sword and could use it. Thinking on it in the morning she realised that all her nights of sleep had been more restful since this wild girl arrived. Not that she told Lucy any of this.

The first substantial conversation between the two of them occurred one night after dinner. It was still early autumn, as Lucy had not been with Cherry more than a fortnight, but it was cold out, and the fire was a great pleasure.

Lucy was cutting fruit for what would be a dessert somewhere between an apple crumble or pie, depending on how it turned out. It was entirely Lucy's idea, Cherry having not been familiar with this particular dish. Lucy intended to use the left over flat bread from the pantry as the pastry or crumble. The bread itself was made from the grains that also grew in the garden, that Cherry ground and stored herself, having learnt how to do so, she said, from that same peculiar book. The fruit for the crumble or pie was not apple, which was not a known word in this world as far as Cherry knew, but a slightly more sour equivalent that Cherry referred to as a ferneara. Without sugar, and given the sourness of the fruit and the stale flavourlessness of the flat bread, Lucy was not confident as to how much this could be classified as a dessert. But there was a sweet nectar made from berries which she would put over the ferneara to make the dish more pleasant.

'Cooked fruit is not so unusual, I know, and yet, the only fruit dessert I recall having was in the palace: plums stewed in wine,' Cherry said from where she sat at the iron table, contently watching Lucy cut. It was a particularly especial novelty, being cooked for.

'Plums?' Lucy said, and laughed, remembering her last morning in Lockerby with Asha. 'So, some things are the same.'

Cherry only nodded, staring into her glass of port. This was the first time she had opened one of the many bottles stored in the makeshift cellar outside the cottage. She was not overly familiar with alcohol, and her suggestion of opening the bottle was purely an impulsive reaction to Lucy's offer to make dessert.

'My father liked plums a lot,' Cherry continued down the memory lane dreamily, 'he could even make the dish himself, which is not usual... for a king.'

In nearly a fortnight this was the most Cherry had ever shared freely about her father or her life before this cottage. Lucy glanced away from the chopping board, only dimly lit by the candles and the firelight, to see that Cherry's expression was warm and not sorrowful. This encouraged her.

'What was he like? Your father?' Lucy asked, she had been reluctant to ask about the princess's past, given both her reclusive persona and the sensitivity that naturally surrounds dead parents, but Cherry's talk of happy memories made it seem the perfect moment, if ever there was one, to delve.

'Oh, he was wonderful,' Cherry sighed. 'He was always so happy. He was so happy, that it was hard for him to appear stern. Although I am told there were times when he was angry, in Dynasty Council meetings. That was a side of him I would never see. But generally, it was hard for him to be hard. My mother was better at that. Which is strange because she was not of royal blood, yet she was the one who seemed more suited to the role. My father, he hated the politics of being king, but in a way...' she paused, reflecting on this almost for the first time, 'that is what made people love him. That is probably why he built such alliances as he did. He was genuine, and transparent.'

Lucy put the fernearas into the clay pot and covered them with the juices of the sweeter red fruits, before beginning to break the bread to place on top.

'You seem to remember a lot about him,' Lucy said tentatively. She wanted to ask if Cherry had had this information passed on from others, but didn't know quite how to pose the question, *'But weren't you only ten when he died?'*

'I only truly remember some things, but they fit well with other stories I have heard about him,' Cherry explained. Outside the night winds raged again, silencing the brook, and making the windows rattle.

'And what about your mother?' Lucy asked, eager to keep it going.

'She was light-filled, but I did not know her as well as my father. She was quite... withdrawn. Serious. Outside of her ladies, she did not like to see people often. I have no memories of her playing with my sisters and I. We went from the wet nurse to the ayah. My mother saw us in formal settings only... I think. I remember a time, it was in a glorious place, it was not the throne room so it must have been her chambers, and we were told by our ayah before we went in, told very strictly, not to climb on her,' Cherry stopped to laugh, but Lucy could not see what was funny, 'but when we went in she picked up Gloria straight away and cuddled her, and oh, Abbie cried. Oh, she cried.'

Lucy put the clay dish of bread-covered fruit into the wood stove. 'Because your sister was picked up and she wasn't?'

Cherry controlled her laughter. 'I suppose. But Abbie was always such a sook. I remember that. I remember her always crying or sulking. But my mother was not mean. No, she was not a mean woman, she was just, she was very serious. Very quiet. She did not play games. But my father did. He played and he helped to teach us, and he showed us many things around the mountains. Both before and after Gloria died, I feel like he was always there. And then when he died… when *they* died,' she corrected herself, 'then it was like there was nothing. There was no one. I was alone.'

Lucy's gothic dream in Archmond Castle was at the forefront of her mind, but as she took her own glass of port and joined Cherry at the table, she felt she daren't mention it now, if ever. The princess only now seemed comfortable enough to share these private details of her past, and that itself may have only been a consequence of the token dram of port she'd consumed. Hearing the strange girl who turned up at your home seeking shelter, claim to have once had an intimate dream about your family's darkest moments, was unlikely to be well received.

Instead, Lucy tried to lighten things. 'But what about the rest of your family? Your sisters?'

'Abbie and I were not really ever close,' Cherry said, 'I was close with Gloria, apparently, not that I can remember. Too young. But Abbie, no, we only played together with father. When he died, well, we were even further apart. As though the only thing that tied us together… was dead.'

Lucy smiled sympathetically, staring into her glass, knowing that to say she was sorry would sound cheesy and insufficient.

'But at least Abbie had Norton,' Cherry went on. 'They were always close. He seemed to favourite her, which was good because no one else did. She was always so surly. But when my father died… I did not have anyone to be with me. Norton loved Abbie, so he went to her. He became her comfort. But my aunt Evaneigh, she refused to see anyone after they died, she was too upset, but she at least had her ladies and her maids. I am sure she saw them. I did not see anyone. Our ayah retired after the funeral, and a new ayah was brought in, but I could not confide in her. She was a stranger.'

These spiraling disclosures were starting to make Lucy wish she'd never asked anything. The princess's past was patently grim, but this revealed a level of sadness she had not been prepared for.

'Is that why you left? Because you were lonely?' Lucy asked nervously, swallowing hard, regretting the words the moment she said them.

'Actually, to tell the truth I do not remember leaving the palace,' Cherry uttered, her hairs standing on end as her fingers gripped the crystal glass a bit too tightly. 'The last thing I remember is being on the boat to the mainland. But I remember being very frightened.'

Cherry shut her eyes then, unwittingly replaying the scene; thrashing waves of dark foamy water terrorising the rickety vessel. She had used gold to barter her passage onto a small fishing vessel bound for Coby. Her hair tied back under a bonnet, and in plain clothes, she tried to present herself as a street urchin. But what street urchin looks so clean and healthy, and barters with gold? She remembered the captain at the helm, shouting at the seamen. She remembered the glint in his eye looking back at her. Until that moment, she had been certain she had pulled off her disguise. But somehow, the captain knew who she was. At the height of the storm, the perilous sea threatening to take them down, he understood that there was more hanging on the fate of their voyage, than the delivery of lobster and mink-tail.

Cherry looked up from her glass, 'I was very frightened,' she repeated, 'and that is what I told the officials in Coby. I said that I was in fear of my life, and that I sought refuge under my father's accord. But I do not remember what exactly I was scared of. They put me in some room in a big building, it was near the ocean. Many days passed and I saw no one. I did not leave the room. Then the small men from Archmond, they came, and the officials in Coby said that Archmond was safer for me. So I went with the small men, and I lived there in Archmond,' Cherry relayed matter-of-factly, and shrugged nonchalantly as she finished her port.

Lucy finished her port too and refilled both their glasses. 'But you are… or I guess were… … a princess, and were the future queen, weren't you? Surely they came looking for you?'

Cherry snickered. 'They did. For years they did. But they did not find me. I was Archmond's biggest secret. Abigail was crowned the winter after I ran away. With me gone, she was my father's last remaining heir. Because our other sister was dead. I said that already? Yes? He only had the three of us.'

Lucy nodded and Cherry sighed before continuing. 'I do not remember it clearly, but before the small men came to take me, I had second thoughts about running away. But when I got to Archmond Castle, Soleman and Ron told me I was right to be afraid. They told me that they believed there was more to my parents' death than it first seemed. They said there was something evil in Verity Palace, but they would protect me until I was old enough to take the Palace back and defeat it.'

She gave an even deeper sigh then, exhausted by how many times she had spoken her own tale in her mind and was suddenly conscious that Lucy hadn't quite asked for this much detail. But having started the process of unravelling the nature of her plight, she was determined to finish the explanation. 'Then, when I was around fourteen, a source in Coby let something slip, and Meta Emery found out where I was. My sister and the Dynasty Council were furious. Archmond were accused of kidnapping. Then when I spoke in public and told the people of Archmond I was not a hostage, but I was being protected from Meta Emery… then I was a traitor. After years of refusing to surrender me, as either a hostage or a traitor, Archmond were attacked. I left then, both because I was scared my sister's army would come for me and scared of how many other people might die because of me.'

A dark feeling came over the room, Lucy gulped. 'That's why you're hiding out here,' she acknowledged, quietly.

'My sister wants me dead. She wants my head on her mantle.'

Lucy was surprised at how shocked she was to hear this, given she already sort of knew it. But to hear it put so crudely by the subject herself was rather jolting.

'Are you sure she would kill you, though, if she found you? Your own sister?'

'I am sure. After Archmond I went…' she paused mid-sentence, deciding to change her answer, 'I went to another city. I lived under an alias. I was Emma, Emma from Winnapea. No one knew who I was. I began to relax. But then some time ago, while I was still living there, my sister's soldiers came and killed residents of the very province where I lived. People I did not know were accused of conspiring to hide a traitor of Meta Emery. I had told no one of my identity. I had never even met these people. But they were neighbours… and they died because of some spurious link to me. I knew then there was nothing that I could do. She would always come. Even in Rumustica I have seen the soldiers come, but here I am hidden. And at least here, alone, no one else will be killed if they find me.'

Lucy took in a shuddered breath.

Cherry was feeling warmed by the wine and waved away Lucy's foreboding expression. 'Do not look so grim! It is all in the past. I am safe now in my mountain cottage. Oh, so much talk of me and *my* past and *my* family. What about you, your family? Tell me about them.'

Lucy was taken aback, she didn't know how to respond, so she got up to check the crumble-pie.

'You do not want to tell me,' Cherry said. It was an accusation as opposed to a question. Lucy felt rude.

'I ahh… well there isn't much to tell. Nothing nice anyway.' Lucy poked the clay pot with the iron prong and embers burst into the room.

'Do not do that. The strange pie is not ready, and my home will catch fire,' Cherry said, but as with most of her requests, it was sweetly put and hardly a reprimand. She then veered them back on topic. 'And so, my story is not nice and yet I have told you, the custom is, the Lores of Terra say, you must return in kind. So, in our case, that means, a story for a story.'

Lucy shut the fire and turned back to her. Now it was she who was tremulous. She sat down and put her hands on the table with her palms facing upward, staring into them as if for answers.

'My father is very aggressive. He drinks too much, and he hits my mother. He does more than hit her, actually. And he doesn't just hit *her*. One night, while typically very drunk, he hit my sister when she was very young. She fell back and her head hit the side of the bed. She died later that night in her sleep.'

Cherry was chilled to the bone; she could not react. Her own story was very sad. But parents who kill their own children was something different entirely. She stared silently down into her drink, and thereafter had more of it.

Agitated, Lucy got back up and went to the sink connected to the water-tank outside, and took a mug of water from the tap. She sipped it slowly, staring at the window which itself, given the darkness, only reflected back a picture of the *amber* room. She looked down into the sink. She had never told another soul about her father before, or about her sister. Well, she had told Bear, but it remained to be seen whether he was a soul. She clenched her fists in the sink, hating herself then. She should not have said anything. She should have made something up. A mundane story. Something close enough to the truth but without its horror.

But just then, she felt a warmth press against her side. A hand, just above her left hip, pressed and fell away just as gently. Cherry. She had come to the sink and now stood beside her, facing the window. Lucy looked up, and could see the perfectly feminine reflection staring back at her from the window pane; supple skin and almond eyes beneath that wild mane of strawberry hair. Timidly, awkwardly, Cherry's hand on the varnished counter-top edged closer to her own, until, eventually, she put her fingers atop of Lucy's and squeezed. Lucy looked at their intertwined fingers, recognising the gesture in complete shock. There had been only tolerance between them until now. Lucy looked toward Cherry's face, and the girl's eyes lifted to meet her own. She recognised then what Cherry had come in this moment to understand; there was something in common they shared, something singular. While they were different people, they shared between them something that few people would ever understand; childhood darkness.

Top ministers in Archmond's upper echelons are in crisis talks today, as the third straight day of rioting continues in the Rolling Hills district. Tensions had already been escalating in our designated agricultural and manufacturing district, after three of the six young men apprehended for attempting to leave the kingdom, currently an offence punishable by up to a decade in the cells, died in offi-cial custody. Protesters in the cotton fields beyond Gathgate, who include relatives of the deceased men, appear to have rejected the government line that the injuries the men sustained were inflicted by the Indawarra tribe, and that the men could simply not be resus-citated once in official custody. But the tipping point appears to be the story in this newscast of seven days ago, where newly liberated Meta Emery journalist, Albert Smithson, has quoted Archmond's own imported heroine Lucy Crypt, alleging she had renounced her allegiance to the kingdom, and herself encouraged the people of Archmond's rural regions to push back against government control.

Archmond's Minister for Agriculture, Aramor Ingress, has issued a statement reassuring the people of the Rolling Hills that additional government forces have been deployed, and that he does not believe the riots reflect any change in the relationship with key farming estates in the region.

More to come.

Chapter 8

Echolalia

The riding cloak whipped behind Lucy as the horse gained momentum down the hillside, and as the trot turned into a gallop, she felt an immeasurable glee rise up inside her. She turned her head to see Cherry was feeling it too, but having ridden proficiently since childhood, Cherry was embracing this glee with a confidence that Lucy and her amateur skills did not possess. There was terror in the excitement that Lucy had, as the two women, each on their own horse, tore down the green meadow towards the lake. Lucy had ridden horses frequently throughout her own childhood, but she was no equestrian, and there was a tremendous uncertainty she felt as the horse gained speed and the meadow dipped. The exhilaration was generating a high she would not come down from all afternoon and evening.

As they reached the cerulean lake, both girls dismounted, letting the horses drink. A scattered formation of altocumulus clouds were drifting slowly across the lake's mirrored surface. Beyond the lake were further undulating pastures of summer-green grass. The hills were modest though, and the woodlands seemed only to preface the steeper hills or the distant rocky slopes that became mountains. On this clear day, in the openness by the lake, Lucy could see further into Rumustica than she'd ever seen before. In fact it was the furthest into the distance she'd been able to see for a long time. She was aware of how exposed this made them.

Cherry was sitting down in the sodden grass, unfazed by how damp it would make her thighs and buttocks. She let her long cream legs unfurl from under the brown dress, and her feet submerge below the lake's still surface. Her horse, who had been thirstily lapping up the cool water, nuzzled against her face as she did so. They had a close, unspoken bond. Cherry had explained to Lucy as they saddled both mare and stallion early that morning, that her horse, Panacea, was, 'this beautiful, speckled creature, whose spirit is as pure and unique as her coat.'

Panacea's coat was a greyish off-white, but it was quite spectacularly speckled with honey and crimson markings, of all sizes, like autumn leaves on the snow. The other horse, an older stallion of black-brown, Cherry presumed had belonged to the owner of the cottage, whoever that had been. She had found him affixed to a post behind the water-tank, seemingly in good health, when she discovered the cottage.

After letting Cherry caress the underside of her jaw, the horse rose up. Cherry tucked a strand of her darkened hair behind her ear, looking toward Lucy as she did so, and now at least, smiling warmly. The previous night, Lucy had helped Cherry put the juices of blackberries through her hair to help hide it's strawberry colour. It was something Cherry undertook routinely when venturing out on a ride, but hadn't done for a while, and given their intentions for the following day, it seemed the most sensible course of action. They were looking for lotus sprites. Lucy's sighting had reinvigorated Cherry, who had been mesmerised with them when she arrived in Rumustica, and then dismayed by their progressive disappearance beginning some months later.

Lucy looked across the pastures again, she could see the steep dark slopes of the rocky mountains jutting out from various points into the distance. They were not imposing mountains, and not tall enough to be snow-capped in the autumn, but they were sharp and sudden as they rose. Between them, there was a sense that the meadows and the sparse woodlands continued indefinitely.

'Are there any towns or villages in Rumustica? The map I have doesn't show any, but Yerkey existed in the tundra, and it's not on my map.'

Cherry hadn't seen Lucy's map yet, but she needn't refer to it. 'There are not any towns, or villages or settlements. But the nomadic families sometimes travel through here and stay a while. Probably because it is so secluded, and they will not be bothered.'

Cherry was looking into the horizon as she said this, at the same pastures and mountains that Lucy had been staring at. Lucy, however, was now staring at Cherry with somewhat of a poignant envy. Envy of her sparkling skin, and the femininity of her elongated limbs. Cherry shifted in the soggy grasses, adjusting her skirt, but even this was done with the most demure elegance, as though every fibre in her was bestowed with an innate grace. Beautiful, graceful, yet completely alone.

'Don't you get lonely then? Without anyone nearby to talk to?'

'No,' Cherry said without having to think about it.

'You don't want a family?'

Cherry seemed somewhat irritated by this question because she feigned a smile, politely, as she looked away.

'There is no family to want. My sister wants me dead. My uncle sides with her. I presume my aunt must too. My only other relative is a distant cousin, Bevant, and he is on the same Dynasty Council that votes for my execution and sends soldiers out to find me. What is to want about that?'

Lucy's stomach churned. She didn't necessarily mean *that* family. But it was a foolish question, nonetheless.

'The berries do a good job of darkening your hair,' Lucy shifted the conversation tentatively, 'but should we be worried about those soldiers now,' she gestured around, reminding Cherry how exposed they were.

'Actually, I have not seen any of my sister's soldiers since the summer before last,' Cherry said, and sighed, then tinkered a bit, scoffing faintly as the connection clicked in her mind. 'Now that I think on it, the spring before that summer, I saw soldiers in spring too, but that spring was the last time I saw any lotus sprites.'

'What are you saying?'

'I do not know… but I used to think the soldiers were coming for me, but maybe there was something else bringing them here. And now it is gone, so they stopped coming back?'

Both girls stared back at the clouds passing across the lake as they mulled on this for a moment, but it was only a moment, for the speculation also prompted them back to the day's cause, and they readied their horses again, to set off in search of the sprites.

There was a distinct glimmer in Cherry's eye as they both grabbed at their reins.

'Race you to where the woodland starts,' she said, to Lucy's disbelief, given there hadn't been the slightest hint of competitiveness or playfulness in her thus far.

But before Lucy could agree Cherry took off, and once again, Lucy was made to chase her.

Lucy incited her own horse and at once it set off after Cherry's at a wild and unsteady speed. Lucy steadied herself on the saddle but took in the broken images of the ground that raced past her in flashes: crumbling black soil and green moss, flattened daisies, jagged rocks, and wild mint. Cherry veered left and Lucy quickly guided her stallion the same way with the reins. As they tore through the shallow stream and the water sprayed across her face, Cherry glanced back over her shoulder, a cheeky smile mocking the terror on Lucy's face. But Lucy felt the rare warmth of the mid-autumn sun, saw the splendour of its colour across this pretty and rugged landscape, and enjoyed the mockery all the same. She felt the sun against her body too, which was tepid from the chase under the cloak, and so she didn't mind the coolness of the muddy water splashing across her. Racing, play, laughter, joy. She didn't mind that Cherry had an adventurous side. This was a good thing.

After they had reached the woodland, and Cherry's subtle smile acknowledged her own victory, they caught their breath before beginning upward. They traversed the rocky woodland terrain, toward the same watering hole where they had met nearly several weeks earlier. But they had travelled a greater distance to be able to approach the watering hole from the opposing side of the mountain. It was a long way from the hidden valley, but it was in this light and airy woodland with its young trees and its crumbling dolomite platforms, that Cherry thought the lotus sprites might have retreated to. Their horses proceeded carefully up the incline, with autumnal light falling all around them. The gentle forest with its soft rain of leaves, a spangled mosaic of ochre, red, and marigold.

'I used to see them all the time,' Cherry remarked. She meant the sprites. They were now on flatter ground and the gentler rhythm made it easier to talk.

'When I first started to see them, in the summer, when I came here, they would dance around the woodlands at all times of the day. But as the seasons changed, it got cold in the late autumn, and I would only see them at night or in the early morning. Every so often a tree would light up. One by one the sprites would go dark, then light up again. When I stopped seeing them in winter, and then saw a dozen or so in the spring, I thought it was the seasons, and that by the summer they would return to dance through the woods again. But summer came and went, and they did not come back, night or day,' she explained.

'When I saw one,' Lucy said, with strained breath as she steered the dark horse back toward Cherry, 'it echoed back to me, things I'd already said. But it was my voice. I don't know if I told you that part.'

Cherry nodded. A five pointed brown leaf floated, spun, and then landed in the crest of her cleavage. She swished it away. They fell silent as they straddled another incline and their horses struggled with the terrain.

'But what was that? How did it…' Lucy said when the path flattened again.

'That is how they communicate,' Cherry said, without certainty, 'I believe. They do not have their own voice, but they can capture sounds, and they can talk to us that way. I think they talk to each other through light. They do not seem to make sound when they are alone, I have watched them.'

They had the benefit of a clear blue sky beyond the auburn trees, and the promise of warmth beyond the cold of the woodland's shadow.

'What did they say? When they spoke to you?' Lucy asked.

'Only things I already knew,' Cherry answered, cryptically.

For all intents and purposes, their expedition was a failure; the pretty golden forest had not a sprite to be found.

When they emerged through the rocky crevices into the clearing with the watering hole, the mid-afternoon had already become awash with clouds. The colourful vibrance that had marked their first meeting here had disappeared. Even the wisteria-type plant, which grew up along and overhung parts of the clearing's rock wall, had significantly paled. Its vivid apricot petals had shrivelled and turned pastel pink in the cool air.

The long journey was not pointless if they enjoyed a swim and collected firewood on their way back, Cherry had said when they were close. But now that they were here, she seemed to decide quite suddenly that she was not in the mood for swimming. Instead, she sat on the edge of the stone platform that encircled the pool, and let her feet slip beneath the cool surface. Beyond Cherry, where the platform stopped abruptly and sharply gave way to the valley below, a flock of ravens flew past the silver disc of the sun.

Looking out at Cherry from under the waterfall, her image blurred through its liquid window, Lucy realised she was starting to regard Cherry as both fragile and delicate, despite her initial standoffish impression. While they had established that Cherry was roughly nine years her senior, Lucy couldn't help but feel a growing urge to protect her. She was reminded then of how she felt in their first encounter at this very spot, when she was met with that inexplicable but powerful desire to pursue this strange girl.

It wasn't the same thing, because she had meant Cherry no harm, but it made her consider for the first time, what it might be like to have been pursued by others your entire life. What it would be like to be perpetually hunted by soldiers, and the reasons why this might make Cherry disinclined to hunt herself. Lucy also started to re-evaluate the rationale of princess's choice to live out her years alone in her valley. If the enemy couldn't be defeated, maybe there was wisdom in finding a place where the enemy would never find you. But, of course, Lucy had found Cherry, and she remembered too then, that there were assassins hunting her, as well. Lucy shuddered at the realisation. How had the assassins found her to begin with? Bear didn't seem to know. What if her presence in the cottage, in Rumustica even, undid all Cherry's efforts, to keep herself hidden, and safe?

'It was a lot more heavenly the last time we were both here,' Cherry commented as Lucy swam back over to where she sat. She took in the image of Lucy's partially disrobed body furtively. Lucy had taken off her cloak and dress and wore only a camisole. As well as being fascinated by her, Cherry envied Lucy's prettiness. The olive hue in her skin made her glow with vitality, and her rich dark hair, when it was dry and not full of jungle litter, sat so sleekly down her shoulders and chest, it seemed as though it had been styled that way by an artist about to paint her. And if all that wasn't cause for jealousy enough, those enormous blue eyes seemed to beckon in a way that was near spell-binding. It was one of many reasons that she found eye contact with her so difficult. Of course she envied what she perceived to be Lucy's relative freedom as well. She would never have guessed that the young girl conversely found her wild hair, pale complexion, and angular eyes beautiful, let alone intimidating.

'It was,' Lucy agreed, but then bit her bottom lip anxiously. Cherry could see she wanted to say something, but it was not in her nature to try and elicit it.

'I haven't told you this yet,' Lucy came out with it, 'but there are assassins after me. Sent from your sister. They came for me back when I was on the Alexandria, but I lost them after I fell into the jungle. But it's possible they're still out there, hunting me. If they find me here, I'll have led them to you. The very people you've been hiding from… Perhaps it's better if I go on, find somewhere else, I don't want to put you at risk after all you've sacrificed.'

Cherry dismissed this instantly, shaking her head. 'You misunderstand. I am not hiding to protect myself, I do not care what happens to me. Before I lived in the valley, wherever I was the people around me were implicated. I wanted to be alone because I did not want *anyone else* to die because of me. That is why I came here. But if my sister's men find you with me, you would not be killed because of who I am, but because of who you are.'

It seemed rather cold to have her death talked about so casually, but Lucy understood the point, and nodded singularly. 'Because of the mission they think I'm on. Archmond's mission, to find you, have you overthrow her, and be the new queen of Meta Emery.' Lucy's tone was laced with a sarcasm that evidently eluded Cherry.

'I will not do that,' said Cherry, with an almost aggressive defiance.

'I know,' Lucy resonated, sighing, and then continued bitterly, 'but they don't know that. They don't know that I don't even consider myself bound to Archmond, or its leaders and their plans.

Whether it's you or whether it's someone else, or it's your sister that rules Meta Emery, I couldn't care less. I am not one of their indentured workers.'

Cherry took in Lucy's darkened face and said nothing. Lucy had already told her what she had discovered of Archmond and the way it was, as she had put it, enslaving more than half of its population. Such comments were not entirely new to Cherry, but the talk she had heard on this before, the people in other cities where she lived, she assumed was half born out of ignorance and anti-Western sentiment. After all, they had never *been* to Archmond, and she had *lived* there. Not that in her concealed identity she had ever been able to disclose that. But, Lucy, on the other hand, Lucy had been to Archmond, and her information was not just second hand. Further so, her own experience in Archmond had been before the attack, before the clink gates, and the emergence of this so-called divided kingdom that people spoke about. Lucy was the only one of the two of them who had any direct insight into that. But still, the wizards had been so kind to her, had sheltered her, loved her, and so the conversation made her uncomfortable.

'So, don't worry,' Lucy concluded, resting her arms and chin on the smooth stone edge. 'When I leave Rumustica I will tell anyone I meet that I never found the princess, and that she probably is dead, like everyone says.'

A sullen countenance overcame Cherry. 'When you leave here? But you said you abandoned the mission?'

Lucy was startled. Was she correctly interpreting, that Cherry did not want her to go?

'I can't stay in the valley forever. I have to find my way home, back to my world.'

There was a sad silence then, as Cherry tried to hide how wounded she was, and struggled to find the words to feign nonchalance.

'Well, how do you get back to your world?'

'I don't know,' Lucy muttered with the soft hopelessness she always felt when she considered that question, 'but there was a way that brought me here, so there must be a way to send me back.'

Cherry thought on this for a moment. They heard their horses whinny somewhere down below.

'Perhaps the book has a charm that can help you,' Cherry suggested, 'actually, it is high time I look at the protection charm again. I am never sure if I am doing it correctly. I understand it, but there are some words I do not know. But tonight, I will try again. All this hateful talk of soldiers and assassins. We should head back soon.'

As Lucy dried herself and dressed, Cherry saw the infinity pendant on the chain for the first time.

'Where did you get that?' she asked, somewhat amused, 'Archmond?'

'Yeah, haven't you seen this on me before?' Lucy said. But there was no occasion where she could have, they had always bathed and dressed separately.

Cherry shook her head, and came closer, lifting the chain from where it had fallen under the wet camisole, so she could examine the pendant. She lifted it and felt it over, it was no replica.

'This was Gloria's,' she commented, 'we each have one, Abbie and I have our own. But I gave Gloria's to Archmond. Why did they give it to you?'

'They thought it might help me prove who I was to people. Not sure why I'd want to do that. But they also suggested it was bewitched, or that it was some sort of key,' Lucy recalled, sceptically.

Cherry laughed. 'It is just lithium. They mine it from the most eastern mountain where the palace sits. The talk of the their being bewitched is simply speculation and imagination getting the better of people. It is such... they used to say my mother was bewitched. Or was a witch. Or a fairy. All because she kept to herself. Ridiculous.'

When they returned to the hidden valley, in the early twilight, the dewy grove was silent and still. It wasn't until they passed through the thicket of trees enclosing the cottage and it's gardens, that they were met with the call of the frogs, the brook, and the chickens. The goats too had once again returned from their jaunts up the mountain, and while some lay contentedly in the soft grass, their knees tucked under their warm bellies, others wandered around eating it, and the sound of their bells chimed musically.

'Did you find any spirits,' Leo boomed, rousing happily from his half slumber.

'We were looking for lotus sprites,' Cherry replied, 'and we did not find any.'

'Oh. Well what about spirits, did you find any spirits?' he pushed.

'No,' Lucy said softly, dismounting the horse and rubbing the underside of his chin. Both Lucy and Cherry had developed an unspoken affection for Leo. They could see that his loitering around the cottage was in part a desire to maintain a connection with them. It was a consequence of his size that he was separated from their company in the evenings. Aware of this, and of the impact it might have on him, they made every effort to spend time outside with him when they could. He seemed to have no great desire to direct or even participate in their conversations, but most of the time he was pleased enough to simply be included.

As the twilight turned to dusk that evening, they lit a small fire in the iron barrel that usually stored the firewood and sat outside with Leo and the goats. Lucy brought out a rug for them to sit on, and Cherry brought out the imposing reference of charms, recipes and creepy sketches that was the Lores of Terra.

Before the firelight, Cherry thumbed the pages until she found the one she was looking for and unfolded the book to this point. She read silently.

Lucy had been, for the latter half of her life, an only child, so she understood the easiness of solitude better than most. She recognised the pattern this could create, and that such a pattern would be hard to break away from. And yet she was still struck by how impervious Cherry routinely was to company.

'Is this the protection charm,' Lucy asked, when Cherry had been silently reading for some time. They were lying on their stomachs on the threadbare mustard rug, but Cherry was closest to the glow of the fire that broke out from cracks in the iron barrel. Having bathed and changed, they were now dressed in their sleeping garments, and using small blankets as shawls to keep themselves warm.

'No,' Cherry replied, pleasantly, 'this is just… information.'

Lucy looked puzzled so Cherry went on, 'the book has recipes and charms, but it also has a lot of information. Mostly it seems to be trying to express a message. It is said within that understanding, understanding of the message, is the understanding of energy.'

'I see, and what is the message?'

'Yeah, what *is* the message?' Leo echoed.

'I think it is that, it is that everything, *everything*, is connected. All of us, all of them, and us to them,' she gestured the goats and the horses, now but mere shadows, 'the energy that can be made to be power, that can be used for will, it exists in those connections,' Cherry said, but added with regrettable honesty, 'but I think it is more complex than I can explain, because these words may have meanings that I am too simple to grasp.'

'What do you mean by connected? I mean we all share the same air, we all eat food from the same earth, is that what they mean?' Lucy asked.

Cherry pulled the blanket more tightly around her and shook her head. Above them the clouds were shifting, revealing the same myriad of stars Lucy had seen on that desert plateau. A moon, full and glorious, was rising behind the perimeter of the mist-woods and pines.

Cherry shook her head again, 'see, the problem is, I know enough to know that you do not understand, but I do not know enough to explain it any better.'

Lucy rolled her eyes. 'Well can you give me an example then, of this connection?'

Cherry thought on this for a time. As she did, her eyes wandered past Lucy, to the brook.

'You drink the water from the tap,' she indicated the cottage, 'and the water becomes part of you. But before that, the water was part of the sky. It fell from the sky and hit the soil, and it travelled down to the roots of the big tree, which absorbed it. It became part of the tree, until the warmth of the sun caused it to transpire through its leaves, and then it went up again into the sky, and when there were many many droplets, they condensed, and all fell down together, and some of them hit the river, and the brook, and my water tower, and gave life to the fish. And some hit the soil again and nourished the trees that bear fruit that we eat, that the animals eat. And in their fall, they became the cause of the weather as well as a consequence of the weather. So, when you drink that water, you drink all of what has happened perhaps a million times before. And when you eat anything grown from the dirt, it is the same.'

Lucy thought her example was more-or-less the same, if not more concise, and found the ideology a bit muddled. She also failed to see how it related to magic, charms, or spells.

'So, what about this concealment charm then, how does that work to use these *connections*?' Lucy asked, trying to amble the conversation along. Crumbs was nestled happily in her lap. Leo who had now fallen back asleep, was snoring loudly beside them.

'I am not really sure…' Cherry whispered, shutting the book. In his sleep Leo shuddered.

'Are you going to try it again, tonight?'

'I think I should, if I can get it all ready.'

'Why don't you let me help you? Is there anything that says it must be done alone?' Lucy pressed.

Cherry hadn't considered having Lucy participate, but she needn't consult the spell. If anything, the connections the book talked about, would be enhanced by a second person, and the connection between them. The fire crackled. The girls both looked up, and so did Crumbs. The sky had not yet gone completely dark, but the stars were bright and they could see the moon was full.

Lucy thought the preparation for the enchantment was no more involved than their usual nightly preparations; they lit the same number of candles. Although, this time, Cherry placed them in groups at strategic points around the cottage. Cherry had also gone out to fetch a mug of water from the brook, a feather from the coop, and a sprig of pine. All three were put in the centre of the iron table, on top of the pages open to the charm. Then a new candle, that was dark blue and smelt of jasmine, was also lit and put on a plate in the table's centre.

Cherry had told Lucy the words to repeat before everything was set up. She seemed to think to do so in the midst of the charm would upset the ambiance. Cherry would say the first line, which was intended as an opening of sorts, and then both girls would recite the incantation.

'From the desert to the sea, from the crypt to the moon, the energy of shadow and light resounds. We open to receive that energy,' Cherry said, and then turned her hands so her palms faced upward. Then together they recited the charm.

'*In solace may you find,*
What is hidden from their eyes.
In the light as bright as day,
What exists they cannot say.

Take the shadow cloak of noon,
And hide the children of the moon.
For listeners chanced to venture near,
Silence the sounds they must not hear,
Take the shadow cloak of noon,
And hide the children of the moon.'

This they repeated three times, and though neither of them intended or sought out to do so, by the time they approached the end of the second recital, their upturned fingers had become so close that they almost touched. Toward the end of the third recital, as they did inadvertently touch, came a spark. They each felt it, but they ignored it, finishing the words with conviction. But as they did, and looked to where their upturned fingers touched, they saw strands of light, blue, orange, and yellow, curling up like a chemical fire. Lucy's hairs stood on end, and all of her scepticism fell away. In fact, she felt a sinking dread of self-reprimand, as she wondered why after everything that had happened, she had doubted anything like this being possible.

The curls of electric light left their fingers and surged upward, hovering, and spinning slowly in a circle around their heads. Outside the night was still. They each drew breath, but they daren't look away from the light.

As the individual lights grew, the blue light dominated over the others. Suddenly all three fused, becoming a wreath of green electric light, which spun above them like a vortex. Neither of them could say a word, as if they both understood that to do so would ruin everything. Then in the next moment the light dispersed concentrically outward, extinguishing all light, and leaving them in darkness.

They each exhaled, and frantically caught their breath.

'Is that what's... was that... did it work?' Lucy asked several moments later.

'I don't know,' Cherry shuddered, abbreviating the words *do not* for possibly the first time. Lucy's manner of speaking was starting to rub off on her.

'Does that normally happen? With the light?' Lucy asked. She thought she knew the answer, Cherry had been pretty forthcoming about the charm, and there had been no mention of ghostly green lights.

Cherry shook her head, which was barely visible in the darkness, and Lucy got up to shake off her adrenaline and stir some light back into the fire.

Lucy woke when the horses stirred. The stirring, grunts, and whinnies were followed by soft hushing. Begrudgingly, still foggy with sleep, she sat up. Even before that she had felt the emptiness of the bed. Her eyes fluttered, adjusting, taking in the crumpled grey sheets beside her. Cherry was perhaps just relieving herself? But then she wondered, why had she never woken like this before, why had the horses never stirred before?

Wearily she rose and went to the window over the kitchen sink. The back wall of the one room cottage had no windows. But in the dark shadows over the kitchen garden nothing stirred. Discreetly, she crept over to the door and peered out of the window to the left of it. A cloaked figure was disappearing into the grove under the moonlight. It was too dark to see the colour of the cloak, but it was undoubtably Cherry. She looked back as she reached the edge of the thicket, ensuring she wasn't being followed.

Lucy ducked back from the window, but it was too dark inside the cottage for anyone to see in. For several moments she tried to understand what was going on. It was incredibly perplexing. Where would Cherry go at this hour? It was nowhere close to dawn, yet they had been asleep for several hours at least. After several moments of hesitant flux, she decided to follow.

'No, Crumbs,' she ordered sternly but quietly, as he tried to follow her out the door. Although by now Cherry had surely descended the sloping pastures and was well out of earshot. Shutting the door, Lucy pulled the hood of her own beige cloak over her plaited hair and hurried through the grove as quietly as she could, her boots dampening with the night dew of the grasses. The light from the moonlit sky made the night world awash with charcoal and silver rather than black. The edges of the horizon, lost to mountains and forests, glowed with a dull and unknown ambiance of green or yellow, or somewhere in-between. In the open pastures at the bottom of the hill, she saw a figure in the distance move toward the woodland. She knelt behind a tall pocket of mayflower, and tried to watch the figure move, but she lost sight of it. Finding Cherry in the dark was all but pointless now she knew, yet somehow, she felt determined to keep going.

Making her way gingerly across the open pastures was one thing, but when she reached the beginning of the woodland, she hesitated. She wasn't certain, but it was among these trees where she thought the cloaked figure had disappeared. But how could she be sure of what she'd seen? Maybe this wasn't Cherry she saw? Maybe the first cloaked figure was, but perhaps this mysterious figure was someone or something else. Another hooded figure had entered the woodland under the dark of night, and she was following this wickedness to her death.

Lucy shook herself, she was being dramatic. Then another thought; where was her sword? She didn't bring it! Curse. But before she could begin to decide what to do, a minute light, aqua blue and pulsating, appeared on a twig nearby. She recognised what it was instantly. This was the same size, and the same brightness, as the first lotus sprite.

She watched it curiously. It bounced, from one spindly twig to the next, whimsically, almost as if doing a dance. When after a time the dancing did not seem to evolve into anything meaningful Lucy spoke.

'Hello,' she said.

'Hello,' her own voice echoed eerily back to her.

She half chuckled at herself, remembering the way these light beings communicated, and yet, for some reason, despite the apparent futility, she decided to persist.

'I'm looking for my friend,' she said.

'Looking for my friend' it echoed.

Lucy sighed, brushing her hand through her fringe. It was both sardonic and somewhat testing, that she and Cherry had looked for these creatures for hours in the day, and she should now so easily stumble across one while looking instead for Cherry.

'How ironic,' she muttered, trying to use the light emitted from the sprite to peer through the trees. Suddenly the sprite darted forward, fifty metres into the woodland. But it stopped there and bounced up and down on the low branch of an ink-wood. Somehow Lucy understood it was beckoning her, rather playfully. *Come on, come on,* its bouncing light called. Against her better judgment, Lucy followed.

After having pursued it twice more, almost a mile into the sparse woodland, the bouncing aqua sprite was joined by another. As she caught up with the light for the third time, thorns and twigs scratching her ankles as she blindly navigated the terrain, Lucy saw a pink light flicker on beside it.

They waited this time, both of the sprites, on the top of a hollow trunk, for her to reach them. She said nothing as she approached but watched them on the broken ends of the dead tree, their glow rising and falling like breath, like heartbeat.

Before she could think of what to say that might carve out some communication between them, the pink light echoed. 'I do not know that I can do this forever.'

Lucy jolted. It was Cherry's voice. They were echoing *Cherry.* Lucy's hairs stood on end, but the lights darted ahead again, their distant glow leading her forward. They were beckoning her. It was without a doubt. More than beckoning, they were leading her somewhere.

When she caught up to them again, the two sprites had become five. There was now aqua, pink, red, orange, and teal.

They had aligned themselves on the one branch, waiting until she was close enough.

She panted, but they wouldn't wait for her to catch her breath.

'Is he okay?' the orange light echoed Cherry's voice, before fluttering upward to a higher branch.

'I miss you especially. I miss both of you. Please, this is a hateful thing for me as well,' the red light relayed her dolorous words.

'Every time the moon is full,' the aqua light relayed several moments later, in a tone of Cherry's that was both uncertain and reluctant, as if Cherry herself was simply repeating something that had been told to her. Lucy was suddenly overwhelmed. Whatever was being revealed to her in piecemeal fashion was enough to instigate a wave of incredible anxiety about what she truly knew about Cherry. But before she could dwell on this any longer, the aqua light echoed her own voice again.

'Looking for my friend,' she heard her voice say, before the lights shot forward in unison, egging her to pursue them.

And so she did. And each time she caught up they darted off again, waiting until she was close enough that she could see them clearly. This went on for several minutes, until the colourful lights led her to where they wanted her to go.

When she followed them that last time, they moved at a slower pace, and much closer to the ground, their light casting across the leaf litter of the forest floor. When she reached them, she saw they were joined by other sprites: cobalt, coral, lime, gold, and lavender. They were all crowded at the base of a rocky boulder. She had been following them in their playful bursts up the gentle gradient of the land, and they had now reached a clearing with an outcrop of boulders. The ambiance of the sky with its enormous moon fell around them. She edged carefully toward the boulder, crouching low, and thought she could almost make out the outline of tiny figures within the lights, when they suddenly all went dark. All but the aqua light. It crept around the base of the boulder, and hopped forward slowly, before it too went dark and disappeared.

She looked around without moving, simply squinting. The sparkling sprites had blinded her, and the outline of the rocks and the trees in the grey night was harder to see at first. But as her vision readjusted, she registered that beyond the rocky outcrop, a network of smooth interlocking boulders, wide and flat, made a long curving platform just above her. A stage. This was the reason for the clearing; she was at the base of the burgeoning mountain steps. Before she could figure out a way up onto that first platform, which is where she thought she must be supposed to go, she saw under the moonlight, Cherry's cloaked figure emerge.

Cherry took several steps across the platform carefully, turning this way and that, before she stopped, and drew back her hood. Something had caught her eye. Beneath the starry moonlit sky her hair glistened, more pink and romantic than Lucy had ever seen it. Perhaps it was the sudden introduction of this light glossy colour into the colourless night, or the way the freshly washed locks were so wispy, free of the berry-tannins that had darkened them earlier that day.

Upon the rocky stage, Cherry was several feet above her, but less than twenty feet away. Lucy pushed herself up against the small boulder in front of her, peering around it. The platform had a row of alternate sized boulders jutting out along its edge, such that Lucy lost sight of most of Cherry's frame as she stepped toward what she had seen. But it was clear Cherry was reacting to something.

Cherry sighed, equal parts relief and disbelief. Then she let out a muffled bitter laugh, also ruffled with disbelief. But there were other breaths and sighs of relief, not belonging to Cherry. Male breaths. Lucy stiffened.

A voice then shocked Lucy to her core.

'I didn't think you'd come,' he said. Lucy's hairs stood on end at once. With a powerful sense of denial, she felt her head spin with disbelief. A dizzy sensation grew as she sought to find the energy to process what she was hearing. But she refused to believe what her auditory senses told her. *No*, she thought, *no it can't be*.

'I wasn't sure if I could tonight, but it has been so long and…' Cherry uttered, trailing off.

He stepped forward and embraced her passionately, and as they kissed and caressed each other they unconsciously edged outward from the shadows into the moonlight. Lucy's heart lifted, and sunk, and then shattered. It was him. It was Hamish.

One arm around Cherry's waist, the other behind her head, hand scrunching into that beautifully silken pink hair of hers, he held and embraced her with a longing and yearning that was as sorrowful as it was lustful. The pain of being apart being wrenched into oblivion. Lucy had never seen an embrace so full of love and desire. And he was more handsome than she remembered, those strong arms, his sun-kissed skin, and his sparkling eyes as he drew his head back from Cherry's, only to cup her face in his hands and gaze into it with adoration.

It was too much to bear. Her vision clouded white from the outside in, her ears muted their soft loving murmurs to each other. As she filled with darkness from the bottom up, she blocked it all out. Her mind rattled through all those moments between the two of them. All that significance she had dreamed up in the jungle, it wasn't real. She'd been but a mere distraction to him at most. A distraction from the one person, the one thing, he truly longed for: a princess. *A princess!* He was in love with a princess, the true heir to the throne of the most powerful kingdom of this world. How would she have ever come close to comparing? It was laughable to think that she ever stood a chance of being close to him. She clenched her fists. Then it was all the more unbearable that it happened to be the very princess she had been sent to find, and that she and Cherry had so warily weaved their differences into a delicately blossoming friendship, for this to now come between it. It was too awful.

Her eyes were shut but she could still see the image of him holding Cherry, tilting her backward with his arm around her waist and his other hand in her soft glistening hair. It was patent, in the way he held her and in the way he had gazed at her. He *loved* Cherry. He could never *not* love her. This strange royal girl that had befriended her was this mystery woman his family spoke of him pining over. She felt as though she'd been shot, as though she couldn't hold her own weight. But she opened her eyes and steadied herself again against the rock. Gently she lowered herself down, clasping her hand to her throat and hoping they wouldn't hear her tortured breaths. As she calmed herself again, she tuned her attention back to their conversation. Their embrace had languished. They were seated on a flat rock in the moonlight and were speaking softly. She could see most of Cherry's face, but Hamish was hidden behind a jagged rock closer to the edge. All she could see was the top of his hair above the rock, and the edge of his coat sticking out the left side of it. She blinked, trying to get the image clearer, and wondered how long she had been in her own head. How long had they been speaking?

'How is he?' Cherry asked.

He ignored her question. 'I miss you,' he said, reaching forward, but Cherry turned her cheek.

'I come here every time, Cherry,' he said, and Lucy heard then the intense and powerful sadness in his voice, 'just hoping you'll show up.'

'It is not as though I do not want to come. Not a day goes by that I do not long to see you and Orran,' she responded, mutely. There was a '*but*' in her tone.

'Then why do we live like this? Me riding out here every full moon, just to hold you in my arms on a damp rock in the cold,' he said, and sighed, full of melancholy, as he reached over and etched his fingers through some of her wind-knotted curls.

'Except when you're on your expeditions,' Cherry teased, ignoring the question. Listlessly Cherry's eyes followed the path of his fingers in her hair. The tenderness of the gesture was different to the passionate embrace. This was habitual care on his part. He couldn't help himself. She looked up then and he smiled at her softly, wanting. Not a sexual wanting. His searching eyes were wanting the same thing they always did, more of her. Cherry's heart fluttered; in his eyes were the memories of Orran's eyes, for those precious few weeks she'd held him. Of course, Orran's eyes were blue at the time, but were otherwise the same as his fathers. They seemed to take her in with the same haunting wonder.

At the mention of expeditions Hamish drew back and his posture stiffened. 'That reminds me. The girl, ahh Lay... Lucy, did she find you?'

Lucy was horrified. Did he really just pretend to not know her name? She quelled her distress, remembering the false name she had given him for most of their time together.

'Lucy?' Cherry asked, startled. 'You sent that girl to me?'

'I didn't *send* her,' he said. 'We found her on the last expedition. She became part of our camp. But it wasn't safe for her to stay with us anymore, so I directed her toward Rumustica. But I did *hope* she'd find you. She has no one, except that dog, and she had nowhere else to go. So, she did find you then? Is she...' he began but Cherry cut in.

'You didn't tell her about us?' she asked.

'Of course I didn't,' he replied defensively, 'but she is staying with you then? I hope she isn't any trouble.'

'You say that as though she is your ward,' Cherry mused, before answering. 'She is staying with me, yes, and she is no trouble. She is not particularly light or sunny, but she is helpful. Her sword has been useful. But why was it not safe for her to stay with your team?'

'We were headed back to Trimany, and we heard there might be war. We couldn't risk it,' Hamish said, deciding to bypass the detail about the allegedly liberated Albatross.

'War?' Cherry exclaimed, becoming distressed.

'It was but mere rumour,' he hushed, stroking her face.

She was not convinced. 'Is Orran in a safe—'

'There is no war, and he is perfectly fine,' Hamish interrupted her needless worry. 'At this hour he'll no doubt be dreaming away. After Lorelai's warm bath, he'll have drifted off to sleep as Star read him passages from one of those history books she uses for bedtime stories.'

Cherry laughed. 'He would not understand stories of any kind yet, I suppose.'

'Hmm,' Hamish considered, 'he is starting to babble, so who knows what he understands. They say children are smarter than we think.'

There was a tension between them then, Lucy realised. It was subtle, it was hardly there, but their words fell quiet, and Cherry looked into her lap.

It was an argument they had had many times before. One that had been exhausted, and Hamish had sworn never to bring it up again, but he couldn't help himself. He felt dishonest not to say how he felt, to pretend he no longer cared about the matter.

'He needs his mother, darling. Star is no substitute. Lorelai is not always around. Please stop this hiding and come back, we can give you a different name, we'll dye your hair, cut it off even. You'd still be astonishing to look at without any hair at all…' he stopped, in part because he knew the futility of his words.

'No,' Cherry said, quietly but sternly, her gaze still in her lap. She shook her head.

'I will always keep coming back to see you, but then it hurts to say goodbye, to be away so long. To not even know where you go when you leave.'

Cherry stood up and stepped several paces forward along the stone ground, away from him. Lucy could see her clearly now.

'I understand you have desires. That is normal. You should marry, I have said that before. Marry with my blessing. I will not resent you for that. It would make me especially pleased to know that you were happy, that you were not alone.'

'Don't be like that. This isn't about my *desires*,' Hamish retorted, offended. 'I want us to be a family. I want our son to have a *proper* family.'

'If you marry soon, to a good woman,' she reasoned, turning around to face him. She was trying to sound cheery and upbeat, but her eyes were already glassy, 'he will know your wife as his mother, and then he will have this *proper family* you speak of.' It was clear in the emphasis she put on the words, proper family, that she did not share his value of the term.

He pushed on, 'I don't want to marry anyone else, and besides that's not the same as him growing up with his mother, his actual mother.'

'It is also not the same as him being shaken dead, or drowned in the river, or burnt alive,' she snapped, more fiercely than Lucy had come to expect of her.

'Cherry,' Hamish called to her softly, coming toward her. He took her hand, but she tore it away and turned back to look over the silver-grey tree tops sloping down to the wider valley.

'You want him to grow up with a family. I just want him to grow up. I will not risk you, I will not risk our son, for the possibility of him having a traditional upbringing. The only way to guarantee he stays alive, is if no one ever knows who his mother is.'

There was silence for a moment. Cherry turned back to check how her sentiments had been received. It was not like her to sound so brash, and she resented having to. She caught her breath in her throat so see that Hamish was calm. His expression sympathetic.

He didn't dispute her concerns. He would never have even considered accusing her of abandoning her son. Her knew her fears were well-founded. He was with her the day they both heard the news about the people in Rusted Bay, the Trimanian province where she'd been living for several years. The government in Trimany were too afraid to impose sanctions on Meta Emery for the Red Army's illegal execution of Trimanian citizens, but it condemned the actions and promised a thorough investigation, which of course never eventuated. The murdered villagers, two women and two men, had never met Cherry, who was in any case living under an alias, but the newscast they read, sitting in a cafe in Trimany's academic quarter, claimed they were summarily executed on suspicion of hiding a traitor to the eastern queen. He had accused her of being paranoid before that, but never again. He would never doubt her fears again. He understood why she feared for their child. But still, while he understood her fears, he did not agree to living one's life by them. He believed there were solutions.

He stepped closer to her still, and put a hand on her shoulder momentarily, then let it drop. Standing alongside her he looked out over the tree tops with her for a time. Then he put his arm around her waist and pulled her in. She let her head fall neatly on his shoulder. Lucy took in the image of them together, their bodies perfectly paired.

But after several moments Cherry pulled away. 'I should go. The girl you sent me might be worried where I am.'

This was a half-truth, Lucy being only part of her reason. The other half of the truth was that his comments about Orran growing up without her had stirred up a deep and horrible void that she worked so hard to bury. Images of him alone without a mother, now whirled a self-hatred inside of her that she found difficult to contain and manage. She felt a desperate need to be alone, and to cry unashamedly.

'Girl I sent you?' he scoffed dismissively before attempting to reason with her. 'Don't leave now, not yet, it's been so long.'

He tried to embrace her affectionately, regretting reminding her of that rift of disagreement between them, but she pulled away all the same, and her slender arms fell gently out of his hands. Lucy saw his heartbroken face as Cherry hurried down the rocky platform, stumbling, and falling onto her side as she did.

'Cherry!' he called, alarmed, but she ignored him, scrambled to her feet, and hurried on, brushing past the stone where Lucy had slid to the bottom and hid in the shadow.

'Will you come again? Next time?' he shouted, just as her figure was about to become enveloped by the surrounding woodland. Cherry stopped and turned. He could still see her clearly in the moonlight. She nodded, strongly, but then pulled her cloak and her hood tightly around her and hurried off.

Lucy sat still in the shadow for several moments, at a loss as to how to handle this. What would she say to Cherry? Should she pretend not to have seen? But how would she go unnoticed crying herself to sleep? But in the silence of Cherry's departure, she heard Hamish's frustrated heavy breaths, and realised he had not left. She knew she needed to get away from this private moment. But as she stepped forward a bundle of dead leaves crumpled and crushed beneath her boots.

'Who's there?' Hamish called, brutishly. 'Who's out there?'

Lucy froze. She stilled herself for several moments, but she heard him creep down the grainy slope, and she heard his knife being drawn from its sheath.

'It's just me,' she jumped out, her arms outward, just as he neared the boulder.

'You!' he said, faltering with shock. 'You were… you were *spying* on us?' His accusation was harsh and she felt it.

'No,' she said, trying to not to weep. First his love for another and now his terse tone. 'No, I was looking for Cherry and then…' she knew the strange experience with the sprites was too complex to convey in this moment, 'and then when I saw her and saw you, I was too shocked, and I froze. I wanted to leave but I didn't want to be seen.'

Hamish let out a long frustrated sigh, before putting the blade back. He shook his head and went to sit back upon the grainy slope that led up to the platform. He ran his hands through his hair.

'So, you heard all of that?' he asked, looking up at her. Lucy nodded, stepping forward.

'You must never tell a soul about Orran. Not the wizards, not that floating bear creature, *no one*.'

Lucy wanted to say that she thought Bear knew everything anyway, but she kept quiet. 'I understand,' she said, agreeing.

'Does she know?' he asked, his voice was softer now, his shock and the derision it had ignited had faded, 'does she know the truth about you? About Archmond?'

Lucy nodded. 'I knew who she was straight away. I didn't want to lie to her. I learnt my lesson about that at least. I told her everything,' Lucy said and then reconsidered, before adding, 'That is, I told her everything about Archmond and the wizards and the prophecy. I told her I met some people in the jungle, but she didn't ask about that and I didn't say anything more.'

Lucy didn't know why she was being coy, nothing had actually happened between her and Hamish after all. But they had both felt the force of what may have been about to happen between them. She wasn't sure if she still felt that electricity now. She was too wounded to feel anything of the sort. Hamish only nodded and looked down into the dirt. His elbows rested on his bent knees, and he was drawing in the dirt with a stick he had picked up.

'Come,' he said, patting the space in the dirt beside him, 'stop lingering over there like a shadow.'

Lucy came and sat next to him.

'So, this is why you wanted me to go north?' she said, grinning up at him.

He grinned as well, without looking at her, and gave a slow nod. 'This is why.'

'But you don't believe in the prophecy?' she posed.

'I do not,' he agreed, 'but I hoped you'd be lucky, find her, and have somewhere safe to lodge. I know she has a cottage somewhere in one of these valleys, I just don't know where it is. And Rumustica has long been uninhabited. If you didn't find her, at the very least you'd find no one, and be safe all the same.'

Lucy was aware that she could lead him to the cottage, but she knew Cherry would see it as a betrayal.

'So, there was no invasion after all?' Lucy asked.

Hamish snickered. 'No,' he sighed, 'though the bird wasn't lying. Just mistaken. Abigail's army did arrive seeking permission to search Arebella, a south-eastern province, for some undisclosed reason, but our government denied them entry. There's been some political fallout from it. But it's old news now.'

Lucy gave a half smile. She felt cheated because she didn't have to leave them after all. But she knew that the pain of being pushed away, had led her to Cherry, and she felt at peace in the woodland cottage, for now.

Hamish sighed again, he was still full of the angst of Cherry's departure, and the talk of war and armies had only circled his thoughts back to that.

'But Cherry is convinced that there is no way she can ever truly hide from them. No one claims to have seen her, seen the princess, in ten years. No one knows what she looks like. I mean the hair gives her away a bit sure, but it's not so unusual. And she could cut it, dye it. But instead, she stays out here, alone,' he looked at Lucy and thought, *well she was alone*, but he didn't say it, 'and every full moon I set out from Trimany before dawn. I ride for hours over the hillsides and wait for her here. Sometimes I try to reason with her to come back with me, but you see what good that does me. Pathetic, really.'

He looked at Lucy more fully then, turning somewhat to face her. They were a foot or so apart. Her eyes met him with sympathy before falling awkwardly away. He remembered then all the intensity he had felt for her in that jungle. When he thought she was just Mary, a lost and likely betrothed nomadic girl. All the moments came back to him in successive flashes, and he remembered heavily how much interest he'd shown her, and the inklings of reciprocation she'd offered, in that demure way females oft expressed themselves. He realised then how confusing this revelation may have been for her. But she had kept hidden things from him too. And he had never been dishonest. He and Cherry were not married, they were not courting, he came here only to try and change her mind about that. But each time he did, even on the occasions where his advances were returned, she still encouraged him to seek out love elsewhere.

Lucy could sense his thoughts swirling with complexity.

'Lucy I…' he began.

'Don't,' she stopped him, not wanting to hear it, 'you don't have to explain anything.'

But then she felt him edging closer. She was looking straight ahead. He barely made a sound, and she hadn't seen him move, but she felt he was pressed right up against her. She felt the touch of his hand on her hair.

'I don't want to explain,' he whispered, and in the next moment he had taken her in his arms. He was kissing her, and she felt herself kissing him back. She let her arms reach instinctively around and rest across his shoulders as he leant her gently down onto the ground.

The kissing went on incessantly. It was like the floodgates that had been holding back their desire for one another all those weeks in the jungle, had finally now burst. He caressed her waist through her nightdress, and then lifted her up slightly to remove the cloak and lay it beneath her before letting her down again.

She kissed his neck. It was sweeter than she could have anticipated, warm, delightful.

He touched her smooth legs, and let his hands trace up them to her soft thighs, but as the desire in him intensified, he regained his senses and stopped. In the same moment so did Lucy. She pulled away.

'I'm sorry—'

'We shouldn't be,' Lucy said breathless, in shock. 'Cherry.'

'I know but I—' he began again, but stopped, 'I'm sorry you're right, we shouldn't. We shouldn't be doing that.'

'She loves you,' Lucy said, 'I could see it in her. The two of you should be together.' Then she was quiet for a moment before saying hastily, 'I should go, she'll wonder where I am.'

Lucy stood up and dusted herself, patted her hair and picked up her cloak.

'Will you— ' he was about to ask her what she would tell Cherry of their encounter. She understood his tone, and his countenance.

'I won't say anything,' she said. She turned away from him to leave through the dark forest. He didn't try to stop her.

As Hamish made his way back to his horse, frustrated and confused, he was startled by a mild violet light, whirling concentrically just above the branch of the small mist-wood where he'd fastened his horse. He had just made his way back to the other side of the base of Mount Nawala, where he'd watched first Cherry, and then Lucy, leave him. He stopped for a moment, fearfully edging his hand toward the sheath of his hunting knife, but the light dimmed some, and he recognised the dark figure within it. He drew in a sharp breath, and then composed himself.

'You're that spirit demon from Archmond. What do you want?' he asked.

'Actually, Spiritual Adviser is my official title,' Bear said, a little affronted by the hostility, 'and I should think it's fairly obvious that I would like a word with you. Why else would I be here?'

Hamish said nothing, but his hand now rested on the hilt of the knife.

'Oh don't be so provincial,' Bear exclaimed, dismissively, 'I'd have thought you smarter than to think that metal could be used against a demon, if that is indeed what you believe I am, *or* that I would come here to harm you, seeing as that certainly isn't part of my known repertoire… or at least, I hope it isn't…' Bear shuddered then to think that he was not aware of what newscasts in other kingdoms reported about him. Although he had never considered his official activities as newsworthy.

'No,' Hamish agreed, approaching the mare, and rubbing the side of her face tenderly, 'but I've not been visited by many talking floating bears in my time, and given that Lucy isn't here, I have reservations about your motives for showing up above my horse.'

'My! So serious Mr. Mathers. I had planned a little small talk to get things going, but,' he paused, sighing, 'seeing as you're keen on being so direct, my motives are fairly straightforward. You are still in love with this princess, yes? Mother of your child?'

Hamish stared Bear down but did not answer.

'I'll take that as a yes,' Bear noted. 'Then I'd think it wise not to be engaging in romantic or… sexual… interludes with her new friend, whose very role in this world is to restore the princess to power.'

Hamish's eyes now narrowed with contempt. Who was this floating puppet of the corrupted western kingdom to judge him?

'You have an attraction to power, Mr. Mathers, that much is clear,' Bear continued when Hamish said nothing.

The rhythm of cicadas pulsated through the dark forest. The horse stirred.

'I am not after your guidance,' Hamish spoke clearly, sternly. 'You are not *my* spiritual adviser. Nor do I seek your counsel, strange demon. And you do not know me, my intentions, or my attractions.'

'Hardly spiritual guidance to suggest you refrain from sexual relations with your lover's friend. That aside, I do know that the only two women you have ever been seen to be powerfully entranced by, happen to be an exiled princess, and a prophesied heroine. But take heed of this and I will be on my way. You must subdue your desires for Miss Crypt, and you will, if you care about your son, your family, or your kingdom. You will control yourself and let this play out, as it should.'

Hamish went to dismiss the demon's concerns as nonsensical. He had no intentions for Lucy; their momentary embrace was a mistake brought on by pent-up lust. But in the same moment the violet light and bear creature within it, were gone. Hamish rode home to Trimany as bewildered and frustrated by Bear, as he was angry and hurt by Cherry.

An energy had been stirring that night. In their separate private ways, they had all felt it build up through the evening: Hamish, Lucy, and Cherry. It had been stirring in the immediate thrill of sunset, stirring anticipation, stirring angst, stirring wonder. It seemed to promise something was coming, this unexplained incommunicable electricity. But as night faded, it vanished, and it did not return in the days that followed. The dull grey air of the following morning, promised and delivered, only rain.

Chapter 9

The Chameleon Effect

'We become what we become, not only through our DNA, or only through our environment, but through their interaction.'
John. A Bargh

When Lucy returned to the cottage, through an open door she saw Cherry, pale and still, gripping the edge of the bed where she sat. A sliver of silver light upon her wet cheeks exposed the extent of her sobbing. Cherry was wrecked with anguish every time she said goodbye to Hamish, and this was no exception, but returning to the empty cottage had amplified her distress. All that held back her utter panic was the lack of visible signs of disturbance and the presence of Lucy's sword and dog.

But when Lucy returned some thirty minutes later, three things had been clear to both of them without word. That Lucy had seen Cherry with Hamish, that her delay in returning was because she too had spoken with him, and that Cherry clearly knew it.

'What did he say?' were the first words Cherry uttered after Lucy had entered the cottage, lingered somewhat, and then removed her cloak.

'That he wants to be with you,' Lucy had said after a careful pause, spreading the damp cloak across the chair so it wouldn't dry creased, and continued to lie by omission, by adding, 'and that there is no war in Trimany after all.'

Lucy had considered putting an arm around Cherry to comfort her, but she could feel the girl didn't want to be touched. Quietly,

Lucy told Cherry the brief version of how the sprites had led her to them. About hearing her own voice, and hearing Cherry's, and about the way they made her chase them, right up until she saw the two of them together.

Turned away in the darkness, Cherry didn't react. She couldn't think about sprites now or what any of that meant. She was anguished by grief. She felt helpless against the doom that her own fate had cast over Hamish and her son. The tremendous guilt that bore down on her as she felt Orran's distance stifled other thoughts. But Lucy had seen, she knew now, and Cherry had to fill in the blanks, to explain, so that Lucy would understand to never speak of this again. Eventually, after slowing her wheezing breath, Cherry told Lucy how she'd met Hamish in Trimany, but was forced to abandon her life there after she became pregnant with his child.

She had relayed part of all this to Lucy before, but she had withheld the names and places. She explained now that the people she'd spoken of who were killed were four residents of Rusted Bay which was the name of the province where she'd been living in Trimany. They had been murdered, effectively, by Red Army soldiers, on a spring day, after being summarily and unlawfully convicted of conspiring to hide her. She explained this was no crime in Trimany, and the Red Army had no power or authority in Trimany to do this, but nothing was ever done about it. Worse still, she reminded Lucy, was that she didn't know the executed people, they were innocent of the accusation, lawful or not. But it meant someone, *someone* must have seen her. Someone knew something, because the soldiers were wrong, but they were very close. This was unsettling; terrifying; disturbing.

The confirmation she was with child was the final straw. Hamish was the only person in Trimany she had ever told about her true identity, and she knew he had not betrayed her. But she knew she had been exposed some other way, the randomness of which set her nerves aflame. What if some passer-by at the markets or in town had simply likened her appearance to the child within an old Verity Palace portrait? She had been terrified that she was being watched; that he was being watched. So she told Hamish she had to leave. Rumustica was the only place she thought of where she could hide and live safely. They agreed to meet at the base of Mount Nawala, on the night of each full moon, and at first, they did so, but she refused to tell him the location of the cottage she'd found, out of fear that he would try to visit her there and be followed.

She told Lucy that she feared if she had let Hamish follow her, he would turn up regularly and those with suspicious eyes would be led to have their suspicions confirmed. Then she and her unborn child would be killed. So, against his pleas to do otherwise, she had had the baby alone, and survived it. Then, against all her instincts, she had given him to Hamish when they met the following moon. She had spent precious little time with her son, but she had cherished every moment.

She implored upon Lucy, not in a tone of justification, but one of deep foreboding, that if anyone had have found her with Orran, whether it be one of her sister's soldiers or a lone traveller, word could get out that she was alive, and had a son. This was followed by a warning in the strongest tone she'd ever used with Lucy. Her face darkened, and she repeated that if anyone knew the child was hers, anyone in the world, they would come for him. His identity, if ever known, would cost him his life. Lucy said she understood and would take the secret to her grave.

Cherry went on to explain that because no one had followed Hamish to Rumustica in those last six moons of her pregnancy, she had, *they had*, to risk that Orran would be safer with his father, as an anonymous love child, than with her. As far as they knew, no one had ever learnt of their brief affair in Trimany before she'd fled. They had been careful. He had told no one in his life about her, and she had told no one in her life (not that of course there was anyone in her life) of him. She'd told no one of her pregnancy. So, Hamish would tell his family the child was born of an unfortunate affair with some rogue whore, who thereafter abandoned him.

After relaying the basics of this history, Cherry ended both sadly and abruptly by saying that despite their original promise to meet every full moon, the reality of the situation was more difficult and painful than they'd anticipated, and their meetings had become more and more infrequent, as the years went on.

After a respectful period of absorption, the two of them both still and seated at opposite ends of the dark cottage, Lucy asked, 'Do you think you will ever see your son again?'

'If the years go by and my sister stops looking for me, if the world forgets about me, then maybe it would be safe, then, to see him.'

'The world already thinks you're dead, Cherry. Even Archmond does,' Lucy insisted.

Cherry shrugged, silently referencing the slaughtered Trimanian citizens of Rusted Bay.

'And will you live here alone forever?' Lucy was empathetic, but at pains to understand why Cherry would see her options so divisively. 'If protecting Hamish and Orran are your primary concern, then you could distance yourself from them, and still live in a society, in another kingdom, under a different alias? Once enough time has gone by, surely then it will be safe?'

The suggestions were not welcome, and Cherry was non-responsive.

Yet still, although pensively, Lucy put forward more suggested solutions to what she saw as Cherry's *problem* of isolation. Perhaps marrying a fisherman and spending her life on the sea, or waiting several more years and moving to Que. Eventually, probably given her delirium, Cherry, without word, turned abruptly away from Lucy, and stood by the window. She undid her nightgown. Then, in the swelling exhaustion of the hour, Lucy was confronted with the growing deformity upon Cherry's back.

Cherry's whole back was in some way raised or inflamed, and Lucy understood then the reason for her candid nature when it came to swimming or dressing. Although generally rampant, the swelling concentrated in diagonal mounds that ran from the far edge of Cherry's shoulders, down towards her middle back. They were large swelling masses, less like blisters, and more like horrid cancerous tumours.

'It began as I started to show,' Cherry whispered, quivering. Her voice was barely audible and the shame in it immense and unsettling. 'But after Orran was born it got worse, kept going. I only saw it clearly… once in the looking glass in my room in Rusted Bay… red and horrible and…' she couldn't finish.

Lucy stood from the chair and stepped forward. The only light was that of the moon, subtle and silver, and cutting in at an acute angle through the brook window. Lucy couldn't appreciate any darkened contusions or general discolouration across the scattered bumps, just the way the shadow and light broke across her back, where it should have flowed evenly. But in places, particularly closer to the shoulder blades, it appeared something swelling was trying to break free.

'I am not just hunted and cursed. I am deformed. I am sick. Please, do not speak again of marrying, or Hamish… or Orran,' Cherry muttered through breaths of alternating clarity. Though she was hushed by her shame, the words *hunted*, *deformed*, and *Orran* were enunciated with a stilling vigour.

Lucy agreed, but later, when she eventually began to settle off to sleep again, she considered whether part of the princess's solitude had nothing to do with the safety of others at all. In an epiphany that early morning moonlight seemed to magnify, she started to question how much of Cherry's solitude was motivated by noble sacrifice, and how much was motivated by vanity and shame.

The days and weeks that followed that night seemed to move more slowly than the last. Around them autumn raced toward winter, and as the leaves were whisked away from skeletal branches, the skies regularly reverted to a palimpsest of white and grey. Life at the cottage fell back into its languid, peaceful routine. But the clouded skies and cold days set their routine closer to home than previously. They set out in search of the lotus sprites occasionally, but not often.

There were still plenty of chores to fill the days. The garden needed extra weeding before winter, which was a simple enough task that Lucy could tend to it unsupervised, while Cherry delicately pruned the roses, and the flowering vines on the lattices. The garden work also consisted of harvesting autumn vegetables like pumpkin, parsnip, leek, and potato, along with bulbous bollikots, which Lucy thought of as smoother, creamier versions of cauliflower. Aside from the fernearas, which she did not particularly care for, the other new food Cherry's garden introduced her to was mila beans, one of many legumes that grew on the vines. Disappointingly though, the beans were as bland and unappealing as any other green bean she'd ever tried.

'You know, if you were queen of Meta Emery, you'd have servants dig in the cold dirt for you,' said Lucy one day, baiting her, as she shook the soil from another bunch of carrots she'd plucked. Cherry smirked, and in return threw a handful of dirt in Lucy's face.

The harvest was bountiful. There was in fact more than enough food for the two of them to consume before it turned bad. But there were ways that Cherry had learnt. Ways for keeping the food. She had taught herself such things after reading about them in the Lores of Terra. So, some of the pumpkin, potato and other vegetables were cut, coated with lemon and dehydrated in the wood-stove, and compacted in glass jars, so they would last the winter.

Lucy taught herself each of the recipes in the Lores of Terra; recipes for soup and bread and broth. The book was more jumbled the more Lucy looked at it, which was not often. She had no desire to learn spells, or be lectured by holistic sentiment, but the recipes were so dispersed she was forced to take in more of the ominous pages than she would have liked. The chapters had no order, no structure, no logic. Pages of seemingly spiritual prose were followed by a recipe for carrot, herb, and goat cheese soup. On other pages, between recipes and prose, were drawings of giant misshapen people the size of trees, and other drawings of smaller but equally odd people, beside giant flowers.

They did not appear to be professionally illustrated to say the least. They gave Lucy the *heebie-jeebies*, she thought, adopting some of Bear's vernacular. So she tried not to look at them, or the adjoining ballads of equally troubling poetry, and tried only to learn the recipes. Given her efforts in the garden had not been particularly well received, cooking was an alternative means of contribution to their lives, and she became quite good at it. It was not a carnivore diet the recipes provided for though, and Crumbs became more savage every day, having to hunt down his own protein, if he wanted more than vegetables and bread.

There were still some pastoral elements of valley life though. The chickens needed to be let out, and watched, a job of which Leo often volunteered for, but was not particularly good at, given his tendency for dozing. The chickens also needed to be reined in before evening too, before the night and shadows spooked and scattered them, and this was not always easily done. Both Lucy and Cherry also tended to the goats, when they came, to their hooves, their injuries, and any apparent malnutrition. In return the goats gave them milk, which Cherry would sometimes make into cheese; the method for which also, unsurprisingly, came from the Lores of Terra. Under Cherry's instruction, Lucy also learnt to sow and sew, both seeds in the earth and yarn from wool.

As the days went on, the brook beside the cottage burbled louder with the onset of late autumn rain. The sky, white and vacuous, drizzled softly but persistently. But the rains would become heavier and more frequent, and Cherry worried for Leo who could not shelter in their cottage. (She caught herself more than once thinking that way; *their* cottage, instead of hers, but did not know what to make of it.) She suggested they begin weaving a cover for him to fasten between the low grey branches of the beech trees and mist-woods by the bank. They would use the wide waxy fronds of the ferneara bush, which she'd used in the past to make the baskets for cloth and dry goods.

'They are doing the same,' Cherry said to Lucy, one dry afternoon, as they sat weaving the long yellow straps together. Lucy had been watching a line of ants marching over the rocks by the water's edge, and down into the dirt somewhere, and Cherry had been watching her watch them.

Lucy let her weaving fall into the lap of her brown tunic and stretched her tired fingers. It was one of Cherry's dresses. Cherry had many. Some had been at the cottage, some she brought with her. Most were brown and beige, or the off-cream colour that white fabric becomes over time. Others were black, or navy. They all fit Lucy, save for being a little long, given their respective heights. Cherry wore a similar heavy brown dress. It was chilly, and they'd both draped heavy winter cloaks over their shoulders and wore woollen socks up to their knees.

'Sorry?' Lucy said, looking over at Cherry. Her intense study of the ant retreat had put her in a daze.

'They're doing what we are, trying to keep out of the rain,' Cherry explained, straightening the grassy-braid she'd begun. Her meagre plait looked pitiful next to Lucy's square, but this was her second square, while Lucy was still on her first.

'Oh,' said Lucy, smiling warmly, 'trying to keep him out, you mean.' Him being Leo. Cherry nodded, smiling at his enormous sleeping figure.

'Is it starting to rain everywhere in the world? Will it be autumn in Archmond now too?' Lucy asked, pondering the onset of rain.

'Archmond yes, Meta Emery, maybe, everywhere, no. For example, in Gemini it will be already quite cold, winter, so probably they have some snow already, not rain. But in Mazouri and down south it would still be quite warm.'

Lucy tried to remember where each of those cities were on the map relative to each other, and Rumustica. She could picture Gemini, having been interrogated on it for those daunting hours aboard the River Princess. But not the others. She almost considered ducking inside to fetch the map as questions she'd harboured for some time started reforming in her mind. Questions on geography had felt foolish to put to Hamish or Star, given they likely wouldn't accept her inquiries as genuine. Yet Cherry seemed to openly accept that Lucy was from another world, so the questions seemed natural to her. Lucy was reminded of another question she'd had when it came to the plight of the poor farmers in Archmond.

'What's west of Archmond?' she asked. She had often, though only ever momentarily, wondered why people wanting a new life couldn't simply migrate in that direction, save for the apparent law against it.

'Swamp-lands mostly,' said Cherry, disdainfully. 'Marshy, muddy plains. Miles of it. It grows with mangroves and weeds. It's not heavenly.'

'And what's west of the swamp-lands?'

'The ocean, and the sea ice.' There was a hint of condescension then, as though this was something even Lucy should have known.

'So,' Lucy paused, digesting this, 'where would you get to if you sailed west on that ocean?' Having finished the square she was working on, she put it down. That made three now they'd done together. Each woven square, about a metre by a metre, when they had done about thirty, would be woven together to form this makeshift shelter Cherry had envisaged.

'Well, *eventually*, if you could get through the sea ice… Meta Emery, or maybe Gemini.'

Lucy looked confused. 'West?'

Cherry raised her shoulders and outstretched her hands. 'The furthest western point is the furthest eastern in the end. You go west long enough, you end up east.'

But Lucy was still grappling with the concept, and her face showed it. Cherry laughed and picked up one of the half-rotten fernearas on the ground beside them. An ant was crawling across it's pale red skin. She held the fruit up, pointing at the ant.

'If he keeps going round long enough,' she explained cheerily, 'he'll end up back where he started.'

Lucy groaned, embarrassed. *Of course.* It was harder to picture this world having only seen it flat on a map, but of course it must be spherical too. Her horizon was spherical after all.

'And what about north? Gemini is by the ocean but are there—'

Cherry cut her off. 'North and south is different. There is a loop back eventually, there must be. But it's not like east and west, it's different. There is land beyond Que, I think there is ocean too. But it's not a journey people take. Nothing has seemed to survive it.'

Lucy nodded in acceptance, but that was about as far as her comprehension went.

The talk of survival felt suddenly grim to Cherry. 'Enough of maps. Let's talk of sunnier things,' she said.

'Like what?'

'Like... what are you making me for dinner?'

Leo was delighted with his thatched shelter when it was finished, and sometimes, when it rained, they would sit under it with him and talk. Lucy would sometimes speak about Lockerby. She told Cherry about the boy she'd slept with at school, and how she in some ways regretted it, and in other ways didn't at all. She prattled on about lots of people she used to know: the horrible girl Mary, her friend Asha, the Breemer children that lived next door to her house on Ursula Avenue. Her sister.

She'd sometimes talk about Archmond and Bear, but it made Cherry unhappy to think of her substitute guardians as corrupt, and even superficial trivia on the topic of Archmond seemed to remind them both of this issue. So Lucy kept talk on that topic minimal. For similar reasons Lucy seldom spoke of Star, Gin, or Lorelai, or anyone from Mathew's team, as they were all too close to the topic of Hamish and Orran. Lucy learned that subject bore a sensitivity no reason could overcome.

Leo in turn would also tell stories from the jungle: the places he'd lived, the times he'd seen the red soldiers, and the adventures he'd gotten into with the Archie he'd once known. However, his storytelling was convoluted and hard to follow. The two girls often feigned comprehension by laughing when he did or mimicking the tone of his more sombre murmurings. Cherry spoke of things too, but she tactically avoided speaking of her life before the cottage, apart from passing commentary on her education in Archmond, and even that was limited to, *I was taught about this,* or, *I studied that,* in Archmond.

All the while amid these rainy conversations and burgeoning friendships, bright winter blossoms, both cobalt and lilac, started to bloom, and let themselves be tussled in the cold wind beside the brook. For the most part these days, as they seemed to amble by with their buried truths and their fragile foundations, were marked both placid and content. Every so often, when the sky was clear, a sense of excitement stirred, and they would ready the horses and set off on a quest to seek out the lotus sprites. But the quests routinely proved fruitless.

On one evening, when they sat on threadbare rugs, keeping Leo company under the makeshift gazebo by the brook, the weather was mild enough that they didn't necessarily *need* the fire. This was unusual at nearly seven weeks into autumn, but they had a small blaze in any event, to allow Lucy to read. The evening had itself not yet gone dark, but the sky was darkened by thick clouds. Rain drizzled slowly over the brook, over the woven-frond roof, drizzling off onto the winter-blossoms at its perimeter. But by the fire at its centre, they were dry.

Leo was telling Cherry about a family of nomads he'd seen fall victim to what he called the devil weed. Lucy had heard the story before, and it wasn't clear whether his meaning of family was the same as theirs. He'd referred to a big man and a big woman, with two little ones, a boy little one and a girl little one, but Lucy was now conscious that he sometimes referred to her and Cherry as 'little ones' too.

'They were doin' okay because they'd got that far, and they looked alright. The big man had a bunch of rope around his shoulder. He used it to tie small branches together and make a roof for them all... like what you girls did. I thought maybe... they're ganna make it. But then I saw the little one, the girl, pick up some fruit o' that devil weed...'

Lucy was flicking through that book again. She wasn't sure why reading it was becoming so habitual, given she was so equally unsettled by it. She told herself she wanted to learn more recipes, to find some she'd missed, perhaps. She knew deep down this wasn't entirely true.

'They packed up and kept on next mornin'. Never saw me. Next time I saw the girl, the little one, probly four, or, ten nights later, she wasn't really all there anymore... know what I mean?' Leo continued. Cherry shook her head.

'She was face down in the dirt, and I thought, no, that's no good, she won't be able to breathe in any air layin' like that. So I turned her over. And yeah, she looked like the animals do when they eat it. All purple-faced. But actual bits of her was missin'. Think the monkeys took some of her.'

As Lucy thumbed the pages in one of the later chapters called Dorum, which had many recipes she'd already tried, she felt a page thicker than the others. She pinned it between her thumb and her index finger and rubbed. It was as she suspected, two pages stuck together. Excitedly, but silently as she did not want to interrupt the conversation, or alert Cherry and have her think she was damaging the book, she pried the pages apart. Whilst very faded, by whatever the substance was that had glued them together, the concealed page appeared to reveal a new recipe for an onion and potato stew. Lucy stirred with anticipation, this was perhaps a meal Cherry had never had before either. In their dull life of increasingly rainy days, a new meal was an exciting thing.

Not wanting to interrupt Leo's story - 'The man? I don't know, I never seen him again. Seen the boy's foot. I think it was his foot. Actually, it could have been the man's. Or maybe it was someone else's foot… But I don't think so. I never saw no one else 'cept soldiers. And it wasn't no soldier foot.'

'Leo would you like some grapes?' Cherry offered him some from the bowl in an effort to silence the gruesome commentary.

Lucy read the recipe quietly to herself: *two white onions, four golden potato, one fifth olive juice,* then followed other items that were too faded for Lucy to read. Parsley? White wine vinegar, perhaps?

But the curious part was actually something Lucy had never seen before, writing that appeared to be scribbled alongside the ingredients haphazardly, in different ink.

'Faut ajouter du sel,' Lucy read it out aloud, astonished. Cherry and Leo looked at her. Lucy had been taught to speak French at school, and her aunt on her mother's side lived in Toulouse. She was hardly fluent, but she could speak and read enough to get by in most simple conversations.

'Have you seen this?' Lucy asked, showing it to Cherry.

'No,' Cherry murmured, but it was the recipe Cherry was focused on.

'No, the words… here,' Lucy said, pointing to the scribble.

'Oh,' said Cherry, then looking more closely, remarked, 'Oh! I haven't seen this page, *but,* I have seen words like these before. They are like the words I haven't been able to make out… in the spells. I don't know what these words mean. It's another language,' Cherry dismissed, perplexed

'It's French,' Lucy said, with mild condescension, but as Cherry's face did not react Lucy quickly understood that the French language would not exist in a world where France did not exist. But then again, neither should English, and that seemed to be what they all spoke.

'Sorry, it's from my world,' Lucy explained, shaking off the attitude. 'As in, it's a separate language, different from the common tongue.'

'Like Mazourian?' asked Cherry.

Lucy didn't know what Mazourian was like, but the analogy would suffice. 'Yes, like that, but it exists in my world. Not here.'

Cherry blinked, disconcerted, and looked at the page and the words again. She took in the context. 'Onion and Potato Stew,' she muttered the words of the title, baffled, before squinting at the scribbled words again. 'So, what does it… what does it?'

'What does it say? It means, I think, well I'm pretty sure it means, *must add salt.*' They both looked at each other then and laughed. Leo laughed too, but it was unclear if he understood why it was funny.

'Wait, you said you saw more words like these?' Lucy asked, several moments later.

'Yes, remember I said in some of the spells, actually in the concealment spell we did, there were these words I could not make out.' Cherry nodded toward the book. 'I mean I can't read them so, I just ignored them.'

Cherry shrugged then, stood up, and curled her long hair into a bun, before heading inside to boil a pot of Lyadell leaf tea.

Lucy knew where that spell was. She didn't make it a habit to read the spells, but she had read that one. How had she missed the French? Sure enough though, when she got to that page, the words were clear. Written quite clearly, not scribbled but neatly hand written in cursive above the title of the page were the words, 'Doit e`tre fait la nuit de la nouvelle lune.'

'Cherry,' Lucy called. But Cherry couldn't hear her. Lucy got up and went in after her. It was good timing, as the rain then became heavy.

'This says the spell must be done on the night of a new moon, that's what this means, *nouvelle lune;* new moon,' said Lucy, her voice half drowned out by the roar of the rain. Outside under the shelter, Leo edged toward its centre, toward its fire which was still glowing.

Cherry was dubious as she placed the kettle atop the wood-stove. 'That seems stupid,' she said, but thought on it a moment more and said half-heartedly, 'I guess though, if you say that's what it means, perhaps then we could do it again on the new moon, for good measure.'

Lucy grimaced, 'I think that was yesterday… or… even, the night before.'

'Was it? Are you sure?' Cherry was taken aback. She was not used to someone more attuned with the lunar cycle than she was. She checked her calendar. It was not a calendar but an almanac of sorts, covering a three year period, which Cherry asserted reset at its end and started again, though Lucy remained just as dubious of this as of all the talk of geographical loops and resets. But disappointing them both, according to the almanac Lucy had been correct, the new moon had passed, and if the clouds had parted, they both would have seen the slender slither of gold resting above the crowns of the conifers beyond the window.

'Well, let's write a reminder so that we remember to do it again on the next new moon,' Cherry resolved decisively.

Several days before the next full moon, Cherry was sorting through garments that needed mending. Cherry could sew quite profi-ciently, but Lucy was still quite sketchy, so Cherry tended to give her socks or scarves or blankets to muster together. Lucy was currently sitting on the bed, doing her best to stitch together the ends of some socks.

Cherry was looking for something else suitable for Lucy to mend, even an old rag that may be used to wash over the horses or clean out the chicken coop.

'You know,' muttered Lucy with a sly tone, after the knitting needle pricked at her for the umpteenth time that morning, 'if you were the queen of Meta Emery, as you could be, we would have servants do this for us.'

Cherry turned to give Lucy a look, but it was not stern enough for her to be dissuaded.

Lucy went on, 'Gowns of endless silk, woollen robes, fires made and tended to.' But Cherry's eyes became fierce and she threw an oil-stained rag at Lucy's face, but it landed on her collarbone.

'Oh, don't be hateful,' Lucy said, amused.

'And what is this we? And us?' Cherry teased. 'If I was queen you would still be here, in this cottage.'

Lucy shrugged the oily rag off her, and then out of it, slipped a little paper box.

'Oh! It is here!' Cherry exclaimed, rushing over.

'What's here?' Lucy asked, having not seen it. While knitting and waiting for Cherry to organise materials, the Lores of Terra was open to a page of strange prose on the bed beside her. She had to admit the book was growing on her. This one seemed to be a long metaphor of sorts, a circular story about a shadow that realised wanting to be whole was what was making it empty, and when it stopped wanting to be whole, it started to be. Lucy made little sense of it.

Cherry walked over to Lucy and reached for the chain on her collarbone. Bringing forward the key turned pendant, she was grinning knowingly.

'You remember I said we were each given one? My sisters and I?' she said and reached down to collect the paper box and hand it to Lucy.

Lucy opened it, and sure enough an identical pendant was threaded through a lacquered black string. Lucy held it up out of the box, looking it over as the string twisted and turned with the weight of the turning pendant. The only difference between hers and Cherry's, was that Cherry's was less worn.

'You made it a necklace as well,' Lucy remarked, curiously.

'Yes, but I don't wear it,' Cherry said, snatching it away, 'it's just a symbol, a stupid symbol, of the past.'

'So why do you still keep it then?' Lucy posed, 'if it's so, *stupid.*'

Cherry eyed Lucy daringly for several moments, as if accepting a challenge Lucy had not intended to make.

'Okay then,' Cherry accepted, and spun on her heels to strut outside.

'Leo!' Cherry called. He was somewhere around the back of the cottage, curiously watching the chickens. He came back though, gladly.

'I have a gift for you, to honour you, for your contributions to both the jungle and the mountains,' she declared.

His confused face tweaked with awe. 'Honour me?' he repeated.

Lucy came outside, 'Cherry, isn't that a key to…'

Cherry turned back. 'To what? A palace I never want to see again? If it even is…'

'And what if you change your mind, in two years or in ten?' Lucy reasoned.

Cherry rolled her eyes at the young girl's foolishness. 'Many people come and go from the palace without a key. The silly rumour that this would somehow be the only way in is *especially* stupid.'

'And what if it's not a silly rumour… I mean… it is strange. This floats on water,' Lucy pushed.

'Well,' Cherry sung cheerily, as she slipped the black string over Leo's enormous head and said to him, 'You are now an Honorary member of the Dynasty of Meta Emery,' before turning back to Lucy and concluding, 'If it is true, we can use yours.'

Their dull days were not without some amusement. One evening when Lucy had forgotten to muster all the chickens back in their coop before sunset, she had to hunt for the missing one by torchlight. Lucy and Leo wandered around outside the cottage for almost an hour before they saw the plump underside of its auburn hide, part way up a young tree. Lucy plunged the burning torch into the ground and balanced on Leo's shoulders as they tried to get it down. It may have worked, but when Cherry opened the window and called out in alarm at their precarious pose, Lucy faltered, and Leo toppled. They both fell forward and tilted the tree. This startled the chicken who for some reason flew straight toward the open window, into Cherry's face and past her onto the bench where she was grinding grain into flour. A cloud of white erupted inside the cottage. After they pulled themselves together, she and Cherry eventually traced the claw tracks and found the ghostly bird cowering amongst the freshly laundered linen.

Leo also took pleasure in spooking Crumbs, which initially was when he came to the brook to drink. Crumbs though, grew suspicious after the first few pranks and was less easily startled thereafter. But the first fright he got when Leo's figure roared up from a pile of leaves sent him catapulting into the icy water. He was not as amused by it as Lucy was. Neither at least was Cherry. While Lucy's eyes were still wet with tears of laughter, the nurturing ex-princess wrapped him up in a blanket and rushed him inside by the fire, where she cooed softly at his cocooned figure, until he was dry.

On the night of the next full moon, Cherry returned in the early hours of the morning from the base of nearby Mount Nawala, and quietly shuffled into bed with Lucy. She had left openly this time, and Lucy had not asked where she was going. So she knew that Lucy was only pretending to be asleep as she returned.

'He wasn't there,' Cherry muttered quietly, swallowing her anxiety, but knowing that Lucy would not respond. 'He wasn't there.'

Chapter 10

Metamorphosis

'My cocoon tightens, colors tease,
I'm feeling for the air;
A dim capacity for wings,
Degrades the dress I wear.

A power of butterfly must be,
The aptitude to fly,
Meadows of majesty concedes,
And easy sweeps of sky.

So I must baffle at the hint,
And cipher at the sign,
And make blunder, if at last,
I take the claw divine.'

Emily Dickinson

That fateful day where they did find the lotus sprites, the day that changed everything, had started out darkly. But the looming clouds they woke to were only the residue of night rain and were soon brisked away by morning winds.

As the sunlight spread over the western sky, and Lucy pegged the last of their laundry on the clothes line beside the water tower, Cherry emerged back through the grove, arms full of kindling. Her face was as bright as the angelic light that cut low through the trees, illuminating her left side, permeating her pale cotton dress as though it were water. She was beaming about something, and Lucy could guess what it was.

In fact, the real reason Cherry had made off through the grove to begin with, was not for wood, but so she could wander down the valley some, where the trees parted, and gauge the horizon. Although they could see grey sky thinning and fading to blue from the small glade outside the cottage, to gauge the future needed more perspective.

Wondrously, it was as Cherry had predicted, as she expected. On the grassy slope, where the pines and the ink-woods grew taller but sparser, she glimpsed down between their trunks and saw that the soft undulations of the horizon were blooming with plumes of white clouds. Breaching these playful shapes, an opalescent light beckoned. The rain was gone, and the day would stagnate as these doleful clouds wandered about a cold blue sky.

'It's clearing?' Lucy asked, all but knowing the answer as she came forward, beaming, the empty basket cradled against her. Crumbs began barking, he would never understand what they were all happy about, but he could sense it.

'It is,' said Cherry, and her face was so primed with childish glee you'd be forgiven for thinking they'd just been given a map to a treasure.

It was several hours before they could get going though. The chickens needed feeding, the eggs collecting, the kindling had to be stripped and laid out inside to dry, as did the wood for the fire when they returned. The other basket of laundry was emptied, wrung out, and hung out. Lucy prepared a packed lunch wrapped in cotton cloth and filled their canisters with water, while Cherry readied the horses. They called it an expedition, but these jaunts of theirs were of course no more than childish whimsy; sight-seeing pursuits of pleasure.

There was no reason they sought out the sprites other than to marvel at their wondrous incredibility. This was more akin to residents of a seaside village, waking early and navigating the coast, in the hopes of watching a whale migration. It was, essentially, something to do. But, of course, Cherry still did harbour hope that she could help their declining population, somehow.

'Now you keep an eye out while we're gone and watch the cottage. Watch out for spooks,' Lucy joked to Leo, as she fastened her sword to her side, and watched as Cherry led both the horses out to the front of the cottage.

'Thought spooks was what yous were goin' after?' he muttered. In times before he had been upset when they left and went off without him. But they had been together, the three of them, for months now, which in their isolated existence seemed much longer, and to Leo felt a lifetime. He no longer feared their abandonment. But he was always happy when they returned.

'Sprites,' Lucy corrected him, 'not spooks.'

Crumbs danced around her more than usual, barking with excitement, energy, and persistence.

'I think this time he *really* wants to come,' Lucy remarked to Cherry as she strutted slowly to a standstill with both horses, a rein in each hand.

'Pity there's no way you can carry him,' Cherry mused.

Lucy remembered then, the very unconvincing lie she'd told to the jungle camp, about riding with him before.

'Wait just one second,' she pleaded, and dashed back inside. Crumbs went in after her, knowingly. She shrugged off her backpack, and shuffled around the contents, putting the cotton lunches to one side, where they would no doubt be squished and trodden. She unzipped the largest outer-most pocket, 'come on then,' she beckoned him in. He was thinner than he used to be, and she could close the zip almost all the way, save to allow his scraggly head to poke through.

'Spirits,' remarked Cherry, disapprovingly at the sight of the dog-bag. She rolled her eyes, but it was nearly noon. 'We're losing time. If that's how you want to ride, then let's ride.'

It was just past mid-morning when they left, and it was an hour or two after that when they began to ascend the escarpment of the first peak of the Alabaster Range, Mount Liox. They would only go some ways up and never in their jaunts did they venture anywhere close to the summit as they were cognisant of their limitations. But the Alabaster peaks were in relative terms quite modest. The range lay north west of Cherry's valley, but they had travelled east first to circumvent the Dolomire Range, sitting just north of the hidden valley's north-eastern aspect. The pass between the Dolomire and the Morgessen Range that sheltered the cottage, was boggy at the best of times, let alone after a night of heavy rain. The horses would become trapped, if not cold and wet.

They had come this way before, around the Dolomires and through the network of interlocking valleys and scattered ranges that made up the northern parts of Rumustica. The Alabaster Range was hidden from eastern eyes by the Karrichore Range just east of it, whose daunting shadow-blue peaks could be seen from as far as the rural fringes of Que.

They stopped to take stock, as a pervasive mist thickened.

'It's going to get worse the higher we go,' Cherry said, craning her neck upward. Lucy nodded agreeing. They were immersed in a young forest, with delicate trees and outcrops of blue-grey boulders. Blooms of baby's breath jutted out around them from small crevices in the rocks.

'And colder,' Lucy added. They had both been shivering whenever they stopped for more than a few moments. Frost speckled across the lichen.

'At some point in the season, the cold is so much that the line between autumn and winter becomes meaningless.' Cherry yawned.

Lucy agreed but was keen to keep moving. 'About the mist though, what do you suggest?'

Cherry looked through the trees. 'Let's go back down a few feet, we'll go around.'

The mist was not so problematic here that they couldn't see ahead. They had clear visibility for a good hundred metres or more, but they realised the mountain became steeper from here. The slopes leading up much of the conjoined Alabaster Range, were gradual. The risk of stumbling to your death off a shrouded ledge was minimal. At this altitude, if the mist became thicker, there was a danger the horse might stumble, but not fall. Nevertheless, ten feet further down things were clearer still, and from here they effortlessly navigated the mountain's circumference.

Waiting with the horses while Cherry relieved herself, Lucy thought she saw something flicker in the corner of her eye. Her head spun quickly; her heart raced. But whether something had been there or not, she could see nothing glimmering now. Her eyes darted about the spindly pale branches, and the sparse blooms of white flowers, but the only thing moving between them was the mist. Crumbs wriggled against her back in the backpack, and groaned, frustrated.

'Shush, you wanted to come so here you are. Stop complaining. I should never have brought you,' she scolded him. He had been able to run and eat and pee less than twenty minutes ago when they'd stopped to eat by a stream.

Then, as Cherry emerged back through the bushes, they both heard the terrifying sound of a deep male voice.

'They'll be here somewhere,' the gruff voice declared. Cherry froze. Halfway between parted bushes, her arms outstretched, she froze. Her face drained of colour. She held the bushes apart, not letting them release, fearing that the sound of rustling leaves might expose them.

Lucy too fell immediately still with fear. But after a moment passed, she bit her lip intrigued, registering something. The voice had been terrifyingly close, but there was no other sound of human activity. No breath, no thuds, no rustle. Eventually Cherry stumbled forward to Panacea, intending to scramble upon her and flee, but Lucy stopped Cherry from sending her into a gallop.

'What are you doing! We have to get out of here.' Cherry seethed quietly in a panic.

When the voice erupted again with, 'Get the container ready,' Lucy had to grab Cherry's wrist, forcefully commanding her attention as she pointed behind them.

A light. A small, bright, white, light, floated among skeletal branches some thirty feet away.

Cherry's terror at first was hindered by the confusion. Wondrous though it was that they'd found one, she couldn't understand why Lucy was risking their lives to marvel at it. But a moment or two later, she got it. The voice. The sprite. They were one and the same.

'Better be more than this bunch. Hell of a journey to make to come back with only a boxful,' the white sprite echoed in a slightly more terse, but equally deep voice. It backed away as it did so.

'This is what happened to you before? It wants us to follow?' Cherry whispered, her whole body trembling with excitement.

'Yes,' said Lucy, quivering, leading her horse forward.

This sprite bounded in more gentle strides than any of those that had lured Lucy to the platforms at the base of Mount Nawala. It led them slowly, with a liturgy of echoed speech giving a combined impression of precisely what Cherry had suspected when they sat by the lake on their first expedition; the sprites were being hunted by Red Army soldiers.

'Be gentle with 'em, they're no use to 'er Majesty dead,' a different voice was heard as the sprite changed direction, leading them upward again.

'Don't be daft. Billions of these things. The mountains are littered with the right bright pests, no chance of 'em disappearin'. Breed like cockroaches.' They heard the same first voice say, as the sprite neared a pass between a dense stretch of tall boulders. They dismounted and tied the horses then, and it waited in the pass for them to do so and follow.

'I'd still like to know what she needs 'em for,' a younger, softer voice echoed, just as the white sprite disappeared into the shadowy crevice of a narrow cave.

The sprite was gone. It was well into the afternoon, and the sun was behind the Karrichore Range now. They stood in the narrow lane between the tall grey rocks.

'Come on, are you coming in?' Lucy said to Cherry, tentative, at the cave's narrow entrance. Crumbs was at her feet now, but he was as reluctant as Cherry to go forward. He barked, quietly, and faltered forward and back, undecided. Cherry stood silently for a moment. Lucy could feel her hesitation.

'Something feels very strange,' Cherry muttered, shaking her shoulders. Behind her the wind tussled the olive leaves of the vine growing up the charcoal rock-face.

'They *are* strange, but I don't think they wish us any harm,' Lucy pushed. 'You wanted to find them, and again they found us. I think this means something, I don't know what but…'

'Okay,' said Cherry with a foreboding sigh, shaking off her nerves, 'let's go.'

They held hands and stepped slowly, hoping their eyes would adjust. They could see but pitch darkness for their first ten or twelve precarious steps, but once the light of pale autumn afternoon had been well and truly swallowed up behind them… a spark.

It came on in the centre of the rocky ceiling above them. The same bright white light, and its illumination revealed a series or a network, of other tiny bumps across the ceiling behind it. Suddenly it went out again. To their right, a pale pink sprite, almost coral, lit up, and went dark again. To their left, a sprite of baby-blue, also lit up and went dark again. Then, majestically, in a display that was as unbelievable as it was enchanting, the entire right side of the cave, across the ceiling and part way down the damp walls, was alight with thousands of coral-coloured sprites. They flickered on and off in sequence; row by row, one by one, segment by segment, before again falling dark. Cherry had stepped forward, wanting to reach out, wanting to touch one, but was startled as the cave fell into instant darkness again.

Then the entire left side of the cave, was alight with the same shade of blue. Mirroring the right side, the chorus of electric blue sprites gave a performance of synchronised illumination and darkness, lighting up line by line, row by row, and one by one, before falling dark again. They had been unwittingly invited to a production they knew not existed. And this was the opening act.

'I've never seen so many in one place before, never more than a handful,' Cherry whispered, her voice echoing, and stepped forward into the centre of the cave, the tight space now clearly illuminated. 'They've never let me get so close.'

As she stood beneath them, her own pink hues all the more vibrant under their glow, they began to drift off the ceiling and the walls, and float to the opposite side of the cave they were in. As they crossed the centre, the coral sprites became blue and the blue sprites became coral, almost giving the appearance that nothing was moving at all. Their movement was sending a melodic sound through the air, barely audible, millions of tiny vibrations, together sounded like the faint and distant ring of a cymbal.

'It sounds like they were being hunted after all,' Lucy said, 'just like you thought.'

'*Any o' you lot got a cigarette?*'

'*We can't go back to Meta Emery without at least one box full o' them.*'

'*Piss off, Yoran, I'm not carryin' it for you.*'

'*There might not be any more left.*'

'*Use your brain, what do you expect will happen if we go back to the queen empty-handed?*'

Three different male voices echoed the fractured conversation in turn from different parts of the cave.

Then Lucy's voice echoed back to them. '*Being hunted after all.*'

Both girls shivered, once again conscious that they were being heard, understood, and spoken to.

As Cherry tilted her head back and spun around slowly in wonder, Lucy twitched suddenly, remembering the day, 'Cherry. Today… *tonight*. Tonight, will be a new moon.'

Cherry straightened her posture and looked at Lucy, understanding immediately.

'We should have brought it with us.'

'And everything else we need: the water, the herbs, and the candle.'

'The water we have, the candle is just for the light, we could light a fire with the flint and the sword but—' muttered Cherry. She was thinking it over.

'But at the cottage, we have to do the spell at the cottage tonight,' Lucy said.

'We can do it in two places, I can't see why not,' Cherry suggested, but her voice was uncertain.

'Can you remember the spell, all of it?'

Cherry's eyes fell to the ground as she concentrated for several moments, her lips mouthing the lines. Her fists clenched in frustration. She looked up. 'No.'

Both of their eyes fell closed, and for a moment they didn't speak. They were avoiding the unpleasant truth that one of them had to go back and get the book. It had taken several hours to get here, but they had been going slowly up the slopes, thoroughly examining the terrain. An expedient ride might see Cherry return in just under three, if she was efficient, and then it would be approaching evening. But she was the faster of the two of them, and faster on her own.

'Crumbs and I will wait here,' Lucy uttered after several tense moments.

'I know,' Cherry conceded reluctantly.

Cherry rode with unbridled determination. She was panicked. Suddenly there was a flurry of things that needed to be done, in a span of time that was vanishing before her. She had to return to the cottage, have enough clarity to gather all they would need, and return urgently to the Alabaster Range. There they needed to perform the spell, with calmness of mind, and then return to the cottage to perform it again before the night of the new moon was over. She would not lose this chance.

At the cottage she found Leo asleep and did not wake him. Once inside, she took three deep breaths. In a moment of enlightenment, she sought to bring not only the book and the candle, but more supplies given it was getting late. She threw the heavier winter cloaks, (normally not worn on brisk rides) spare woollen undergarments, wash cloths, ointments, and other small essentials into the saddlebag. She was suddenly worried that the spell might take too long, that early night would be too dark, and they would have to sleep there in the cave. In the surrounding comfort of her comforting walls, she revolted at this thought, but she knew she had to be practical. She decided to bring food as well, but in her haste, she grabbed a whole handful of dried vegetables and bread, more than enough for dinner and lunch, but it was faster to bring it all than to have to think about it.

When Cherry returned, the sun was fast dropping on the eastern horizon, and she knew that evening would soon be upon them. She found the pass and the cave easily, from memory, and found Lucy sitting inside it, peacefully, the sprites floating around her, in a swarm of blue light.

Lucy looked up with gleeful relief, but she tried to shake off the relief in her expression.

'That was quick,' Lucy lied. 'Did you manage to bring everything?'

She needn't have asked. Cherry held a hessian bag in her arms, and her usually demure countenance bore a level of determination that told them both they were ready to do this thing.

The sprites were silent as Cherry set up. They had echoed things back to Lucy as she'd waited: voices from strange men; her own voice; things she had said to Cherry; and in Cherry's voice, things Cherry had said to her. They even echoed Leo at a point, she believed, but the words were so succinct, 'Guess so,' that she couldn't be sure. But once Cherry had reappeared into their cave, they had fallen silent, as if, somehow, they were shy around her.

'Are you ready?' Cherry asked as she lay the blue candle and water between them. She needn't have asked. Lucy's eyes told her she was ready.

As the sprites continued to float in seemingly aimless circles around the small cave, the two girls positioned themselves, Cherry read out her habitual opening line, and then the two of them read the incantation just as they had before.

'In solace may you find,
what is hidden from their eyes.
In the light as bright as day
What exists they cannot say
Take the shadow cloak of noon,
And hide the children of the moon.
For listeners chanced to venture near,
Silence the sounds they must not hear,
Take the shadow cloak of noon,
And hide the children of the moon.'

Toward the end of the first verse, the colours began to rise out of the pages of the Terra, just as they had done before; blue and yellow. The girls locked eyes with anxious anticipation as the colours swarmed like curls of smoke as they rose, becoming green as they melted into each other.

Part way through the second verse, Cherry faltered with pain, rushing a hand to her side at the edge of her rib cage, but paused only for a split second. Lucy had paused too, about to ask, but Cherry's fierce gaze warned her against interrupting and together they kept going.

As they finished the third verse the circular ring of green light dispersed as it had done before, but this time it left a spell of sparkling, fading green light, glittering away to the relative dim glow of the sprites. Lucy was twisting her head this way and that, taking it in, but as she tilted her head back down and her eyes refocussed, she saw Cherry contorted with pain.

'Cherry!' Lucy gasped, a panicked whisper.

Cherry was gasping with pain, closing her eyes, and pushing her palms into the rocky ground. She whistled in narrow tubes of air, trying to contain the agony.

'I… don't… I don't know, I don't know what is happening,' was all she was able to stutter out. The sprites, returning to their coral colour, began to migrate toward her, but kept a comfortable distance.

When she cried out in agony again, Lucy rushed over to her, but in the same moment she put a hand on Cherry's thigh she jerked it away again. Cherry's skin was too hot to touch. Lucy inched back, terrified, but powerless. It was plain that Cherry was undergoing something horrible, some dire calamity, but Lucy could do nothing. It dawned on her then, how much Cherry meant to her well-being. What would she do if the young lady died here, in the dark cave, on this cold night, part way up a mountain? Would she take her place and live alone in the cottage until she died?

In tortured breaths, Cherry began to lifts her arms up, and then outward. It appeared to be a reflex of sorts, as if it was her only mechanism for relief. The sprites hovering around her began to spin, repeating Lucy's initial frantic call, '*Cherry!*' in a manner that was both disturbing and surreal.

'I'm too hot,' Cherry whined, her eyes red and tearing. She shrugged off her cardigan, her dress, and all her undergarments until she was sitting there, completely naked, her porcelain skin awash with shadow and coral light. Inside she was terribly ashamed, but the torment of her physical condition was too demanding to warrant giving heed to shame.

Crumbs rushed into Lucy's arms, terrified. Lucy had no idea what to do. She thought of throwing the water on Cherry, but by all accounts it was part of the spell, and it was the spell that seemed to have started this. As she held Crumbs tightly, a sudden and powerful vibration pulsated through the cave from its centre, in the image of great white light. Whatever the source of the energy, it sent Lucy sideways to the floor, her face collided with grainy ground, and she fell into unconsciousness for more than several daunting moments.

As the sensation parted, and the ringing in her ears shook her awake, Lucy opened her eyes and pushed herself up off the ground. Her face was stinging where it had grazed, and she could feel the blood running down from her temple. She worried her eye was damaged, but as she brushed the back of her hand against her eye, it was just the blood running into it, not out of it, thankfully. The sprites were still present, but they were simply hovering, not spinning, above the anguished girl. Cherry's arms were dripping with streaks of blood.

'Cherry…' Lucy muttered, breathlessly, too quiet to be heard. Cherry was looking down into the flickering flame of the candle. She was silent, shaking, but alive.

Then in a somewhat fractured moment of surreal disbelief, Lucy registered, in horror, Cherry's shadow. It was this change in her shadow she noticed first and came to understand what had happened. Where Cherry's shoulders should be falling down in slender lines, instead were bulging protruding shapes. Cherry was still trembling with pain. Lucy shut her eyes, thinking it was perhaps her vision, still distorted from the strange blast, and looked again, looked directly at Cherry this time. But her vision was clear. Emerging from the girl's back, clearly outlined by the glow of the sprites, were two crimson wings.

'Cherry,' Lucy began, carefully, 'are you okay?'

'My… my back.' Cherry grimaced. 'I can't move. It hurts so much.'

'Cherry… I need to tell you something, something's happened,' Lucy went on. Cherry was silent. She seemed completely unaware. Lucy was unsure how to go on.

'The thing on your back Cherry, it's grown, it's grown to what it was becoming,' Lucy stopped, she felt so nervous saying something so preposterous. Cherry gave no reaction. She was trying to absorb her pain. Her eyes glazed, she swayed, swathed in the delirium of the transition's aftermath.

'Cherry, you have wings,' Lucy declared.

'I'm going to throw up,' Cherry replied. In that moment all the sprites went dark and seemed to vanish from the cave.

Lucy rushed Cherry out into the milky light of the steep pass, steadying her as she leant forward and regurgitated, in lurid lurches, everything Lucy had prepared for their lunch.

This would be one of only a few times that Lucy would ever be able to truly appreciate the intricate intensity of these magnificent wings. They were speckled with blood from where they had burst out of her skin, but this was barely noticeable given their colour. The diagonal wounds from which they'd emerged were little more than thirty centimetres, but the wings themselves stretched down past her buttocks. They were longer than they were wide, they arched up above her shoulder blades much like the image of an angel, but they were not much wider than her torso. Their underlying cream structure was finite, almost delicate, joined by crimson webbing, that alternated under light between shades of magenta, pink, and red.

'Get them off me! Get them off!' Cherry shouted at Lucy between her wet, spattered breaths of vomit.

'I can't,' Lucy explained, repeatedly, 'they're coming out of you, Cherry, they are part of your body.'

'No!' Cherry whined and choked miserably, sickly, throwing up again.

Lucy looked up between the dark rocks, the sun would soon be setting. The white horizon was emanating a gold glow. But it would just as quickly desert them.

'We have to go,' Lucy said sternly, putting Cherry's arm against the rock, forcing her to support herself. She fetched Cherry's clothes and then packed up their things.

Cherry groaned miserably as Lucy helped her down the gravel path back to where they'd left the horses. She was unsteady. Her balance was distorted with the weight of the wings, now hidden beneath the thick winter cloak draped over them.

'This is what the deformity on your back was, this is what has been happening all this time,' Lucy tried to enlighten her.

'Stop.' Cherry resented the spin, 'I just want to get home. Just let us get home.'

'Yes. That's where we're going,' Lucy responded, curtly.

Cherry winced with pain as she mounted Panacea, the speckled mare momentarily aghast at her master's strained and stumbling presentation. But once she was atop her, she managed to balance her new form by leaning low, the weight of the wings pushing her down. Once they descended Mount Liox, they attempted to travel home through the pass between the Dolomire and the Morgessen Range, chancing that it might be manageable now, given the clear day and given Cherry's desperation to return to her cottage as soon as possible. But although the day had been dry, the weeks of rain meant the pass was still boggy, and the horses would not go through it.

Cherry veered her own horse back as Lucy approached the muddied grass plains.

'Stop,' she called, 'he won't manage it, neither will she.'

Colour was fading from the world around them as the hidden sun dipped below the horizon. The wind was picking up.

'Will we have to go back around the Dolomires?' Lucy asked, despondent. Her face too, was forlorn with exhaustion and at the prospect of journeying through the cold night. Cherry looked at the Morgessen Range beside them and shook her head. They turned right and ventured up the more gradual slopes on the western side of the range. It would be a long journey up the gradual western gradient and down the southern side of the range, but it would see them home far quicker than the alternate route.

Though the terrain was steep in parts, and certainly unwelcomed by the horses, it was not impassable. The western slopes took them to the brow of the lower peaks, which were more hill than mountain, where gravel planes eventually wound their way back to the eastern edge, where between the base of two escarpments, the slender depression of skeletal autumn forest awaited them.

But as they passed the V-shaped valley from above, ascended the final crest of the plateau, and began left as Cherry directed them down the southeast slope… *smoke*.

They both saw it at the same time. The sun had set, but the early evening was still full of residual light. Against the darkening white sky, the thick black wafts of smoke were a stark awakening.

Wafts of destruction drifted up from the grove in the valley.

'The cottage,' Cherry gasped, dismounting.

In the panic she forgot all about her new body parts, and in her ignorance of them her balance was wondrously restored. But before she stepped any closer, she and Lucy locked eyes. It was a dry day, but it was wintry, and the evening air was becoming thick with dew. There was no possible way the cottage could have caught alight on its own. Even an inadvertent Leo could not cause such destruction. Without a word, as frosty evening gusts whipped around their cloaks, they both acknowledged that to each other, grimly.

'Slowly,' Lucy said to Cherry, nodding in the direction of the cliff, acknowledging too, the unstable crumbling at the edges. Staying low, they crept over rocks, around to where the ground began to fall steeply down toward the sharp edge. From this vantage, they could take in the entire valley. Lingering light had retreated from the range and swirled only in the sky. With hoods drawn on their long cloaks, the outline of the two dark figures was barely discernible as anything other than small boulders between the frail young ink-woods. Pensively, in shadow, they took in the horrible scene below.

Soldiers, more than a dozen of them. Some at the base of the valley, waiting, watching, peering out into the wider meadows. Others moved about within the grove, their flashy red armour giving them away. Where the glade had been, was now an inferno. In the newly hollowed space, the crumbling black outline of the cottage could just be made out at the inferno's yellow centre. Ruthless angry flames that raced up the trunks of naked conifers, roared and crackled into the evening air. Others were licking up the sides of the ink-woods, the mist-woods. Devouring them. Devouring everything.

Cherry dropped to her knees, gripping the jagged edges of dolomite in front of her so hard her palm's bled. The pit of her stomach so instantly ached with despair. Lucy only looked on in disbelief. She took in the blaze, the smoke, the devastation, the men. They had both been yearning so much to go home, now there was no home to go to.

It would not rain tonight, but Lucy could see the condensation settling on Cherry's forearms, as her bloodied hands gripped the cold stone. She felt the same wet air dampening her own hands, and she wiped them on the inside of her cloak to better steady herself against the rock, worried she'd lose her footing and slip down several feet, creating attention.

'Cherry,' she said firmly, kneeling down, clutching the girl's wet forearm. Cherry looked a ghost, her pale complexion drained of the last of its colour, her eyes nearly as hollow and dark as the frame of the burning cottage below. In shock Lucy glanced back at the burning valley once more, but she shook off the terror. With a hand she turned Cherry's cheek back toward her, forcing those wet swollen eyes to meet her own. The wind continued to howl around them, gusts of ice and pepper bush seeds tore past, the sides of their cloaks ballooning outward every other moment. But the shadow on the range concealed them.

Lucy steadied her voice and spoke firmly.

'Cherry, listen to me. In the jungle an albatross from Meta Emery said a war was coming to Trimany. Hamish wasn't there to meet you on the last full moon, and now soldiers have burned your cottage. Cherry, Hamish is in Trimany and so is your son. He is no longer safe there. It is time to stop hiding. We have to find your son. We have to go to Trimany.'

Twenty-two people have died today after rioters clashed with officials as they bandied around the latest cargo of produce en route for the Wooden Floor Borders. This was the latest and most extreme move from a group calling themselves the United Farmers Front, or UFF. The UFF are a growing movement from the arable region of the Hills, that are insisting upon equal conditions for people on both the land and the wooden floors. They claim the government has not only abandoned but enslaved its rural population, and that farmers will no longer accept medicine as an appropriate payment for labour and produce.

Andy Tunnable, one of the founding members of the UFF, spoke to our journalist exclusively:

'What we're seeing here is a move towards transparency. For too long what we have done is accepted a reality that was imposed upon us. If even she, if even the girl that they have brought here to advocate their cause, can see the fallacy of the lies of this government, then it's time we see it too.'

But the sentiments of the movement are not supported by those working in ancillary industries closer to the border, with many labelling the movement as reckless, with the government now proposing to restrict the flow of Clorix if protests continue.

But Tunnable has rejected concerns surrounding the medicine's supply. 'Dependence on Clorix has ruined us. And we've fallen into this trap of believing it's the only way to stay healthy. East of Gathgate the crops are already healthy, the cattle is healthy, and so are the people. We have been sick for a long time, but our land is healing, and so are we. The Clorix mythology has to stop.'

More to come.